Praise for You or Someone

2.00

"Chandler Burr's debut novel, *You or ....-read for any book group serious enough to spend m..... .... discussing the book at hand instead of what wine to serve during the meeting. But the book group plot constitutes only one of the unfolding stories in this smart novel, which is, primarily, a very tough reflection on the idea of 'group-ness' itself—who's in and who's out; who's considered a full person and who's not. *You or Someone Like You* is sure to stir up controversy because it doesn't just stick to the safe pieties of descrying discrimination in terms of race or gender; instead, it confronts what it sees as a more socially acceptable form of discrimination practiced by organized religion—specifically here, Judaism. Chandler Burr's provocative new novel weighs in on the issue of identity politics and also makes a powerful case for why great books are a great danger to small minds."

—NPR's *Fresh Air*

"In his first, well crafted, and thoroughly enjoyable novel, *New York Times* writer Chandler Burr presents a sweeping spectrum, set in Hollywood, of contemporary religious and social issues. . . . Woven into the novel's relationships are conflicts over intermarriage, children of intermarriage, orthodox versus secular observance, gender choice, career paths, friendship, and immigrant aspirations. Howard Rosenbaum, a studio executive, encourages his wife, Anne, an accomplished literature scholar, to start a book club. Her book selections are brilliant and her discussion skills are penetrating. Using classic literature as the lens through which all is examined, the club becomes the in-group, a touchstone, and an engine for Hollywood decision making. Anne's success is personally empowering but surprisingly disruptive to her long and healthy marriage. Ultimately, in a stunning performance, orchestrated to reach out to her crisis-ridden, beloved husband, she delivers a radical opinion of Jewish political and religious ideology. It is an enormous risk. Agree or not, it is well worth the read."

—*Jewish Book World*

"*You or Someone Like You* is a pitch-perfect, often very funny novel about why, in this crazy world, we still bother to read. It's for anyone who defiantly clings to the belief that a book can change our lives."

—David Ebershoff, author of *The 19th Wife* and *The Danish Girl*

"This new novel questioning the merits of religion comes as a bit of a surprise from the *New York Times*'s perfume critic . . . but Burr has proved to be a Renaissance man. Who knew?" —*The Daily Beast*

"Burr's fieldwork serves the novel well, with depictions of Los Angeles culture that feel spot-on. . . . It's a genuine thrill to read what people like Albert Brooks, to give just one of many examples, might think of *Jude the Obscure*." —*Time Out New York*

"A savvy novel that deals with Hollywood from a cultural rather than a tabloid perspective." —*Kirkus Reviews* (starred)

"A true celebration of intellect . . . examines the personal decision each of us must make to run from, or embrace, our identity." —*Publishers Weekly*

"Burr luxuriates in wordplay. . . . *You or Someone Like You* is loaded with smart and sassy insights about writers and writing." —*Jerusalem Post*

"*You or Someone Like You* finds trend-loving Hollywood in a bookish trance and a certain studio exec's wife as literary guru du jour. . . . Burr's tale touches on marital strife, prejudice, and identity struggles with intoxicating realism." —*Flavorpill.com*

"Few authors are willing or even able to come across as well-read and painstakingly familiar with both the literary masters and religious convention, yet Burr freely spouts the words of Byron and Keats and follows up with an intricate discussion of Jewish culture and identity. . . . The author has a lot to say in this novel, and he says it all beautifully." —*Edge.com*

You
or Someone
Like You

ALSO BY CHANDLER BURR

The Perfect Scent

The Emperor of Scent

A Separate Creation

You
or Someone
Like You

—— *a novel* ——

Chandler Burr

An Imprint of HarperCollinsPublishers

YOU OR SOMEONE LIKE YOU. Copyright © 2009 by Chandler Burr. All rights reserved. Printed in the United States of America. No part of this book may be used or reproduced in any manner whatsoever without written permission except in the case of brief quotations embodied in critical articles and reviews. For information, address HarperCollins Publishers, 10 East 53rd Street, New York, NY 10022.

HarperCollins books may be purchased for educational, business, or sales promotional use. For information, please write: Special Markets Department, HarperCollins Publishers, 10 East 53rd Street, New York, NY 10022.

Grateful acknowledgement is made for permission to reprint from the following: "November Songs" by Elaine Feinstein, from *Elaine Feinstein: Collected Poems and Translations*, Carnacet Press Limited, 2002. *Sexual Perversity in Chicago and the Duck Variations* by David Mamet, copyright © 1974 by David Mamet. Used by permission of Grove/Atlantic, Inc. "There Was a Saviour" by Dylan Thomas, from *The Poems of Dylan Thomas*, copyright © 1943 by New Directions Publishing Corp. Reprinted by permission of New Directions Publishing Corp. With permission of the author, ideas and quotations from "Goodbye, 1939" by Nicholas Jenkins, from *The New Yorker*, April 1, 1996. "The Sloth," copyright © 1950 by Theodore Roethke, from *The Collected Poems of Theodore Roethke* by Theodore Roethke. Used by permission of Doubleday, a division of Random House, Inc.

P.S.™ is a trademark of HarperCollins Publishers.

A hardcover edition of this book was published in 2009 by Ecco, an imprint of HarperCollins Publishers.

FIRST ECCO PAPERBACK EDITION 2010

Designed by Mary Austin Speaker

Library of Congress Cataloging-in-Publication data is available upon request.

ISBN: 978-0-06-171567-9

10 11 12 13 14   ID/RRD   10 9 8 7 6 5 4 3 2 1

This book is dedicated to Eric Simonoff. Who else.

Author's Note

This is a work of fiction. But my fictional characters live in two worlds—the movie industry of Los Angeles and the media world of New York—and because of the nature of the novel, I have used real people from both these worlds in a fictional context as characters in this book. In the case of figures in the movie industry, the motivation is simply authenticity. Their actions and the words I've put in their mouths, with one notable exception (which I've been granted permission to reprint verbatim), are entirely fictional and of my creation. With those from New York, the reason is more complex; the people who appear as characters here have written extensively about ideas that bear directly on the issues the novel raises. I have added some minor fictionalized dialogue, but the ideas and opinions ascribed to them they themselves have written or said. In the notes, I have identified the sources of, and credited, all such original material.

Regarding excerpts of Pound, Keats, Shakespeare, Yeats, et alia, my source is in almost all cases my very battered volumes one and two of *The Norton Anthology of English Literature* (4th edition). I have changed or abridged certain words in certain quotations to make the quotations clearer in this context. This novel is not a literary reference guide. That said, I have sought to present these quotations with as much fidelity as possible.

One important point. The scene in this novel involving the fictional Samuel Rosenbaum's two weeks in Israel and what happens to him there happened to me, in real life, more or less exactly as described. There are a few minor differences—Sam arrives in Israel on a flight from New York whereas I entered from the Sinai with a backpack; Sam is seventeen, I was twenty-three—but otherwise every detail is identical. Over the years I've come to an understanding of this incident—my interpretation of it, its implications—via friends and strangers with whom I've discussed it and the writing of those presented as characters here who have addressed the central problem substantively and intelligently, sometimes directly, sometimes indirectly, even unintentionally. For example, there is the question posed by Nancy Franklin. What is our capacity to step back and see ourselves as we actually are?

You
or Someone
Like You

IT IS 4:18 A.M. WHEN I realize Howard has come home.

I watch his outline in the still, dark bedroom stripping off the trousers of his navy suit, stained with sand and Pacific salt water. After a moment, I ask, Who has the life he wants?

He says nothing, standing in the shadows. I say, Wystan Auden did, one could argue.

Howard cuts in, "We're not fucking talking about Auden, Anne."

I am, I say with a calm I do not at all feel, talking about Auden.

We wait in the dark, in the silence, and I realize Howard is crying, his shoulders shaking beneath his stained, unbuttoned dress shirt, the tie gone, his chin down almost to his hairy chest, bobbing up and down with every sob, his eyes closed, his fists clenched. I am so stunned I cannot move for a moment, this big man in his underwear, crying, but then I jump out of the bed. I take him in my arms. He is large enough that his jerky, rough sobs push me back and forth, as if I was grasping an oak in a storm.

Howard, I say. Howard.

He is wiping his nose on his sleeve. He turns away from me.

"It's bad," he finally says, his back to me.

I retreat the tiniest bit. What do you mean, bad?

"No," he says. "I mean it's really bad. I've thought a lot about it."

He fills his lungs, and he looks out and down over Los Angeles. The fury in his head and the pain that almost cripples him baffle me. He frowns, turns his eyes from L.A., and I watch him riding it out as they wash through him. They push him, shipwrecked, onto some distant mental shore. After a moment he manages to say, "I can't help feeling like I did something wrong."

I say after the briefest moment, You mean we.

He doesn't reply. Then he says, "No, actually I mean I."

Too small for a commercial flight, out the large dark windows the taillights of a tiny plane draw a dashed line across the sky.

I hear the "I." I feel something very cold start to climb.

The suddenly strange man who is my husband says, "There was something wrong before, and now I see it." He raises a hand like Caesar and adds in a loud voice, "Don't argue with me, Anne."

His anger is gasoline vapor filling the room.

I already know, of course, what the anger is: I am now, for him, a different kind of person. Howard discovered this only recently, when he picked Sam up at LAX after our son's flight home from Israel. Simply by telling him what had happened in Jerusalem, the boy made Howard realize that Sam, too, is a different kind. It was inadvertent—Sam, who is asleep down the hall, never intended to lead Howard to the conclusions that have brought him to standing here in the dark, covered in sand and half-naked and sobbing—but inadvertent hardly matters now.

I watch Howard get the suitcase down from the walk-in closet, go to the dresser, and start taking out the soft white T-shirts Consuelo folded yesterday. On my bedside table I look at my Modern Library *W. H. Auden: The Collected Poems*. I was reading it last night as the hours ticked by and Howard didn't come home. I have selected it for my next book club—the studio executives—for one very specific reason: Unlike Howard, Auden, the adamant universalist, saw all people as the same kind. He called the human species "New York-ers," and to him they were, otherwise, nameless.

I hear Howard murmur. I have to focus on it to clarify the words. "There's something missing, Anne."

I cast about for the thing to say. I say, as quietly as if I'm afraid of shattering something, There was never anything missing before.

He merely breathes for a moment, wincing. Then, "There is now."

He is walking to and from the suitcase in the shadows. The sun will be up in about fifty minutes. I hear his feet.

Howard, I say.

(I can't bear the silence.)

Oh, Howard! I implore him, please talk to me.

"It's not necessarily rational," he says, his eyes on the things in his hands, and adds, his jaw tense, "To you that means it's suspect. I used to feel that way. Now I don't."

As he packs, he begins to speak about having left an island long ago and wandering in the wilderness but the little island never forgot him, about a home that he betrayed, about a man in exile (in exile? I ask; in exile from what, Howard? but he doesn't stop), and about longing without realizing he was longing—and my saying, How can you long without realizing it? and his digging in his heels at this, putting his head down, his voice rising by several decibels as if sheer willpower could win the argument.

He wraps some black shoes in felt. There is a suit bag. He is leaving our home.

Who will you be staying with? I ask.

He is struggling with the suitcase. "I'll be in touch," he says through gritted teeth, working on the lock. He snaps shut the case, hefts the suit bag. Glances heavily at the dresser to check that he hasn't forgotten anything.

Who will you be staying with?

It takes an instant for his feet to begin to move.

I hear his footsteps going down the hall. The kitchen door opening, a moment of auditory void, then the sound of it closing. An eternal period, and the car's powerful German engine wakes again, calm mechanical equanimity. I listen to the recessional down our driveway. The faint sound of gravel crunching under tire comes through the open window, then the engine, the car leaps forward, and Howard vanishes into what is left of the night.

The movie cliché is the woman reaching out her hand, touching his pillow, and only then remembering. But I, when I wake again, find by contrast that my brief sleep has been entirely drenched in a blue distillate of his departure, such that even awake I confuse waking with sleeping and believe dreams to have become merely mundane. Unlike in the movies, there is never a single instant I don't know that he's gone.

IN THE SILENT LIVING ROOM (the sky is pale white-blue now) I search the vast, clean, neat shelves for a large dark-blue children's book. The search is merely movement, an attempt to rein in the vibration of my emotional state. I am a very rational person, even though I am at the moment, not altogether rationally, searching up and down for this children's book that is at the moment incidental.

I have a thought in my mind like my pulse, not under my control, and though I am shattered, the thought is crystalline, coherent: Everything that I have done has been connected. All these pieces of literature, the poetry, the novels, all of it. The lines that I spoke to express what I felt instead of using my own words because, to me, the authors were just better. And that connection, that thread, was, in every case, Howard. Now that Howard is gone I realize with a terrible clarity that the quotations were really always and only my way of talking to my husband. Throughout the book club I was speaking to them, yes, of course, and everything I said was meant for them, but it was also meant for Howard. This narrative, this conversation I have had with Howard from the very start, if it was imperfect and at times obtuse and, most recently, interrupted, it was entirely our own. And those authors' words: When I used them, Howard always interpreted them the way I did. Or I thought he did.

When Sam was a very small boy, I would open the tall French doors of our house up in the hills from which we looked down over Los Angeles and sit him next to me and read to him from a big dark-blue children's book of Bible stories, one my mother had found at Camden Market when I was a girl in London, called *The Lord Is My Shepherd*. I read all the stories to him, as my mother had to me, but *his* story, and Sam made clear the possessive, was Samuel's.

"'Hannah was barren,'" the story began.

(It means she couldn't have children, Sam. She wanted to, so very, very much; she wanted a little boy, like you. But she couldn't.)

"'And she vowed a vow, and said, O Lord of hosts, if thou wilt give unto thine handmaid a man child, I will give him unto the Lord all the days of his life.'"

The Lord answered Hannah's prayers. "'And she called the boy Samuel, saying, Because I have asked him of the Lord. And Hannah took him to the temple in Shiloh and gave the child to Eli, the priest. And the child Samuel grew on.'"

"The sleep part!" Sam ordered, four years old, looking at the book. (I heard a laugh and looked up. Howard was leaning against the doorway, amused. He uncrossed his arms briefly to make a saluting gesture, "Yes, sir!")

"'And it came to pass,'" I read, "'ere the lamp of God went out and Samuel was laid to sleep, that the Lord called Samuel, Samuel. And he ran unto Eli, and said, Here am I; for thou calledst me. And Eli said, I called not; lie down again. And he went and lay down.

"'And the Lord called yet again, Samuel. And Samuel went to Eli, and said, Here am I. And he answered, I called not, my son.'"

It was years before I explained to my son my reason for reading him this story. It would have been impossible to explain infertility to a child, and undesirable. The trying and the disappointments—we were still young, and then not so young—our growing fears, our visits to the doctor and sitting in that office with the large gray clock as they gave us the diagnosis. "Never," they said. I felt Howard's body stiffen at the word. Then the banally horrible fertility treatments, the injections, the needles, the plastic tubes, and all those decisions in those sterile white clinics. The drugs. And then, miraculously, there was Sam.

I used the story's words to say this for me.

"And the Lord called Samuel the third time." (Sam liked the third time.) "And Eli said unto Samuel, Go, lie down; and if he call thee, that thou shalt say, Speak, Lord; for thy servant heareth.

"And the Lord came again, and stood, and called, Samuel, Samuel."

Now, I always found this odd. The Lord came and *stood*, it says. When Sam was fourteen, a high school freshman, this came up at the dinner table, and I said intently, Right, I always meant to ask you: The Lord came and stood. How did you understand that? Elbows off, please.

Sam thought about it and shrugged and said, "I always pictured Dad. Standing at the top of the stairs." And then he laughed, his fork in his right hand.

I looked at Howard, and Howard wore the most indescribable expression on his face.

I have to assume Howard never fully recovered from this comment. What father would? And I thought I understood everything it meant to Howard. I was wrong. "Father" in Hebrew is *Aba*, and that, of course, is in turn "God," and though I'm certain he was at the time unaware of it, Howard heard Sam's fourteen-year-old remark as he had been prepared to by his parents long ago when Howard himself was a boy at a shul in Brooklyn. The word came back years later and claimed him, and he was defenseless. Words have such power. As a schoolgirl, I had read Jesus' cry, "Aba!" Father! and was astonished, as a grown woman and my first time in Israel with Howard, when I heard a boy call out on a street "*Aba!*" and a man turned around.

"Samuel answered the Lord," I read to my son. "'Speak; for thy servant heareth.'"

And then, says the text, God revealed all sorts of visions to Samuel.

I glanced up from my child to my husband. He was watching me, simply listening. He made no comment. At the time, I assumed Howard understood these words the same way I understood them. I still think we do.

When Sam turned seventeen, we discovered that he had had visions, too, though I use that word simply to mean that he was suddenly, in several ways, not the boy we thought he was. To Howard it seemed that Sam was being torn from him, and Howard was in torment.

When I read from this book from lovely old Camden Market, I always tasted the Holy Land in my mouth and nose: the polyester of the 1970s jetways and the fuel vapor from the old El Al jetliners, the hulking X-ray machines, the grim baggage searches for bombs and the faint clink of the automatic guns, the tension, the dry Mediterranean breath of Tel Aviv. Howard when Howard was that younger person he no longer is. The ancient stones and the dust cooked by the sun, the aged date palms, and a sharp, hard something you got in the Israeli air coming through the hotel windows at night.

My only child and I sat on the sofa with the children's book, the world thousands of feet below us outside the open French doors as the desert sun burned through a luminous particulate molecular mesh spun by millions and millions of automobiles on the Los Angeles freeways. When I began going to Israel with Howard, I was struck by the palms, and even after all these years I'm still conscious of them since, where I come from (or at least one place you might plausibly say I'm from), they are potent, exotic symbol and metaphor. (But then so is the place I live now, this dream factory that is Howard's job.) Palm trees look, one discovers, quite the same poking up beside the ancient, dusty passages of Ramallah shading fly-infested donkeys hitched to knock-kneed Arab carts as the palm trees standing at the foot of our smoothly curving asphalt street as it meets the stop sign on Mulholland Drive, across from Cahuenga Peak, just the other side from Universal Studios and above the 101.

THE VARIOUS BOOK CLUBS STARTED a year ago during one of Howard's Shakespeare recitations at dinner at the Hamburger Hamlet on Sunset Boulevard. Howard told a reporter at some point that the credit was mine because I mentioned something that set him into motion that evening. But it wasn't. It was Howard.

On the other hand, we were eight at the table and had just ordered when Stacey Snider asked me about a reading list, so you could say that Stacey began it.

I had stopped there in the afternoon to make the reservation; it's an industry place, but in a low-key way. "Certainly," the hostess had said. She wrote it down. She gave me a delicious smile. "So where are you *from*?"

New York, I said. She seemed to find that logical, somehow. Mine is such a strange accent, neither entirely one thing nor another, and naturally people become curious. I thanked her and went outside where the valet, a well-scrubbed boy, had watched over the convertible, and I tipped him.

Howard had brought Casey Silver with him from the studio as well as Jennifer, Howard's assistant. Sam had gotten his driver's license a few months before and had driven down Coldwater Canyon from school with his friend Jonathan Schwartz. They'd been playing intramural basketball, and their teenage bodies, though they had showered at school, were still flushed from their exertions and the residual thrill of driving without adults. I had come from Griffith Park (via the flower shop, via the house), where I had spent the afternoon reading on one of the benches near the tennis courts. Stacey came on her own. Josh Krauss, an agent, dashed in as the waitress was handing us menus.

Stacey and Howard had a mutual interest in a feature to be produced by a good friend of hers. Stacey would executive produce, if it went through. She was on my left, we were chatting about an actor she'd gotten to know during a recent shoot, and she leaned over to look at my book, which I'd placed next to my bread plate. John Ruskin, 1819–1900. One of the great Victorian art critics. I had just read his description of his first ever view of the Swiss Alps, at sunset, and Stacey picked up the book, opened to it, and read it to me: "'The walls of lost Eden could not have been more beautiful.'" Ruskin was fourteen at the time, Sam's age three years ago. "'I went down that evening from the garden-terrace of Schaffhausen with my destiny fixed in all that was to be sacred and useful.'"

She turned some pages slowly. Smiled, glanced at Sam. "College a year from now."

I was startled, and I hesitated. Though it was barely September, she had sensed the loss I already felt from Sam's future departure.

Am I so obvious, I said.

"You're never obvious, Anne," she said, smiling. Her gaze moved back to the Ruskin. They often comment on the fact that I always have a book. The tone is sometimes vaguely curious, as if reading were an eccentricity. Usually they glance at the cover, then turn to the menu.

Casey looked at the book in Stacey's hand, and it reminded him. "So, Howard," he said slyly. "We're here."

Howard, who knew exactly what he meant, just gave him an owlish look, so I explained to Josh, who was not following, that it was because of Sam. Hamburger Hamlet was where we had introduced Sam to Shakespeare. And I turned to Howard, because the subject had come up, and we were with friends, and it was a beautiful evening, and, moreover, it was time.

"When young Hamlet came from college," Howard explained, looking around the table at us, each in turn ("That's mine," he told the waitress who had just appeared, pointing out the iced tea), "full of new ideas and knowledge, he was shocked to learn his pa, the king, had lately passed away."

"Perrier," the waitress said. Casey raised a forefinger.

"But his discomfiture was greater," recited Howard, "when he learned his dearest mater had been married to his uncle"—and here Howard raises his eyebrows menacingly and pushes out the word—"*Claude* without the least delay!"

"Another iced tea?" Mine. Cokes for the boys, pear juice for Jennifer, beer for Josh.

"For it seemed to him indecent," explained Howard, "with his father's death so recent, that his mother should prepare herself another bridal bed. And there seemed to be a mystery in the family's royal history, but he failed to follow any clue, for fear of where it led."

With a curious glance over her shoulder at Howard, the waitress retreats to the kitchen. Perhaps it is Howard's narrator accent, a crisp and remarkably authentic 1950s BBC British. "While he's in this sad condition he's informed an apparition is accustomed to perambulate the castle every night. That it looks just like his sire, both in manner and attire, but is silent, staid, and stoical—which doesn't seem quite right." Howard puts on a quizzical look, like a demented peacock: "Having heard this testimony from Horatio, his crony, he decides to take a peep at this facsimile of his pop." Two matching plosives.

> *So at midnight's dismal hour*
> *Just outside the castle tower*
> *He confronts the grisly phantom and he boldly bids it STOP.*

Josh leans to Jennifer, whispers something, and she smiles and nods. Casey is loving Howard's *Hamlet*. He has already heard *King Lear* this way, lines that both send up and honor the play, at a party at our home, and *Romeo and Juliet* on, I believe, a tennis court in Santa Monica. Howard memorized these parodies in college.

Those in the industry recognize us. They recognize Stacey and Casey and Josh and Howard. They watch Howard, the waiters who are actors, the dishwashers who are writing screenplays, the hostess who is waiting for a callback. They know his face from the trades. They know he can help green-light a movie, buy a script, make a career. It is Hamburger Hamlet on a Tuesday evening, and we are in Los Angeles, and anything is possible.

Howard tells us Shakespeare's story, of anger and greed and violence and pain. *Then the grisly phantom faded / Leaving Hamlet half persuaded.* The tables around us, one by one, fall silent to watch and listen, those next to them notice the silence, then the focus, then the words, and they too still. *Spends his time / in frequent talking to himself / of suicide and other subjects tinged with doom.* And Howard, because he is an innate performer, increasingly projects to include them, so that in this room the circumference of his words enlarges to fit the expanding circle of attention paid to them. The waiters stop to watch, and so their busboys' busy motions gently still, and they too turn to our table.

And so then one after other / King, Laertes, Hamlet, mother / With appropriate remarks / They shuffle off this mortal coil.

When he reaches the end, everyone dead, we all applaud. The room fills with the sound. Howard bows to the stalls, accepting the declamation. Amid the applause people murmur. "Howard Rosenbaum," they say, and his title at the studio, and the last movies he worked on, as if his name were a powerful enchantment and they were spinning a spell. I love Howard's golden light when he is in his element, the vigor of my husband's love of these words and stories, but I dislike the hunger this city focuses on him, their celluloid obsession. And I quietly prepare to withdraw into myself as usual and leave them to this world. But this evening, something is different.

It is, I realize, the play. Even in this permutation, I notice, the story holds its own. I look around in wonderment. Casey is looking, too.

"I'd forgotten the power of the goddamn thing," he says. "Look." Stacey and I turn. Two Guatemalan busboys attack each other with invisible rapiers. The restaurant's manager, coaching them, tilts the hand of one of the boys as it holds an invisible sword, pitching it, like Howard's voice, into a perfect affectation of Elizabethan style. *There*, the manager says with satisfaction, good boy, that's how we'd have done it on the set. We hear him say, "Shakespeare," and hesitantly, in heavy accents, the busboys repeat the strange name.

Todd Black, a producer Howard knows, comes over to our table to say something to Howard. Stacey leans toward me. "Listen," says Stacey. "Anne." It's a proposition. "Would you make me a reading list?"

I look at her. She is quite serious.

"What you think is important," says Stacey. "No," she corrects herself immediately, "what you think is good."

Well, I say. Why me?

"You read," she says, simply enough.

Howard overhears. He turns slightly, toward us. "Make her a list, Anne," he says to me, smiling.

I don't really know her that well. She's Howard's friend, not mine. They invariably are. Stacey is waiting, Howard and Casey and Sam are watching me. I think, Well, Howard has the same degree, after all. And he has the teaching position. She could ask him. She works with him, not me, on the movies; it would be more professionally strategic for her. Yet she is asking me. And it is impossible to overestimate the pleasure of being included. Even for one who has never much wanted to be.

Certainly, I say. If you like.

I assume it is merely because I have the doctorate in English literature, which impresses them more than it should. That I read a lot is one of the only things they know about me, even though Howard and I have been here for twenty-five years. I have always preferred it that way. In fact I assume that I myself am not actually material. I just happen to know the books.

But I smile, thinking about some titles. I say to her, I think we can come up with some very nice possibilities.

Todd registers this exchange. He returns to his table, where there are several people on Paramount's production side, and I see him lean down and say something to Brian Lipson, who then makes a comment to a woman from the Universal lot.

AT 11:00 A.M. THE FOLLOWING morning I park next to our house, open the kitchen door, temporarily compromised by all my packages. Denise appears, and I hand her a large wrapped bouquet of flowers. The cone of crackling cellophane is like a lady's inverted organza ball gown, the flowers many delicate feet. Denise accepts the cone from me and sets it on the kitchen counter. She will deal with the flowers when she's ready.

They're from Mark's Garden on Ventura, I say.

"You was there?" She is not making conversation. She hadn't thought I'd had time to go that far. I say, Yes, I was, there was an alarming lack of traffic. She goes back to her work.

I deposit the car keys next to the flowers, go to my office and lay down my books, the old ones and the three I just bought at Book Soup. I carry my new blouse upstairs, take it out of the bag, and hang it in the closet. I wash my hands and face and brush my teeth, use a clean white towel, and then go to the library. I sit down and stare at the shelves. I take out a pad of paper. I am slightly irritated. I have been thinking about Stacey's list, and it will not coalesce. I hesitate. There are her interests to consider, there is topicality. What would resonate with her. Then it comes to me. I write down the first title. My eyes move along the shelves. I write down another. I open up my *Norton Anthology,* which leads to other things. Soon I am fascinated, suffused with pleasure. When the phone rings, I am writing down the eighth. Melanie Cook says hello, we talk, in abbreviated manner, about a deal she is undoing. She is one of the industry's top entertainment lawyers.

Howard's friend. She says, "I heard Howard gave another stellar performance. Does he do those Shakespeare things in class?"

One per semester. They won't leave him alone till he does.

"Listen. Anne. I heard you're starting a book club."

I pause. After all this time, I'm still amazed at the velocity of information in this odd little world.

I realize, with a flush of annoyance at myself, that the idea of creating a book club interests me. Really, I say to Melanie.

"You're not?"

No, I say, I'm afraid I'm not. I say that someone (I don't mention Stacey's name, that would be tasteless, and Melanie already knows anyway) evinced an interest in my making her a reading list. That's all. Melanie is endearingly disappointed, but like a good lawyer she has prepared an alternative. She presents it in the form of a confession. "We were at a screening," she says. "Spike Jonze, a rough cut." After the screening, Bob Zemeckis had gotten into a debate with Jonathan Kaplan. Bob, she tells me, held that Spike was being derivative and cited *The Ugly American* to support his position. ("The book," she stipulates, "not the movie.") Zemeckis paraphrased a passage. Kaplan had responded that *The Secret Agent* was actually a better reference and that Spike was in fact *starting* where Conrad had left off. "Carla Shamberg agreed," she said, "then Marc Lawrence brought up Saul Bellow." She mentions a Bellow title. (I correct it slightly, which she accepts with grace.)

"It was visceral," she says, "we could *feel* it, and I suddenly thought—" She pauses, remembering, a little awed. "I thought, my *God*, picking up the damn books with your hands. Not the Columbia Pictures version of Edith Wharton with an Elmer Bernstein score pushing you through. The Wharton itself." She sighs. "How long since I've done that." I know what she had felt, standing there as they spoke the book titles that appeared in the air, one by one; the titles conjured, they were spells. Literature is a power, like a foreign language you possess. The titles had clearly been played like cards.

And her feeling was also of guilt, and I think: So she is, in fact, confessing. But no matter. Wanting to appear capable is not an illegitimate reason to read books.

She comes to her point. My name had come up. What if they read the books with me? She mentions a few people who are interested. "It's your field," she says.

I rub my fingertips on the desk. I love the particular spell she is under, it is one I know well, and because she is under it, at this moment I love her, but I simply am not in the position to pursue this. In order to put her off gently, I tell her I'll consider it.

"Good." Melanie has, she thinks, planted a seed. "Great." She hangs up as if tiptoeing.

I retrieve the salad Consuelo has made me and carry it and *The Way We Live Now* out to my chair by the *Campylotropis macrocarpa*, which I transplanted the week before. I check its small purple-white flowers, which are healthy. I start to read and forget about the list and the call.

Then I remember it again on the studio lot, and under a translucent California evening mention it to a man outside Howard's bungalow. I am waiting for Howard so we can drive home together. I've known this man since we came here, he started in production design at Warners, and now he has his development deal and his sleek office. Three overweight union members in T-shirts are pushing a blue 1950s-era car across the lot. The car has no engine, it's fake. When I mention the book list, he squints into the sun, then laughs. "Anne," he says.

What?

With a look he apologizes for the laughter but explains very patiently, "Nobody *reads* in Hollywood."

IN MY DESK THERE IS an ancient letter I scribbled to my mother in gray, chilly London.

I was not, I'd written, happy at having left London, at having turned down Cambridge, at Barnard's class offerings now that I was actually in New York. At the color of the New York sky, for that matter. I was not even happy (for reasons so juvenile I prefer not to recall them now) with my apartment, 808 Broadway, above the antiques dealers. (My mother kept the letter, gave it back to me a decade later; "It's not revenge," she said, smiling, and I knew it wasn't; reading yourself in immature, overwrought version is instructive.) And the *Americans*.

One example: I wrote to her about a largish bespectacled left-handed boy with curly black hair who focused intently on whomever was speaking in the 2:00 P.M. Columbia English literature seminar. On our first day of class I had shared the briefest of opinions. Anne Hammersmith, I said to them. I observed that Trollope made few claims for the durability of his own fiction. Which was, in my prim opinion, appropriate humility. But George Eliot? "Eliot's novel *Romola* will live forever." I'd been emphatic and a little breathless about that.

The other students shot me sideways glances. Except for the black-haired boy. He did *not agree*. He felt ("Your name, please?" "Sorry: Howard") that Trollope created fully real worlds where Eliot tended to write over her readers' heads. Howard was impatient with George Eliot and impatient with *Romola* and, clearly, with me. I turned away.

The next day, driven perversely by a fury, I drifted into the orbit of a Formica-topped table near the back of a Greek diner on West 96th, a table he always inhabited accompanied by several thick paperbacks. I walked slowly, unwrapping my scarf and pretending to look for someone, but he didn't care about the pretense. "Hi. C'mere. Siddown. You want some coffee?"

Crisply: No. Thank you.

"You sure?"

I'm sure.

"So, you English?"

Sort of, I said, you American?

"Hey, funny."

Look, he explained, Eliot just couldn't make up her mind whether she wanted to be the writer or the goddamn reader—she barely got a character invented before she started responding to him. Turgenev, on the other hand, stayed the hell out of his stories, let you do your own damn responding, and that, said Howard, was the way to write literature. Present the characters *as the world sees them* and get the fuck out of the way. Hey, did I wanna go see a movie? Oh, perhaps I disagreed about Turgenev, but he would convince me. I was astonished by all the various conversational pieces he pushed furiously at me. And then he came back to the accent.

Yes? I said of the accent. And?

He grinned, repeated the phrase about "inventing characters," and it took me a second, but then I gasped. You think, I said, that my accent is *fake*! Well, I assure you—

"I think it's lovely whatever the hell it is." Before I could explain it, he proposed we see a film by Some Important Director Or Other. He rushed through the director's filmography, explained why he was great, how he stacked up next to *other* directors, and *this* movie was a literary adaptation—

I was so thoroughly put out with him that I cut him off and agreed to go to the movies. Howard seemed to still. We sat in the sudden silence. His eyes were on me, and so I glared at the chalkboard menu on the wall. I dislike people trying to work me out, I always have. An old waitress trudged past with a Pyrex globe of coffee and a sigh. A customer entered at the other end of the diner, shivering. He began to talk to me, more quietly now. I can't remember taking off my coat, but at some point I did.

We talked about New York versus London, and then important variations on this theme, like winter versus summer, and which was better, hot chocolate in winter or ice cream in summer.

I think I asked if he believed in God as an attempt at being witty. Howard's gaze was so focused, I thought there was going to be a punch line. On the question of religion, he said, he was agnostic. I took him seriously, then realized. Oh, I said, you *are* joking.

He shrugged. He seemed completely uninterested in discussing it. "Joking and not joking," he said.

I considered this. You're Jewish, though agnostic.

That he was Jewish was, Howard stipulated, clear. "I'm as Jewish as they come, culturally." He quickly listed several words I didn't know ("They're holidays"), recited something in Hebrew quickly.

As for God? Yes, yes, he said impatiently, he had some sense of God. "Or, you know. Something."

At the time, perhaps because I was young, what I spotted here was nothing more than a delicious chink in his armor. To divert his attention I trailed an ostentatiously casual finger in some spilled sugar. God or not, it wouldn't matter, I said, licking crystals from my fingertip. Belief in God is irrelevant to Judaism. You can be completely Jewish and completely atheist. Exhibit A: Karl Marx. Exhibit B: Disraeli, a confirmed Anglican. Ergo, I said, Judaism was not most fundamentally a religion, it was most fundamentally a race.

Ah *ha*: Finally the boy truly objects to something! No, he said, it was most fundamentally a religion. We had an intense argument on this, and I won with *Daniel Deronda* by (I *so* loved saying it) George Eliot! (He glared at me.) You'll recall, I said, that Eliot's Daniel is raised Christian, is culturally Christian, knows nothing of Judaism whatsoever, but is considered Jewish by the writer, the reader, the other characters, and the Jews for the sole reason that he is racially Jewish; ergo the fundamental definition of Judaism is racial.

Howard, irritably, asked me what was my obsession with Eliot, for Chrissake, and then he looked at his watch, grabbed the movie schedule, swore floridly, threw his paperbacks in some sort of deteriorating bag, and pushed me at high speed onto West 96th's sidewalk.

After the movie, I will take him back to my small apartment. The sheets will at first be cold with this early, very chilly autumn, and then very warm. It is said by the Greeks that the breath of the Minotaur was so hot it ignited parchment.

But why should I need more than him? I asked her. We were in the Columbia cafeteria.

She frowned, took a quick (slightly exasperated) breath. "Jeez, Anne, you can't just stay *consumed* by him."

Oh, honestly. I'm hardly "*consumed.*"

"Well, what would you call it!"

God, I thought furiously, this is why I avoid people. I wouldn't bloody call it anything, but I can't exactly say that to her. She was my best friend. I couldn't say, "I've found an entire world to live in, and he is enough." We used to do homework together, this girl and I, go to the movies, paint our fingernails at midnight. She was looking at me. I hunted for a response.

I said, carefully, He is mine.

She gave a single, lithe shake of her head, but when she spoke, her voice almost broke. "I never see you anymore." She pushed a glass on her plastic tray. "It's class or him."

You can see them disappear before you, vanishing away in sadness or incomprehension. Oh, I've never been good with people. You rely on them, and you love them, and they love you vaguely from some distance, they kiss you and fly away on a plane, and then suddenly they're gone. Either you hurt them too easily or they hurt you. Am I wrong, I wanted to plead with her, to find one strong, anchored island and stay safe and contented upon it. But she had simply left her plastic tray behind.

It was shortly after we met that I told Howard a story about a teacher who had taught me Greek mythology. Howard loved the myths. At the time, it was simply something I mentioned to him, casually and entirely abstractly, one of the bits and pieces that had happened to me that he absorbed avidly.

I was in England, I think age thirteen and almost seven months at

this particular school just outside London, for me a relative eternity
in one place, and I listened with fascination as she spoke about the
gods. She was an older, starched woman, but she would allow me to
linger with her after class, when the other girls had recrystallized into
their well-established structures that did not include places for me.
I was one of the prettier ones, just beginning to fill out, but in that
single-sex school there were no boys around to elevate my status. She
was, for example, the only logical person I could tell of my father's
announcement at dinner that, once again, we'd be going overseas.

For seven months I had hovered by her desk. She would murmur
to me bits and pieces about the myths as she frowned at her papers
and jotted notes on things. The Greek god Proteus, she said, when
he fought with you, had the power to change himself into any shape
he wished—lion, serpent, monster, fish—trying to twist away and
escape. But there was a trick, she explained sternly. If you could just
hold on to him throughout his transformations, he would be compelled in the end to surrender, and resume his proper shape.

She had paused. "This is a new posting for your father."

Yes. (I would be gone within the week.)

"And where are you going this time, Anne?"

My parents, I said, would be transferred to Jakarta, myself to a
British boarding school in Kuala Lumpur.

"Remember Proteus," she said, fixing me, looking into my eyes.
"Just keep tight hold of him, and it will all be all right."

Despite the hole I felt in my chest, despite the incipient loneliness
of another distant country that would soon replace the present loneliness, I understood what she was doing. She was giving me strength
via erudition, a particularly, and particularly lovely, British tradition.
She was sharing her secular faith. A literate knowledge of the Greek
myths to get one through. Very English. I nodded. When she was
satisfied, she turned back to her desk. "Right. Off you go," and she
was back to work.

I told Howard this story.

————

ON THURSDAY MORNING, HAVING FINISHED a few other things, I called Stacey.

One of her assistants put her on. "Anne." Her voice was hopeful.

I've made a list. If you're serious.

"Of course!" She was thrilled, she said. I realized her voice had quickened my pulse. She had the unique, fresh hope that springs up in us when we are about to begin reading a good book.

Oh, said Stacey. A small cloud passed over the voice. She had been at a meeting the other day and in the parking garage had run into Melanie Cook. Melanie had heard I was starting a book club.

Yes, I said that Melanie had called me, we'd straightened that out.

Ah, she said. Well. The thing was, what Stacey and Melanie were wondering was whether, if I had time of course, if it wasn't an imposition, would I like to read *with* them? Obviously I'd already read the books, it was my list after all, but they were thinking an evening every month or so—they would come to me, of course! I wouldn't ever have to get in a car.

I thought about it. Well, maybe I could do that. Once every month. Or so. Why not. Perhaps we could start three weeks from today? I was looking at my calendar. Thursday evening. At my house.

Stacey said, "Josh, pick up, please."

A click on the line. "Hi, Mrs. Rosenbaum."

Hello, Josh.

Josh would make the entry on her calendar. I told Stacey I would leave it to her to coordinate all this with Melanie.

"Of course. Josh?"

"Got it," he said.

This is not a book club, OK?

"No," she said, "I understand." Oh, and she wondered if J. J. Abrams might join us, because she'd mentioned it to J.J., and he loved the idea.

Who was J. J. Abrams?

A director, she said. Great energy.

Oh, yes. Of course. (I had met him somewhere.) If you'll call him, that's fine. So that's three of you, then.

A studio executive, an entertainment lawyer, and a director. I thought about it, potentially pleased.

I went to warn Denise. There always has to be food.

HOWARD AND I WERE MARRIED by a justice of the peace just before 8:00 P.M. at City Hall. My parents were in Burma. They sent their blessings.

Howard's parents were more complicated. On a frigid February day about two months before the ceremony we took the 1 subway from Columbia in Harlem, changed to the 2 train at West 96th Street, and got out in Brooklyn at Borough Hall. Down Court Street, across Atlantic Avenue, left on Dean Street. This was when one scanned the sidewalks in that neighborhood for danger. They had gathered in the living room, his mother and father, several aunts, an uncle and so on. I was nineteen; Howard, twenty. Stuart, Howard's brother, was three years his junior. They kept kosher. They handed me cookies and cups as if I was infectious. I tried to catch Howard's eye, but he was engaged in a side argument with his father about LBJ.

At one point he slipped me upstairs to show me his boyhood bedroom. Well, I whispered to him, the conversation is as iced as the weather.

He was looking around. "They turned my room into *storage*."

Howard?

After a moment he said, "Things are fine."

I said, Well, I'd hardly call this "fine." You know perfectly well they're against it.

"It's none of their goddamn business," he said gently.

His reticence at discussing it was an emotional default, I knew.

As we walked back down the stairs, he held my hand till our knees became visible to the living room and then he released it. He said, moving toward the large kitchen, "When do we eat!"

His mother glanced at me, very briefly. "This one eats?"

I don't think he heard.

Still it seemed simple to me at the time. Upstairs in his room, Howard had put his arms around me, bearlike, carefully so as not to make noise. "I love you," he had whispered simply. So I take it back; we did discuss it, or, to be precise, Howard gave me what seemed to me at that time the only response I could have asked from him. I thought it was the only thing either of us needed. And it was, then.

Stuart made it tolerable. He offered me chairs when they didn't. It was subtle and typically Stuart, the instinctive diplomat and negotiator, pouring oil on the waters. He talked with me. I asked about kosher. "Kashrut," said Stuart with a smile. So what was eaten with what, how did they do it? He rolled his eyes, said with equanimity that his parents were self-delusioned, and, in whatever was not self-delusion, hypocrites and fakes. "Do you see two fuckin' sinks?" He dismissed it. I gleaned that he and Howard had given definitive, if not violent, notice on the Kashrut Question several years ago, and a delicate truce had been forcibly established in which the parties had agreed not to issue statements.

It was Stuart who explained—Howard had never mentioned it to me—that up until a matter of months before he met me Howard's mother had contrived to introduce him to a succession of Orthodox girls. I said, Really? with some astonishment, and before I could ask more, Stuart added, "They wear *wigs*. OK?" It was Stuart who, when they weren't looking, put his hands around his neck and pretended to strangle himself. "Why are you guys laughing?" Howard asked, annoyed. The odd thing, in retrospect, is that I never explained to him what we were laughing at. It belonged to Stuart and me. At some point in the presence of Howard and his parents I had understood that Howard had compartments, hermetically sealed off from each other, and if these were not to communicate with each other, on a

certain level I accepted this. My acceptance was automatic. I had
been raised that way. It was how I had survived.

One word they used to his face was *inappropriate,* which I know
because I overheard it, and which was a very mild word, but they'd
already used all the others.

In the spring, his mother and father came to the wedding. Then
we went out for dinner in Chinatown. Conversation was stilted. The
food was mediocre. They paid. We said good-bye, walked up Mott
Street, waited till we'd gotten to the corner and ran as fast as we
could up Canal to the lip of the Manhattan Bridge and we kissed and
kissed. We walked up Bowery, bathed in the greasy scent of hot oil,
past the kitchen supplies stores, wandered through Union Square
where the April buds were just starting to come out.

He told them he loved me, and they knew it was true. That their
view didn't infuriate him infuriated me, at times, and baffled me at
others. I didn't care so much that they disapproved. I cared that he
didn't seem to care and that I had no idea why he didn't. We had
a few minor fights over it, but then it simply became background
radiation. I always knew that he loved me. That—and we agreed on
this, Howard and I—was what counted.

When Sam was born, we lived inside him.

We soothed him with tiny promises.

We fed him orange flowers from blue islands and imported sun-
sets to his nursery.

He had the fingers of an artist, the lungs of a stevedore, and the
ears of an artilleryman.

We cursed the clock, that it did not give us more hours in a single
day to spend with him.

I taught him words: *flower.* And *tree.* And *clematis,* at which Howard said, "Oh, boy," and rolled his eyes. I was not deterred. I would
bring Sam with me to lectures at West Valley Nursery on Ventura,
educated, interested women sitting on wooden benches with our

coffees in paper cups, the smell of mulch curling around our ankles, evaluating forsythia in arid Southern California. I never join in the decrying of eucalyptus. It is not indigenous, an import to this area, but then so am I, and it thrives here. Besides, it smells heavenly—astringent, fresh earth. When Sam was a baby, he slept. When he was older, he toddled around among the seedlings, and the nursery's salespeople watched him. In grasses, they knew him by name; I love grasses. At age two and a half, Sam pointed at a vine I was planting in the garden—which was coming together very nicely—and said, "Clematis!" Howard, reading a contract on a teak lounge chair, sat bolt upright, then burst out laughing.

His febrile intelligence, his curiosity, were obvious. As we watched him moving about the garden with his toys, placing a truck just so, investigating a bee, Howard murmured a line of Keats to me: "The creature hath a purpose, and its eyes are bright with it."

There is a pop song Howard and I heard on the radio. I thought it was so lovely I used to sing it to Sam, when he was little and afraid of the Disney villains.

> *I'm stronger than the monster beneath your bed*
> *Smarter than the tricks played on your heart*

Howard would watch me hold Sam and sing to him. Years later, Sam said that he had been conscious that I was focusing on the line about being stronger than the monsters. But actually, he said, he himself as a child was relying on my being smarter than the tricks the animators sought to play on his heart. Those fake villains they drew into existence. Imagined sources of threat.

EVENING, THURSDAY, THE L.A. AIR is darkening and lovely. It is almost 6:00 P.M., and I ask Consuelo to set the table next to the crape myrtle. Jennifer calls from Howard's office just to check in. No, I have everything. Oh—I tell her to keep Howard away for at least an hour, and she says she's already arranged that. She's very good.

J.J. arrives first. We introduce ourselves. He stands, self-consciously deferential, in the entryway in his suit, pressing the book over his testicles like a sporran. "Oh, I'm first?"

Quite all right.

He frowns at his watch. "She said . . ."

It's quite all right, J.J., honestly.

"Well. Terrific evening, huh."

Yes. We'll be talking outside.

"Great!" he says enthusiastically. Then: "Oh! Should I . . . ?" He makes a quizzical hand motion toward the back.

Please. After you.

"Great!" He moves out, like a one-man platoon taking the garden.

We hear two car engines die in immediate succession, and Consuelo brings Melanie and Stacey. The candles are lit, we sort out the drinks. Are they hungry? Denise has made some things, so I hope we'll all eat. It's marvelous of you to do this, Anne, they say, to take the time, and so on. I say I'm happy to. Now, first of all, everyone finished, yes? Good, a well-thumbed copy there, nice to see.

I slip into the role as if into warm salt water in some pleasant ocean. They're watching me closely. I introduce myself very briefly, my literature degree, what this book means to me. It's an odd sensation, but I like it. Usually I only talk to Howard. This is pleasant. I stop speaking for a moment, clear my throat. Then I say, Right, now you. Who enjoyed the book and who did not?

But the conversation starts out painfully, haltingly. They are hesitant, their ideas cramped, and I don't understand why, and I find myself suddenly disappointed. Three days later this will be explained to me when I get a phone call from Jeremy Zimmer. It's the doctorate in literature, he will inform me decisively. How does he know this? Oh, he will say—Jeremy, like all talent agents, speaks with dead certain authority—he'd been to a dinner party last night, seated next to a woman J.J. knows. She talked about it all night. They'd loved it, by the way, the whole evening, *really* loved it. Oh, and the English accent, too, that also intimidates them.

I will be struck by the fact that even in Southern California, every human being connects a knowledge of books with self-respect and self-worth. I will say to Jeremy, It certainly didn't occur to me that I was intimidating them.

They found you masterful, Jeremy will say.

So (he adds smoothly) the reason he called, he was wondering, could my book club take another person.

I will be slightly flustered but react by stipulating, It's not a book club, Jeremy. I will give him the next title, which it turns out he already knows, and the date, which it turns out he also already knows. I will say we haven't set the where yet but it might as well be at my house again. This, it turns out, he will have assumed. Right. In that case, I say, would he please take charge of logistics and coordination.

"Bronwyn"—his assistant—"pick up, please."

Click. "Hi, Ms. Rosenbaum," says Bronwyn.

Hello, Bronwyn.

"Oh, Bronwyn," Jeremy will begin, "we'll need you to get us a dessert. A really good one."

But in the garden on that first evening, it is not working, and I am feeling my way forward tentatively. I think, Why would they listen to me? but I am careful not to show this because in my experience showing doubt never serves any purpose.

I tell them: Please understand. You won't *offend* me if you do not like this book. I happen to love it, but a book is like a person, and one's reaction to a person invariably has more to do with one's own personality and life experience than with the actual person herself.

I add, Unfortunately.

After a moment I add, That always seems to be the case with others' reactions to me, for example. They watch me when I say this. I flush very slightly at having made this statement. I'm the least self-revelatory person I know, but they were listening so intently. Well then. I return to my point. Half of any book, I say, is just a mirror in which you do or do not see yourself. But, and this is just my opinion, the best readers try to fit themselves into the writer's mind rather than the reverse. Take a step toward your authors, and they will repay you twofold.

They listen. And still the conversation stumbles along. They take no risks. They have, I think grimly, no courage.

I'm losing patience and about to look at my watch. And something occurs to me. If you were directing this, I ask them, how would you cast it.

Within two minutes J.J. is waving a cell phone like a switchblade and threatening to call Bonnie Timmermann, the casting director, because obviously such-and-such an actress, who Bonnie happens to love, possesses *ex-act-ly* the qualities the book's author ascribes to her main character. Considering the actress's latest performance, I personally find J.J.'s a rather unusual reading, and I tell him this, and so he immediately cites three different pages from the book at me, slams down a suddenly forceful, precise critique, and I see his point. Stacey dismisses the actress (as does Melanie, though for wildly different reasons), brutally details a *New York Times* review (eviscerating), suggests a different actress and two supporting actors, and quotes text from the book to support all of it (she has, to our surprise, underlined these sections), but J.J. will not be quashed and says oh, hell, if Stacey casts the supporting characters that way then she has totally missed the author's whole point, and Stacey is arming herself with her own cell phone and citing filmography right and left and saying fine, then why don't they just call Stephen Gaghan and ask *him*, and Melanie is championing her own choice, a young Golden Globe winner two years earlier ("Too young," snaps Stacey; "Not if Tony Gilroy directs her," retorts Melanie and with a certain menace goes for her own cell phone).

I make my first rule, which is No cell phones, and they back off, somewhat. I excise the extraneous comments, supply some textual pieces they missed (I am severe with them about a character they have all, to my mind, grossly misinterpreted), guide them back from a silly subplot they've gotten lost in. But essentially the textual work is theirs, and from that point onward it is decent work. Not brilliant, but, for a first outing, quite competent. We also arrive at what I must admit is a rather fascinating cast, which would, were the book filmed, add a radical and contemporary spin to Brontë's original intent. At 7:00, I stand up. Howard will be home soon.

J.J. peers at his watch again, this time with surprise.

I was seeing them to the drive when they asked me how I'd gotten here. In those words. The question confused me at first; I thought they meant our Realtor. I tend to be literal. They said no, no, Los Angeles. As in *living* here. "You were raised in London, yes?" they added.

Ah. Yes. Well, actually I was raised many places. My father, Matthew Hammersmith, was in the British diplomatic service. My mother was American. (They waited.) Where: Hong Kong, I said, for several years when I was young. Rome. Oh, lots of places.

Where had I met Howard?

New York, I said. Howard and I met at Columbia.

And so? Stacey indicated our house, and J.J. pointed at the hills, the Pacific beyond, and I finally got it. Right.

How I got here. We came to L.A. because in 1970 we ran—quite literally—into Bennett Cerf, the head of Random House. The old train from Paris to Avignon swerved, and I lost my balance and flew outstretched-hands-first into a well-dressed man as Howard tried to catch me. Providence.

I'm *so* sorry!

In a carful of Frenchmen, "Ah, you're English!" said Bennett.

Well, sort of, I said.

Howard: "She's half American."

"Well, you," Bennett turned to Howard, "*you're* American."

We wound up moving to the dining car. Bennett went and fetched his wife, Phyllis. "Phyllis, this young man is a newly minted Ph.D. in English literature." "Anne will be one soon," said Howard quickly. (It would take me an extra year; I'd been supporting Howard.) "Ah," said Bennett. Howard was quite thin then, and Bennett had a fatherly hand on his shoulder and, clearly, an idea forming in his head. Almost immediately, unbidden, he brought it up: There was a job in—well, it didn't really have a name, not yet, Cerf was thinking about it (he looked at Phyllis as he said this), but he had this idea of having a Random House person work directly with the movie studios, selling books to them.

I did not dare look at Howard. I could feel him holding his breath while his brain was shouting. Howard was twenty-five.

The only question Bennett asked directly, indeed almost immediately, was: "You two are married?"

"Oh!" said Howard. "Yeah!" He indicated France with a chin. "Delayed honeymoon."

Cerf nodded warmly at me. ("Such a lovely English girl," said Phyllis to Howard.) I found them very sweet. I held up my poor little diamond ring, which I adored, so they could admire it.

We got home and started packing up our cramped apartment in Greenwich Village and moved to West 70th and Amsterdam. My mother flew across the Atlantic to help. She thought our brownstone "kind of *dark*, Anne." She looked around with raised eyebrows. *She* was from the *East* Side. She helped me cover everything in drop cloths and plan the tiny patch of soon-to-be garden out back as I rollered the walls with a daffodil cream I'd seen in a Macy's catalog.

Howard walked to Random House's offices in the Villard Mansion on Madison near 50th Street. Within days he knew them all—Donald Klopfer (who trained him), Jason Epstein, Jim Silberman, Bob Loomis, Sally Kovalchik, who did the "how to" books. They all had two-digit phone extensions then. He used to play kick-the-can in the hallways with Howard Kaminsky, who helped him develop the movie sales. Kaminsky was Mel Brooks's cousin, and Howard worshipped him. He met people at Simon & Schuster and Alfred A. Knopf. He basically lived on the phone—it was considered a bizarre job, neither publishing nor movies, a hybrid of the two that at first only Howard and Bennett understood—and he had to earn people's trust. Bennett gave Howard the phone numbers of a few of the studio heads to start him off and introduced him to the writers, who didn't exactly know what to do with him. Philip Roth actually thought he was an agent. Saul Bellow thought he was an editorial assistant and would call to ask him to run a manuscript down to Saul's friend so-and-so on Bleecker, which of course Howard did.

And he met Shawn of the *New Yorker* at a party on East 88th, and from Shawn to the writers, and then Bob Gottlieb and the writers Gottlieb hired. They were interested in Howard because Howard, as Mark Singer once put it to me, "kept the writer's entrance to Hollywood, like Cerberus. But," said Mark, "with only one head."

I loved that image. Howard guarding some fiery hole on East 50th leading to Paramount.

Through Mort Janklow, Mike Ovitz heard of Howard, and called him, and Bennett, after thinking it over, said absolutely, Howard should interface with Creative Artists Agency. CAA was constantly searching for material for the movies, and Howard would ensure that material would come from Random House. He prepared his pitches, walking into their meetings holding a book in his hand. "Your next blockbuster," he would announce. He explained to them why it was a perfect vehicle for this or that client, a career maker, and so he started getting to know the actors. CAA was doing surprisingly well, and Howard was flying more frequently to L.A. "He's gone a lot," observed my mother but left it at that. Through Mike, the studios noticed him. The idea of this hybrid literary-to-film job he was doing was no longer so strange. Howard came home and looked at me

sideways and said, "So. What would you think?" One of the studios
had made an offer. Executive in charge of new properties. He was
elated. They had said, in essence: Be our book eyes.

Howard would say in the future that his job descended directly
from Samuel Goldwyn because it was Goldwyn who first tried to
marry literature and movies. The semiliterate Eastern European
immigrant, desiring the elevation of his art through literary good
taste, hired as a screenwriter the dignified Belgian Nobel Prize
winner Maurice Maeterlinck. Maeterlinck spoke no English, and
Goldwyn, as he would have been first to acknowledge, spoke no
Belgian. Hollywood legend has it that Maeterlinck's first effort
for his new employer was an adaptation of his own *Life of the
Bee*, and Goldwyn ran from his bungalow screaming "My God,
the hero is a bee!" Still, Goldwyn liked having the author around the
lot. He proudly pointed him out to everyone who stopped by as
"the greatest writer on earth! He's the guy who wrote *The Birds
and the Bees*."

I started packing up the brownstone.

In my driveway, the light was becoming golden with evening as
they listened to me. I frowned. I asked the three of them, who've
worked with Howard for years: Howard never told you any of this?

No, they said, with some amusement because obviously I didn't
have the faintest idea how Howard behaved with them. "You know,
Anne, Howard doesn't really talk much about himself." And after a
moment one of them added, not at all unkindly, "He's like you that
way, yes?"

I hadn't known this about him. I suppose he is, I said. They realized that I had always taken Howard's easy friendliness with them,
his colleagues, as friendship. They realized that I had not known that
he was rather circumspect with them. They watched me learning
these things about my husband.

Very warmly they kissed me good-bye on the cheek. Their car
keys were tinkling cheerfully. They called, "See you in a few weeks!"

I went inside and thought about our next meeting. Well! Next time, I decided, I'd cut some fresh flowers from the garden.

THEN THERE IS WHAT I did not say.

When Howard and I arrived in Los Angeles in 1979, I was, I realize in retrospect, in shock. The sun was pouring down like the rain in London. Unlike London, there was no context for anything. Stuart called from Brooklyn. "So! Anne. L.A."

I replied, with an eye on Howard, who was emptying boxes, that L.A. was "the ninth circle of hell." Stuart misunderstood me to say that Los Angeles was "the nicest suburb of hell." He repeated this to Howard, who readily acceded to the description.

Almost immediately I said to Howard that they were all ridiculous. I actually said (I'm embarrassed to admit it now) "all." They certainly all *seemed* ridiculous; I have learned over the years that this is not the point. First, Hollywood people are ridiculous and they are not. More important, even the dullest and crassest of them have a certain startling animal perceptiveness. Who would imagine that pathological narcissism could foster such external awareness? Howard took David Geffen to lunch one day, and David, his eyes taking in the entire restaurant, snorted, "These are people who talk on the phone all day." But perhaps because of this, they are deceptively febrile with words. Counterintuitive, to my mind. Utter disdain for the written word and still this immense value put on language.

But I had to learn this.

We would walk in the front door. "Oh, Howard, good, you're here." "Howard, haven't seen you in ages!" "Hey, kid, come and meet a friend of mine who works with Lew." "Great to see you, Howard. Oh, hello, Anne."

Hello.

Sit at the Hollywood dinner party listening to one more reference to one more deal, another drama being played out at another studio. You are sitting next to the producer of the kind of movie where, Howard says, you not only have to suspend disbelief, you have to stab and gang-rape it. To amuse yourself, if you are, say, only recently arrived, if you have left the West Side of Manhattan for the nicest suburb of hell with a young husband who was only a few months ago avidly discussing Shelley and Donne and is now equally avidly following the crafting of a vapid sitcom (and, yes, if you're trying to understand being faced with this young man you thought you knew who is revealing an unguessed-at capacity for what he himself calls "crap"—how to interpret him now, here where all is cars and valet parking and no one reads), you just might express ever so slightly too much enthusiasm for the utterly vapid sitcom characters being created before your eyes. If you generate a slightly wild-eyed enthusiasm for the idiocies trotted out by a breathtakingly ambitious recent Harvard graduate, one more self-serious Jewish boy from an urban eastern suburb (who looks disconcertingly like your own recent Columbia graduate Jewish husband from an urban eastern suburb). If you evince an ever-so-slightly condescending fascination toward yet another facile ad-agency concept that they confuse with narration and plot as they present it to you with a gravity fit for Spinoza—then it would be understandable for you to imagine that your sarcasm was sailing right over their well-groomed heads.

Howard told me gently that I was wrong. In the cocoon of our already relatively nice car, returning from a dinner party that had run much too late thrown by moneyed people in a large house where, as my friend Ellie Trachtenberg once put it to me, the cuisine was haute and the conversation trash, he told me that I was wrong. That their little antennae were picking up all sorts of signals I would have thought beyond their wavelengths.

Hm, I said. And then: Really? Those people?

"Your incredulity is adorable," said Howard.

Don't be patronizing, I said, my incredulity is completely sincere.

"And therefore more adorable." Howard looked back at the road. He said that any literary work can be measured in purely commercial terms. I pursed my lips at this. It would take me approximately a decade to admit he was right. Which was just silliness on my part. I was being a snob. Howard understood this. Me with my nineteenth-century novels, my Trollope and my Dumas— had I already forgotten that these were the commercial hardcovers of their day? ("Trollope made few claims for the durability of his own fiction.")

As for the signals I had been emitting, imagining them lost on all those Californians, well, he had a response to that, too. He cleared his throat in the faint green light of the dashboard and quoted to me, loosely, this. It was (the point was not lost on me) from George Eliot's *Daniel Deronda*: "'Gwendolen meant to win Miss Arrowpoint at the party by giving an interest and attention beyond what others were probably inclined to show. It followed in her mind, unreflectingly'"—I looked at Howard sharply—"'that because Miss Arrowpoint was ridiculous, she was also wanting in penetration, and Gwendolen went through her little scenes without suspicion that the shades of her behavior were all noted.'"

He took my tensed hand. It took me all the way to La Brea to let out the breath I'd been holding.

In the end, Howard turned out to be absolutely right. Many of them are ridiculous and very few are actually stupid. One of the many oddities of this place.

It was quite early on that a UCLA trustee—I think we were at a cocktail party?—had asked me about my Columbia degree. "A Ph.D. in English literature." That's right. "And Howard just earned his as well?" Yes, I said, but Howard's focus was sixteenth century, mine nineteenth. He said, "Hm!" and then, enthusiastically: There was a faculty opening. "Intro level, part-time, be warned, but it's a terrific position."

(I paused, quite excited.) You're suggesting I apply?

"Absolutely!" he said. "Both of you."

I didn't go on about it, but I did think a teaching position would be wonderful—we agreed it would be at least a small contribution to our income—though I was, in fact, quite apprehensive about standing up before two hundred students in an auditorium. "They'll love you," said Howard. I wasn't sure. I balked. Howard wound up applying as well in order to push me into it. "Stop second-guessing yourself, Anne." We submitted our fresh Columbia doctorates. Howard had written his thesis on Shakespeare's approach to adaptation from other sources, I on the intellectual origins of the Romantics.

In my very first interview, in Haines Hall on the central quad, the professor—an Americanist, he taught ENGL 179A, "American Fiction to 1900"—seemed curiously distracted, the conversation diffuse. He glanced at a paper in front of him, switched gears, and said, "You're married to Howard Rosenbaum." Now he seemed intently interested.

Yes.

"Of Random House?"

I said yes, then, *formerly* of Random House.

"He's with a studio now, right?"

Yes, that's why we moved here.

He cleared his throat. "You know," he said, "I've written a manuscript for a book. I think its quite filmic." He named it: the biography of an American author of several twentieth-century novels.

I was a bit off balance, so I said, A minor writer.

"Yes," he replied, managing his irritation, "but he shouldn't be."

Well, we'll disagree.

He knew it was not going well but still said gamely, "Maybe I could talk to Howard about it." Looked again at the paper. "I see he's also applied for this position."

They interviewed both of us.

The letter from UCLA, which arrived quickly, asked Howard to come in for a final interview. He found it before I did, opened it, and, after a bit, brought it to me. He cleared his throat. "Maybe I'll just tell 'em to go to hell," he said.

I looked down at my shoes.

"Anne?"

I raised my head to him and smiled and said, Don't be ridiculous. You'll *love* teaching, you were born for it.

He paused a moment, gauging the sincerity of this. He hadn't, honestly, given it much thought, but now that it was here. "They're idiots," he offered. He was earnest. "You're twice the scholar I am."

Well, I said and cocked my head brightly. At least *you* know that.

I turned away and pretended to organize some papers.

"It's just because I'm more flash." I noticed his eyes were back on the letter, rereading it. You could feel his excitement. "It's the movie studio, they're suckers for that." He was still reading. Then he looked up at me. "And I'm male," he added, darkly. (This I thought was laying it on a bit thick.)

I kissed him briefly. True, I said. I made a gesture as if I'd forgotten all about it.

I went out to work in the garden while Howard called the department head. I moved out of earshot. I had decided that I could indeed stand up in front of two hundred students, I could do it, and I *would* do it. It wouldn't frighten me. I would teach them, I would choose all sorts of wonderful pieces of literature and they would listen to me and we would read these texts together and discuss them, and I would explain why I loved them.

I pushed my trowel deep into the earth.

UCLA looked over his thesis, asked a few questions, and then offered him a little freshman requirement backwater called Introduction to Shakespeare. He began the fall semester three days after he started at the studio, where everyone considered his "teaching thing" a harmless eccentricity. He had a few students in a small basement room.

Today his classes are held in a huge lecture hall and invariably oversubscribed, which makes for a perennially hectic second week of September, desperate lines outside his door, and all manner of add/drop subterfuge. He moans about it every fall. "These nubile eighteen-year-olds panting for me," he sighs at dinner, "their pert nipples, limpid blue eyes, the blond hair that kisses the napes of their tanned necks." He pops an olive in his mouth. "And that's just the football players."

He genuinely loved them, and they responded in kind. He disliked "Doctor" ("Only my mother calls me doctor," he told them; this was in fact true) but got a kick out of "Professor." Then a colleague saw him coming out of Rolfe Hall after class and shouted at him, "How are you, Howard?" and he shouted back, "I'm great box office," and he was afterward known by all of UCLA and eventually everyone at the studio as GBO.

In class, Howard was not overly prudent. It was just discovered, he told his second freshmen seminar, that Shakespeare actually wrote three plays about penises, one four-inch penis, another eight inches, the last one ten. They got the first one immediately—*Much Ado About Nothing*—and the second, *Midsummer Night's Dream*. But the third?

"*Othello*," said Howard.

The dean looked very grim as he listened to the single complaint by an intense young woman from Walnut Creek who lectured him on Professor Rosenbaum's racism, patriarchalism, and sexism. He ushered her out with solemn tones, and then called his wife, an Elizabethan scholar, and repeated the joke to her, laughing hysterically.

Howard paces the dais of the amphitheater enthusiastically. He is not bothered by doing the elementary stuff. Contrary to what all of you weaned on Warner cartoons think, he tells them, star-crossed lovers does *not* mean that Romeo and Juliet, a boy and girl three years younger than you are now, are so in love they have Chuck Jones animated stars circling their heads. *No. What does it mean?*

An expectant glance at them over his reading glasses, his favorite prop. I bought them for him at the Rexall drugstore near the Beverly Center. Time's up! Yes, possums, it refers to astrology, which used to be the state religion in Elizabethan hangouts. "What's thy sign?" It means that this boy's and girl's respective astrological houses are at odds. Also, "Wherefore art thou, Romeo?" does not mean "Where the hell are you?" but "Oh, Christ, why do you have to be Romeo Montague, and I Juliet Capulet, two families at war, what a *pain!*"

The first year, GBO rewarded their curiosity with a few juicy industry tidbits, was it true that such-and-such a star who *Variety* reported was working with him had signed for such-and-such a movie? He began rationing this sort of thing for moments when he found himself losing their attention. He stood at the lectern with his drugstore reading glasses and his notes and used sex to glue them to the text.

"Every culture and society renews its religious injunctions against sex as perennially as sexual desire is renewed, which is to say every third of a nanosecond. The reflexive whitewashing of the past that we do with respect to sexual mores, which In My Humble Opinion derives basically from our desire to avoid imagining our parents doing it, leads to a really silly view of human nature. People use sex for many purposes. Certainly Shakespeare did. And his contemporaries. Take John Donne. Slightly younger than Bill. Donne 1572–1631. (Shakespeare's dates? Hm? You in front, with the Lakers T-shirt. A guess, then. *Dude*, you can do it! What? Not bad, Shakespeare, 1564 to 1616.) During Vietnam, a war that we sort of fought before all of you were born, young men gained exclusion from military service if they got their wives or girlfriends pregnant, which gave the slogan 'Make Love Not War' a certain, shall we say, piquancy. 'Better to make a person here than kill one over there.' John Donne made the same argument in a poem called 'Love's War,' on page 1068, where for example—ah, the sound of those pages riffling—where there are a few choice lines that never fail to bring a smile to my face. Just ask my wife. She's sitting next to the big blond hunk in the sweat-shirt, the one who looks so much like me. Wave, Anne. Thank you. Donne sees love as a constant, eternal war, only to him there are two kinds of war. You, yeah you, with what I'm sure is an absolutely lovely mezzo-soprano, or perhaps a basso profundo, please read and think of my marriage."

The boy unslouches a bit and begins to read aloud.

> *Other men war that they their rest may gayne*
> *But wee will rest that wee may fight again.*

"Get it?" says Howard with a grin, and, after a rushed silent reread of the lines, frowning at the page, and finally equating "fight" with sexual activity, their faces say: "*Oh . . .*"

> *There lyes are wrong; here safe uprightly lie;*

"Donne means that telling lies in love is par for the course."

> *There men kill men; we will make one by and by.*
> *Thousands wee see which travaille not to warrs;*
> *But stay swords, armes, and shott to make at home;*
> *And shall not I do then*
> *More glorious service, staying to make men?*

"Thank you. Nice voice. Where were you when we were casting Nemo? Now, Shakespeare, in his sonnets—quatrain, quatrain, quatrain, couplet—addresses the usual Elizabethan themes of immortality and beauty and constancy and all that crap, but we will skip Sonnet Number 18, the famous 'Shall I compare thee to a summer's day?' where he modestly tells the girl that summer may fade and the sun grow dim in the commuter smog but *she* will remain eternally fair for the inarguable reason that he is presenting her that way in Sonnet Number 18, and we will skip Sonnet Number 29, which opens with the paradigmatic iambic pentameter When *in* dis*grace* with *fo*rtune *and* men's *eyes* new line I *all* a*lone* be*weep* my *out*cast *state* that makes such an icon of Sonnet Number 29, and we will skip Sonnet Number 87, the delicate Ode to Paranoid Insecurity that uses a cheesy flashback not even the schlockmeisters at Carolco would have touched, and stop at Sonnet Number 116, which treats sex a bit more seriously than does Mr. Donne and by which you should all prepare to live your lives or suffer failed marriages. I say this sincerely. Am I revealing too much? Remember that my wife is in the audience. You, in the black lycra cat-suit—page 809. People"—he looks up, projects to the very last rows of the amphitheater—"this one's about expectations and reasonableness."

> *Let me not to the marriage of true minds*
> *Admit impediments. Love is not love*
> *Which alters when it alteration finds*
> *Or bends with the remover to remove:*

"In other words, Shakespeare is saying hey, stuff happens in relationships. Deal with it."

> *Oh, no! Love is an ever-fixèd mark,*

"Bill means love is an unmoving landmark."

> *That looks on tempests and is never shaken;*
> *It is the star to every wandering bark,*

"A 'bark' is a boat."

> *Whose worth's unknown, although its height*
> *be taken.*

"The star's 'height' is its location, for use by navigators."

Love alters not with Time's brief hours and weeks,
But bears it out even to the edge of doom.
If this be error and upon me proved
I never writ, nor no man ever loved.

"You will decide for yourselves, of course, but when I first read this I took him to be warning me that if my girlfriend ever cheated on me, I'd better be able to work through it." He eyes them pointedly. "Just my interpretation. Either that, or he's being hopelessly idealistic, which you may come to believe. I don't know. But in the final couplet Bill's saying he's betting everything he ever wrote on being right on this baby."

And Howard laughs.

It was his theory that what they actually liked was hearing their own conversations, their own dark dorm-room thoughts and secret masturbatory interests and desperate erections and romantic young dreams, in late Middle English. As for Howard, he adored the words themselves. With his own son, he was somewhat stricter in his literary choices, attempting to find less NC–17 literature. He started with words. "Why is there no egg in eggplant nor ham in hamburger?" Howard asked when Sam was five years old, and Sam's eyes got big as saucers, sitting up straight at the dinner table. "English muffins weren't invented in England nor French fries in France."

"Really?" asked Sam, very seriously.

Sam already knew from my father that sweetmeats were candy, and he knew that sweetbreads were calves' glands because months before in Paris, at Le Train Bleu, after I placed his seat so he could see the trains arriving at the Gare de Lyon, and having gravely considered the long menu I translated for him, he had ordered them from the amused yet respectful waiter. But when Howard pointed out that sweetmeats aren't meat while sweetbreads are, it surprised him.

We went skiing in Aspen, and Howard's outburst prompted Sam to ask how it can be cold as hell one day and hot as hell another. I've spawned a tape recorder, said Howard to me.

What's "spawned," Dad? said Sam.

Ask your mother, said Howard.

Howard measured Sam's developmental phases both by his increasing linguistic sophistication and by the way he reacted to Medieval poetry. Sam absorbed it without a hiccup. Sitting on his six-year-old's bed, bedtime promptly at 8:30, covers up around Sam's chin, Howard perched his reading glasses on his nose and read.

"I Have a Yong Sister," intoned Howard.

I have a yong sister
Fer

"Far," said Howard

beyonde the see;
Manye be the druries

"Druries are gifts, Sam."

That she sente me.
She sente me the cherye
Withouten any stoon,

"Stone," said Howard, "cherry pit."

And so she dide the dove
Withouten any boon.

"Without any bones," Howard said to Sam. "Cool, huh!"

"*Dad,*" shouted Sam, twisting the sheets, and then set about repeating the lines back.

As he grew, the sheets of Samuel's bed became glowing, luminous membranes. Howard had bought him flashlights. I had to make him stop. Bedtime was bedtime. At least I didn't fear fire. In Virginia Woolf's comic novel *Orlando* I saw Sam exactly: "The taste for books was an early one. As a child he was sometimes found at midnight by a page still reading. They took his taper worm and he bred glow-worms to serve his purpose. They took the glow-worms away, and he almost burnt the house down with a tinder." I took it as a warning, but I didn't tell Howard. He would have been alarmed had I told him I was using *Orlando*, which is about an immortal boy who turns into a woman, as an operating manual for Sam.

Why do you park in the driveway, Sam asked Howard on the 405 heading for a Lakers game, and drive on the parkway? When the inevitable question came at fourteen—"Can I drive?"—and Howard gently replied, "Fat chance," Sam sulkily pointed out that a slim chance and a fat chance are the same and was further irritated that his verbal dexterity didn't get him behind his father's wheel. When they were getting up at 4:30 in the morning to go fishing on Lake Castic, Howard noted that your alarm clock goes off by going on. Sam, why when I wind up my watch do I start it, but when a screenwriter winds up a screenplay, as screenwriters are only occasionally known to do without extensive prodding from long-suffering, overworked movie execs and the proffering of absurdly large sums of cash, does she end it?

I tried to play once, early on. I put down my fork and said, Why is it alumnus, alumni, but hippopotamus, hippopotamuses? Howard froze. He looked at Sam and mumbled "Ha!" with his mouth full, and clear as a bell I heard "Look, pretend, OK?" But the ten-year-old was having none of it, nor did I want him to—I was fascinated by his sudden scornful agitation. "Mom, *no.*" It turned out that, yeah,

yeah, he already knew that the plural "-i" ending is due to alumnus's Latin provenance, but the animal's English name derives from the Greek (hippos were known to the Greeks), thus "es."

Hm, I said. I had been under the impression that quirky information was the point. No?

No.

Ah. I see.

The point, Howard explained to me, was . . . well, it wasn't *that*. Sam rolled his eyes unempathetically and stuck potatoes in his mouth. The thing, done rightly, had to "make you go *hm*," offered Sam, as if this was ridiculously obvious. Sam had given a concise working definition of irony.

I gathered their plates and left the dining room for the kitchen, experiencing the amusing sensation of being expelled from a nineteenth-century men's club.

This exclusive connection Howard has with Sam makes Sam openly love Howard, look up to him, be complicit with him. And I know, if I don't fully understand, how almost desperately my husband needs that link to his son.

Denise loaded me up with the pie she'd made, sent me back out so I wouldn't be under her feet.

"You know, Sam," said Howard as they did a decidedly mediocre job of trimming a hedge—we needed a gardener—"when a house burns up, it burns down." "Dad," said Sam at fifteen when he was *finally* old enough to apply for his learner's permit and they stood in the fluorescent lighting of the L.A. Department of Motor Vehicles office, "you fill in this form by filling it out." They were staying out together at night, practicing Sam's driving on the empty roads near the Hollywood Reservoir, and, "You know, Dad," said Sam, "when the stars are out, they're visible, but when the lights are out, they're invisible." Sam pointed at the stars overhead, and my husband tried to name the constellations as my son gently made fun of him. They were lying on their backs on the hood of the Volvo looking up at the dark sky, side by side.

"It's like a snapshot of fireworks," said Sam of the stars.

"The poet L. E. Sissman described fireworks," said Howard.

A small white integer appears,
Bears a huge school of yellow pollywogs,
And, with a white wink, vanishes. The boom
Takes twenty-seven seconds to arrive.

An airplane blinked away behind the hills.

The dandelions of light now go to seed.

Sam was watching something far, far up.

I MYSELF TOOK A DIFFERENT approach to Sam with words.

At Columbia I had bombed into Howard's dorm room one evening and said, Burgers! And, I'm starved! He'd gotten a funny look. He was fasting, he explained. It was Yom Kippur.

Oh. (We'd talked that morning between classes. He hadn't mentioned anything.) I considered this. Well, why do you fast? He began to say something. Then he stopped. Howard will work out things right in front of you. He looked at his watch. "Let's get a burger," he said, a bit slowly, as if he was rather unsure of the syntax. He processed the psychology of this his way: public statements, humor. "It's just like your parents warn you!" he would say, loud and menacing, a few years later to a group of us. We were in our twenties then, taking menus from the waitress at Gennaro's on Amsterdam and 92nd. "The hot blond shiksa asks why, and you abandon all your morals!" He said, "So a Catholic boy marries a

Jewish girl. And one night, not long after the wedding, she starts reaching down under the bedcovers, but he freezes up. 'It's Lent!' he whispers to her. 'Oh,' she says, surprised, 'can you get it back?'" We laughed.

That evening his parents were at Kol Nidrei services.

He always took me to the seders, though. He never wavered on that, and so I went. Howard's mother put us at the far end. Howard held my hand, though under the table. He had grown up going to seders. He had such strong memories, of his grandfather reading from the Hagaddah, said Howard, of looking for the *afikoman* and the resulting minor skirmishes when someone found it. Of how bad the food was. Of that time alone in the year seeing all his cousins, gathered in Brooklyn. Of everyone singing together.

No one bothered pretending. I wasn't welcome, but Howard had married me, and so they gritted their teeth. When Sam was born, I sat at the far end of the table, holding him for five hours. He fussed and squirmed, and my arms ached, and I was miserable. They shot me looks when he got noisy or cried.

When he turned three, to distract him, I began whispering to him a word to learn—Stuart would listen, never saying anything—or perhaps a line from a children's poem, bits and pieces of Milne or Potter. Sam, I would say very quietly, holding him at the table.

Listen.

Nobody seemed to know where they came from, but there they were in the Forest: Kanga and Baby Roo.

"What I don't like about it is this," said Rabbit. "Here are we—you, Pooh, and you, Piglet, and Me—and suddenly—"

"And Eeyore," said Pooh.

"And Eeyore—and then suddenly—"

"And Owl," said Pooh. "And Eeyore, I was forgetting him."

"Here—we—are," said Rabbit very slowly and carefully, "all—of—us, and then, suddenly, we wake up one morning? And

we find a Strange Animal among us. An animal of whom we had
never even heard before!"

(A small child, he knew these were our secrets. Another way of
saying I loved him.)

At six, Sam, I murmured. You know Cinderella's glass slippers?
They actually weren't glass at all. Cinderella is French, Sam—her
name is actually Cendrillon, just as Pinocchio is Italian and the Little Mermaid is Danish—and she wore shoes made of the fur of a
squirrel-like animal the French called a *vair*. But as the story was retold, French people confused *vair* with *verre*, which means glass. So
the whole thing is a corruption. Pretty, though, isn't it, I said quietly
to Stuart. "Glass slippers." Stuart was smiling, his arms crossed.

What began as a simple distraction at the seders I've now been
doing for years. As I drop him off at school. When he's checked in
with me before practice. As he's turning out the light, ready for sleep.
Sam, I say. Listen:

Assorted vocabulary: litotical, apposite, liminal. (He knows liminal.)

French words that do not exist in English: *nombre* (a number that
is a quantity, ex: 1,004 people) as opposed to *numéro* (a number referring to a position in an order, ex: the fifteenth).

A line from an Elaine Feinstein poem: "The air is rising tonight
and the leaf dust is / burning in cadmium bars, the skinny beeches /
are alight in the town fire of their own humus. / There is oxblood in
the sky." Isn't that marvelous, Sam?

AT OUR SECOND MEETING, DENISE and Consuelo and
I set up in the garden. Drinks and ice on a small table before the
tall Argentine grass, sparkling glasses lined up, linen napkins for the
food, which Consuelo will pass. When we're done, the three of us
step back and look it over. Yes, perfect.

They arrive, we find our places and open the books.

The next morning I run into a producer at King's Road Café. We're both getting coffee. Hello, how are you? He sees me moving on, gets to his point. It was great that they wanted to read literature, he said. Though of course there was the *other* aspect to it. (He makes a show of choosing a sweetener. This manipulation, making me wait, is completely conscious; like pathological physicists they measure everything here in iotas of power.) Stacey, he says, has an informal relationship with a star, a major one. He names the first name in the way they do, that false nonchalance, the implication (unverifiable) of intimacy. And Jeremy, another. Both stars have made known a desire to commit to a project with serious subject matter, not the usual explosions and romantic pablum off which each has made at least fifty million dollars. Something image-enhancing, he says. Challenging. And, well, he says, I did have a wonderful mind to exploit toward this end. (He uses an apologetic voice.) Thus their, uh, "interest"—he makes the quote marks with his eyebrows—in books.

He just thought I should be aware of their motives.

I say, That's very interesting, I wasn't aware of this. I'm going to have to rethink the list now.

"Oh," he says, and affects a glum look. "Well, that's too bad." He begins to move in now, to deploy whatever stratagem he has prepared into what he believes is the vacuum he has just created, but I slice off his leading edge.

No, I say, thoughtfully. I take off my sunglasses so he can see my eyes. I mean, I say, that there are several works I can think of that would be beautifully adapted to the screen, and I'll have to include those.

An instant goes by. "Oh," he says.

In fact, I say. (He stands there, warily.) In fact, I can think of several works perfect for both these actresses, and now that I think about it, I'm actually baffled that no one has snapped them up. They've taken some obvious ones, *The Age of Innocence* is so hugely cinematic despite the psychological backstory, and anyone could see the strong

visual narrative in *House of Mirth*, and *Portrait of a Lady* has that marvelous transformation arc, you can just storyboard the whole thing in
your head. But: I mention a Faulkner. A little-considered one. You
could do it period or better yet, updated. I mention a Chekhov story
that is a tiny, perfect movie pitch. I say that a certain actress has mentioned to Carla Shamberg and also to Lucy Fisher that she would
like to stretch, to do serious now, and the Russian would suit her
wonderfully, and come to think of it, Thackeray created a character
perfect for that new boy they just put on the cover of *Vanity Fair*, the
one with the woolly hair. What was his name? (With the Tourette's
reflex they have when given the least opportunity to provide a piece
of industry data, the producer supplies the name.) That one! I say,
Sam loves him.

He is trying to take mental notes on the titles I am naming, and
failing.

I know that he is an enemy of Stacey's. An associate producer
credit that, long ago, purely out of spite, he made sure she didn't get.
I've always disliked him.

They should have said something! I say happily, meaning Stacey
and Jeremy.

As I get back in the car, I feel simultaneously slightly repelled and
thoroughly excited. I jot down the titles I've just come up with. I'm
looking forward to telling Howard. I think, No, I'm not an executive, like my husband, or a producer, but I do have *some* instincts, and
really, they would make marvelous movies.

L.A. IS COVERED WITH FLOWERS. Gasoline pink, mint
crimson, moonlight white, deuterium violet.

We drive past them, tuxedo next to evening gown, two elegant
Saturday evening pupae in this rushing metal-and-glass cocoon,
migrating by infrared night vision toward some disease fund-raiser
or cinematic party where we will metamorphose and spread our

wings, seeking the heat lightning of the cameras. Diamonds fili-
gree on my neck. *Click click click.* "Mr. Rosenbaum, over here, sir."
"Howie! Great to see you, how've you been?" "Howard, how *are*
you? Hello, Anne."

Hello.

Before we leave the house, I put my flowers to bed. The bou-
gainvillea simply waits in the dark in its gaudy purple glory. Stupid
plant. Infragrant. Ambitious and showy and thorned, but if pruned
that sort has its uses. As Howard pulls the car out, I check my new
Stewartia koreana. I have just transplanted it, and it is wet and upset,
bewildered and off-key, but it will be fine in a day or two. The lilies
are overwrought from the heat. The butterfly bush is sullen but will
perk up later. The kumquat is simply delighted with everything. My
horticultural nursery is innocent, sleepy, except the delirious moon
vine, which is waking up late, delicately, waving and stretching and
looking around, asking, "Where is everyone?"

Everyone has set with the sun.

Out here on the streets, the tough flowers grip the walls, cling to
the gates, and skirt the concrete sidewalks, self-saturated with their
delicate scented particles and infused with the even more delicate,
invisible fizz of television and radio waves, their opalescent petals
shot through with the quantum mechanic buckshot of millions of
cell phone signals from millions of cars. The street flowers bathe in
catalyzed exhaust fumes. The metallic night is cool as tinted glass,
hung with the thick odor of indolent Los Angeles blossoms, groan-
ing silently with their own weight, glamorous and petulant. On thin
vines, the honeysuckle climbs the concrete barriers behind which
they hide the big houses, the long driveways. Everything in L.A.
aspires. Even the flowers. Aspiration ladens the bloom-opiated air.
They stand, waiting for someone to notice them. As we swoosh up
to the brilliantly lit entrance in our car, they languorously shift their
svelte, gorgeous bodies, forests of thin-waisted women, covered in
the most expensive silken sheaths and suits, slit their eyelids as we

emerge, desperate to know "Who are they?" and "Can I use them?" even as they seek to broadcast "I don't care." They always greet each other with only one eye; the other is on the future, the rest of the room. As we carve our way through their bright colors and pass by into the hall or home or screening room or backlot, their hot interest blossoms into flame and burns in the next instant to a cinder. They turn back to gaze once again at themselves, straining to determine whether or not they are impressed.

HOWARD HAS TOLD ME HE loves me in so many ways. Some have taken me by surprise.

When Sam arrived, he looked, Howard said factually, like poor-quality dough. His eyes changed colors. He had boils, rashes, his teeth came in, fell out. He screamed, he vomited. He was fat as an infant, and short, then he shot upward and was thin and awkward. We waited, apprehensive, for puberty. And then we had to relearn him physically. The newly tight skin, the slender muscle mass. We could almost identify the day people began to look back when he passed by (he was oblivious), the mascaraed glances of teenage girls in malls, the way they began to track his movements.

I asked Howard: Is he? Really? But what did the word *handsome* mean, exactly? How does this boy look, Howard? And Howard explained. "Sam looks," he said, "the way we all look when, cocooned in sleep, we are the heroes of our dreams."

When he was fifteen: That evening he had (unbidden) put on a crisp new shirt and a navy blazer, which cut his broadening shoulders and framed the short, dark-blond hair. He buckled himself into the driver's seat, Howard next to him, and caught me in the rearview mirror. Sam had come to know a certain look in my eye. He knew I thought about the Thornton Wilder character, a mother whose daughter asks her anxiously, "Am I pretty?" and gives the starchy New England reply, "My children are good-looking enough for all normal purposes." He knew I found it unfortunate that he was more than good-looking enough for normal purposes.

He sometimes shrugged off Howard's directions and used the gas aggressively, but that evening, learner's permit in pocket, he eased the large automobile down our curving drive, across Macapa, and gently right on Mulholland.

I had commented on my fears to a friend. He had been in Los Angeles long enough to understand the potential toxicity. He knew what it could do. In the car, Sam, I said. Listen: Yeats. 1919, "Prayer for My Daughter." (Driving, he kept his eyes on the road.)

> *May she be granted beauty and yet not*
> *Beauty to make a stranger's eye distraught*
> *Nor her own eye before a looking glass, for they,*
> *Being made beautiful overmuch,*
> *Consider beauty a sufficient end,*
> *Lose natural kindness and maybe*
> *The heart-revealing intimacy*
> *That chooses right, and never find a friend.*

"I hear you," he said, very briefly, and to the windshield. But he did.

Howard adores Sam's looks. He loves the strong cut of jaw made satin with thickening peach fuzz, loses himself in the green eyes. Howard stares at them like a lover, but always obliquely. (Sometimes we watch our son from a distance. "I wonder what he's thinking," Howard will say.) Howard watched as Sam negotiated the left turn down Laurel Canyon, assessed the traffic both ways, taking the care that fifteen-year-old males take when under their fathers' gaze.

Howard stood with me on La Cienega's cement curb (the starched maître d' at Mark's restaurant waiting to lead us to our seats) while on the asphalt Sam just a bit shyly handed over the keys to the valet, a Vietnamese teenager his own age. Seated at our lovely white-linened table on the sidewalk, Howard watched as Sam got up, started to jog across the street to examine a sporting goods store. It is Howard's own flesh that moves like this. That's what got him, Howard murmured to me as we held our menus. That sleek young animal loping across the pavement came burbling up from his testicles and shot out his penis, it is his flesh and blood, and it looks like this. Look at it! Look at the way it moves.

Howard's eyes are black brown and somewhat close together, his nose Roman, the crinkly black hair tamed only to a degree with an expensive silicon gel (I don't know where he gets it) that lies on the tight curls and says, "I am doing what I can."

The intensity of his personality, the slight thickness of his mannerisms, the Brooklyn that formed him and will never let him go. For Howard, that he, this particular Jew, should have produced the tawny creature gliding unaware among Mark's cool white tables on that blue evening where the tanned men tracked him from behind their menus and their golden hands—that was remarkable.

Not so long ago I happened to mention to someone that I am as surprised as Howard is that, given Howard's looks, he has produced this boy.

She paused. "Don't," she said in a low voice, "ever say that to Howard."

I thought about this for a moment now as we sat at our table. What would Howard say? I lay down my menu and talked about my surprise at Sam's looks given our genetics, given Howard's dark eyes, and what used to be called olive skin. Given the hair. I observed that genetically it was quite odd, wasn't it, Sam's having got virtually all his coloring and his skin from me. I wanted to know what he would say.

Howard put his hand on mine. He considered me for a moment. His eyes flickered over—Sam was heading toward our table. He smiled at me. He said softly, "Don't you see, Anne?"

I waited.

"The reason I love the way he looks," said Howard, "is that he looks like you."

I moved my hand across the white linen and caressed his warm skin. I loved him so deeply I wanted to cry, and laugh, to melt into this warm skin, to rip his clothes from his back and feel him inside me (after all these years still I want this).

"Dad!" said Sam very seriously, hauling back a chair, "all their ski stuff's on *sale*."

"*Cool*," said Howard, and smiled.

So Howard had offered a reason for the pleasure he took in Sam, and it was me. I felt my heart skip a beat. A clichéd expression, the heart, a beat, but it feels that way. A surge of love causes brief cardiac arrhythmia, and for some reason we aren't alarmed.

At the same time, I'm fully aware that Howard thinks of Sam very much in terms of his own flesh, because in everything Sam is and in everything Sam does, Howard sees himself.

WE HAVE EATEN DINNER, AND Howard is on the sofa watching a TV show a friend has produced. He holds the remote as if it were a shotgun, menacing the screen on the wall. I come, stand in front of him. He glances up and freezes the image. I sit, he puts his arm around me, and I briefly summarize my encounter with the producer at King's Road Café. Howard merely grunts a fillip of disgust and says, "Asshole." Howard has seen it all. He aims the remote, and we watch a bit of the show together. "Hm," says Howard. Yes, I say, agreeing with him. Dismal. It will be a huge hit.

I go to my office to get the list of books I've jotted down, and I come back and spend a half hour on the sofa showing him my list and talking to him about What Is Visual, or as he concretizes it, What Literature Is Translatable to the Screen. I mention the Thackeray, and he gives me the odd look it deserves, then waits patiently as I sketch out one of the subplots, and his look changes, and he starts nodding. And, Howard, look at Boswell for that matter, not just the work, although the cinematic case could be made for that, but look at his papers, the diaries, believed destroyed, all miraculously discovered in the past fifty years. I said it struck me that Darren Aranofsky (Howard had just met with him) could have a postmodernist field day. I meant, well, *Boswell*: Now here was a genius both charming and repellent, someone both completely honest and, by good fortune, graphomanic, who by the age of twenty-three, when he met Johnson and began the biography, never wrote down a single thing at the time he heard it, as he had trained himself to remember, verbatim, every word, every gesture, every tone and remark of social discourse.

Here was the Scotsman who guided the very English, London-centric, devoutly anti-Presbyterian Johnson on his improbable, ultimately wildly successful tour of Scotland's primitive Highlanders. Now that was a buddy movie. Boswell knew absolutely everyone in literary England in the last half of the century, and he was a social genius, a literary artist, a brilliant conversationalist, and a deeply imaginative interviewer. I list a few actors I'd idly envisioned in the roles, two production designers Howard admires, an excellent costume woman from Cardiff, now living in Santa Monica. Howard mentally ticks them off with interest.

So the next day I redid the book list. I enjoyed it immensely. That evening we have dinner with our friends David and Ellie Trachtenberg. David does some kind of technical sound editing I don't understand. Ellie, script doctoring. Sam sits next to Rachel, their daughter, and instantly the two fall into a mysterious murmured teenage communion. As soon as we've ordered drinks I get out my notebook and run my ideas by them, with Howard annotating verbally. David does the conceptual criticism, Ellie hits the practical logistical points (practicality is her strong suit; one book she nixes for sheer length, which is smart and which I, stupidly, hadn't thought about). We're excited. David and Ellie and Howard and I, grinning at one another. We feel like kids building a tree fort.

I call Jeremy Zimmer the next morning. I email him the list.

The day after that, Max Mutchnick calls. He is wondering could he join my reading group? Oh, and he's already ordered every book on the list from Amazon.

I pause. You have the list, I say.

Well, ah. (He feints, trying to decide if he should admit what he's just stated.) Yee-*eah*, he's got the list.

It's odd. I am on the phone with this boy, a very nice boy, Max, and here he has my list, which is to say a somewhat intimate part of me, and I didn't volunteer it. I didn't offer it. But he wants it, and that's lovely, actually. And I should be put out, and I am, a bit, who do they think they are, passing around my list.

Oh, who am I kidding. It's lovely.

That's fine, Max, I say. I add immediately: But you only have five days before the next meeting, and the book must be read. (I can't be a complete pushover.) "Of course!" he says, wounded, and I want to kiss his cheek. I tell him that's an absolute rule, could he please convey that to everyone. Just so we're all clear. He says he will. He hangs up before I can ask him if he knows everyone who is coming. I do my own recount and go down to see Consuelo about seating.

Denise will glance at me and look away again and say to the dish she's wiping, "What you smiling about." Which will startle Consuelo: Is Ms. Rosenbaum smiling? She doesn't look like she's smiling. But Denise knows.

I will say to Denise, Well, we wanted a new teak dining table for the garden anyway.

"Mmm hm," she will say skeptically to the dish.

It is a pleasure to suppress laughter. It bubbles into other parts, effervesces through you. This book club, I say to Denise, is doing unexpected things. It seems they want to know me.

She considers me for a moment. She nods matter-of-factly. She is happy for me. She turns back to her work.

And, I say to her, I want to know them.

I'M GETTING INTO BED, AND Howard is getting in on the other side, his breath minty from the paste. I ask him very casually, So what I said to them about Elizabeth Sewell. Do you think I was off base, then?

The comment was one that, when I made it, I knew perfectly well would be over their heads. It was aimed directly at Howard; years ago he'd told me I was misunderstanding one of Sewell's poems. Howard looks startled. "How would I know?" he says, turning off his light. "I wasn't there." He shuts his eyes.

I continue to look at him.

Howard waits, for good dramatic effect. Then, "I think," he says, and with a grin, and with his eyes closed, makes a precise tweak to the point I'd made in my garden.

I *thought* so, I say triumphantly. I knew someone would pass my comments to him. I hadn't realized they would reproduce them with such fidelity. He's rolling around to get in a comfortable position. "It was an interesting discussion," he says. He reaches for me.

I turn out my light. So you agree, I say, sliding toward him, with my view of Sewell.

"Yes," says Howard. "Actually, I do."

All these years later, I say, and you make some sense.

"Never too late," he says in the dark and kisses my shoulder.

DOUGLAS WICK CALLS ME. AM I reading spec scripts? he demands.

Doug, what are you talking about?

He names the producer from the café.

Him again, I say.

"Did you bring that jerk some fabulous literary adaptation?" (He names an eighteenth-century author. It's the wrong author.) *No*, I say very precisely.

"He's trying to rush Paramount into it."

I reassure him: I'm reading no scripts. I never have. Ask Howard.

Doug is still not reassured.

I tell him it's the wrong author.

Doug is reassured.

Because I'm interested in his reaction—he by contrast is a supremely competent producer and has twice worked with Howard—I run the Boswell idea by him. "*Huh*," he says. We discuss it for a few minutes. "I might take a look at this," he says. He adds, "With your permission, of course."

I'm surprised he's asked my permission, and then immediately, for a split second, I feel the possessive greedy neurosis toward my idea that they must feel all the time. I want nothing to do with that feeling. I am not a producer, I say to Doug, and it is not "mine." By all means, I say firmly.

After we hang up I find myself wondering what he will think of it. It's such a *good* idea, I think. I make a mental note to call Doug in a week.

FRIDAY I HAD ASSIGNED THEM William Golding's *Lord of the Flies* and noted a few thematic points they should look out for, and instantly I began to receive questions. These were innocuous enough but made it apparent that they were reading my analysis of the book's literary points as being hugely bound up with my own past—Golding and I both English, his dates roughly contiguous (they assumed, correctly) with those of my parents, and so on—and so they began to read between the lines and interpret me via the text. Rather annoying.

At my kitchen table Sunday morning I had been flipping the pages of John Peters's criticism of Golding, pen in hand. I'd already taken my notes on the author's dates and background, but there was a particular citation I was after. I had a real need to find it. As I searched the Peters, I muttered grimly to Howard: I've realized I'm inadvertently in analysis.

"*And you*," he had murmured dramatically, not looking up from the newspaper, "*hate that.*"

I'm not going to do some (I searched for the image) literary strip-tease for them. I didn't sign up for this.

He was turning a page. "Apparently you did."

By the next day, I've gone over the matter in my head. Why not use a personal approach to *Lord of the Flies*? It was an idea. I've never taught before. And Howard doesn't do it this way at all. But maybe for me it will work.

In my garden on Thursday evening, I preface for them why the book has particular meaning to me. I don't really talk about my own past much—and as I begin to speak I realize that, oddly, Howard and I have never talked about this novel—and I feel my way forward.

My father, I say to them, was born, in London, in 1914. I was born, in 1949, in Islington, where he had imported my mother after their wedding in 1938. She, languid and smooth as a cat, was from the Upper East Side, born in New York's St. Vincent's Hospital in the summer of 1918, "in the middle of the war," she liked to say, though of course it was not; the Central Powers were collapsing, and it was only months before the Armistice of November 11.

I was a certain time in distinguishing war from militarism, because militarism was my father's culture. One could live as an Englishman then, as he did, never actually in the Royal Army, as he was not, and yet be of the Royal Army in almost every way. That was British culture. The books he read as a child, a diet of Kipling, the poet laureate of Victoria's Imperial rule, and volumes of *Chatterbox*, a series of Edwardian "boys books" that contained a sampling of moral rah-rah, semi-Byronesque male poetry of the over-the-top variety, and heady adventure fiction—shipwrecked English boys on sunny desert islands, English boys solving murders on holidays in the Scottish Highlands, "endlessly brave, resourceful, and Christian," as Ian Gregor once put it. William Golding's *Lord of the Flies*, which would be published in 1954 (*Catcher in the Rye* had just come out three years before), cruelly took this romantic story, turned it inside out, and showed it in a nightmare version. "We've got to have rules and obey them," says Jack at the start, above the lagoon, before the darkness comes. "After all, we're not savages. We're English, and the English are best at everything." So when I read *Lord of the Flies* as a schoolgirl, my father snapped into focus.

A diplomat in the British foreign service, my father was a proud member of the "pinko-gray" race, as E. M. Forster called the masters of the British Empire. It was a better world then, and they were better people. "Alas," a friend of my parents' once said longingly, "for the time when civil servants somehow connected the well-being of the British Empire in India with a quotable knowledge of Browne's *Pastorals*." Browne, 1588 to 1643.

> *A rose, as fair as ever saw the North,*
> *Grew in a little garden all alone*

If my father did not engage me in conversation, he did impart to me something else, verse, lines he'd memorized as a schoolboy. My mother simply listened and smoked.

My father had his tastes, and if Browne ran to them he also enjoyed more pungent—and in a sense more viscerally English—English pastorals. There was an old British army lyric, which he recited while he shaved; I loitered quietly in the hall:

> *The sexual urge of the camel*
> *Is greater than anyone thinks*

In time of erotic excitement
It frequently buggers the Sphinx.
Now the Sphinx's posterior passage
Is washed by the sands of the Nile
Which explains both the hump on the camel
And the Sphinx's inscrutable smile.

("Matt," remarked my mother dryly as she passed by, "you're gonna have to explain that to her."

"Right!" Frowning down at me with great surprise, "Now what are *you* doing here?" he said every time.)

The provenance of that one is pretty clear; poetry born among innumerable Tommy Atkinses, the Queen's soldiers, defending Her Majesty's interests in distant, dusty countries. I overheard a friend of my father's fondly recounting a different kind of informal sexual education.

The King was in his counting house
A-counting out his money
The Queen was in the parlour then
Eating bread and honey
The maid was in the stable
There a-teaching of the groom
That the vagina, not the anus,
Is the entrance to the womb.

(Why, one wonders, the British obsession with sodomy?)

I mention to them that Howard adored this one. At parties he would beg my mother to recite it. She obliged, in a decent imitation of my father's accent.

My parents attended to each other, and they attended to me as necessary, and they defined "necessary" in their own way. I was never lacking, though being a diplomat then, or a diplomat's wife, meant lengthy separations from one's children, Asia to Europe, Europe to Africa, going away, leaving me behind, but there were nannies of various colors and various languages—I tended to absorb the languages—and various schools. I assured my mother and father that I never minded because they wanted that assurance, and they chose to believe me. I grew very good at taking care of myself, and the older I got, the better I got at it.

So. William Golding, I say, looking down at my notes, born in Cornwall in 1911 and educated at Oxford, awarded the Nobel Prize for Literature in 1983. Of course he had seen the systematic destruction aimed at the Jewish race and the two mushroom clouds in Japan, so he took the sunny desert islands and the brave, resourceful boys, and the rest of my father's world, and turned them inside out and made them the Holocaust. One understands the resentment in the trick.

I go to my next note card and say, John Peters commented in 1957, "Like any orthodox moralist, Golding insists that Man is a fallen creature, but he refuses to hypostatize"—(it means "to treat or regard as a separate substance or reality") —"evil or to locate it in a dimension of its own. On the contrary Beelzebub, Lord of the Flies, is Roger and Jack and you and I." The novel, and its literary precedent, Conrad's *Heart of Darkness*, defined a thing for us. It was this thing that my Anglican religion teachers, then on the theological cutting edge, identified as Original Sin.

All of this, in my father's youth, was yet to come. I tell them how my father at age fourteen would put each new precious *Chatterbox* in his book bag, ride his bike in his schoolboy coat-and-tie up Sloan Street, and eagerly plunk down somewhere in Hyde Park, a glorious green garden inviolate since assured by Her Majesty's Police, who patrolled like stern, blue-suited nannies. (I have a distinct memory of my father as a boy, with a book, in a garden. Which is, of course, impossible, I wasn't alive. But I can see the garden.) He would read until closing time, when the light grew dim and the calls of the blue-suited nannies would bring him back from the hot, dusty depths of India and Burma and into the city of London.

In England, even paradise must close.

HOWARD, IN THE MORNING, DRESSED for work, whis-tles. It can be Mozart, it can be Radiohead. He leaves a trail of musi-cal notes down the hallway to Sam's door, opens it. "Sam-oh, get *up*." When Sam was younger, Howard would go to the bed and with great innocence sit on Sam, humming Irving Berlin and pretending not to see him, and Sam would battle him, howling with laughter. Then the car keys, and a trail of Bob Dylan out the kitchen door to the car. The times, they are a changing, he whistles.

Stanley Jaffe called to chat. So this club of mine.

It's not a "club," Stanley.

"Whatever the hell it is. What are you reading next."

Glengarry Glen Ross.

"*Huh*," he said. "Stanley Zupnik will like that. He produced the movie. You invite him?"

No, actually.

"You should invite him." (Of course, Stanley's right, I need to improve at this.) Perhaps, Stanley added as if stretching his limbs, he himself would come, too.

Well certainly, I say, if you like. It will be our sixth.

"Your sixth book group."

It's not a book club, Stanley. Call Max Mutchnick. He'll give you the details.

So the reason I've assigned the Mamet, I explain to them when everyone has a drink and is settled into the garden, is that during

Sam's class trip to New York last October I had a run-in at the Metropolitan Museum of Art. And, I say, I would be interested in your views on it.

They smile, nod. I thought I would open the evening by situating you in my personal relationship to the work.

Sam's art history teacher had organized the thing. Three days, four museums. I went as support staff and kid wrangler. Howard and I know two of the trustees, and the trip was doing double duty: I would attend a Met fund-raiser one of the evenings, and Sam would be blissfully without his mother.

Our group was standing around on the second floor of 1000 Fifth Avenue at the entrance to European Paintings, waiting for it to clear out a bit. We happened to be bumped up next to a New York City public high school group. Sam goes to a private school since the United States has, fascinatingly enough, decided that educating Americans in good, well-funded, safe public schools is unnecessary. An interesting policy. The public school group's docent was taking her time with a not overly competent, in my view, lecture on portraiture.

So there, I said to them in my garden. That's the scene. Now, the Met is, as everyone is, obsessed with "the democratization of the museum experience." They bring groups of public school students to the museum on Saturdays, guide them through exhibitions, give them a talk, and so forth. The public school students were dressed in what Howard calls "Bergdorf Goodman of Papua New Guinea," huge, untied shoes, layers of garbage, underwear out. They shuffled in place, vacuous. Our teacher checked his watch. That was when a sullen young woman wearing a T-shirt with the Puerto Rican flag interrupted the docent midstream. (I'd noticed her fascination with a Vermeer; she had attempted to conceal her interest from the other students.) What, she now asked loudly, was the Metropolitan doing to "combat elitism." She was very smart, and—one saw instantly—politicized in that juvenile way. She'd learned the question recently, and her immature intelligence had pounced on it. She had been holding it in her little arsenal of resentment and launched it now to gain her moment in the spotlight.

The docent had a small cardiac arrest. So I, wanting to get them done but also because it was such a silly question, replied quite clearly across the narrow channel of marble that separated us, "You're an elitist."

Everything froze. Our students stopped bumping theirs. Our teacher's eyebrows went up his forehead.

The young woman stared at me. Then she vigorously and haughtily denied it. The denial, stated with admirable self-possession, was formatted in the standard leftist terms, peppered with clichés (she used the verb "to marginalize" repeatedly), and predictably dogmatic.

After she'd gone on a bit, I cut in and said, This is Saturday, and you're not hanging out on a street corner by some bodega in Queens. You've come here because you want to learn something, to better yourself in some way. That makes you an elitist.

No, no, no, elitism, she said, was patriarchal people who think they're better than other people, who they then marginalize.

If, I said, she meant "to act pompously and insufferably," those people are called "snobs," and they are fools. I said that elitism, by contrast, is acknowledgment, in word or action, of the fact that some people are better than others. I'm not interested (I cut her off) in an epistemological treatise on the word *better*. I mean that they know more, and more sophisticated, things, that's my definition. More things than the kids hanging out on the street corner or watching television will know. They like Vermeer, for example. (I pointed at the painting she had been covertly absorbing; eyes swiveled over to it, then to her, then back.) That means *you* are better, I said to her, assuming you're paying attention to him (the painter), which you seem to be doing. You're elitists. All of you are better.

I'm an elitist, too, I added. And smiled at them. They were lovely kids, and I wanted to hitch up their sagging trousers and touch their cheeks.

The docent hurried them out in the direction of Nineteenth-Century Sculpture. (One of Sam's friends leaned toward him and in a very low voice said: "Whoa." Suddenly I thought, Oh, dear. Had I embarrassed him? I looked at Sam. He wore one of Howard's unreadable expressions.)

I noticed that their group, on leaving, shuffled a bit less.

And that led to Mamet. To me, the thing about Mamet, I said, is that it is art—we're all in agreement here? (they nodded)—that is stylistically accessible but substantively elitist (according to my definition). Art must communicate, I said to them. (Yes, they agreed.) "Democratizing" art just means "to the greatest number possible." And I thought Mamet was arguably the most interesting elitist democratizer around. No matter what you thought of him, here he was creating a devastating, often hilarious, often vicious new idiom in which a great number could, in the most sophisticated way, follow his dissection of the follies of American life.

Some of Mamet's personal affectations I could do without. "The crewcut is an honest haircut," he has written, "of the two-pair-of-jeans working man." Please. This sort of thing bleeds into his writing at times as well. And though he gives a voice to a sort of close violence that absolutely exists, that voice can be rather melodramatic. "You take a knife" (he said this came from a blues singer), "you use it to cut the bread, so you'll have strength to work; you use it to shave, so you'll look nice for your lover; on discovering her with another, you use it to cut out her lying heart." You see what I mean. But accept it as the art form it is, and here is a refreshing, a wondrous, exhilarating helix of language that ascends, I admit, to nowhere in particular, but who cares. "It was stuff you heard in the street," said Mamet. "It was the stuff you overheard in the taxicab. It wasn't writerly." Mamet's drama teacher, the renowned Sanford Meisner, at New York's Neighborhood Playhouse, urged him to "fuck polite," and he did. What he wound up with was inherently, biologically male writing that a New York public school student understands immediately:

DANNY: *So how'd you do last night?*

BERNIE: *Are you kidding me?*

DANNY: *Yeah?*

BERNIE: *Are you fucking kidding me?*

DANNY: *Yeah?*

BERNIE: *Are you pulling my leg?*

DANNY: *So?*

BERNIE: *So tits out to here so.*

This is elitist language, I said to them, in that it is presented, it is calibrated. Who cares if you can hear it on the Staten Island Ferry. And by the way, you can't, actually; on the ferry you hear its raw material. Mamet mills that to manufacture an artistic product. He puts it in our hands and makes us think all sorts of things, and the rhythm of it is intoxicating. Nor is it lawless. It is, in fact, drowning in rules. Only idiots believe hip-hop kids are less socially cosseted than country club members. Rather the opposite is true.

Now, the mere flow, which is by itself narcotic, can be achieved any number of ways. One feels "So tits out to here so" inside these four lines from Samuel Johnson (I lift my book, preparing to read, and everyone in the garden lifts theirs), where as you'll see the flow is essentially imagery. It's Johnson giving us an elegant, proto-Mametian necklace of adjectives:

> *At once is lost the pride of* awful *state,*
> *The* golden *canopy, the* glittering *plate,*
> *The* regal *palace, the* luxurious *board,*
> *The* liveried *army, and the* menial *lord.*

Mamet's flow is *rhythm*, I say to them. Meter. We are similarly borne, compelled, rushed forward by William Shakespeare's iambic pentameter (í-amb: from the Greek, "iambos": a metrical foot of two syllables, the first unaccented and the second accented, Ex. "to stríve + and nót + forbeár"). Each matches the two-stroke "lub-*lub*" of our hearts.

The meter is: Iamb, iamb, iamb, iamb, iamb. And repeat.

I pick up another book. From the close of *Julius Caesar*, I tell them.

> *This IS not BRU tus, FRIEND; but, I as SURE you,*
> *A PRIZE no LESS in WORTH. Keep THIS man SAFE,*
> *Give HIM all KINDness: I had RA ther HAVE*
> *Such men my friends than enemies. Go on,*
> *And see whe'r Brutus be alive or dead;*

Elitism personified. And here is Mamet, no pentameter in sight, only twenty-seven iambs jammed back to back in a single, opalescent, perverse, sickening unraveling string:

> "But all I ever ask (and I would say this to her face) is only she remembers who is who and not to go around with her or Gracie either with this attitude: The Past is Past, and this is Now, and so Fuck You."

As if, said David Levy, we were listening to him through a stethoscope.

Exactly. And, I say to them—and this is truly wonderful—one can combine rhythm with yet another tool: syntax. Mamet takes syntax, twists it inside out, and uses it to reveal the interior of a mind. The character Teach enters. Page 142, I say. (They all flip to the page. So this is what it's like for Howard at UCLA, he speaks a word and books fly open obediently. Now that's fun.) Teach is furious at a lesbian who has insulted him for eating a piece of toast off his plate. A critic described it as "hearing a syntax that reels backward like his fearful scrambled mind":

"Only (and I tell you this, Don). Only, and I'm not, I don't think, casting anything on anyone, from the mouth of a Southern bulldyke asshole ingrate of a vicious nowhere cunt can this trash come."

Mamet himself commented, "The beauty of the fugue comes from the descant." (I put down my notebook and pick up the card on which I've jotted the note. Descant, I read quickly, *noun*, Latin *dis- + cantus* song. "Music played at the same time as the main tune, but higher.") Now. Words are aesthetic of themselves, but the auditory key to the music of this social class is not the notes (the words) in the piece but the counterpoint. I'm speaking personally now, all right? I simply believe that any human being of any class who can speak this beautifully, who displays the full range of human emotions, who suffers and bleeds and laughs and dreams, including the losers, including the formally uneducated, is self-evidently a three-dimensional person. Including the sociopaths.

A snob, incidentally, I tell them, is interested in a person because they are of high class. An elitist is interested in a person because they are interesting. That's the difference. At least in my view. Mamet, at his best, is interested in those who are interesting. And that's where he opens our eyes.

They are not UCLA freshmen, and I do not, happily, report to a dean, so I say to them, Here is one of Howard's favorites. A guy walks out of a theater on 42nd at Times Square and stumbles over a bum.

The bum says, "Spare a buck?"

"*Neither a borrower nor a lender be!*" snaps the man. "William Shakespeare."

"*Fuck you!*" says the bum. "David Mamet."

THE NEXT WEDNESDAY, DAVID LEVY took a meeting with Lizzy Weiss on the Sony lot and was critical (extremely, according to Bob Balaban, who heard about it immediately afterward) of Lizzy's fourth draft.

Critical of what, exactly, her agent asked her.

Of her meter.

Your *meter*? her agent said to her. He thought perhaps it was bad cell phone reception.

Her meter was off, apparently. And so, she sobbed, was the entire project, potentially. (Wait. Your *meter*? said her agent to the phone.)

According to Chris Silbermann, who was actually in the meeting, David, who suddenly felt that his position as producer should touch on this, had simply raised the question of executing greater care with the rise and fall of the words. Iambic accents. Lizzy began by doubting that this would translate to the screen (an action-adventure). "Hello, it's a *Rob Cohen* movie!?" someone kept saying, where the hell this fucking sudden interest?

Anne Rosenbaum, said David simply, and explained.

Lizzy left the meeting, called her agent, who called Howard, who called me. I said yes, OK, although I'd never met her she could attend the next book club (I covered the receiver and told Denise that we'd be twelve now), though I said she'd have to start the next book immediately.

"Oh, I'm sure she will," murmured Howard.

Actually, the more I looked at Lizzy's specific point, the more different it seemed to me from the question of Mamet's rhythms. Our next evening, I decided to bring up what irritated me and get it out of my system. I chose Houseman's meter, I told them, because some things he does drive me insane. I picked up "To an Athlete Dying Young" (they passed around the photocopies), and I said, Right, look here:

And silence sounds no worse than cheers
After earth has stopped the ears

I realize I'm belaboring this, and Houseman's sudden shoving of the rhythm into reverse gear is not the end of the world for his poetry, but he does it *everywhere*. Here one is led to expect the "Af," the first syllable of the second line, to be the up-beat like the "And" of the previous line, but it isn't; "And" is up and "si" is down but the "Af" is down and "ter" is up, and you find yourself head over heels, with the irritated sensation one gets when an unexpected German verb pops up at the end of the sentence like a demented gopher and makes you rethink the whole goddamn thing.

But wait. There's worse. Could you? Line 42.

"Uh," says the person I've pointed at, someone from Weed Road Productions I don't really know, "where . . . ?"

Runners whom.

"Oh." He finds it.

> *Runners whom renown outran*
> *And the name died before the man.*

Now *what*, I ask you, are we to make of this, I say to them.

"It's completely wrong," murmurs Eric Roth.

It is, I say.

"The first line is dah-dúm," Eric says, "but Houseman wants you to read it"—he frowns at it; like many writers, he heard about Lizzie's situation, so he's focusing—"I mean, the *the* is so weird—"

How would you do it?

I notice that it doesn't even occur to him to be fazed at the idea of reengineering A. E. Houseman. It's just another rewrite. Eric scowls for a second, calmly, everyone watching him, but they do this on location burning $450,000 a day with the DP breathing down their necks. "OK. How about

> *Runners whom renown outran*
> *The name, it died before the man.*

Ah! You see, rhythmically *that* scans, I say, delighted. Now, I want to be—

"Wait."

The name would die before the man.

Even better, I say. We all brighten and look around at one another. Now, I want to be clear, I say, that in some writing—less overtly classical, perhaps—a bit of this gear shifting is actually bracing. It works marvelously for Dylan Thomas (the single-page photocopy? that I handed out earlier? does everyone have it?), who starts out all satin and smoothness and then snatches the carpet from under us, all but holds a gun to our heads to make us—quite intentionally—say "*ass*-embled" and "*to* hear" and then, just below that, gleefully pushes us into a hole after the "Prisoners of wishes" phrase, willfully setting rhythmic stones ("In the jails") in our path to make sure we trip about them. It's all on purpose. I nod at Noah Baumbach. Read, please:

> *There was a saviour*
> *Rarer than radium*
> *Commoner than water, crueler than truth.*
> *Children kept from the sun*
> *Assembled at his tongue*
> *To hear the golden note turn in a groove,*
> *Prisoners of wishes locked in their eyes*
> *In the jails and studies of his keyless smiles.*

The last line a minefield of arrhythmic beauty. We all sat back and, after a moment, exhaled and looked at one another with glistening eyes. One of them made a note to himself. You notice, I said, each syllable, because of what he's set before it, obligatorily a crisp, precise component machined to a zero tolerance, separate pistons functioning seamlessly in the turning verbal engine block. It actually transcends iambs.

You'd have to shoot it as a period piece, someone grumbles.

So shoot a period piece! retorts someone else.

I was about to reply when a producer of particularly commercial blockbuster-type stuff said that this kind of rhythm could be "used *great*" in action-adventure. A development executive cleared her throat, shot him a withering glance, and looked away. He raised his shoulders: "*What?*" Apparently everyone knew everything about the dynamic between them except for me.

I cut in to say that in fact I agreed. And when she got a look of satisfaction on her face, No, no—I agreed with him (she raised her eyebrows), and completely. Consider that essentially William Shakespeare's *Julius Caesar* was *Lethal Weapon* in iambic pentameter and that to my mind the violence of *L.A. Confidential* was drenched in the balletic quality of its noir-prose origins: "He could muscle the money out of her," writes James Ellroy, "glom some pimp scuttlebutt, close out the Cathcart end, and ask Dud to send him down to Darktown." It was the art of subcutaneous violence.

It gave me an idea, and I rejuggled the schedule in my mind and told them their assignment for the next session—it's in the Library of America's Hammett collection, I said; they broke out their devices to write it down—was "The Scorched Face," which Claudia Roth Pierpont and I agree is a perfect short story.

THERE ARE THINGS THAT I would notice. But how does one, passing through the millions of touchpoints of one's life—a look, a particular word, a missed lunch, the click of a seat belt—pick out those that preface an event. Clues to the future seem to me to be particularly opaque.

It is four years ago. He is in his home office on a cloudy, gray

Saturday early afternoon. I come down the stairs and freeze, listening. Howard has a junior producer on the speakerphone. Shooting is going very badly, and the movie is generating serious overruns, and Howard is methodically, coolly flaying the man alive. Howard enumerates the studio's points—this had been promised, that date had passed, they had been told such and such, fucking lies, you little prick. With every thrust, there is an inaudible gasp from the speakerphone. Howard's back is to me. After three minutes I sit down on the carpeted steps, a ringside seat. I'm bringing him a FedEx package I've just signed for, and I watch, transfixed. The FedEx is another screenplay. Several hundred of them line the high shelves, neatly categorized, and I read their titles one by one as I sit there.

He stops for a moment, clicks over. It's Jennifer. So-and-so's rewrite just showed up at his office; should she messenger it to him? No, he says, just open it, put it on his desk, he'll get it Monday. He clicks back and continues.

Howard hangs up, turns around. He sees my face, which is ashen. He is a little bit startled. Somewhere we can hear a lawn mower.

"I'm sorry," he says, slightly on his guard.

I nod.

After a moment, he says, "Is that for me?" He gets up, approaches softly, takes it from me. He sighs heavily and sits down on the stairs next to me. His body does not touch mine.

"Someone has to," he says. "They've burned through the entire fucking budget, and they've only got *half* the thing in the can."

I nod. But I have never been afraid of him before.

"He's stupid." This he offers as a mitigating factor; he watches my face. He clarifies, "He's not just young. He's actually stupid. And arrogant." His eyes drift over to the milky window, his mind still partly engaged in the conversation. He speaks poisonously to himself. I have never seen his face so ugly. He looks exactly like all of them when they go into this mode. "An arrogant little shit who cost us three million dollars yesterday for two very, very bad reasons."

He swallows to keep down the anger sloshing in his lungs. We stare at all his screenplays.

I say to him, They all do that. (I mean the applied cruelty.) I just didn't know you did it, too.

We sit on the steps, on the tasteful, putty-colored wool carpeting, looking at Howard's clean, spacious home office, the walls painted a muted straw. "Don't think you don't know me, Anne," Howard says. "You know who I am."

Not entirely, I say. After a moment I add, But I suppose that's OK, isn't it.

I add, It just surprised me a bit, that's all.

DENISE SHOPPED FOR FOOD TWO days before the Woolf. She stated that she didn't want to prepare everything last minute, as she'd had to do with the Thackeray, when Double Features Films had suddenly asked if a small contingent could come. I'd begun cutting off the guest list one week before. It seemed a weekly event now, which given that they couldn't possibly be finishing the books in seven days I found bizarre until I realized I now had in essence two alternating biweekly groups. Consuelo began her setup outside at around 3:00 P.M., wiping down the big teak garden dinner table, bringing out linens and glassware and fighting back a few of my vines, dying of curiosity, and a small regiment of grasses staging an invasion. She noted that we needed a gardener. I agreed. Consuelo had a not-indecent eye for table placement, I found. She and I had gone to Crate & Barrel for extra plates and silver because I wasn't about to use paper. My job, which Denise and Consuelo assigned me—it was the only one they felt me competent to perform—was buying and arranging the flowers, although as Peter Chernin pointed out, "Anne, you're holding these things in a *garden*."

Well, I said. I just thought it would be a nice touch.

He grinned at me. He considered something. "Who from Fox comes to your clubs?" And from then on Peter sent flowers with whoever came from the studio. Calla lilies and delphiniums and jonquils in fresh, crackling paper.

The unwritten rule was that they brought dessert. In typical industry fashion, like emerging nuclear powers, they rapidly escalated the desserts in intricacy and number and size and exoticism and, quite predictably, cost. The boxes they came in, covered in glinting gold filament wrapping or scented sheets of rare Indian cinnamon bark, irritated Denise. After several weeks of this I said to them, I am terminating this brinkmanship. The coordinator for each successive club will choose one of you to bring dessert, and it will be appropriate.

The Woolf dessert was appropriate in size (small), but it cost eight hundred dollars and came in four cream-colored bamboo boxes lined in silver paper and tied with raw Andalusian hemp. Some kind of chocolate-flecked foam. Denise grimly got out a sharp knife for the hemp. Consuelo carried it out to us. We were just finishing a conversation about novelistic conventions and writers who broke them importantly. That was when Amy Slotnick asked me a question. What, in my opinion, was the single most important work of literature in the twentieth century?

They watched me carefully, sipping white wine. Two of them leaned on the large rocks with which I'd framed a lovely Latin American wisterialike vine I found two years ago.

I said that this hierarchization of literature—"the first most important work, the second"—is ludicrous, given art's complexity, and yet it rivets all of us.

I paused. I actually do, I said, happen to have an answer, because something happened that decided it for me. It started when our friend Daniel Rose called.

Sam was eight at the time. Daniel had landed at LAX at 3:00 P.M., checked into the Ermitage, and called us. Hello, Daniel. "Hey, Anne, how are you. Howard there?" Howard: "Daniel! You in town?" Daniel had three tickets for the Bulls, floor seats. "Sammy," Howard had hollered, "we're going to the Forum!" Into the receiver he said snidely, "So we're your latest philanthropic effort—I commend your choice."

"Ya ain't much," retorted Daniel, "as charitable causes go." Daniel funds his philanthropy through his real estate.

But when they returned much later that evening, their mood was somewhat dark, and Daniel was watching Sam intently. Some of the players, Howard explained, had gotten up to speak after the game—an antidrug message mated, naturally, to a product endorsement—and Howard and Daniel had both realized that Samuel was registering Black English. The boy had listened to them, and, after a long moment, had turned to Howard. "Why are they talking like that, Dad?" It had bothered him.

I was pouring Howard some coffee. The way they spoke, Sam?

He wriggled in his chair, eyes on the wall. "Yeah."

What did you think about it?

Daniel, his head cocked slightly to one side, observed Sam vaguely kicking the air.

"I don't know."

Articulate it, Sam. Say what you're thinking.

My son thought about it, and we ate cookies. "Well, it was, like—"

Don't tell me what it was "like," tell me what it was.

"Mom!"

Sam.

And then more cookies and then, gradually, with no "likes": They were famous, he understood that. He knew their names. And they were rich, and they slid gorgeously through space with the sleek agility of cats, gleaming and graceful, but when they opened their mouths to articulate their ideas, the words squeezed with visible effort through the neural tubes. In their bodies they were athletes, but in their minds they limped. Sam was reacting, we understood, to the sudden realization that intellectually they were cripples. Then Howard picked him up to put him to bed. I made some fresh coffee for Daniel.

Howard came back and sat down. "It was the contrast," said Howard, adding that he, too, via the kid, he said, had seen something for the first time. That all of us who reflexively cringe (and just as reflexively hide it) at the stumbling ineloquence of these black men are not alone. That our children can sense, too, this vast difference. The great divide had opened for Sam for the first time, and they— Daniel and Howard—had witnessed the boy's learning at the Los Angeles Forum that we are not all equal. Howard sighed.

Tell me about it, said Daniel. They didn't know how to speak, how to *walk*, for God's sake, look at them, either strutting like peacocks or shuffling like convicts—and you were supposed to hire them? One of the philanthropic projects he'd recently funded was the Harlem Educational Activities Fund. It tutored bright Harlem junior high students and then supported them in high school with mentoring and special trips, and in college with a special HEAF 800 number they could use, and money to come home on holidays—and, he said, it was a great program, if he did say so himself. But. He'd just been at a HEAF awards ceremony, and, Jesus, you just watch these kids, he meant the way they moved with tentative, awkward embarrassment, how the hell are they going to look at their Harvard interview, at their Goldman Sachs interview? They didn't know how to act, said Daniel.

I said that, in that case, he should be providing them with acting lessons.

Daniel gave me a look.

Socialization is acting, I said. You needn't change the person, you simply need to change the façade they present others. We spend our entire lives acting, Daniel.

Daniel gave me a different look. He looked at Howard. Howard said, "Sounds right to me."

(My eyes rest on Amy Slotnick, seated in my garden. She's carefully following my answer to her question.)

Daniel went back to New York and called Juilliard, and Juilliard talked to one of their voice coaches, Denise Woods, a black woman, and Daniel wrote a check, and the teacher created a class called "Express Yourself!" and they started enrolling kids. Daniel called me and said, "Come," and so I wrote a check to HEAF, which Howard and I copied to our accountant as a charitable deduction, and HEAF bought me a ticket out of that amount, and I flew to New York and met the teacher. Denise was a delight. She had been raised at the foot of the Williamsburg Bridge on the Lower East Side. "I used ta tawk like dis," she told me, "I kid you not."

We argued out every aspect of the program. I sat in on a class. I watched her illustrate different accents to the students, acting out texts with her assistant, Justin Diaz, a Juilliard drama major she'd borrowed. Justin was smooth and very serious and good-looking (he was rather conscious of this). I assumed a dash of Quechua blood had added exotic to his handsome. She used me as an exhibit. She said, "Everyone, this is upper-class English, listen to the vowels," and pushed me into the middle of the room and said "Speak." Twenty-five underclass black and Hispanic kids all turned their eyes to me and waited, expressionless.

I spoke, about Samuel. What my son liked to do after school, who his friends were. I clipped my Ts with positive cruelty. I selected words of no more than three syllables, simplified my structures, was chary with relative pronouns (but did insist on the subjunctive), intentionally used a predicate nominative, referenced Tennyson, which I pronounced *tenisin*, as one used to at Oxbridge. I made it a point to sound in all ways like the unreconstructed, pre-Regionalist BBC. I modeled for them an impressive façade. I elocuted and circumlocuted and shan't'ed and cahn't'ed. I even—twenty-five years in America, and you feel that it's overkill, but—pronounced "opening" as two syllables. I loved it. I was absolutely passionate. They were my children, and I treated them as I treated Sam. One is not, I suppose, supposed to touch students nowadays, but I did, put my hand on their warm skin, patted their backs. It is like putting one's hand on something electrical, or a wild bird. One feels so much startled life inside those small bodies.

A light-skinned girl asked, What use is all this? Her tone was calculating, slightly hostile.

I said: Wealth. Power. Social standing. Success. Access. Money talks, I said. Speak its language.

Denise shot me a look; she agreed completely with me—her point was simply that to them, I was sounding glib. Hm. I looked back at the girl, estimated her at around fourteen. I said to her: The phone rings at my house. (This is two weeks ago.) I answer, cover the receiver. "They're inviting us to go sailing," I say to Howard.

"Sailing!" cries Howard, then adds suspiciously, "On a boat?"

I confirm that the sailing will take place on a boat.

He says, "'*To mew me in a Ship is to inthrall Mee in a prison / Long voyages are long consumptions / And ships are carts for executions.*'" John Donne. Howard hates boats.

I uncover the receiver and say I am terribly sorry, but it turns out we have lunch plans that weekend.

I hang up. Howard says approvingly, "You sound so English when you lie." I say yes, an English accent is marvelously effective for lying. People buy it much more readily even when they don't believe a word. I said to the light-skinned girl: This is a matter of culture. British culture assumes duplicity for the conveying of manners to a much greater degree than American, and it also more highly values privacy, which is guarded by manners, and sees this kind of duplicity not in moralistic terms (the American reaction) but in terms of simply making things flow better. Hypocrisy saves you trouble; your interlocutor accepts this because he shares your culture. The accent—the expression of words and thoughts in this particular manner—is a finely tuned tool, and you use it to *get what you want* in life.

"I can see that," the girl said approvingly, and I saw her eyeing the cut of my clothing, taking my measure, and plotting a new persona. I thought I detected her planning to steal wholesale this exterior I have developed. I hoped she would. It is, for all its defects, one I've always found useful. You children, I said to them, you need weapons, yes, but you also need protection; the personae you've developed for survival on the sidewalks of Malcolm X Boulevard don't work in fortieth-floor conference rooms in offices on East 57th or the sleek lofts of SoHo where their dinner parties are held.

"You will breathe deeply from the ribs and not the chest," the teacher told them. "Now, what are the sounds?" She turned to me.

The rain, I said, in Spain stays mainly in the plain. In Hartford, Hereford, and Hampshire, hurricanes hardly ever happen. (I look at Amy Slotnick. It takes her only an instant to put the connection together and see, before anyone else, that I have just given her the answer to her question. "Ah . . ." she says, smiling.)

A jet-black girl repeats this. In Hartford, Hereford, and Hampshire. I appraise her.

"Where are you from?" she asked. She carefully included the predicate. You could see her doing what the teacher had taught them, you could see her turning her three-word sentence into four.

I was raised in London.

"They all talk like that?"

Yes, they all talk like this. Excuse me, *some* of them talk like this. It depends on which part of the city and which social class. (This they understood implicitly.)

The teacher directed me. "Hah!" I said. "Hah-tfuhd. Hereford. Hampshire."

The teacher looked at them a trifle narrowly. She spoke with a street accent. "Y'all gone get up an leave here. They gone be stan'in' aroun', drink malt liquor from a can, 'Yo, mami! 'nuthin' gone change, see?" And continuing in Standard English, "So do *not* think you're going to use this sound on 131st Street. You will use it when you need to adapt to different circumstances."

She turned to me, and I added (I deeply enjoyed the rhythm of this with her, our collaborative performance in the conveying of these ideas), Yes, let's be very clear about something: This sound is the mark of a specific culture with that culture's history and values (symbolic and real), and that culture will claim you when you use the sound. You will metamorphose, you will be, to the degree you choose, a different person. I mentioned the accent of a famous large black opera singer from Georgia who had created a regal, refined accent for herself so she could fit into her new international world. *Affectation* is an ugly word. Transformation, on the other hand, is self-improvement. It is the business of living.

Build vocal graciousness, I said, standing before the assembled. Not ax but asks, not mumfs but months—T H, months.

The teacher handed me the book I'd brought from L.A. I gave them a very brief historical and phonetic lecture on Cockney, a few biographical words on George Bernard Shaw, found my page in *Pygmalion*, and, recalling Howard's coaching on how to do this ("Sell 'em, put your body into it, make eye contact"), I read with Justin Diaz, as we'd practiced. He turned out to be quite the professional and did the male parts expertly.

HIGGINS [BRUSQUELY]: *Why, this is the girl I jotted down last night. Shes no use.*

THE FLOWER GIRL: *Dont you be so saucy. You aint heard what I come for yet.*

PICKERING [GENTLY]: *What is it you want, my girl?*

THE FLOWER GIRL: *I want to be a lady in a flower shop stead of selling at the corner of Tottenham Court Road. But they wont take me unless I can talk more genteel.*

Now, in the garden, I looked up from the Shaw (it was the same copy I'd read from at Juilliard a decade ago; I still have it). I saw the same intensely quiet expressions I'd seen in the children as they'd listened carefully. I turned some pages. Shaw's introduction to the play, I said, 1912. Ah, here we are:

"Finally, and for the encouragement of people troubled with accents that cut them off from all high employment, I may add that the change wrought by Professor Higgins in the flower girl is neither impossible nor uncommon. The modern concierge's daughter who fulfils her ambition by playing the Queen of Spain in *Ruy Blas* at the Théâtre Français is only one of many thousands of men and women who have sloughed off their native dialects and acquired a new tongue. But the thing has to be done scientifically."

As I left, I had the incantatory experience of hearing a roomful of black American teenagers from Harlem repeating exquisite, crystalline phonemes with fierce concentration, breathing deeply from the ribs and not the chest, as if choristers preparing an offertory canticle for Edward V in a cool, pristine, echoing marbled Wren nave.

Daniel sent us daylilies and baby's breath, which I put in our bedroom.

On this lovely Los Angeles evening, I pick up a card with my note jotted down on it. William Blake, I say to them.

I must create a system
Or be enslaved by another man's.

Blake's truth was what Shaw illustrated, I tell them. Shaw showed the adoption and mastery of the system—culture, which is simply a system, its accent being merely the face it presents—and portrayed that as the key to all the wealth and power of the world. Becoming a lady in a flower shop. And that is why *Pygmalion* is the single most important work of literature of the twentieth century.

When I go back inside I find Howard is already home. He's putting his clubs in his golf bag. He kisses me. "They liked it?"

They seemed to love it, actually.

He frowns at me, curious.

What's the matter?

He returns to the golf bag. "You're lit up," he says.

Oh, honestly. I put the back of a hand to my forehead. It is, in fact, slightly warm. I say, We're discussing things that matter to me. I suppose it's that. I turn and smile at him.

"How many tonight?"

Eighteen. Believe it or not. I ate with them, by the way; what would you say to your and Sam's going to pick up Chinese tonight?

He shrugs his acceptance. "By the way," he adds, "next week you'll have six more."

Howard! *Six*.

"Paul's got someone from Heel and Toe and might show up himself. Steve Zaillian made some comment to Fred Weintraub, apparently repeating an opinion of yours on Cervantes." He looks suspicious. "I thought you weren't big on Cervantes."

I'm trying to warm to him, I say.

He's eyeing me. "It was a pitch meeting at Imagine apparently. Neal Moritz was there and called me. Neal asked if he could come with Lou Friedman. And two women from a production company on the Universal lot. I said OK on your behalf." He smiles. "So?"

So, I say. And then, Well. Fine. Steve had run an idea by me, and

I'd gone and gotten *Don Quixote* and after some searching found the passage I'd been thinking of, which he loved. Imagine was the perfect place for it, and Cervantes fit Steve's pitch like a glove.

The Chinese menus are in the drawer there, I say to Howard. Sam likes the Hunan place.

"You enjoying it?"

Yes. For the moment it's fun. Actually, I say, drawing a breath, it's rather wonderful.

"*Sam-oh!*" yells Howard. "*C'mere!*" He sticks a hand in the drawer and automatically says, "Anne, the menus aren't in here."

Look, I say very patiently.

ONE EVENING I SAID TO them—it was a comment entirely in passing—that I questioned whether one could claim, ultimately, that any body of literature belongs to any particular culture. I had read somewhere that Heinrich Heine, the great German-Jewish poet of the mid-1800s' late Romanticism, wrote that he carried his patriotism on the soles of his shoes.

I stopped short; this appeared to bother a location scout slightly. He put the question to me, very directly. Here in L.A., did I feel at home? Did I ever miss England?

It's a question I think about, of course. My son has a thoroughly American sound and speaks differently than I do, and every so often I find myself startled. I replied to the scout's question this way.

It was many years before, we were just out of college. We'd been walking down a freezing Sixth Avenue on a wintry afternoon when Howard had asked from behind his muffler, what would I think of taking a U.S. passport? "It's more practical. Here, let me carry that."

Thank you.

"Christ, it's cold."

How is it more practical?

"So we don't have to do two lines at passport control anymore," said Howard. "When the kids start arriving, four or five of them," he grinned, "or six, or seven, hanging on us." We'd been arguing it, I wanted three, maybe four children, Howard was rather serious about a string quintet. "Obviously the passport's your decision."

Four, I said.

"Agreed," said Howard. "After the fourth, we can negotiate."

I told them I had thought of W. H. Auden. It allowed me to become whatever it is I've become here.

At some benefit dinner in New York—at the NYPL on Fifth, I believe—Nicholas Jenkins once said to me it seemed likely to him that Auden would turn out to be the only poet of world stature born in England in the last hundred years. I said to Nick that this struck me as harsh (for England), but the "born in" was certainly crucial in his case. The soles of Auden's feet took him from England, where he was born, to New York City, where he started the process of getting an American passport. Auden's former countrymen did not understand this movement. He was attacked in Parliament. Philip Larkin declared that when he renounced his English citizenship, he "lost his key subject and emotion . . . and abandoned his audience together with their common dialect and concerns."

Nick put it directly: They felt Auden had betrayed them. Despite his essential Britishness—someone called him "a communist with an intense love for England," and he produced sensuous, devoted, longing portraits of England's mines, millscapes, her Lake District, diagnosed her prewar phase with a chilling and pitiless eye clearer than any other's, "this country of ours where nobody is well"— despite all of this, the British never forgave him. Most British critics feel he was never as great, once quit of England.

Auden, I said to them, didn't care. He was a contemporary of the traitors/spies Burgess, Blunt, Philby, and Maclean, and in the 1950s he told a friend, "I know exactly why Guy Burgess went to Moscow.

It wasn't enough to be a queer and a drunk. He had to revolt still more to break away from it all. That's just what I've done by becoming an American citizen."

But as for me, I was not a queer and I was not a drunk, so those were not my reasons.

And so, years ago, Howard and I walked out of the State Department office, blinking in the winter sun. I was holding my bright new American passport in a gloved left hand. "Now," said Howard, "you're officially home."

I pulled away from him at this, turned and said rather loudly, "I am officially on the corner of Varick and Houston." I was about to cry.

"OK," said Howard, gently.

My British passport I planned to turn in to the Foreign Ministry. When they demanded of Auden, angrily, resentfully, now that he had left his nation, What Then Was He?, he replied that he might have given up "English" but he had not—please note—taken "American." Auden was, he said, a citizen of a polyglot world of transients, misfits, rootless and chaotically blending souls, placing themselves as they wished, or as they were driven, jealously guarding old identities in order to furiously stomp them out, cooperatively and energetically defiant. He was, in short, "a New Yorker."

So, then, the question: Did I feel at home? Well. Auden had a concept of home, and it wasn't a particular place. He had transcended physical location. He had made a choice. His leaving Britain, for whatever reason, did not necessarily reflect poorly on Britain. I would say the same thing for myself. Howard and I talked about it, of course. Perhaps because Howard never changed passports, or because he encountered the Robert Frost lines first, in high school, Howard sees it Frost's way:

> *Home is the place where*
> *When you have to go there*
> *They have to take you in.*

It reflected Howard's experience, of course, I said. After marrying me, for example. The place where they had to take you in.

But Auden's view, I said to them, is a bit different from Frost's. And I myself hear Auden's voice more clearly because it involves choice and emptiness without faith. Which is to say, it would be emptiness *but for* faith—or (much better) "trust," Auden's word. Auden, Nick observed, had gone from one mental place to another and discovered in going there that he had arrived nowhere in particular. That he had shed everything and constructed something nameless.

When I read this to Howard, I said that I didn't know if there was any better synonym for "New Yorker" than Nameless. Free, if you prefer. Liberated from the old ologies. Howard disputed it, but he didn't understand what Auden meant. He meant you shed the old names and assume new ones, and the new names mean what you want them to. In 1942, just three years after he arrived in his new home, Auden wrote that home is—the meter alone makes me weep—

> *A sort of honour, not a building site,*
> *Wherever we are, when, if we chose, we might*
> *Be somewhere else, yet trust that we have chosen right.*

Auden remarked to Benjamin Britten that New York was one "grand hotel in a world so destabilized that everyone had become a traveler." I am a traveler, and that my son does not share my accent bothers me in the end not at all. I was and am that thing Auden described, feared, and in the end loved more than anything. I was—I am—nameless.

SOME JEWS, SPEAKING TO HOWARD under what they considered the right circumstances—they were friends of his family, they had his best interests at heart, they knew him from Brooklyn, they had gone through it with his mother when he married me—asked him gravely whether he considered Sam Jewish. They wanted to know how Howard was "going to deal with this."

Howard would change the subject. I didn't really understand why. It seemed an odd reaction. Just answer them.

"I don't want to answer them," he said. "It's not their business."

I agree, but you can still answer them.

"It doesn't concern them," he said, which was not exactly what he meant. Obviously it did concern them. In any case, I didn't give it much thought.

At the time I thought I knew what Howard's answer to them was. I thought I knew because of what he'd said to his mother, often, including in front of company a few times. (She was less bothered by what was said in front of me. I got very, very good at not betraying the pounding heart, the reflex of my throat to swallow with anger.) When he told his parents about me, Howard's father had enumerated the standard arguments: the perpetuation of the Jewish people after the Holocaust, the continuance of Jewish culture. He had even, if without much confidence in the stratagem, proposed that it was Howard's being ashamed of being Jewish—"Give me a goddamn break, Dad" said Howard and burst out laughing. When that didn't work, just once his father had tried the word *God* and the word *faith*, in the theological sense; Howard's reaction to this, on the other hand, had been so blistering that his father went immediately back to cultural justifications. But it was his mother who had pressed him. It was she who asked. Why? Why? Why her? (I stood, my hands folded in front of me, outside in the hall, staring at nothing.)

I knew what he replied. He replied that I was, simply enough, the woman he loved. He'd assured her that he himself was not changing, that he was still the son they both knew, that he could promise them that. The culture, the people, remained with him. (We were both twenty when he was saying this. His father would die when he was twenty-one.) Anne, he said to them, is the person I want to be with.

He said at one point, We don't live in a vacuum. (They didn't reply. I interpreted Howard's meaning.)

So I thought I knew what Howard's answer was when, once Sam hit fifteen, the Jewish mothers of Los Angeles's Jewish teenage daughters began to notice and evaluate Sam and to ask Howard the question. They gather their information. They have Sam's last name, they have Howard's curly black hair, his vestigial Brooklyn accent, as they pursue their mating strategies. And they have their fears, bred into them: Look at the mother, they say, worried, suspicious. My looks throw them. And so they will, subtly or directly, ask, though never in these words.

Is Sam Jewish?

And Howard doesn't reply, "Go fuck yourself." No. Gravely, my husband will appear to consider the question.

Faeder ure, thu the eart on heofenum, si thin nama gehalgod.

We have lost so much. "Father our, thou that art in heaven, be thine name hallowed." Look at this sentence and see what has gone. We got rid of English's lovely familiar second person and its correlative possessive form (*thou* and *thine*, of the Old English *thu* and *thin*), and we replaced that regal genitive ending *heofen-um* with the modern, if a bit chrome-plated, preposition *on*, soon to become our mass-manufactured, ubiquitous *in*. Around 1400, we downsized the muscular past participial *–ode / -od* of Middle English, restructuring it into the more concise *-ed*. Of all the richness from our highly inflected paternal Middle German verbs, only the poor little third-person singular conjugation still hangs on: "He *reads* a book." And we surrendered to the Germans the elegant Teutonic prefix *ge-* of *gehalgod* along with capitalized nouns and the luxury car market. (Surely the delightfully antiquarian silent *e* after "name" is not long for this life.)

But we have through some perversity or other kept a treasure trove of odd little adjectival suffixes; what we think of as "English" is a conglomerate of everyone. We have *-ish* (Old English *-isc*; cognate German *-isch*, Gothic *-isks*, and Gk. *-iskos*). Thus: "Irish," "Scottish," "Finnish," "Spanish." But "German," "Eritrean," "Alaskan," of *-an*, and its variant *-ian*, "Latinate suffix denoting places ("Roman"; "urban")," now productively forming English adjectives by extending the Latin pattern. This one denotes provenance or membership ("American"; "Tibetan"), social class ("Republican"), religion ("Episcopalian"), sense of time ("Elizabethan"); ME < L *-ânum*. (Not to be confused with the prefix *an-* < Gk. "not," "without" ex: *anelectric*.) The Latinate *-at* ("Democrat") and its variant *-ate* ("Italianate") denote offices or functions ("triumvirate"), collective bodies ("senate"), or periods of rule ("protectorate"). Interestingly enough: Can also form nouns ("advocate") and verbs ("calibrate"). And the decidedly Italianate *-ese* starting with "Milanese," "computerese"—(this is also actual Italian, "scozzese")—and on to "Japanese" and "Chinese" (rather than Chinish or Chinan or Chinate).

Ah, *but*, Howard notes to the mother of the Jewish girl, or the grandmother, or to the curious rabbi, who is listening to Howard's disquisition and wondering a bit uneasily what she or he has gotten him- or herself in for and where all the etymology fits into this, this meant there was a grammatical ambiguity, did it not? Yes indeed it did. Why, for example (Howard pointed out), consider the adjective "Jew-*ish*" (he motions to the mother who has asked "Is Sam Jewish?")—which used the suffix denoting "sort of, but not exactly." ("Not large," one might say, "but large-*ish*.")

I love this. (I listen to Howard's extremely serious exegesis during the Silverman bar mitzvah from behind a plaster pillar in a rented party room of the Beverly Hills Hotel. I listen to it a few feet from our table at the Shapiro bas mitzvah in Brentwood.) I love it first as mockery, which it is, and second as a point of grammar. We need here, Howard vigorously argues to them, a better adjective, don't we?

But what should it be? "Jewate"? "Jewese"? "Jewan"? *No.* Howard Rosenbaum proposes the grammatically sturdy "Jew" (still capitalized) as the English adjectival form of the nominative "Jew." Consider the benefits, argues Howard, leaning toward his colocutor, the aunt of the bar mitzvah boy, her eyes taking on a gleam of panic. Now *that* is a straightforward adjective, truth-in-packaging. Not the hushed, chin slightly lowered and to-the-side whispered-in-your-neighbor's-ear "So, the boy . . . is he Jewish?" but rather, asking it plain: "Is Sam Jew?"

To your tablemate at the friendly family seder: "What great Jew food!"

A knowing appraisal: "He certainly *looks* Jew."

Remarking of the klesmer: "Boy, I love Jew music!"

A: "Hey, are you Jew?"

B: "Why, yes! In fact I am!"

Certainly, says Howard, the other person could see the benefits. (The other person nods, very tentatively.)

Because the thing about the *-ish* suffix is that it signifies "a mixture or alloy," which Howard, a full Jew, is not, but which Sam, Howard explains, is. ("Oh," says the woman. Her worst fears are confirmed.) "*-ish,*" points out Howard, as if he had picked up nothing at all in her face, happens to be precisely the adjectival suffix that takes adjectives and forms new adjectives ("reddish"; "sweetish").

See, that's what's great about the adjective "Jew"! It would mean "racially pure Jew." ("Which describes me!" chirps Howard brightly.) And adding the suffix "*-ish*" would form a second adjectival (see above), one whose denotation would be "alloyed with pure Jew, or mixed with pure Jew," as one might say of white paint into which some green has been added, "Not green, exactly, green-*ish.*"

This is what Howard tells them, when they ask him. When Jews worry about purity, as Jews worry about purity, when they firmly circumvent me as one would something whose cleanliness was not up

to par, when they frown and cough meaningfully, I simply fade back
and let them take Howard aside by the elbow a centimeter or two to
ask him gravely of our son, Sam: "Is he Jewish?"

And Howard frowns with equal gravity and appears to ponder
the question deeply. And then, solemnly, he replies, "Well, he's Jew-
ish." And smiles at them.

Which, given me, and given that Howard loves me, and that he
loves his son, is really just a way of replying, Go fuck yourself.

HOWARD CAME HOME TO FIND me quietly cursing twenty-
four voice-mail messages. I was on the point of throwing the whole
thing over.

"Need help?" he said.

Do I need *help*?

He assessed the situation. "I'll have my people call your people."
He turned.

I don't *have* people, Howard. And then as it dawned on me
what that look meant: And I don't *want* people. Howard! Do you
hear me?

"I'm going to make a phone call," said his back. I could hear the
whistling heading toward his home office. Some bit of Gershwin he
likes that I can never place.

A few days later I was informed by a friend at The Ant Farm
that Howard had somehow gotten me onto the UTA Job List. *Quite*
insider. The following morning at 8:00 A.M. there were, sitting politely
in my kitchen under Denise's stern eye, five candidates for the position of my full-time assistant, all intelligent, capable young men and
women. I began interviewing them. By 8:12 A.M. three more had
arrived. One was Justin Diaz from Juilliard. My former acting partner from HEAF, now having left New York and already a veteran
of the Los Angeles movie audition. I'd forgotten how good-looking
he was. "Howard gave me an 8:30," said Justin, "but I figured I'd get

here early." I politely dismissed the others, handed him the code to my voice mail, and drove off to buy a small amount of fertilizer and, while I was at it, coffee beans.

By the time I got home, Justin had organized my book club files, cleaned off my desk, sorted my voice-mail messages in categories of urgency, and written out the current book club membership lists, annotated. I took a moment to acclimatize, glanced at the lists, and said, Fine. I noticed that he had, in those two and a quarter hours, manifested a completely different demeanor. One knew he owned this space.

"Of course," said Stacey when I mentioned it. "He now manages a Rolodex people would kill for." She meant Howard's.

I don't see this, I said. He's an actor.

"Then he's taken an excellent day job," she said.

I described my frustrations with the book club to Justin. I felt things were becoming diffuse, unfocused. We looked over names and affiliations. As we were doing so, Justin fielded calls from Harold Ramis and Joel Zwick and handed me the messages; it was heaven. Also, I explained to him, lots of them were calling Howard, not me, and Jennifer was trying gamely to do the gatekeeping, but she already had a full-time job, and her efficiency was suffering and so the numbers were becoming unwieldy.

Justin had a suggestion. "Let's divide them up."

I frowned.

"Why not, Ms. Rosenbaum?"

Um, Anne.

"Anne." Despite the Ms., I'd noticed that he'd become instantly familiar in the way he spoke to me.

I was in fact resisting the idea of making the club official, just as I was trying to get used to the idea of a personal assistant. I suppose, I murmured to Justin, we might as well.

So we split them into categories on different nights, producers with producers, studio people with studio people. It made them at once more competitive, which was to say sharper (particularly the agents), which I enjoyed, and more relaxed, since among their own. They mix very poorly, these people. Justin started playing basketball with Sam in the driveway, which Sam loved. I took Justin to the lot to meet Jennifer (she had already started forwarding all book club calls to him) and Howard. ("Mr. Rosenbaum," said Justin, reaching out his hand with his eyes slightly wide. "Indeed," said Howard very gravely. I kicked him.)

Steve Tisch came out of Howard's office. He wanted to know if I'd done Dumas. (Howard said "Oh, boy" and went back into his meeting.) Steve had been toying with a Dumas idea for a while. Someone I took to be an assistant came to get Steve, twice, with increasing urgency. "Take a message," he said tersely. And also he had this idea about Henry James. What did I think of him? I said that James's genius is detail, meticulously observed. Ah, said Steve, in that case I should definitely give James to my line producers. (Steve, I said, I don't have any line producers.) Those guys live and breathe the details, he said, locations, shooting schedules, when did the writer fuck up the continuity.

Three days later I got my first request from two line producers, but I apologized; Steve Tisch notwithstanding, I just couldn't see creating a line producers group yet.

I gave *Mansfield Park* to my directors. We were in my living room that evening; it was raining. It clearly surprised them when I said that Austen, to me, was writing about movie stars. Odd looks all around, so I tried to clarify: I meant, actually, our perception of ourselves vis-à-vis the stars. Not their own lives. (Widespread skepticism.) She's writing, I explained, about moral systems. (Still unconvinced.) Hang it, I said. You. Read aloud, please, this is Lionel Trilling's 1954 essay on Austen, "The Opposing Self."

He raised the photocopy. "It was Jane Austen who first represented the specifically modern personality and its culture. Never before had a novelist shown the moral life as she shows it to be, never before had it been conceived to be so complex and difficult and exhausting. Hegel speaks of the 'secularization of spirituality' as a prime characteristic of the modern epoch, and Jane Austen is the first to tell us what this involves."

"Well!" said a director. He looked at each of them. "That's definitely us," he said.

I said, Carry on. You, please.

"Secular spirituality's dark and dubious places are more numerous and obscure than those of religious spirituality."

I absolutely would choose to grapple with the secular variety, I told them, but I understand why the disoriented and afraid prefer the reassurance of the religious kind. (Still unconvinced.)

It clicked when Trilling said that Austen wrote of the need to ensure that our lives and styles "exhibit the signs of our belonging to the secular-spiritual elect." You see now? I said. (Oh, they certainly did. They understood the star's need for the newer Lamborghini. They understood the need to be seen lunching with the star.)

To me, I said, almost the only surefire secular-spiritual elect are the movie stars.

They now acted as if it had all been obvious from the start.

I tell them a story to illustrate: It is a relatively recent evening, just south of where we are sitting, when everything is bathed in white-hot light. The studio has paid for the searchlights scorching the night sky above. The two of us, Howard in a tuxedo and I in a gown, are alone among a thousand people pressed fervidly together in a plush, electrified place. Howard watches them progress up the red carpet and murmurs to me: "Everyone here"—(he means Hollywood)—"lives as Lucifer, the definition of hell always being one's distance from the stars."

Howard is good with the stars. We are standing somewhere behind the actress who has gotten her name above the title, who has just stepped out from the long black car. I watch Howard's face flicker with the flashes aimed at her. She is escorted by her new agent. She has just dropped her previous, longtime agent for him, for his youth, and for his aggressiveness, which she believes she needs now, and for his looks and his clothes, and he has made hot professional love to her. Then, back at the curb, another car door opens. A younger actress emerges, the one they've run on the covers instead of her, the one she didn't get along with on the set. (This is what they've written in the tabloids.) The cameras swing away from her, back toward that car, the voices move in a vast wave from her, creating a void where she is standing, she is in free fall, and she needs an anchor.

But the young agent is not an anchor. His talent is pyrotechnics, not strength. A sea of whispers rises around her, she falters, one or two cameras, smelling blood, swing back now. They would love to record her as she drowns before them on that linear pool of red. But Howard is moving. The studio security know him, he passes through them like smoke. From nowhere, it seems, Howard slips his arm through hers, sets her ringed hand onto his tuxedoed wrist. To the young agent's shoulder Howard briefly applies what looks like a fatherly hand; it serves to separate the agent from the star. His arm in hers, he begins to walk her down the long carpet to the theater's doors. Had she heard the story, Howard murmurs to her, his mouth close to her diamond-tipped earlobe, of Jean Harlow's meeting Margot Fonteyn? The two divas hated each other on sight, but it was a movie premiere, and the cameras were watching. (The star remembers to relax her face. She grips Howard's arm.) In front of the reporters, murmurs Howard, Harlow was pure sweetness, and it was "Oh, Margot this!" and "Oh, Margot that!" (He maneuvers her perfectly into place, stand, stand, turn slightly, stand, so they can get their shots.) Except that Harlow pronounced it "Mar*gotte*," with a hard consonant. (He looks ahead, catches security's eye, and they prepare to open the front doors.) "Mar*gotte*, darling!" Finally Fonteyn leaned over to Harlow, not quite out of reach of the microphones, and murmured "Oh, darling. Actually it's Margot. With a silent T. Like Harlow."

The glow blossoms onto her face again. She regains her composure. The two of them pass into the cinema with elegance and grace, and none of those watching dare to breathe, because they are in the presence of a star.

The person truly unimpressed by celebrity, says Howard, is impossibly rare. He himself claims to be susceptible to it, but I've never believed him.

I abhor the fear that is a plague here. I despise the vanity and the wanton waste and the vast and utterly boring emptiness, the breathtaking unoriginality of their meretricious visions. I am aware of the Terror that rules their moral situation, but Jane Austen has already told us about it. The emptiness is on view for us all to gaze at, their Plexiglas castles on their hilltops, the baubles in their garages, and their spectacular parties. The sad littleness of their rudeness and intimidation, the sinister, garish motifs of their grossly false friendships. As Anita Loos tartly observed, in the 1920s "the stars were moving out of the Hollywood Hotels and beginning to live in their own private houses with servants, most of whom were their peers in everything but sex appeal—which pinpoints the reason for the film capital's mass misbehavior. To place in the limelight a great number of people who ordinarily would be chambermaids and chauffeurs, give them unlimited power and instant wealth is bound to produce a lively and diverting result."

Everyone is inside the cinema now, waiting for the movie to start, and Howard is watching over things. The director of photography is relaxed as a cat. An associate producer fairly shakes with agitation, wondering about the critics. That asshole from the *L.A. Times*? It's a fucking vendetta, Howard, that guy! Howard just nods, his eyes locked on the director across the room. The director gets physically ill at premieres and is trying to appear stoical.

I remembered something I'd always meant to tell Howard. That I'd read a description of all this in a book on God. "Yeah," he said. "What was it?"

"Millions fuse the real lives and the screen lives of movie actors, assign the combination an importance greater than any they concede to the real human beings whom they know, and then suffer the melancholy consequences. Their flesh is sad, alas, and they have seen all the movies."

"Nice," Howard replied. "Mallarmé?"

Yes. (An update of Mallarmé's great lament: "The flesh is sad, alas, and I have read all the books.")

The distributor's trembling fist grips the forearm of Howard's dark-blue suit. "Howie, that bitch wants to fire our publicist." Howard removes the fist but speaks reassuringly, leads him forward like a calf.

In my quiet living room, the directors listened in silence. They know these evenings. One of them sighed and made a comment. I found it particularly perceptive. He had touched this heat, he told us. Of the blond, handsome movie star who years ago he'd intimately orbited, he said: "As if glancing at a menu, he was able to choose his life." He had been spellbound. "The truth is, the temperament and impossible behavior of stars are part of the appeal. Their outrages please us. The gods themselves had passions and frailties. Modern deities should be no different."

But they'd drifted apart, he said. He came, on one of these white-hot evenings, to watch the star from the back of the theater at yet another premiere, the top of that famously casual, ever-boyish blond head visible as it moved down the aisle. (They all knew who he was talking about. It was his saying this that surprised them; these people have a rule: Never, ever bring up failure.) Watching in that white dark, a line of Falstaff had come to him. *King Henry IV, Part 2*, act 5, scene 5. He put on his reading glasses. Falstaff is watching the coronation of the new king, his former bright intimate, and murmuring to console himself for the stretch of this dark, unfamiliar space between them:

Falstaff
Do not you
grieve at this; I shall be sent for in private to
him: look you, he must seem thus to the world:
fear not your advancements; I will be the man yet
that shall make him great.

When they have gone and my living room is empty but for Howard and me on the sofa, I will mention this to Howard. He will take
a Miltonian view. He will appreciate the Falstaff reference but, at
the same time, shrug and comment of the movie stars, "Even when
you're with them, you're not with them."

I will decide that the following week I will give my producers—
how could I not—"Ozymandias." Shelley, 1818. I know. Too obvious.
But they will love rereading the poem. Each perfect, cruel line will
feed their narcissism. The plush suites off Lankershim and Alameda,
the law offices on South Rodeo and Wilshire, the glass fortresses in
Century City. The hearts that feed. The wrinkled lip and sneer I saw
on Howard's face in his office on that cool afternoon.

In the early dawn hours, while the world is still bluish and I am
driving my powerful car very fast and alone on Sunset in the desert's
chill, I sometimes look up to see the billboard men in their blue jeans
scaling the sheer concrete sides of the tall buildings above Sweetzer,
and I see the forty-foot-high faces looking down on the cold, empty
concrete. Their names are written in letters as high as people. The
workmen peel down their faces and strip away their names in tat-
tered rolls. The movie having closed, the stars disappear. Nothing
lasts in this desert.

FOR MY FIRST LINE PRODUCERS group, I give them *Crime
and Punishment.*

I give them this particular novel because a literary agent mentioned to me once that since it was published in serial form and on deadline, like Dickens and much nineteenth-century fiction, some of the facts got flubbed in the process. So I have Justin send out an email. "In *Crime and Punishment*," asked my message, "where are Fyodor Dostoyevsky's continuity errors?"

Two of them find the first one almost immediately: Dostoyevsky puts the office of Porfiry, the police detective, on the fourth floor, and some eighty pages later it reappears on the sixth. Jennifer will call me to say that in a people-watching item, the *Los Angeles Times* has reported the producers' names.

THEY ASKED ABOUT THE ACCENT. One of them thought I was Australian, but then Americans are almost completely incapable of distinguishing non-American English accents. And—how many languages did I speak? Wait, *Chinese*, right?

Right.

I don't know why I've kept the degree of British phonetically that I have. People think it's on purpose; it isn't. Things stick with me. My German, which is rudimentary, has a marked French accent. I suppose it's the order in which I learned the languages. (I explained that we were in Paris for fourteen months, an eternity, before my father was again transferred, to Bonn, and I switched schools for, it seemed to me—I believe I was twelve—the three hundredth time.) The Spanish I learned because when Consuelo came to us, she spoke no English at all. I bought a small Spanish grammar book and spoke with her and it came quickly.

My Italian is good. My father was on special diplomatic assignment in Milan for a year (my mother put me in an Italian school that time), although all his assignments seemed oddly special. Howard thinks he was MI6, and that's what he always told Sam in a melodramatic whisper. "Sam, your grandfather was a spy!" I think it's a fun idea, father as James Bond. I never saw any direct evidence for it, even when, as a girl, I myself suspected it and snooped among his papers. I assume he was an ordinary diplomat, but I admit that is only a default assumption; he had a strange, secretive life in a multitude of strange, constantly shifting places, and I've often thought of contacting British intelligence and simply asking. My parents are dead; perhaps MI6 would give me an answer.

In Cantonese, interestingly enough, I am utterly invisible. By accent, obviously. Not English at all, purely Cantonese, except for an inexplicable hint of Mandarin (which I don't speak at all) in my slightly Beijing "r." Seven-year-olds—my age when we arrived in Hong Kong—absorb grammar like sponges but will not necessarily become phonetically native, and China's northern "r" is almost weirdly American. I listened to the servants and to my ya-ya, eavesdropped on the Star Ferry, and followed Cook around the market as she haggled. All of this from the top of Victoria Peak, where we had an apartment with the most breathtaking Hong Kong view. The view was virtually free, since the apartments, which were quite modest and functional, were owned by the British government and given to its officials. Nineteen fifty-four to 1958 were lovely years to be in the colony, when the British ruled, the expatriates played polo, the Chinese had their unknowable lives in their fragrant mazes of alleys and noodle shops, and we understood everything.

The Chinese hate not being able to categorize me. (Who is she? they mutter to each other in the greasy fluorescent-lit dumpling palaces of Los Angeles, the walls white ceramic tile. What does she want?) I order a soup, dispute a check, and they give me suspicious looks and twist the conversation, not very subtly either (they are Chinese, after all), to try to make me say things like "dental floss," which they think is hard for foreigners to pronounce. It is, but not for me. *Nga h'cxin.* I say it and smile sweetly at their sullen reactions until one of them laughs, declaring victory in my favor. I give them no ground, ever, no foothold. I remain free from their expectations. It was very important to me as a girl. I am not in- nor out-group. I am always myself. A year of hanging around Cook, and I was able to entirely escape their categories, the expectations they could nail on one, and I did so loving it. They glared at me and said with distaste, "*Lei-goh lui-je ye-gang mo je-gai geh gun-yuen.*" This girl, her own origin-lacking. And talked snottily of seven thousand years of history.

I said to them, "*Lei-goh lui-je ye-gang ghai-fong-jeo je-gai geh gun-yueni.*" This girl, origin-free. Or more literally, This girl is liberated from the idea of origins.

THE QUESTION OF WHICH RELIGION in which to raise Samuel was not one we ever discussed. There was no need.

Rarely—a bar or bas mitzvah, maybe—we go to synagogue together. There, Howard is the object of omnipresent feelers. "Howard! *Great* to see you here. You're joining the temple!" It is a question. Sometimes, when they know about me, the interlocutor, jocular and earnest, avoids looking in my direction. "Nope," says Howard pleasantly. After Yom Kippur, people drop hints. "Howard, we didn't see you in shul." Or "So Howard, listen, ever tried Temple Adat Shalom?"

"No," says Howard pleasantly, "I don't think so. Anne"—(turning to me)—"have we ever tried Temple Adat Shalom?"

No, I say, we never have.

"Nope," says Howard. "Never have."

Then my mother found *The Lord Is My Shepherd* in Camden Market just after Sam was born, and that solved my question about his cultural education. I simply read him the biblical stories, Old and New Testaments, as literature.

Howard, on the other hand, read Kipling to Sam. He mentioned it once at a PolyGram meeting. *Kipling?* said a talent manager, with a severe frown. Very not-done. Racist. *No*, Howard had responded slowly. Kipling once said he worshipped "The God of Things As They Are," which meant he was a brutal realist. But race? Kipling's poetry is "not," as an English friend once put it to me, "just chaps in pith helmets keeping the wogs at bay on the Northwest Frontier." Here was a man who intimately knew Hinduism, a theologically justified racialist social order. One was born this caste or that one: Brahmin, Shatriya, Vaishya, Shudra, Thakur, Prabhu, Kayshth, Untouchable. The color of the skin went (surprise) downward from light to dark. And Kipling is quite pointed about opposing it. Howard used him to teach this to Sam. I gave my agents the poem we'd years ago given our son and asked Billy Lazarus to read it.

> *All good people agree,*
> *And all good people say,*
> *That all nice people, like Us, are We*
> *And everyone else is They:*
> *But if you cross over the sea,*
> *Instead of just over the way,*
> *You may end by (think of it!) looking on We*
> *As only a sort of They!*

The agents were surprised to hear this from Kipling, but, without thinking about it too much, they all nodded vigorously in the usual self-congratulatory way and said how much they liked it. It's the sort of thing Americans automatically take as self-evident truth.

I take it as a self-evident truth as well.

Kipling was as far textually as Howard went into religion. A few years ago we were approached by two of those smiling zombielike people who asked about "our faith." Sam replied, "We worship the French fry," and Howard enjoyed that. When Kabbalah arrived, to blossom and wither inside the industry like every other fad, Howard met it at first wordlessly. People in meetings at Paramount enthused about their Hebraic scholars, lunches at Imagine and Amblin where they plumbed the cryptic mysteries of the Kabbalist texts. He said nothing. "It's great, Howie!" I'm sure it is, he replied. "Have you *tried* this?" (He was in some meeting with three Triad agents.) "It'll unlock secrets for you, seriously." Hm, said Howard genially. The agent to Howard's left—his rabbi guru had, after months of study and thousands of dollars, pinpointed his Hebrew consonants *daled* and *nun*, which gave *dan*. "So, see?" he explained to Howard, according to Kabbalah, for him any word with "dan" in it held power. You had to find the words. That morning he'd been pondering "laudanum," "a mysterious and powerful opiate." And "danburite," "a mysterious rare mineral contained in crystals." And, of course, "danger," a rich semiotic vein.

Howard considered gravely and then brightly suggested "dandruff." He looked around the antique cherrywood table. "A mysterious and powerful seborrheic condition."

As for Sam, he had from the very start had ideas of his own, thank you very much. When he was five, Howard had read the Adam and Eve and serpent story to him. Sam was at that point obsessed with defining, in all narratives, who was "the bad person," and so Howard asked him whether in that story there was a bad person.

Sam thought about it very gravely. "Yes," he said, his face serious.

"And who was that?" asked Howard.

"God," said Sam.

WE ARE DESCENDING IN THE elevator with David Remnick. It is a year ago. The air-conditioning is freezing. Howard has come to New York for a meeting because there is sudden interest in L.A. in one of David's pieces.

Immediately on arriving, Howard had ducked off to Alex Ross's office to negotiate this evening's logistics. Howard loves Alex, loves that he is the music critic. I have never possessed whatever madness is necessary to be an opera fan, and so it suits me that he is happy trundling off with Alex to the Salzburg Festival. The two of them get their hotel rooms and spend the week hearing Kurt Weill and lieder and Mussorgsky and Ernest Chausson's Poème de l'Amour et de la Mer. "The musical version of Cannes," Alex once explained it to me, not altogether kindly, "a glamorous watering hole for classical super-stars and tycoon sophisticates and tourists sharing in their aura."

"Tonight?" Howard had asked, sticking his head in the door. "Quarter to eight," replied Alex, "in front of Will Call," and threw him out. From there he went to find David. I waited outside the office, reading about threats to the world's food supply. Parasites, pollution. They emerged, twenty minutes later, talking about David's article, which now may become a movie, and we go to the elevators.

"The Afterlife" was about Natan Sharansky's imprisonment by the Soviets and then, after he'd emigrated, about his political career in Israel. David wrote it several years ago—"but," says Howard, "you never know when they'll discover what"—and David is recalling the tiny, freezing cell in Perm-35. Sharansky'd take a cup of hot water, says David, put it on spots all over his body to warm up. David taps his fingertip on his shirtsleeve to indicate it.

"I'm telling you," says Howard emphatically, "it's a long shot, OK? But there are people interested, and it matters. I've talked to him"—(Natan)—"and I've talked to Avital"—(Natan's wife)—"a lot to her actually. He's interested. She's not crazy about the project." Howard and David share a look. "Avital's religious—"

"Yeah—" says David.

"—so, you know. . . ."

"Uh-huh—" David, nodding, is holding the elevator door for me but concentrating on Howard.

"—so Avital talked a lot about the religious issues, Jewish law, the way that would be presented."

David is ambivalent. "Natan did support a conversion law that effectively disenfranchised half of world Jewry," he admits. "His personal political survival depended on his caving in to ultra-Orthodox ultimatums."

Howard says, "Yeah." David wouldn't, Howard indicates, necessarily need to bring this up with Natan. I notice Howard seems to be lost in David's comment about the conversion law for a moment. He comes out of it. "Look, they're open to discussing it," he says, then, "By the way, I liked the way you opened the piece—"

"The hats."

"Yeah, when he makes aliyah. *Very* nice," says Howard. "Tribeca likes it."

"Did you like the hats?" David asks me, intently, just as I enter the revolving doors to 42nd Street ahead of him. The first interest had come from Jane Rosenthal, she loved it, and HBO and Participant were quite serious, so David is now having to rethink things in terms of the screen. Howard actually thinks it less of a long shot than he's letting on, but with David he wants to err conservatively. David looks at me through the doors, impatiently, each of us in our moving slice of glass as the air-conditioning disappears into early summer in New York.

Actually I haven't read it, I say when David emerges; they sent a copy to Howard's office.

So Howard describes David's opening to me. The Lubavitchers have felt fedoras. The Moroccan Sephardim wear multicolored skullcaps. The Modern Orthodox Zionist has a small knitted *kippa*, a slightly larger one means a right-wing settler. A black velvet model is ultra-Orthodox. And then there was Sharansky, who wasn't much of any of this except he wanted to be Israeli. When the Soviets freed him (Sharansky was the most famous political prisoner of his day), and he got on a plane to Israel, "people were betting whether or not I would put on the *kippa*," Natan had told David, and added with an irritated grimace, "because it is impossible for Israelis to stay in one room together if they haven't got their headgear coordinated."

"Taxi." Howard's pointing at the sky, glaring toward the street.

"He put on an Israeli Army hat," David says to me with a laugh. "It solved the identity problem. Thanks, Howard." The taxi has slammed to a stop. David slides in. "299 Park," he says to the driver, then to us out the window, "Allegiance to the national institution, the army. It was a secular statement, so it said, 'I'm secular.' But it covered the head, so it said, 'I'm not completely religiously indifferent.'"

"I'll call you from L.A.," says Howard. The taxi driver, who is wearing a Muslim tupi on his head, hesitates, sniffs the traffic, leaps into the flow.

"I admire that," Howard says, looking after the yellow car. "Great solution." He glances with irritation at the sky. "Christ, it's hot as hell, and it's not June yet."

Why admire it?

Howard says, "Sharansky's smart."

That's why?

He focuses on me now. He asks, "What's a better reason?"

I say, I suppose it seems to me that the question is inherently silly. Playing political chess with these factions, each one madder than the next.

"It is silly," says Howard, logically, "but if you have to deal with it."

But why should one have to deal with it, I say. Why should one have to put up with this kind of ridiculous garbage.

He is getting the slightest bit impatient with this. "That's the way things are, Anne," he states.

That's precisely my point, I say.

FOR THE SCREENWRITERS, MY INITIAL choice was (retrospectively) so obvious it refused to jump out at me. One thinks "screenwriter" as one goes through lists and pages, brow creasing, one thinks (with a grimace) "writing . . ." and then "well, *creativity*" and then "oh damn it all," and then it stands up on the page and waves at you. Light verse. Nonsense writing. Of course.

The persecution complex is so deeply rooted in the Hollywood screenwriter and the parameters of their lives so tenuously lived between studios, directors, and stars, all positively barking and all viewing the writer as a sort of personal Rorschach blot, that Mark Singer once described Hollywood to me as "where the writer is that laughable schmendrik so low in the food chain he gets flossed after breakfast." I assumed nonsense verse would catheterize them. Sure enough, they loved it.

We began with Edward Lear (1812–1888). I rummaged around in the basement book boxes marked "Sam, childhood" in green Magic Marker and found the copy I'd picked up in London, a later edition of Lear's 1846 *Book of Nonsense*. The original was printed for children, but my edition had already transitioned to adults. (Sam, at six, had been put off by the lack of pictures.) I'd had Justin photocopy it, carefully. Akiva Goldsman handed out the copies. I asked a writer with an action-comedy in preproduction to read "How Pleasant to Know Mr. Lear." Mind the meter, please.

"How pleasant to know Mr. Lear!"
Who has written such volumes of stuff!
Some think him ill-tempered and queer,
But a few think him pleasant enough.

His mind is concrete and fastidious,
His nose is remarkable big;
His visage is more or less hideous,
His beard it resembles a wig.

He reads, but he cannot speak, Spanish,
He cannot abide ginger beer:

Ere the days of his pilgrimage vanish,
How pleasant to know Mr. Lear!

Their appreciation was purely neurological, reactive; discussion was limited almost entirely to an unspoken sense of complicity. I did get a clear-cut reaction to "Cold Are the Crabs," which begins with the blissfully incoherent mess

Cold are the crabs that crawl on yonder hills,
Colder the cucumbers that grow beneath,
And colder still the brazen chops that wreathe
The tedious gloom of philosophic pills!

and careens contentedly along through the lusciously meaningless *"tardy film of nectar fills / The ample bowls of demons and of men"* to end, with brilliant aplomb

Yet much remains——to weave a solemn strain
A pea-green gamut on a distant plain
When wily walruses in congress meet——
Such such is life——

It was, one of them said, what he thought every day while driving on the Santa Monica Freeway, these shadowy scenes in the dark.

I repeated their comments to Anthony Lane, and he got interested and wound up writing a piece on the subject. He noted of light verse that these very British constructions are "indeed funny but also curiously macabre in their imperturbable accounts of disasters, cannibalism, and murders." My writers agreed. That, too, reflected their experience. To them Lewis Carroll (I found the dates: 1832–1898) "encapsulated" the movie pitch: the randomness, the weirdness, the pell-mell rush forward, the brutality. I'd made a mistake with Carroll's "The Walrus and the Carpenter" (you know it:

"*The time has come,*" *the Walrus said,* "*To talk of many things, Of shoes—*
and ships—and sealing wax—Of cabbages and kings"), which ends with
a calculatedly and breathtakingly cruel deception-cum-genocide of
a group of oyster children. The mistake was reading it to Sam at
age six, for of course he grasped all of the horror and none of the
linguistic gamesmanship, and sobbed for an hour, Howard glaring
at me the whole time.

IT IS ALMOST TEN YEARS ago. Kate and I are watching Sam
and Sawyer playing on some sort of jungle gym. Mostly we just watch.
By moments we talk about something, someone, an idea. Sam, hold on
tighter, please. "Well, *this* year," says Kate, "he looks a little more like
Howard." We compare the two boys, which one looks like his mother,
which looks like his father. And what that will mean for them, how it
will encumber them, the famous parent problem, and so on.

I am conscious of the fact that she converted and I didn't. We
are physically similar, Kate and I, hair and eye color and skin tone
and so on, and we resemble each other ethnobotanically, except that
she's from Texas. The fact of her having converted when she married Steven and my not converting when I married Howard is not
greatly relevant to us, personally (this is my perception; I don't know
if it's relevant to her), but it is immensely relevant to the two children
on the metal rungs above us. And to her husband, of course, who
needed Sawyer to be Jewish. This we don't discuss.

She tells me about a trip they might take to Italy in September.

NOT EARLY ON A ROSEATE orange evening when the first
guests are just arriving and the staff and the sunset are still fresh, nor
when walking over the marble threshold into the cool, exquisite restaurant, hungry, and the thick white linen tablecloth under the silver
and crystal is clean and starched and pressed and inviting as a pool

of clear, blue water. Not then, but later, when the party has dragged on too long and the drunk ones are still there and a cigarette is floating in whomever's pool, or when the paying of the check becomes a Byzantine process and the conversation was not so stimulating and, hunger now sated, one realizes that it was, as it always is after all, just food—then I think of the line from the Roethke poem: "I run, I run to the whistle of money." And when we did not run to it.

Or at the parties where everyone's clothing is perfect and mannered and where they announce—always with the glass raised, and the grin—the new three-picture deal, the latest opening numbers. And suddenly everyone is toasting and the eyes are moving in their slots and smiles are brittle and the food tastes of cardboard.

I shoo out the last guests, tell the caterers to send the cleaning staff the next day (it is just too late, no fault of theirs), and sit in the dark. He finds me there and joins me on the sofa. Puts his arm around my shoulders.

All that planning.

He sighs. "Yeah, but it was great."

Hm. I know I shouldn't say it. But I hate, I say, and list several things and, maybe, even a person or two.

"Yeah, I hate them, too," he says.

No, Howard, I *really* hate them.

"I hate them more!" he says. "I hate them more than life itself!"

Thank you.

"Don't mention it."

Your breath smells like a wine cellar, I say to him, and he shrugs, acknowledging it.

I slip from his arm, take a volume from the bookshelf there, slip back under his arm, turn to Charles Lamb. The paper is textured beneath my fingers. When I assigned this to my producers, who jammed their Jaguars into my driveway, I had Justin photocopy for them a short biography of Lamb (1775–1834), a contemporary of Coleridge and Wordsworth and a good friend of both. What I like about Lamb is what he is generally noted for, his immediacy and entirely human observations of life (so different from the Romantic craziness). His simple, ruthless account of landing as a young boy at Christ's Hospital, the London boarding school for sons of middle-class parents in straitened financial circumstances, is typical: "I was poor and friendless. My parents, and those who should care for me, were far away. Those few acquaintances of theirs, which they could reckon upon being kind to me in the great city, after a little forced notice, which they had the grace to take of me on my first arrival in town, soon grew tired of my holiday visits. They seemed to them to recur too often, though I thought them few enough; and, one after another, they all failed me, and I felt myself alone among six hundred boys."

A woman I know was of sufficient ill-humor to dismiss Lamb as the Mitch Albom of Imperial Britain. This is truly cruel. And false. A stuttering, shambling, fragile man who was known for his smoking, drinking, and inveterate gentleness, he became a successful writer, actually a one-man publishing industry. Money began to flow to him. So it went. He and his beloved older sister Mary, to whom he devoted his life, gathered on Wednesday nights in their home the leading artists and writers of England. But after these artists and writers had cleared out, when they were alone again and it was late, Lamb thought about the difference in his now-rich life. Listen, I said to my producers, sitting in their expensive clothing in my large home atop this expensive hill. This is from Lamb's "Old China."

"I wish the good old times would come again," Mary said to me, "when we were not quite so rich. I do not mean that I want to be poor; but there was a middle state in which I am sure we were a great deal happier. A purchase is but a purchase, now that you have money enough and to spare. Formerly it used to be a triumph. When we coveted a cheap luxury (and, O! how much ado I had to get you to consent in those times!)—we used to have a debate two or three days before, and to weigh the for and the against, and think what we might spare it out of, and what saving we could hit upon. A thing was worth buying then, when we felt the money that we paid for it.

"Do you remember the brown suit, which you made to grow so threadbare, till all your friends cried shame—and all because of that folio 'Beaumont and Fletcher,' which you dragged home late at night from Barker's at Covent Garden? Do you remember how we eyed it for weeks before we could make up our minds to purchase it, and had not come to a determination till it was near ten o'clock of the Saturday night, when you set off from Islington where we lived, fearing you should be too late. And when the old bookseller with some grumbling opened his shop, and by the twinkling taper (for he was setting bedwards) lighted out the relic from his dusty treasures. And when you lugged it home, wishing it were twice as cumbersome—and when you presented it to me—and when we were exploring the perfectness of it (collating, you called it)—and while I was repairing some of the loose leaves with paste, which your impatience would not suffer to be left till daybreak. Was there no pleasure in being a poor man? Can those neat black clothes which you wear now, and are so careful to keep brushed, since we have become rich and finical, give you half the honest vanity with which you flaunted it about in that overworn suit for four or five weeks longer than you should have done, to pacify your conscience for the mighty sum of fifteen—or sixteen shillings was it?—which you lavished on the old folio.

"Now you can afford to buy any book that pleases you, but I do not see that you ever bring me home any nice old purchases."

WE WERE ACTUALLY STANDING IN the spotless, luxurious hallway of the Four Seasons on East 57th—we'd arrived from Los Angeles the previous day—and Howard was in loafers and a business shirt, ready to go down to the lobby (I think he'd already pressed the button) when I suggested that, well, it was a bit last minute, but perhaps I actually wouldn't go to his family's seder this year. I'm not wanted, I pointed out forthrightly.

Howard said that, yeah, he did have to admit, I wasn't wanted.

And so how about if I went to the spa? I proposed. Perhaps I'd get a nice massage. I'd be here when he and Sam got back.

"OK," said Howard.

I mean, why should I go? I said to him. I'm not Jewish.

"OK," said Howard, "no problem." He'd take Sam. He turned his head toward the open door to our room. "Sammy!" (Sam was eight.) "We're leaving for Bubbe and Zaide's!"

(Well. I had to say that a casual "no problem" was not quite the reaction I was expecting. I was only his wife . . . ! I paused, trying to work it out.)

But why do *you* go, Howard? You don't believe of word of it, the religious stuff and all that.

"Tribal identity," said Howard. Calling into the room, a bit more irritated: "*Sam!* I'm waiting."

But you're completely opposed to that benighted sort of thing.

Howard shrugged, breezily. He scratched his nose. A moment later I heard the elevator ding, and they descended to get a taxi. I stood in the plush hallway watching the space they'd disappeared from. I went into the room, kicked off my navy pumps, picked up the phone, and called down to the spa.

Was the shrug a nonchalant acknowledgment of the irreconcilable nature of life? Or was it, as the expression goes, shrugging it off. If I play the scene again, it could be either.

On the Lexington Avenue train that evening back to 59th Street and from there the Four Seasons, Sam swung his legs over the plastic subway bench and asked Howard about the end of the seder. They had concluded with, "Next year in Jerusalem!" "We always end the seder with that," explained Howard. "It's a promise."

"To who?"

"To whom," said Howard. "To ourselves. We promise ourselves to be in our own land."

Sam thought about it for a moment and asked, "Will Mom be there?"

The reason I know this is that many years later Sam told me. At the time I knew nothing. And Howard, reported Sam, gave no response.

("Now Anne no longer goes and I go," I heard Howard explain once to someone. It struck me that Howard was being simplistic.)

SAM HAD HIS FIRST FORMAL lesson in Talmud at thirteen while hanging out at the AMC Century City movie theaters. A boy Sam remotely knew from the Buckley School was asserting that his mother's recent transconjunctival blepharoplasty was for her health.

The transparent idiocy of the argument threw Sam—"She had an eyelift for her *health*?" said Sam—but it was the aggressive vehemence of the boy's response that drew him into what rapidly became a well-attended shouting match in front of the ticket booths. The vehemence was generated, it turned out, by theology; Sam learned that categorizing plastic surgery as Health was crucial because Hebrew scripture categorically forbid "mutilation of the body" for any other reason. A tattoo, pierced ears, a medial pedicle mastopexy (breast tuck), and a Jew could not be buried in a Jewish cemetery. But for the observant—the Buckley boy's family kept kosher—the cutting-and-pasting of his mother's features, this elective surgery—"*Elective!*" shouted Sam, "like, did her *health insurance* cover it?" and eight teenage heads swiveled to the other side for the retort—could indeed be categorized as "health," turning the word into such a large theological umbrella that arguably anything you wanted could be made to fit under it, including pop sex books.

A girl in the group threw Sam a scornful, slightly disgusted look, which he interpreted instantly. He had grown to thirteen, half the kids he knew lived in Beverly Hills, and he was only *now* discovering that this intellectual contortion of wealthy Jews regarding their plastic surgeons, this gross hypocrisy, was as universal as it was perfunctory? Please, her look said.

When he arrived home grim and furious, Howard, with a bit of work, extracted the episode from him. Howard thought about it, then went and dug up the *New Yorker* of a few weeks earlier and found a letter to the editor by a certain Arthur Daniels of Brooklyn—Howard showed it to Sam—which read "In discussing whether Ophelia can be given a Christian burial, one of Shakespeare's gravediggers asks another how this would be possible 'when she wilfully seeks her own salvation?'" ("He means 'Since she committed suicide,' Sam. That's a sin to Christians.") "His companion responds that Christian burial is possible for anyone who drowns, since 'if the water come to him and drown him, he drowns not himself.'"

"A perfect example of Talmudic reasoning," said Howard with a smile.

"Well," objected Sam, who was sick of being exasperated, "but that's just a way of getting around the—you know, the whole *point*."

"Exactly," said Howard, that was exactly what Talmudic reasoning was, the selective assembling of tendentious arguments from a completely arbitrarily designated body of text in order to justify the conclusion you had already arrived at through your biases based on your difficult personality, past mistakes, tax bracket, lousy conscience, and so on. Sam should understand that Judaism was divided into two distinct phases, that when Temple Judaism, a primitive nomadic-tribal religion typical of its historic context with all the gewgaws of such religions (priestly castes, ritual purifications, fanatic xenophobia, nutty dietetic and sexual rules; Howard ticked them off on his fingers), was destroyed in—let's see, was it around the second century CE?—rabbinical Judaism began, the study of text rather than the performance of temple ritual, since the temple was gone but the text could be stored and parsed in any Russian shtetl or Warsaw ghetto or Brooklyn tenement. Or (a significant look) the AMC Century City movie theaters in Los Angeles. OK? And this particular theological product has broken all the records. Outlived them all. Immune to internal incoherence. Here was this young idiot from the Buckley School, said Howard, engaged in exactly the brilliant adaptive strategy that has kept Jews Jews. And—this was the genius part—the simple act of arguing about it *was Jewish worship itself*. Not *literally* worship but something infinitely more important: the preservation of the tribe as a tribe. Marking the boundaries. What mattered was not that there was actually a right answer to whether or not you could get an eye job. What mattered was that Jews argued about these things. And non-Jews didn't. Drawing that line was the point.

And Howard cited to Sam several specific examples of reasoning from the Talmud. Sam rolled his eyes and left the room, spitting.

But I was more interested in Howard. In bed later I remarked to him, You can really reel those off.

He shrugged.

I said, Really, I'm astounded at the extent to which you have these examples at your fingertips.

He said, "They program you well." He was reading the newspaper.

Where do they program you well?

He said, "At Hebrew school." He turned a page, skimmed. "And a couple of weeks at a yeshiva." Turned another page. "Jerusalem, I was a teenager." He closed the paper, lay it down, turned out the reading light on his side, and closed his eyes. He chanted in a mumble, "*Hamotzei*, the blessing for bread, *mezonos*, the blessing for wheat, *hagofen*, the blessing for wine."

I thought about this for a moment. I said, I didn't know you actually went to Hebrew school.

"Are you going to read?"

Yes, I'm going to read.

"Kiss me and read."

I reopened the book and looked for my place. I couldn't remember if I'd read this page or not. I said, So how many years did you go?

AS WE ARE SETTING UP for that evening, Howard appears in his suit with a bag over his shoulder and kisses me gently on the forehead. That was sweet, I say. I take it this means LAX?

He suddenly has a meeting in New York the next day with Natan Sharansky and David. "The Remnick project," as HBO is referring to it, has led to Howard's becoming friends with Natan and, surprisingly, his wife, Avital. She has become a correspondent of a sort, and Howard spent Shabbat with them during his last trip to Tel Aviv.

"What did you give them?" he asks me, already moving toward the car. "It's the directors tonight?"

Yes, I say. Christina.

I see more than hear him give a short laugh. It's an obvious choice. "Knock 'em dead," he calls, his key almost in the car door. "I'm back tomorrow night."

To the directors, I give Christina Rossetti. Who else? Less overtly visual than Keats, yet imagery so compelling one can't turn away. She reads like film. We taught Sam about drugs with "Goblin Market," which is about heroin addiction, whether Rossetti knew it or not. And she accomplished her splendid work without Sexton's insanity or Plath's crippled mind. "Do you know," Virginia Woolf wrote to a friend, "she was about as good as poetesses are made, since Sappho jumped." She masters the sensual act, slips it into our ears like a snake disappearing into a hole.

You cannot think what figs
My teeth have met in.

Say it slowly, out loud. Pronounce each final consonant. Go ahead.

"CHUPPA" SIGNIFIES "WEDDING" TO ME now, after all this time being married to Howard. (That's the tent thing over the couple, I had asked years ago, yes? "Right.") And at the same time, it doesn't. It is another system, and I have adapted to it. The verb of culture. I didn't have to create my own system, and I was not enslaved by this one, because I was able to exist parallel to it. But I did not own it, nor it, me.

This is how it goes. Say it is two years ago. Say we arrive in New York for the weekend. They decide that we will visit the Jewish Museum, 1109 Fifth Avenue at 92nd Street, because Stan and Rebecca want to see the Alex Katz exhibit.

Afterward, for lunch, we descend to the Café Weissman, a paradigmatic museum café: the ivory walls, the still-life-under-glass feeling, like eating in a huge bathroom. The sign reads "Glatt kosher" and is guarded by a yarmulked, bearded, portly thirty-year-old. Because Howard called him last week, Donald Kuspit, of the museum, joins us, and Rebecca and Howard interrogate him about the art, the Katz. Regarding the Chaim Soutine exhibit last month Donald says things like, "Soutine's shudder is a sublimation of the trauma of being born a lowly shtetl Jew and becoming an absurd Jew by becoming a painter."

They nod gravely at this, give it deep thought.

I sip my tea.

Lawrence Weschler joins us, apologizes for being late. "Anne!"

How are you, Ren.

Rebecca tells him about the Katz. They talk about the Jewish Museum. They discuss the place of Jews as outsiders in various societies. Someone says that the Jews are chosen, yes, "but it's not that the Jews are *better* than other people, just that we answer to a higher moral standard."

They all nod gravely. This time I simply have to stare at Howard. Howard seems to notice nothing, and after a moment I look away. Ren, Howard, completely unaware.

This is how it goes. Say it is just a few months ago. I am perhaps waiting for Howard in the canteen on the studio lot.

I am drinking hot water with lemon and reading *The Bacon Fancier*, by Alan Isler. A friend of Howard's has recommended it to me. Isler is an English Jew who won the 1994 National Jewish Book Award. In the novel, which is actually four novellas, there is a discovery of a mystery monster baby in the ghetto (it is the seventeenth century), and Isler has his Catholic Canon of the Cattedrale di Ferrara write a letter to the ghetto Jews. Isler's character writes: "Think well what this portends, O Jews. Is not this monstrosity given as a sign that ye follow along twisted, wicked ways? From such as this may we not suppose that ye plot diabolical evil against us? Are ye not by this clearly possessed of Satan and his demons?"

As I read this, at the table next to mine sits an anxious young man with dirty blond hair. His hands are moving around a paper cup, constricting, releasing. Constricting again. He looks toward the door every time someone comes in. I glance at my watch, get up to leave, but I ask him: Are you OK?

"Oh!—" He laughs, clears his throat.

He is working on a pilot, *maybe* he is working on a pilot (a nod toward some decisive meeting going on in offices upstairs). Creative differences. The network wants, you know, light, but serious, and original but familiar, and meaningful, but not too much. All the clichés. He wants: darker.

I think for a moment. I refer him to a play by Wendy Wasserstein.

His tension springs the response. "I'm so fucking sick of Jewish angst!" he says. And immediately the hands freeze in a choke hold on the coffee cup. "Oh, I don't mean to offend you if you're Jewish."

No, I begin slowly. The Isler is in my mind. He takes the slowness for something else.

"Oh my God, I am *really*—"

I smile. I'm Anne Rosenbaum, I say by way of self-introduction, and, when he immediately starts again: It's my husband's name. Not that that matters, it doesn't.

He waits. I am smiling. You have no idea how refreshing it is to hear, I say to him quietly. I'm beaming with mirth.

He stares at me.

I tuck my purse under one arm, and offer him a hand. I want you to know what a pleasure it's been to have spoken with you.

He doesn't know what to say, so I just smile at him. Howard says I always smile with my mouth closed, and I make sure to let my lips part because I like him and want very much for him to know that, and he does, I think.

On the 101 going home, Howard driving, I reread for the eighth or ninth time the dust jacket copy of *The Bacon Fancier*, which some copywriter or perhaps an editor at Viking has written. This is, reads the copy, "a book in four tales set in successive centuries and linked by a common theme: The Jewish experience in the Gentile world."

There are the boundaries that they clarify incessantly, neurotically. The drawing and redrawing of the line, which constitutes the sole purpose of the devotion. There is the constant clarification that I am not inside these lines. It is simply a fact. There is the shocking poverty of their perception, the vast depth of their narcissism. "Not better, just a higher moral standard." The constant hypostatizing of evil, always locating it somewhere else. And this dust jacket copy. It is always, I notice, the Jewish experience in the Gentile world. It is never, I notice, the Gentile experience in the Jewish world.

YEARS AGO. WE ARE IN New York visiting Howard's family in Brooklyn Heights. Howard has disappeared into some conversation somewhere in another room. I don't know where Stuart is. I linger in the dim front hallway that leads into the living room, where Sam, age six, his skin like the freshest peach flesh, is playing on the floor and where Howard's aunts sit back on the sofa, viewing him, like queens on cushions. He is childhood itself, says one. Beauty itself. ("Beaudy" she pronounces it.) The other says, "Yes." And then with dismay, whispers (but not all that quietly), "But the wrong half!"

Sam, of course, takes no visible notice, but he has ears.

In the dim hallway, the wrong half takes a sharp breath, freezing like a deer where she stands. The large, airy brownstone is dark and cool despite summer's best efforts, the sun burning the Callery Pear trees (*Pyrus calleryana*) outside. A breeze zooms happily through the large open windows and up to the high ceilings, bearing with it Brooklyn's streets and a bit of roast chicken with onions and a garrulous delivery boy and a passing car radio. In some other room, the correct half laughs briefly at a story an uncle is telling him.

In the doorway, the wrong half peers into an old mirror. She examines herself. Hair. Nose. Trim breasts. Slim hips. Cotton sundress. A thin gold bracelet and small earrings. She feels that she looks normal. Not abnormal. Not wrong. She enters the room smoothly, sweeps up the two halves of her son without a word to the aunts, and cooing something in his small ear, bears him out the open door and into the streets, down the brownstone's steps past the amorous delivery boy (chatting up the gum-snapping teenage Puerto Rican babysitter from the bottom unit), moves swiftly across the glowing concrete sidewalks and the fragrant asphalt, and deposits him on the other side. Together, they rush pell-mell down the street with crazy big steps to where they will stand, he with his thumb in his awed mouth, to watch the sweating young men wearing gold chains carrying plastic bags of ice from the truck into the Italian grocery on Dean Street near Hoyt.

Stuart comes walking up Dean Street past the Italian grocery. He's got a brown paper bag. He'd gone out to run an errand. "Hey, Annie!" Stuart says.

Sam rushes to him, cheering. Stuart grabs Sam, holds him by his ankles so Sam can scream. Looks at me for a moment. "Whaddya doin'? You waitin' for somebody?"

No, I say.

"Where's Howard?"

At home.

Stuart flips Sam right side up, and he holds him in his arms as he considers me. He blinks. He puts Sam down and hands him the brown bag and whispers to him, "You take that back to Bubbe." Sam tears off. Stuart looks at me, waiting patiently until I am ready to speak.

I AM IN THE BLACK Saab, having pulled onto the dusty shoulder of Mulholland at Franklin Canyon Drive. The top is down, it is a spectacular day, almost no smog. I apply lipstick, matte it down with my lips. Burst out laughing at myself. Acting like an ex-actress driving into Bel Air. (Howard would have a field day, were he in the car. But he'll be at home, and I'd like to look a bit less windblown when I arrive.) My head is tilted up with the laugh, which is why just beyond the mirror I catch sight of a slightly battered Toyota pulling up from the Sooky Goldman Nature Center, an occluded exit. I watch. My fingers run distractedly through my hair. The Toyota's driver, a white man in his late thirties, leans forward over his steering wheel with a frown, trying to see one way, then the other. The Toyota pulls out into the far lane, then cuts across the shoulder of the road, where a gardener descends like a cat from behind a mass of dahlia, huge purple flowers and dark-green leaves (my mind will light on the variety: *Pierre chaumier*) and the old Toyota's right front edge plows into the man's flesh at the hip.

Time stands still, one hears birds chirping, all the clichés. I semi-register the jerk of the car, how it stops like a confused animal, and the brief, awkward arc of the gardener's body to the ground. Then he gives a choking cry, the Toyota's driver begins to judder, and the event is no longer celluloid.

Gripping the steering wheel, I check both ways with care, then send the Saab over the road and into the strip of dust on the far side, shaded by ficus, where I put it in park and turn the engine off. I extract the keys, put them in my purse, get out. The driver of the Toyota has the gardener, Hispanic, perhaps early forties, by the armpits and is frantically dragging him into the backseat. I glance at my cell phone. We are perched atop the world between city and valley, and there is no service. I think about the time to find a house with someone at home, the time for the ambulance to come. For it to return. I take a breath and think: OK, Anne. Steady on. You can do this.

I say, You're not supposed to move him.

They both freeze and stare at me like truants caught wrestling. The gardener seems to be lucid, with neuromuscular control (he is clutching the driver, whose worn khakis already have a small blood stain), and is clearly in great pain. I look around: No one. I look at my watch, mentally run through traffic patterns. I look through the Toyota's open door; the backseat is larger than mine, so that's that. I toss my purse onto the floor of the front passenger seat. Right, I say in my best authoritative British, put him down and hold him like this. I motion to the driver to support the man, under the armpits. No, lock your hands together. Across his chest. (I observe that the driver is not stellar in a pinch.) "Like this?" he asks several times in anguish. "Like this?" Yes, I say, like that. Calm down. On my command we're going to lift, you're going in backward, and I want—no, calm down—

"How can you *see* anyone!" he pleads, panicking. He means at the intersection.

Listen to me, I say. He freezes. I fix him with my eyes. It's a technique I've practiced on my son. I want his head in first, your end, OK? Slide him in slowly.

I've got my hands around the gardener's legs, and that's when I notice the blood. To the driver, I say: Ready? We both breathe in and lift together, but the legs are heavier than I'd expected. The driver awkwardly pulls the gardener inside, more or less on top of his own body, but it works, until the hurt man screams, then closes his eyes and concentrates on the pain. When he opens his eyes, they are looking directly at me.

I look at the driver, who almost seems in worse condition. Are you OK? I ask him.

There's a muffled sound, and he says, "I think so." With a bit of shifting he edges out from under, and the gardener lies back on the seat, head almost touching the car door, his hands in tight fists. I gently bend his legs and, stepping back, very carefully shut the door. I gather myself for a moment and realize I am not breathing. I let out my breath.

I walk briskly around to the other side. We'll take him to Cedars Sinai, I say.

The driver is scampering around the other way. "Not Good Samaritan? It's closer. Wait. Is it closer?"

Cedars does better osteopathy. (I'm thinking of Marty Silverstein.)

"Laurel Canyon!"

I think, again, about traffic. Coldwater Canyon, I say.

"Maybe we shouldn't have moved him," he says, almost literally wringing his hands.

I give him a brief, sharp look, and he flies for the door, jams the key into the ignition so that it almost breaks off. I push the passenger seat as far up as it will go and then find the lever and flip the back forward. I squeeze into the back, near the man's head, which I lift and then lower onto my lap, and look down at him. There is a surprising amount of blood on his hip and thigh. I start unbuckling his trousers. I'm sitting behind the driver on the passenger's side. Drive, I say, fast.

The Toyota jumps forward. I put a steadying hand on the back-seat and continue with the pants. I'm going to look at the wound, I say to the man in Spanish, and he nods. I pull up his shirt, unfasten the belt, unzip the trousers. OK, I say, I need you to help me. You seem to be able to move.

"I can move," he says, and before I can stop him, he shifts his hips, gritting his teeth. Stop, I say very quickly. Don't move. (That much I know from watching television shows.)

I say to the driver, in English, He's moving, so I don't think there's serious damage to his hip structure, amazingly.

"Oh, thank God, thank God," he says, and he gives his version of what happened, which of course he needs to do. At a very mild, brief wave of nausea, I realize that I myself am coming out of a bit of shock. I let it flow and ebb. I am gratified to see that the gardener is not modest. He slips the trousers down, uncovering gray, worn underwear, the agony showing in his neck. There is a huge gash along his upper hip, already purple and swollen, and I hold it closed with the fingers of my left hand. The blood stops flowing. The underwear is becoming soaked with blood. I look down and see that I, too, am covered with blood to my elbow.

I glance up, indicate a rapidly approaching street. Turn there. The driver does, and we almost go off the road. The driver is trying to look at us in the rearview mirror. Eyes front, please, I say. I say it very crisply to control the tremble I feel. I close my eyes for a moment. Steady on, Anne.

"Is it bad?"

I breathe deeply, open my eyes. What should I say. He's going to be fine, it looks much worse than it is.

"Ask him if he's legal," the driver says.

It takes me an instant to process this. I find it interesting he has the presence of mind to pose such a question. Then: hospital, questions, papers, police, Immigration. I put my right hand on the side of the man's head and ask him. He says that he is. I don't bother to ask if he has health insurance. He moans, and the driver, already unnerved by the blood, becomes so agitated I'm certain all three of us are going to be hospitalized. He's going to be fine, I say, and then gently, *Please* keep your eyes in front. I'm more frightened by his driving than by the blood; normally I would find this funny. But I can hear him hyperventilating, and I realize I must stabilize him. What do you do? I ask him.

He's staring ahead. His mind spins a moment before it grips. "I'm a screenwriter," he says, close to tears.

That's interesting, I say. My husband works at a studio.

He blinks. Focused now. "Oh yeah?" He attempts a casual voice. "Who's that?"

Howard Rosenbaum.

He gasps without making any noise, which is a feat. He is looking at me in the mirror even as he turns right at high speed. "You're Anne Rosenbaum?" He is literally wide-eyed. Why do emergencies generate clichés? A car trying to merge into our trajectory honks at us.

Yes, I say. (He pretends not to be staring into the rearview mirror.) What are you writing?

"It's a," he says, clears his throat, "romantic comedy. Set in Vancouver."

Ah. Vancouver is lovely.

He frowns, clears this throat again, says quickly, "Well, the movie's not *about* Vancouver, and people don't get that the characters don't—"

You mean script readers don't get it.

He makes a scoffing sound. He hasn't even gotten as far as script readers. He's gotten to the person who answers the phone.

You don't have an agent.

"To get an *agent* you'd have to—"

Would you like me to give your script to Howard?

His eyes fill the rearview mirror. "Would you?"

I will if you keep your eyes on the road.

His eyes are instantly on the road. Eyeballs motionless.

The gardener moans and shifts. I raise and lower my left hand as he moves to hold the skin together. I ask the driver, Do you have a cloth? He starts flinging things from the glove compartment, though it's clear this will produce nothing. He stops when he notices I'm shimmying out of my sateen slip, which is quite awkward in the backseat. I rip it into wide strips. It's inappropriate bandage material, but my cotton shirt is too thick to rip, as is my linen skirt. I mop the blood that started seeping the instant I took my hand away. Then I try to tie the strips around his thigh to close at least part of the wound. The cloth seems to hold. I cradle the gardener's head in my lap. He has become conscious of the blood now, and he is terrified. I tell him he will be OK, we are going to the hospital. I ask him his name, and he says José Pineda. He moans something about death and invokes Jesus and the names of several of the saints.

I remember a professor marvel once as he told me that in his view, strangely enough American poetry had become gentler and more reassuring to readers than it had in a century. I was dubious. He waved this away. Yes, yes, modernist technique had become the norm—difficult and complex allusion, fractionated reality. But forget the style; much of poetry today had reassumed its nineteenth-century role, Wordworth's comfort and consolation, Blake's even earlier haven from the cares of the world.

Including car accidents, I think now.

I look at this man lying in my lap, close up. I see the pores in his skin, the thick hairs of his eyebrows. I see all the busboys—come up by means I don't ask about from all the unnamed impoverished countries—who have stood beside me to serve me glasses and glasses of cool lemon water, who have reached an intimate army of hairless cocoa-colored arms gently around my body to set a palace's worth of gleaming white detergent-washed dinner plates before me. Smiled and nodded at me as I have smiled and nodded at them. But I think, now that I think, that I have never, ever, in all these years and all these plates actually touched this skin or this jet black hair that I am stroking. So I will give this man in my lap comfort and consolation. I murmur to him

> *My mother bore me in the southern wild,*
> *And I am black, but O! my soul is white;*
> *White as an angel is the English child:*
> *But I am black as if bereav'd of light.*

I hold the cloth tightly, but not too tightly, to the leg of the man in my lap. He looks as if he is concentrating. "William Blake," I say to him.

> *My mother taught me underneath a tree*

I glance up to verify we are going the right way.

> *She took me on her lap and kisséd me,*
> *And pointing to the east, began to—*

There is a faint scream of rubber on asphalt somewhere, but it seems unrelated to us. Turn left here, I tell the driver. He turns. His eyes are in the rearview mirror, watching me recite, but somehow he seems to be able to drive like this.

—began to say:

"And we are put on earth a little space,
That we may learn to bear the beams of love,
And these black bodies and this sun-burnt face
Is but a cloud, and like a shady grove."

I'd take Civic Center Drive, I advise, to Beverly Boulevard.

He executes it, runs a red light. Both the face of the driver and the face of the gardener are focused now, kinetic, consoled.

Thus did my mother say, and kisséd me;
And thus I say to the little English boy:

José is listening. I don't know if he understands any of this, since I haven't heard him say a single English word. The driver's mouth wears a strange smile.

When I from black and he from white cloud free,
And round the tent of God like lambs we joy,

I'll shade him from the heat till he can bear
To lean in joy upon our Father's knee;
And then I'll stand and stroke his silver hair,
And be like him, and he will then love me.

They are both calmer now. Better.

"*Más,*" he asks from my lap. More.

I hold the gardener's head as I used to hold Sam's when I put him to bed, stroking the man's hair down behind his ear with my right hand as my left holds his skin together. His hair is the color of Howard's, black and very thick, but utterly different in texture, and boar-bristle straight. I think of one of Sam's favorite poems, a Roethke called "The Sloth." I remember only a random bit. Roethke, I say.

> *In moving slow he has no Peer.*
> *You ask a question in his Ear,*
> *He thinks about it for a Year.*

The driver is grinning. I cannot remember the Spanish word for "sloth" but I describe the animal to the gardener, its habits, and he nods. He laughs, then winces. We proceed, three strangers, down West Beverly Boulevard.

When we get to Cedars Sinai, the ER team—young women in white coats, two Jewish and one Indian—extract him from the car. They act as if this were the most normal thing in the world. As they are taking him out, he says, apparently to me, "What you say." English words. He gulps air. His accent is thick.

"Señor," one of the doctors orders him, "por favor acuéstese. No se mueva."

"Lo que usted dijo," he says to me, cooperating with her but looking at me. "¿Me daría un duplicado por escrito?"

Yes, of course, I reply, surprised. I'll write it down for you tomorrow. He lets his head fall back on the gurney. He is examining the scarlet gumminess all over his right hand. I particularly enjoyed the last stanza, he says politely in Spanish. His Spanish is, phonetically, thoroughly lower-class Mexican, yet grammatically impeccable. He looks me in the eye, adds, just to make sure I understand, "En inglés." He wants me to write it in English.

I smile broadly. Yes, sir, I say.

I turn to one of the doctors. Is Dr. Silverstein in today, I ask.

"Do you know him?"

He's a friend, I say. There may be hairline fractures.

My diagnosis amuses her, but she is not entirely dismissive. "I'll let him know."

I'd like him to get good care, I say. Here's my card.

Having stabilized him, she turns to me, looks at the card, accepts it. Very rapidly, she scans my skin for breaks—"You were hit?" No, I just held him—checks my fingers and cuticles. "You'll need to come in for a hepatitis A test. You've had your B series?" I nod. "And syphilis, and in a few months HIV." She purses her lips, satisfied, releases me, indicates a sign on the wall. "Call that number." She turns away, passes through the swinging metal doors. In them I see a distorted image of myself covered in blood, streaks on my face, in my expensive hair. My shirt has dark-red patches. Half my pearls are tinted hemoglobin. The diamond earrings alone are untouched.

The lipstick is not entirely gone.

I look toward the driver. He's watching me now, utterly exhausted. I smile at him, and he smiles back, the first time he's smiled, and for a moment we grin at each other, out of panic and relief and whatever it is you feel when you experience something of this kind with another person.

We sit together, in companionable silence, waiting for the police to arrive.

The breeze coming in the window and the setting sun make me realize how energized I am. An adrenaline high.

"You're English, right?" he asks. He makes a careful left, heading back up into the hills toward my car.

Not exactly, I say. I'm half. Well, yes, I mean, I suppose I'm English. I never know how to answer that question.

"Ah," he says. "Well, everyone thinks you're English." He adds, "Your Spanish is really good. I'm jealous."

Thank you.

There's the slightest hesitation. "My partner is from Mexico." Then, "Well, his parents are."

Ah, I say.

I wonder if that is why José's immigration status occurred to him.

When we arrive at the Saab, he stops, and I get out, and he follows. "Well," he says with hearty sincerity, "listen, thank you. I mean, thank you. If it weren't for you——"

I smile. You did fine, I say. Do you have that screenplay with you?

"Oh!" He dives into his trunk, comes up with it, clean, nicely bound, three-hole punched, hands it to me. "A Screenplay by Paul McMahon." His home address and home phone number, neatly typed.

I give him my card.

He accepts the card as if it were rare metal. He motions deprecatingly at the screenplay. "I really appreciate . . ." He looks hollowed out.

I take his chin between my thumb and forefinger, covered with dried blood, draw him toward me, and kiss his cheek. You did very well, I say.

As I drive off, he's still standing there next to his Toyota, looking after me.

At home, I stop at the kitchen door and call inside, Howard?

"Yeah!" says his voice. "Where were you? I can't find the——" I hear him coming toward the kitchen door. I say loudly that the blood isn't mine, Howard, I'm perfectly fine, don't be shocked. Then he rounds the corner and sees me.

I hand him Paul's screenplay and start to explain what happened. He tosses it on the kitchen table and talks agitatedly about tests and medical exams and what the hell was I thinking and picks up telephones and waves them about. I hold his hand and tell him I've talked to Dr. Blum. I'm to go in tomorrow morning. Howard and I are not to have sex for a while.

"We're going to the damn emergency room," he says, digging for his car keys. "They can give you something tonight."

I say, Don't forget the screenplay, please.

"Goddamnit, Anne!"

I give him a firm, warm kiss on the cheek. I head to my study to look up sloth. "*Perezoso*."

Up in our bathroom, I strip off the earrings and the necklace and set them aside for Denise to clean when she gets a moment. I place my shoes on the bathroom tile and fold my clothes in a neat pile on top. I take a very hot shower and wash my hair and scrub under my fingernails. Halfway through my shower, I begin to hyperventilate, and my body shakes. I grip the walls until it passes.

I throw out everything except the shoes.

I HAVE BEEN ASKED WHETHER the proximity of this number of women, this nubile, this interested in Howard or his job, bothers me. They glance pointedly at his assistant, Jennifer.

"I can hold my liquor," Howard once said to me. I told him I both appreciated the metaphor and believed him. He happens never to have let me down, as far as I know.

Byron wrote, in 1821 in a letter to a friend, of his difficulties in finishing his epic poem "Don Juan." He had "not," he said, "quite fixed whether to make him end in Hell, or in an unhappy marriage, not knowing which would be the severest. The Spanish tradition says Hell: but it is probably only an Allegory of the other state."

I am certainly aware of the blind genetic stupidity of men. Howard understands it as well. At our table at a charity dinner in Beverly Hills—I think it was Woodland Drive, we were in white tents in someone's backyard—Howard talks about it in the way he does. Why do men have a hole in their penis? he asks everyone. So oxygen can get to their brains.

What's the difference between men and pigs? Pigs don't turn into men when they drink.

Why does it take 100,000 sperm to fertilize a single egg? None of them will stop to ask directions.

Why do so many women have to fake orgasm? asks Howard. Why? our table replies in unison. Because so many men fake foreplay.

I am truly aware that many women get from men the things they don't really want and don't get what they really need. But then, so is Howard. He too has a Byronesque view of marriage. He knows what can turn it to hell. If the sensitive part at the head of the penis is called the "glans," he asks the benefit table, what is the insensitive part at the base of the penis called? The man. The table roars. A thousand dollars a plate. Cancer, I think.

Certainly it is best when the man you are with is aware of the illusions men have, the confusions these cause. A fly is buzzing through the jungle, says Howard as we sit in our seats in the Kodak Theater (the giant gold statue is on the screen; we've just started the fifth commercial break and only two Academy Awards have been handed out). The fly hears an elephant trumpeting with annoyance. He asks, "What's the matter?" She says, "It's this damn bug in my ear!" The fly marches into her ear and shoos out the bug. She says to the fly, "Oh, how can I thank you!" "Well," he says, "I've always wanted to have sex with an elephant." The elephant tries not to laugh at the obvious, but she agrees. The fly swaggers around to the rear and begins thrusting while she waits for him to finish. Suddenly a gigantic coconut falls on her head. "Ow!" says the elephant. And from the rear, the fly roars, "Take it all, bitch!"

"OK, back in five!" they warn, "four, three," the cameras swing into position, and on the stage Billy clears his throat and looks into the prompter. Our row is still choking with laughter, and a minion wearing a headset glares at Howard.

We have had our moments of solitude. Disappointments, a few disagreements that lasted days. A silent late-night flight eighteen years ago to Prague. We had experienced our second terror in the middle of the night, both of them boringly identical in the way they uncoiled themselves, my waking in the darkness of New York to some vapor-ous pain, the textbook-style cramping where my own flesh raged inside me. And yet each nightmare managed to distinguish itself, the blood, Howard's voice, my screaming. They were paradigmatic miscarriages of myth and legend, both fetuses lying on their backs on the porcelain bottom of the toilet bowl gazing up at you, doomed swimmers in their agony, the water, blood filled as if from a shark attack, sloshed gently over their tiny heads. The first was male, the second female. We couldn't afford it at the time, but we'd stabbed a random finger at the globe, and Eastern Europe had seemed so far from all the doctors telling us we would never have a child, that I would never survive it, in the extremely unlikely event that I ever did manage to become pregnant again. Never. Sam, for whom I would have sacrificed anything, had not been conceived yet.

Years later, we rented an apartment in Rome, and one of the first things the elderly signora who lived below us taught Sam in Italian was a dictum: "Love makes women strong and men weak." (After summers and vacations there, Sam spoke Italian fluently, with a blunt-instrument Roman accent. The kid sounded, Howard once told David Simon, like a miniature Fellini character.) I liked the dictum, and remember repeating it to someone, and he thought it over and replied, "Maybe Howard is actually a woman." Love seemed to make him strong.

All the young agents and hopeful writers and ingratiating producers, who came to Howard and minutely detailed for him in some Hollywood canteen the examined, transporting joys of oral sex. Invariably their joy derived less from the act itself and more from the man's not being married to the woman involved. Howard recounts these tales to me, sitting at the kitchen counter still holding his car keys, his shirt hanging exhaustedly on his shoulders. They lay every minute goddamn detail of this lubricious facsimile of intimacy at his feet, he sighs, their aim to create yet another facsimile of intimacy, this time between them and him. "Bonding," said Howard sourly, hooking two fatigued fingers around the word; thus was cunnilingus recycled, gaining infinitely more meaning by its recounting (they were hoping it would seal a production deal) than by its actual performance.

More astonishing, said Howard, is that these men consider their emotions—these tendentious fillips in torrid afternoon moments in bungalows, the surge of tiny hormones they feel when their organ is in some moist, dark hole—real.

The movie industry operates on a mentor-protégé system, and Howard has his protégées. Generally women, though again, this is to be expected. Protégé derives from the French, "to protect," and Howard does, as much as he can. He looks out for their interests.

Jennifer walks into the meeting room. "Hi, Howard!" She is lovely, her hair gleams, her body is thin. She is carrying a trashy legal novel, on which she's just submitted her coverage to him, plus three different scripts based on it. (By that afternoon they will throw out all three.) "Where would you like these?"

Howard touches the table near him. She lays them on that spot, flashes a smile. "Anything else?"

"We're OK," says Howard, "thanks. I need you at three fifteen."

"You bet."

Even before the door closes, the short man meeting with Howard is leaning over the desk. "She single?"

After a moment, Howard says, "Yes, in fact." He doesn't look up.

"Set me up with her." Now Howard looks up. The man bats away Howard's look. Insistently: "So set me up with her!"

Howard returns to a script, searching for a problematic page. "She's not Jewish, Barry."

"*How* ard," Barry says.

Jennifer has been with Howard since she graduated from USC. She is twenty-six now. She began as a production assistant on the lot, and six weeks later she came to the bungalow. She herself suggested babysitting Sam, and he adored her from the start. Howard knows little about her private life—she has an almost breathtaking maturity,

which includes discretion toward her boss regarding herself; I know
her a bit better: favors she's done me, the logistical planning of Howard's time that she and I manage together, her evenings looking after
my son while we attended some function she had arranged for us.
Howard knows she is sweet. He recently overheard that she is single.
She is under his jurisdiction, so she is his protégée. Protected.

"Howard," Barry says. He has not heard the edge in Howard's
voice (actually he has, but he ignores it because he is intoxicated by
her teeth, her perfect shoulders, her breasts). He spreads his arms,
the hands open palms up, raises his shoulders. "She's got a box,
right?" Confidentially: "*Ya don't marry a box, Howard.*" The hands say:
Am I right?

Howard sits there for a moment. Equanimity. He knows Barry.
He says, "You're the kind of guy I'd want dating my daughter." He
holds Barry's gaze.

Barry doesn't say anything. Howard goes back to thumbing a
script, daffodil yellow. Barry thinks: "Fucking prick."

The breakdown was over morality, Howard explained to me.
There were, he said, just two different moralities at that table. He
and I were in the living room, the sound of Sam's music distantly
from his bedroom. I was eating seedless grapes.

And what was your morality, I asked Howard.

He took a grape. His morality, Howard said, was that not in a
million years would he let some guy use her as a sexual toy. Some
little shmuck with a corner office on Wilshire who knows going in
what he's after and what he's not, and why he's not after it: because
she doesn't, as Howard put it, have the right stamp on her ass. A guy
who would never drag her out of bed to meet his parents because his
parents definitely wouldn't wanna know. If Jennifer had the full info
going in, she'd never go in. She'd say, Are you *kidding* me?

And what was Barry's morality?

He seemed to be thinking about something else. He roused himself. "Well!" he said of Barry. "*His* morality." Howard didn't, actually,

dislike the guy per se. He'd known him a while, they'd done a couple of projects. "She isn't Jewish." He shrugged.

JOSÉ APPEARED TWO WEEKS LATER, on crutches, wearing a carefully ironed cotton shirt. He somehow lent a dignity to the crutches. Denise answered the door, and although José cleared his throat and launched his best effort in English, she just turned and called Consuelo.

Consuelo's eyes narrowed at the figure in the doorway.

When I came upon them, she was grilling him like a Mexican Himmler. He was enduring it but evinced relief at seeing me. I led him to the sofa. Would you like something to drink?

No, thank you, I'm fine. Thank you, by the way, for the poem by Mr. Blake.

You're welcome. Did you understand some of it?

He paused. I read some in the hospital, he said. Then he said, in English, "My mother taught me underneath a tree."

I tried not to appear startled. That was excellent, I said. Then: How is your leg?

La herida está sanándose. He shrugged. Crutches for a few more days, perhaps.

This about the crutches was, I assumed, a lie.

Consuelo swept in to inquire, in English, if Madame would like something to drink.

No, thank you, Consuelo.

She turned imperiously to José. "Would you like drink something?"

"No," said José. "Thank you."

Well then. She swept out.

I asked him, How did you get here? To the house.

By . . . He merely motioned arriving, supplied no details. I didn't pursue it.

I realized as we sat there and he asked me for a job that I did not exactly know, when I saw him the instant before Paul McMahon struck him with the car, how I had known he was a gardener. But he was. His price was reasonable. He wondered if perhaps there were not others nearby needing a gardener. I said the Fishbeins—he at TriStar, she at Paramount, four doors down—hated their garden service, I'd give him their address as well. (Miriam had ordered rocks. Marvin said that spending $20,000 on *boulders*—boulders!—was crazy. "It's a *rock* garden, Marvin," said Miriam. Marvin looked at me. "Who are we?" he said. "The Flintsteins? We live in Bedrock?") As for us, I told José what his duties would be, stressed that I needed him to do exactly, precisely what I asked. No more. No less. I had all the equipment. We would work out a schedule.

He nodded calmly. Mr. Taciturn.

Howard accepted José with a friendly handshake and benign indifference. Howard was conscious that he was now employing three people in his home and with the usual American awkwardness regarding servants began referring to them sardonically as "our baptized property." This was what the Russian gentry called serfs attached to landed estates. Not within earshot, though, since who knew who understood what at this point.

I LOST MY TEMPER, AND the press coverage started, and Howard said I deserved it. It was in public, too, so I was at fault.

Rather than have the next book club in my garden, my agents group suggested we meet at Orso. A few of them had a thing for Dos Passos. Dos Passos, who has strange punctuation that I dislike, which irrigated the affair, but what made me blow up was the *New Yorker,* specifically a profile they'd run just the previous week. It concerned a black woman who was a vocal coach, this serving the *New Yorker* writer as a platform for an examination of why blacks do not get jobs as easily as whites and Asians, and the vocal coach unconsciously provided the answer by stating, "African Americans don't associate proper pronunciation and grammar with intelligence, and it is a shock to us when they are."

First of all, I said. I don't believe this for an instant because it is absurd. But leave that. The rule that a comma is placed before a conjunction joining two independent clauses is, I think, one of the few truly indisputable points of grammar. This was the way the sentence appeared in the *New Yorker*: "African Americans don't associate proper pronunciation and grammar with intelligence and it is a shock to us when they are."

I had Dos Passos's *U.S.A.* on the table. I'd propped it open with my bread plate. The waiter kept moving the plate and losing my place. More water, yes, no, leave the plate, please. I glanced at the book, saw one of Dos Passos's ellipses (he uses millions), and it triggered my irritation over the *New Yorker* piece.

There are, still, a few things one should be able to count on, I said to them. If we are to reverse this country's insane lack of support for public schools capable of educating our children—and what is more important than the public school system, nothing is, *nothing*— we need to begin with correct punctuation. I said, The *New Yorker* somehow managed to remember the period at the end of the sentence, but really, why bother with the period *if you can't remember the goddamn comma between the two independent clauses.*

Their heads moved back just slightly. Well! Look at Anne. The waiter had stopped moving. But they were amused and interested, and it gave me permission to continue. (A thought came to me, from years of observing this industry: The freakish, the odd, the abrasive, the larger-than-life, when they are put before the camera, lit with halogen, presented on the screen, can become compelling. Context is everything. The act of going to see a person transforms that person. They had come to see me here, hitting my mark on this swank set, and I was suddenly conscious of being a different person.)

Spelling, punctuation, grammar, vocabulary, I continued. These things *matter.* They are not just the backbone of literature, they are reflective of education and intelligence and capability. I thought about how Howard would express this. Oh, of course. I said to them, So there was a letter to the editor of the *Times* of London in which the writer, whose children went to one of London's most posh and expensive schools, had just gotten the tuition bill. This exclusive, august institution had printed the figure in "pounds per anum." He wrote a reply to the school noting that while he didn't mind the amount so much, could he perhaps go back to paying through the other orifice, which was to say the nose.

Just look at this article, I said to them. I picked from my bag my copy of the *New Yorker* and flipped the pages. Here. For the moment, at least, I said, the *New Yorker* is still using the comma of direct address. (I read from the article.) "Hey comma baby!" (It was talking about street slang.) The meaning here of course being completely different from "Hey baby!" which means a baby named Hey. "You all curves an me wit no brakes." No predicate, *and thus no comma necessary.*

I cleared my throat and smoothed my napkin. I flushed just a bit. I'm sorry, I said, for this pasquinade. But honestly, we all must understand this. It sounds silly, it sounds minor, these sorts of things, but they slip, bit by bit, and then suddenly you're the Congo, and nothing works, and the government is corrupt, and it's all shit, and you *hate* it.

A man at the next table kept glancing at me.

Howard met a lovely, rather breathless young actress recently, I said to them. She told him, "I'm about, like, self-expression!" Howard replied that that was nice, because she certainly was not about eloquence.

Either you can parse a decent sentence or you can't. The great French grammarian, Dominique Beauhur, wrote as his last words: "I am dying." He then appended: "I am about to die. Either is correct."

I looked up. Several of the agents were watching me with huge grins. The grins said that if I was a lunatic, I was their lunatic. Their warm complicity, their willingness to consider my linking punctuation to the rise and fall of civilizations, caught me off guard.

I loved them for it. And that caught me off guard as well.

For one moment I forgot about the punctuation and saw that they were enjoying me and liked me for who I was, and I let myself go into that, and I smiled back at them. I had to blink a few times and make a show of organizing my papers, and I said to myself, Honestly, Anne! but then I thought no, no, it's perfectly fine.

So, I said, and I laughed. So we were talking about John Dos Passos.

Nick Paumgarten wrote the *New Yorker* Talk piece on the lunch. The man at the next table turned out to have been Philip Gourevitch, and he mentioned it to Nick on the phone. The waiters must have been listening closely, or perhaps it was Nick's reporting skills, but the detail of it was startling. To my mind, the piece was about my agents group, and Nick, naturally, had spun something very nice out of that. But, "Uh, *no*," said Sam, looking at me as if I was insane, "it's about *you*, Mom."

The *New Yorker* did at least wonder about having elided (as Nick put it, rather self-exculpatorily in my own view) the comma. Which was why David Remnick called. "Anne!"

You deserve it, I said to him. Every bit.

"I'm having all the copy editors shot," he promised solemnly.

I got a call from Amy Kaufman. Focus Features has just bought a spec script from a UTA client, said Amy, and she was wondering, could I look at the (she hesitated, choosing the word) flow? The writer's word use.

I paused. Are you asking me to look over the script's syntax?

Yes! she said. The syntax. (She hadn't wanted to say the word so bluntly.) Could I?

Well. Yes. I supposed I could. I was intrigued. I knew the writer. As we were talking, a messenger service dropped it off. I hung up and asked Justin to handle it. He immediately called Amy back and negotiated a five-figure agreement.

The next day Jeff Berg gave a quick call to say hi, he thought the script checking for Focus was an interesting idea, and he was wondering if I needed representation, but I said Justin was doing quite well. I wrote Justin a check for 15 percent. Justin started spending more time on the phone, which irritated Sam, an orphan under the basket over the driveway. José installed a separate in-box for Justin's mail on his desk in my office. Justin's attitude began changing, and Howard noticed immediately. Howard, walking past my office, would say loudly, "ICM's hiring, Justin."

Justin, I said, not glancing up, stop walking like that.

"Like what?"

With your chest out. Stop it. This needs to be mailed, please.

I would like to shoot, or have shot (either is correct), every fourth-grade teacher who is not regularly drilling their pupils in the diagramming of sentences. Sam, at twelve, came home one day and asked me what a predicate was. I explained it to him carefully, questioned him till I was satisfied, got my car keys, and drove straight to Harvard-Westlake, where I collared the school's head. Borys Kit of the *Hollywood Reporter* called to ask me about why I'd done it; he had apparently heard about the four-year-old incident because Sam had mentioned it to a classmate after the Talk piece, and that classmate's father was (of course) in the industry and passed it to Borys. So I explained to him that I'd said to this teacher that, my God, at age twelve my son didn't know subject from predicate, and who, exactly, was going to hire him? McDonald's? My son did not want to be limited to carting dirty dishes, and given, I'd said, that he was not African American, if he didn't use proper grammar and pronunciation, people would think him ignorant. I told him my favorite knock-knock joke:

Knock, knock.

Who's there?

Fuck.

Fuck who?

Fuck *whom*.

At the same time, I said, hysteria over split infinitives is ridiculous. English isn't Latin. So I'm hardly a purist.

Borys wrote it all down and reprinted the knock-knock joke in full in his *Hollywood Reporter* piece. It was generally taken as my throwing down the gauntlet.

WE'D JUST FINISHED A CHEEVER story on the subject of loss, and people were leaving when an actress stopped me. The Cheever had made her recall something. She laughed, almost embarrassed.

The tantrums she threw in the kitchen as a Trenton fourth grader before her tearful and uncomprehending mother. "An immigrant from Budapest," she said. "She would knit me these absolutely exquisite Hungarian sweaters." She did the accent perfectly: "'Is good!' she'd plead, 'Is varm!'" She cleared her throat. "I used to drop them in the woods in the snow on the way to school. I told her I lost them. *Now*, of course . . ." She exhaled deeply, hooking a finger around a thin gold chain. "I'd kill to get my hands on them. I mean, you can't *buy* that shit today. I could have given them to my daughter. But they're gone. And I broke her heart." She thought about it. Matter-of-factly: "And she's dead."

We stood and both looked up at the palm fronds making a gentle scything sound, like blades harvesting the night air. José had just trimmed them. "You miss your parents," she said.

Some comment of mine about the Cheever had obviously elicited this from her. I considered it. I think about my parents, I said to her. Often, actually. Though not exactly like yours. Mine (I laughed briefly) never gave me anything I had to pretend to lose.

"A car accident, right?"

I was startled. Yes.

She frowned. "In Malaysia?"

For a moment I was confused, then understood. No, I said, it was the Brooklyn-Queens Expressway, coming from JFK. Quite prosaic. I talked about the accident?

She paused. "You alluded to it. A few details."

Malaysian Airlines.

"That's it."

I'd said to them that when we read fiction, we pour our own particular store of emotions—say, the sense of loss we feel for those disappeared from our lives—into the characters set before us. We take the few words with which the writer sketches these characters, the thing he said, the pain she felt, where they were, and our own emotional stockpile magically creates people. As the human eye fleshes out the pixilated image. Fictional characters are highly sophisticated Rorschach blots, and we, along with their author, are their authors. When you read a fictional character, you too are creating her.

I had commented to them that my mother and father made Cheever's characters real for me.

It was a pileup of some sort, I said to her now, in a thunderstorm. Theirs was the last car into the mess. I paused. I think it's called hydroplaning? When the tires do that. They had just landed. Their luggage was in the taxi's trunk, but it burned.

I felt my heart constrict again. Such a strange sensation. It never changes, yet always surprises.

I too have such regret, I said to her, these vast black oceans of regret. Their simply being alive was—(I hunted for it)—the possibility that they might change. Some day? Their dying took that away.

She pulled a strand of hair behind an ear. "Their dying didn't really change anything, Anne."

The stars above the palms disappeared and reappeared as the fronds moved in the air, like the warning lights on the tops of sky-scrapers. She was right, of course. I remember, I said to her, when we got the call. I remember stumbling to a chair and putting my face in my hands. Howard's voice, his hand on the back of my neck.

I took a breath, eyes opening. I looked around. I said, I've never really talked about this.

"Yes," she said, smiling, "I know that."

Howard's mother, cancer. And very fast. Not as fast as a pileup on the BQE, but fast. His father, a stroke, six years before that. They exit one by one, or sometimes two by two. You scatter pieces of them on the snow in the woods and run away as fast as you can, and then you turn and run back toward them, once they're beyond your reach.

I did not know Sam had felt this great loss from his bubbe dying, or rather I didn't know he was feeling it to such a degree. He was sev-enteen. The young sometimes show much less, and I simply didn't see it, or wasn't looking, or didn't know how to look. Degrees of culpability, I suppose, but little difference in the end.

Sam had gone with Howard to New York to sit shiva for his grandfather, but it was his grandmother's death—it was just last September—that had shaken him. He had watched Howard crum-ple as the beeping hospital machines finally silenced themselves, the heart rate line flattened, and her hand went lax in his father's. How-ard lay himself along her cooling arm, eyes closed, facedown on the metal gurney, and the nurses skirted them for a few minutes as Sam watched this man hold his mother's body. He put a hand tentatively on his father's shoulder and in that gesture, seeking to comfort, expe-rienced the moment that the child starts to become the parent. Sam sensed that in his grief something had also changed inside Howard.

For years, every year, when he saw her in that house in Brooklyn, "Next year in Jerusalem!" his bubbe had said to him. It's the way the seder always ends. He'd been told it was a promise.

The first time I heard it, at age nineteen, I said brightly to Howard's father, "Oh, you're going to Jerusalem?" They fell over themselves, and she had laughed hardest, one of the few times I'd seen
her do this. She had looked at me, for the first time and briefly, with
a kind of affection. She told and retold the story every year at the
end of the dinner, Sam listening. The aspect of rebuke and its function as identification of the outsider, which were crystaline, Howard
simply pretended not to hear. The Anne/Jerusalem story became,
to Sam, a part of his grandmother. And now she had left, and he
himself was leaving us, and (this is my interpretation) he got the idea
that he would follow her. One last time.

We forget that they also mourn incipient loss. High school will
soon end, and they are reassuring one another that they will all be
friends forever, and they are about to discover that this is false. They
cover the sadness and fear. They bluff. The college applications are
in, the tests are taken, the doors are in sight, the control tower is
guiding them to the take-off point, and they have absolutely no idea
how to navigate this flight.

It is also only in retrospect in which I see where Howard was at
this moment. That Howard's son, whom he loved more than anything, was disappearing before his eyes and he could do nothing
to stop it, and I had amazingly noticed nothing at all. I can argue
responsibility—Howard should have said something, led me, given
me the end of the thread. But that would be meaningless.

As for Sam: They might seem a bit needier than usual, they might
slow just the tiniest bit their trajectory away from us to adulthood up
ahead, and waver for a moment, their longing palpable. Exodus is a
disorienting affair no matter where or when. Sam decided—I did not
know any of this till later—that out of love, out of habit, out of pro-
gramming, out of hope, because he had to, because he was mourning,
because he had nothing else to do, because it had been implanted in
him, because he was restless, or abandoned, or afraid, or optimistic,
or lost in some strange stratosphere, that he would go to Israel.

He would be leaving for college in September. He would be leaving us. Next year in Jerusalem.

His entire life, Howard had trained his son to come to this conclusion. Naturally he could never have foreseen what Sam would find there. Or what it would mean to himself, Howard.

FAULKNER, I SAID TO THEM.

I said, This will make you uncomfortable, but that is what literature is for.

My paternal grandmother's campaign to hire and retain a butler in her Knightsbridge residence was unending. I learned early a bit of H. H. Munro because Grandmother repeated it, acidly, at regular intervals: "The cook was a good cook as cooks go, and as good cooks go, she went." The entire serving class in that era seemed to be evaporating bodily from London.

Denise, to contradict Munro, is a cook of ever expanding achievement. When Sam was eleven we proposed, and after quite a bit of consideration she accepted, the two-week course at the Culinary Institute in Napa. I'd seen their glossy ad in, I think, *Gourmet*; this is the kind of cooking school that has a spa attached. Howard wrote a check for the substantial tuition. There was some trepidation at the setting out, but Roy told her to "go on, do it," so she went and did. She had not spent a night away from Roy, nor outside Compton, in twenty-two years (nor from Kelvin, since he was born, though he decreasingly slept at home), and her face was an unreadable mask as she prepared to get on the Greyhound. (She refused to fly.) I had touched her arm. I was a bit anguished and suddenly as uncertain about this as she. She had paused. She had not given me her hand in return, but she had focused on the weight of my hand on her and let it anchor her for a moment. Then she had nodded briefly and gotten out of the car and climbed onto the bus.

On the return she registered suave equanimity. (I do this all the time, said her shoulders as she descended from the bus and smoothly into my Saab.) For her initial report, she merely stated that it had been odd sleeping in a bed not her own. And that was that. Very Denise. But she communicated in her own time. We learned that she had enjoyed the lush, crisp cotton sheets, the maid service that turned them down every evening, the chocolate on her pillow, her own big white bath towel by the tumbled-stone shower, having everything laundered. All the things that occupied her day at our house, done by other people, and done for her. She would not get a massage, though she visited the spa's steam room twice. This, she liked. She dangled her legs in the Jacuzzi, once. And she allowed the Filipina women to give her a pedicure, which she loved.

What had she studied? Sauces. Soups. Garden greens. After much consternation, she had tried horse and liked it, and buffalo and ostrich, and liked them even more. She at first categorically refused, then slowly acquiesced to, then eagerly participated in sampling from everyone else's sauce pans as the instructors required them to do. She learned the names of fungi. She wrote them down. She learned knives: cutting from paring from chopping. She did reductions and daubes and tasted cooking wines and had the cork waved under her nose (she glared at the sommelier as if he was crazy).

And everything changed. She herself came back different. Her sauces were now light and delicate and complex. They had done an entire day on Asian flavorings, and we started finding Thai and Vietnamese fusions. Kaffir leaves. Tangerine zest in surprising places. They'd made them keep a detailed, very lengthy notebook, which the instructors had supplemented, and which the school then had printed and expensively bound, and I caught her glancing sideways at hers next to the stove. Eventually she just kept it open on the counter and didn't care who saw. I bought her a Plexiglas cookbook holder for it. She made nasi goreng and an amazingly authentic Indonesian es campur, with the gelatin and the condensed milk. I took her to Chinatown's grotty food shops, and she read M. F. K. Fisher in the car after shopping for rice noodles and nuoc mam. She made gigot d'agneau and risotto primavera and a buttermilk African American catfish fry into which she improvised lemongrass and a dark-green Asian citrus leaf whose name she never told me. Sam gingerly picked up a piece and took a small bite. After a moment I said, Slow down, Samuel.

"Have you *tasted* this?" said Howard with his mouth full.

She began watching us with a critical eye as we sampled. Then she would turn and go back to her affairs. We willingly showed our enthusiasm. She was batting high 800s, said Howard.

By complete chance I got a secondhand report. The woman thin, blond highlights, perfectly bleached teeth. It turned out she had been in Denise's class. How *interesting* to send your maid, she said. Perhaps (she cleared her throat) a better cook than anyone else. And she'd been so very interested in the school's *cookware*. (I knew this. I'd had to spend a breathtaking sum at Williams Sonoma when she got back.) Not very *talkative*, though. And she had been, you know, the only black person taking the course.

I said that yes, in fact I imagined she was the only person with a net worth below four million dollars taking the course. The woman laughed, ah ha ha ha ha.

I gleaned from the exchange that her fellow students were distracted by the degree to which Denise is reserved. I sympathize. It is extreme. Though it happens to be the quality that most attracts me to her, and her to me. We get along quite well. She will point at a tomato variety in a farmer's bin, one eyebrow raised, and I will give my opinion with a nod or shake my head, and she will make her decision. I feel comfortable with her.

Actually I feel protected.

Then there is the part of Denise's story that I tell them, but in shadings and not as a story per se; obviously I will protect Denise. But I have asked her, explained my textual and personal reasons for wanting to discuss this with my readers, and she has given me her permission. She, of course, is fully aware of its import. She lives it. It went like this.

I had been in the lower study when Denise appeared in the doorway. She was agitated. There was a problem, her car was in the shop—a friend had dropped her off this morning—and Kelvin had just called. Do you need to go home? She considered her answer. Yes, she said. She meant instantly. I picked up my car keys and stood.

I had never been to Compton. She sat in the passenger seat with her seat belt fastened, eyes on the road. It is quintessentially Faulkner (which is why I gave Faulkner to my studios executives, why I was talking about it now; I was talking more frequently in book club about myself and my life) to be a privileged European-American woman driving your underprivileged maid to her house. And here's what is so fascinating, I said to them. Faulkner's powers are such that he still defines what this scene means today. When the difference is no longer, as it was in his time, race. Race is completely irrelevant. Today, the difference is culture. Race is merely a proxy (and an increasingly inexact proxy) for culture, and culture, I said, is much, much more difficult.

Denise and I drove in silence, Denise saying only "Left" or "Right" as we approached traffic signals. Sometimes pointing to the turns. When on the rare occasions I am sick, I think of Oscar Wilde's statement that the vastest distance between humans lies between the sick and the well. But I tended at that moment toward Karl Marx's view: It is between the employing and the employed.

I pulled up outside the battered bungalow and turned off the engine. Would I care to come in? she asked. Certainly I would come in. Don't forget to lock the car, she said.

She beat back an ancient screen door, still trying its best. She held it open for me. I saw that she had hung a small frame on the wall in which there was only text. "I will call them my people which were not my people; and her beloved, which was not beloved. Romans 9:25."

Though I'd heard nothing she suddenly turned her head upward and said loudly, "Dat you?" An instant, and Kelvin's voice, from somewhere: "Yeah." And then he said something I didn't understood. She responded. I understood none of this. She yelled that he was to come down. He pounded down the stairs, a large boy of nineteen, the house's wooden frame shaking, and froze at seeing me.

"Miz Rosenbaum brung me," she said to him, which was reproving his rudeness.

Hello, Kelvin, I say. I do not hold out my hand.

He nods briefly. "'lo." Shaking hands is not his custom. We note a bandage around one ankle, some fresh blood.

He speaks to, but does not look at, his mother. He says that it will be not only highly unlikely but possibly dangerous if a thing, which he references but does not describe, occurs.

She stipulates that she is quite familiar with the problem. More familiar than she'd like to be. Kelvin seems concurrently bored and passionate. They disagree on a course of action. There are apparently three distinct alternatives, which they lay out, although both disdain the first for some reason, which leaves the second and third. I still have not caught the subject. Everything is verbs, "don matter" and "gone" and relative pronouns in the place of all propers. Verb conjugations bear no relation to person or number and "to be" is never conjugated at all. I understand approximately 70 percent of this English. In her opinion, it is evidently futile to pursue the unnamed problem through certain authorities (not, it seems, a reference to the police) since they have demonstrated a clear disinterest. The proof of this, she proposes, is self-evident. Kelvin, whose financial situation I gather the issue touches on, though only tangentially, disputes this. He is not helping the situation. His last name is Williams, like Denise's, while Roy's last name is Parker, which is odd because I'd always understood Kelvin to be Roy's son, although I know there is some complicating aspect to this story involving a separation of several years. Kelvin is recalcitrant and vituperative.

This cognitive/interactive process is standard among humans. Howard goes through it with Sam all the time. The variable is how it is done. What strikes one here is that the ideas are poorly expressed, the analysis reductive and unimaginative, the frail logic overpowered by emotion. I stand, watching as they sling these odd, semicomprehensible phonemes at each other. Denise's face registers dull fury.

I drive us back. I am not clear why Denise's presence was needed—although it was, and she is evidently appreciative of my help—but I think that something was supposed to happen that didn't. It is impossible for me to tell.

Kelvin is a sullen boy, ineloquent with internal gravity, like some collapsed star. He is an exhibition of limited capacity. He projects a dark tunnel. And though he debates options and logistics, at nineteen his reasoning is inferior to Sam's at eight. Sam's friends, hyperarticulate, slightly neurotic, typically aggressive Jewish boys and girls, ambitious and verbally off-the-charts, Denise has known for years. And then Kelvin. I think: No, Wilde and Marx are both wrong. Not the sick and the well. Not employer and employee. The greatest distance between any two human beings is the greatest possible distance between any two cultures. She looks out her window at Los Angeles rushing by, and finally she says darkly, "Din raise Kelvin. Street raise 'im." Her voice claims that she accepted this reality long ago. But it's obvious she never really has, nor will.

They all sit with their copies of Faulkner, which I had assigned them two weeks ago, the day after I drove Denise to Compton. They listen to me telling these stories, staring at my hyacinth or the Los Angeles sky overhead or glaring at their hands. What I am saying makes them uncomfortable. I can see that. I hesitate, trying to be gentle. It is simply observation, I point out to them. Perhaps we don't discuss it. But if you're going to tackle Faulkner, you're going to have to tackle this bitter empirical reality, although Faulkner of course does it through fiction.

Half of all black men between twenty-four and thirty-five have no full-time employment. One black man graduates from college for every hundred who go to jail. Almost half of all black children live in poverty.

I glance down at my notes. In a letter, dated August 30, 1791, Thomas Jefferson wrote to Benjamin Banneker, a black astronomer and mathematician whom he had had appointed official surveyor of the District of Columbia: "No body wishes more than I do to see such proofs as you exhibit, that nature has given to our black brethren, talents equal to those of the other colors of men, and that the appearance of a want of them is owing merely to the degraded condition of their existence, both in Africa and America."

They glance at one another. The book they hold is *Absalom, Absalom!*

I get two glares. I say to them, I understand the desire not to wound, but it has been long observed that literature, if it is not ruthless, is nothing. They do not capitulate, but they turn the point over in their minds.

I can feel a breeze moving up from the Los Angeles side. For an instant it carries the sound of a radio, the music then blown toward the valley. No one says anything. I repeat to them, to clarify. Remember, I say, that in this context, this is a literary question.

THINGS HAPPEN. YOU ANTICIPATE THEM without knowing it. This one had waited for us, quietly. Then it arrived.

Out of nowhere, Sam announces that he will go to Israel by himself for a few weeks.

"Out of nowhere," says Howard to me, looking surprised and pleased. (It wasn't, of course, out of nowhere at all, but I do think that is the way Howard perceived it.)

Naturally we debate the timing. It is mid-January, but his college applications have been in "since forever," everyone is (Sam points out) just waiting for the letters to come, and his grades essentially can't be higher. By the way, Josh Weinberg's parents are letting him go.

What's it hurt, Howard argues, missing one short week your senior spring? (He said two, I say. Howard promises that one of the two will be spring break, which makes it one. Yes, Howard will handle the school, don't worry about it.) Howard is very excited about it. He buys Sam the ticket. Economy class, a window seat, 14A, so he can sleep, on the El Al flight departing just before midnight.

JUSTIN IS GOING OVER A list of things and mentions an email from a Paul McMann. "He says you know him?" It takes a few seconds and the word *screenplay* and then it clicks.

Mc*Ma*hon, I say to Justin, the man I met on Mulholland, yes. I'm trying to help him with a project.

I think to myself that I have truly been remiss, although, given the book clubs . . . I ask Justin to respond with my apologies, that I promise to get to it. Then, Never mind, Justin, I say, I'll do it myself. I send the email to Paul and mentally file a note. I've got to read his script. And I've got to get Howard to read it, too. I know I'm not going to trust my own reaction till I get his yes or no.

SAM WAS DRIVING WEST ON Fountain when he asked Howard for some advice. He put the question: Stanford or Berkeley. Howard was struggling to position his visor against the morning sun flooding the windshield.

"What the hell's the matter with Columbia," said Howard, squinting to cover his surprise.

"Dad," said Sam very patiently, "I like California. My third choice is Occi. Jon and I went a couple months ago. We compared courses, the teams, all that stuff."

"Well, if you've made up your mind," grumbled Howard, surprised as well at the research, proud Sam was being serious about it. Personally, said Howard, he'd take Stanford, but nothing wrong with Berkeley if Sam chose his subjects carefully.

Sam held the wheel easily, accelerated from the light. But what did Howard and I want him to be? he asked. What did we intend for him?

Howard blinked.

"I'm just wondering," said Sam, oblivious to the effect he was having. He sighed, very teenager. "God knows you guys have ideas about everything."

I have always thought Howard did wonderfully when it came to Sam's future. We never dictated a word. We never told him what he must or mustn't be. We pointed out certain options and certain directions. Years ago, Howard had read Sam a passage from George Eliot's novel *Daniel Deronda*, and later that day, when they'd gotten home and Sam was out of earshot, he told me he'd found himself heading right for it as an anchor. He knew Sam would remember. In fact he suspected Sam's question had come from it.

Eliot's Daniel is freshly returned from his Young Gentleman's tour of the Rhineland with his Eton tutor, and he presents himself in Sir Hugo's library on a morning, and asks "What do you intend me to do, sir?" Naturally if Sam ever called Howard "sir," Howard would choke.

Howard had always indicated to Sam that he would have to make his own money, and I had said the same thing, much more directly and much more often. At the same time, Howard argued to me, he didn't seem the sort of kid you had to worry would be corrupted by his parents' bank accounts, and I carefully agreed. He appeared solid. We never caught him showing off. He rarely coveted the expensive toys that surrounded him and quickly shook off the episodes of jealousy when they arose. We had given him a decent allowance, increasing with his age and experience. "'Perhaps,' said Sir Hugo, 'I had better tell you that you may consider yourself secure of seven hundred a year.'" And so, said Howard, as they crossed Mansfield Avenue, we would pay for either Berkeley or Stanford. Graduate school, we would pay tuition; room and board would be his responsibility. Obviously we would ask that he live modestly. We would ask him to study, to be serious. No live-in girlfriends; that was nonnegotiable.

OK, said Sam.

As for what Howard "intended"? Well, said Howard, whatever Sam wanted to be. Howard comes by this sort of liberalism naturally. Yes, he had some ideas. He mentioned journalism and sports agent-ing. ("'You might make yourself a barrister,' said Sir Hugo to Daniel, 'be a writer.'") Howard brought up, well, studio work. ("Or take up politics," says Sir Hugo. "I confess that is what would please me best. I should like to have you at my elbow, pulling with me.") But he said to Sam, You will do what you want, and you will be the one to find out what that is.

I am inclined to be more directive, but I found that Howard's point of view had, at some moment, become indigenous to me. Per-haps because I had read it in a book.

And still the boy Deronda says nervously to Sir Hugo, "'I hope you will not be much disappointed if I don't come out with hon-ours.'" And Sam said, basically, the same.

Howard made a face, waved this away with one hand and put the other to his eyes. Luckily they were at a stoplight, because he grabbed Sam and kissed him hard on the head. Sir Hugo says, "'No, no. I should like you to do yourself credit, but for God's sake don't come out as a superior expensive kind of idiot, like young Brecon, who got a Double First, and has been learning to knit braces ever since. What I wish you to get,'" quoted Howard gravely from Eliot's novel, "'is a passport in life.'"

"They don't offer that," said Sam, turning right toward the hills.

"Yes," said Howard firmly, "they do."

OUR FRIENDS HAVE ALWAYS TOLD me that press attention functions microbially. The one-celled creature suddenly becomes two, which become four. Howard assumed it was the *Hollywood Reporter* piece that generated the article in *Entertainment Weekly*.

It was by critic Gary Susman. Gary had not attended the clubs—he hadn't, in fact, ever asked to—but he clearly knew many of those in them quite well. He said, in fact, that I had changed his view of filmmaking. He did not say how, which disappointed me. I was interested. The article reported a breathless account of a secretive book club for the Hollywood elite. It made me sound like a guru. The aura of exclusivity was carefully appointed, a paparazzi photo of me in sunglasses carrying dry cleaning into the house over my shoulder. I have to say, the photographers were very quiet. I had no idea they were there. If they had just asked, I would have certainly posed for a shot or two, outside, without the dry cleaning.

When *Us* magazine called, they said they wanted to take a "different approach," which was to photograph me in my home. I said absolutely not. Well, would I talk with a reporter? I put them on hold and asked Justin what he thought. He said, "Are you kidding?" as if it was obvious. They sent a nice young woman, and Consuelo brought lemonade to the garden, and I found it surreal. The piece wound up consisting of literary recommendations by actors, most of whom I had never met. What Will She Choose Next? Sandra Bernhard was quoted as saying she didn't fucking care, she hadn't fucking been invited. Bette Midler proposed D. H. Lawrence for some unusual reasons, and it started me thinking—I actually went back to take another look at *Sons and Lovers*, though I am conscious of Max Beerbohm's evaluation of Lawrence: "He never suspected that to be stark staring mad is something of a handicap to a writer." Perhaps. I sent Bette a note. Howard worships Beerbohm; Joseph Epstein once delighted Howard by telling him that Beerbohm "took out Freud with a single sentence: 'They were a tense and peculiar family, the Oedipuses, weren't they?'" Bette enjoyed that.

Justin interrupted me with a slip of paper, quickly jotted: "Jane Sarkin. *Vanity Fair.*" He mouthed "Line 2."

Hello, Jane.

Hello, Anne.

It was to be a cover, she said. (Oh, *honestly*.) No, no—they had *just* come out of the editorial meeting—a cover, a cover, she repeated the word, incredulous, which I found rather amusing seeing that it was she who was trying to convince me, not the reverse. Ludicrous, I said to Howard. (He agreed but shrugged.)

Julie Weiss, the *Vanity Fair* art director, called four times. "Anne Rosenbaum at Home."

"Why not?" said Howard. "It's your home, show it off."

Oh, for God's sake, Howard, it's invasive, that's why not!

But I was so bewildered, and so intrigued, that I agreed.

"And," Julie added, "Howard would be in some of the photos, naturally."

I covered the receiver again, ran this by him. Yes?

"Sure," he said.

Fine, I said.

"And," (papers ruffling) "now, you two have a son?"

My tone of voice must have finally taken, because she moved immediately to the stylist.

David Margolick arrived from New York and was very pleasant, and quite handsome with his gray wavy hair, and direct. Did I agree I was very opinionated? I said I supposed I did. Good literature is strong opinion, intelligently expressed. (Water, please, I said to the waiter. Thank you.) *Complexity* of opinion does not dilute its strength, incidentally. And then there are various styles.

David ordered a salad. "And you?" He glanced at the attentive waiter, back at me. "Nothing? You're sure?"

Honestly. I'm not hungry.

How, I asked, can one not be in awe of Oscar Wilde's opinionated snottiness on every imaginable subject? Take art. Samuel Johnson humbly praised Shakespeare, writing, "Shakespeare is above all writers the poet of nature, the poet that, like Hamlet, holds up a faithful mirror of manners and life." Wilde responded, "This unfortunate aphorism about art holding the mirror up to Nature is deliberately said by Hamlet in order to convince bystanders of his absolute insanity in all art-matters."

David jotted rapidly and managed to eat lunch at the same time. I, with my elbows on the Lucques's table, playing absently with a bracelet, was slightly uncomfortable with the method of it; sometimes he wrote, his notebook laid next to his fish knife, sometimes he didn't. It seemed random. Please, I said, it's getting cold. He smiled. He said he'd eaten cold sea bass before.

Annie Leibovitz stopped by the restaurant to look at me. She sat with us for a few minutes. The only thing she said was, once, "Anne, could you look left a little." I lifted my chin, and she said, "Mm hm."

"Wasn't there," David asked, "some controversy over your politics? George Eliot?"

Ah. Right. Well, I had—unintentionally—begun a conversation about feminism: I'd assigned *Middlemarch*. I'd said that in my view George Eliot had perfectly described in the character Dorothea Brooke virtually every woman "building a career," in Eliot's prescient phrase. Of these women, she wrote, in 1871 (notice that, in updated language, this is *exactly* what you read last week on the same topic), "Their ardour alternated between a vague ideal"—the career—"and the common yearning of womanhood"—children, staying at home—"so that the first was disapproved as extravagance and the other condemned as a lapse." Remarkable.

When I read the quote, there had been a collective intake of breath from everyone in my garden, then a visceral, disgusted reaction from a woman from Roadside Attractions. There was no "*common yearning of womanhood*," she said. "Jesus!" That (she said) was just "sexism."

I said that "sexism" was possibly the most overused, and therefore useless, word in the damaged American lexicon after the now-meaningless "racism."

How could I say such a thing? she demanded. Did I believe women were actually biologically different from men?

Obviously women are biologically different from men, I said, including neuropsychologically.

Well! . . . she said, nonplussed. Well, then—so I believed women were *inferior*?

Don't, I snapped, be ridiculous. I was now very seriously annoyed.

But, she said, George Eliot—! (Heads were moving back and forth between us.)

George Eliot, I replied, was making an empirical observation anyone not clinically insane recognizes as perfectly obvious. All cultures create social ideals for men and for women—what each should do, feel, value, wear, et cetera—and at the same time to varying degrees these mirror what men and women actually are, how each is evolutionarily programmed to feel and think. But biology is not necessarily *prescriptive*.

And as for literature, literature is not, and George Eliot is not, about politics. Literature, well done, illustrates the reality of human nature.

She glared at me.

Although obviously, I added, ignoring the truths of literature in our laws and customs and politics is silly.

It became a debate, and after they left the debate continued both at an afternoon pitch meeting at Miramax and at what became a quite volatile client conference at Endeavor. I didn't gather this information. It flew at me. This is what they're saying, Anne. And this. With the name of each person saying it. In Los Angeles, gossip comes with an index.

I was right, no, no, I was wrong, I was deluded, I was retrograde, I was "sexist" (of course), no, I was not sexist but realistic. I had guts (said a handsome young defender of mine heatedly; he had a political thriller coming out next month from Paramount), and if she (the one who said I was sexist, she had a three-picture deal with Sony and a vengeful look on her face) would just *read* Dorothea Brooks's character correctly—!

She had *read it* correctly, she said, but he, a male, was incapable of seeing that Eliot was merely reflecting a socially constructed sexist norm of her time and culture, not a biological universal, and no wonder he never dated anything not clawing its way up the Wilhelmina roster.

He: Utterly untrue, not to mention insulting, and frankly it should be obvious to everyone not a prisoner of her time and culture. (He meant liberal Hollywood.) (She: Oh, *please!*) Hadn't she felt, exquisitely delineated in every anguished passage of Eliot's prose, all that complex, conflicted shit women feel when boarding yet another flight to New York or London before the kids have even woken up—

"There was also," said David to me in the restaurant, "your views on making moral judgments."

You have done your homework, I said to him, and laughed.

"Mm," he said, taking a bite of bass.

Well, the moral judgments, that was the Browning. Browning killed certainty. And I believe in this, in closing the book and wondering, "Wait—is our narrator a genius or a fool?" The Modernists say, Your man Browning is simply stating, There's no truth, it's all viewpoint. But I disagree, strongly, I said to David. Browning is saying, There *is* truth. And we must find it. We must take what we see, and we must judge it to find truth.

"Oh, but we can't judge!" they argued to me at the chic bistro where we, at a large, prominently placed table, were holding our book club. "Who are we to sit in judgment?" (they argued). "Whose values should we say are better or worse? Everyone has a point of view, and all points of view are equal."

I said to those of them making this argument, You vote for the Republican or Democratic party, and you have absolutely no problem with imposing your party's view on abortion on everyone else because you think your view on abortion is right. That's Browning. And, if you're even minimally honest, that's you, too. I can't abide these idiots who say "We can't judge!" and spend their lives judging and writing checks to political organizations whose very existences are axiomatically judgments. I reiterated this at a cocktail party the following night in a voice loud enough to carry: These good Hollywood people who "didn't want to judge," which was not a Modernist perspective but simply the head-in-the-sand vapidity of mindless leftism. And then someone aggressively demanding of me, "Why do we have to judge?" and my retorting rather hotly, "Opposing child prostitution," and then "Supporting separation of church and state," adding pointedly, "Those are judgments," and being rescued by Ilene Chaiken, who saw I needed rescuing.

"It's that political, then," said David, raising an eyebrow, looking at his pad and writing quickly now.

Well, I said, and put down my teacup. I assumed he was referring to the book club in this case, not literature itself. I smiled, briefly. Yes, I suppose it is. It became overt when we read the Dostoevsky, and it seems to be continuing.

David said, "It does indeed seem"—he was reviewing some previous notes; I wondered who in the world he had been talking to— "that that's what makes them most uncomfortable. Your divisions into right and wrong."

Yes, I said.

I turned my teacup one way, and then I turned it the other. David simply waited. He didn't move a muscle. Some people walked past his chair. I was finding this extremely odd. Actors and directors have told me, but I was now discovering it personally: The most out-of-body experience one can have is being interviewed. I was anxious, but I tried not to show it.

I told David: I said to my son, Samuel, You *will* judge. You *will* say This Is Right, and you *will* say This Is Wrong.

"And?" asked David.

Oh, I said, Sam understands.

David wrote this down. He put away his pen, picked up the menu. "Dessert?"

At some point, David made reference to my world being "the Hollywood elites." I almost responded with something quite sharp, but I didn't. I simply said, These are the people we know. The quote was dutifully reproduced in the article. It was my impression that it set straight David's implication that I had somehow "sought out" names you saw in the coming attractions. As we waited for the valet to bring his rental car, David asked about their new passion for literature. What did I think of it all? I juggled a few variables and thought, Oh what the hell, say it. I replied that Oscar Wilde once described the basis of literary friendship as "mixing the poisoned bowl"; naturally, I said, Hollywood has taken to it like cats to cream. (I figured the ones who knew me would get a kick out of that.)

David shifted his car keys to his left hand, got his pen out again, and wrote this down.

The piece was not, as I fully assumed it would not be, a cover. It was, at the same time, longer, with larger and more numerous photos, than either of us had expected. "Good God," said Howard, holding the brand-new copy of *Vanity Fair* at arm's length. Then he said, "Stop scowling at me." Then, "You think I had something to do with this?"

I said nothing. I was peering at a photo of myself, Alan Levine, and Peter Mehlman.

"*No.* Anne. I didn't." Then he said, "Fine, call Margolick and ask him. Call Sarkin. Call Si if you want!"

Haven't you been talking to Annie Leibovitz about directing something?

Gritted teeth: "Anne . . ."

We both looked at the magazine. Turned it this way, then that.

It is pretty, I admitted.

"What does it say, anyway?" asked Howard.

Oh. That.

All right, so there I am, swimming in an ocean of my own creation. I'm all these Things, and I didn't even know it. The trick of journalism, I now understand, and it is a trick played on the reader, is to create the illusion of a coherent whole where none actually exists. It is to take the complex, unkempt pieces of a real life and stitch them together and generate a neat sum with neatly interlocking movable parts that exists for the reader but not, actually, for the person written about. There was a quote from Nancy Meyers: "She's one of the smartest, toughest people in town. Anne has the trick of knowing everyone while remaining, herself, unknown, which in Hollywood is an interesting choice." (So. I have a trick, too.) Any idea why that choice? asks Margolick. "I think it's her personality," Nancy says. "Anne doesn't need anyone except Howard." There are comments from Sid Ganis on my marriage to Howard; apparently we're a "rock solid" couple. "There's a lot of trust there," Margolick quotes Sid as saying.

I could not tear my eyes from the photographs. I stared at the pages. It hadn't started out well. I'd been planning to cut back my vibernum that afternoon; I didn't want José doing it, because while he was an inspired gardener—well, *I* wanted to do it. They had put me in a gown by some designer or other and had led me into the living room, where Annie Leibovitz assessed me. I was awkwardly trying to look at myself in a wall mirror. Annie, I said to her, I do have my own clothes. "Listen," she said, smiling and adjusting the tripod, "it's just dress-up." The makeup person came at me again, and I held up a hand—I felt so uncomfortable, I explained, in that ridiculously expensive dress I was sure should be covering someone much younger and sexier than I. Some starlet, say. The makeup woman cooed and shushed me and I felt the pancake going on my skin. I stood there, looking skyward as she'd ordered, very unhappy. Annie was questioning Howard, who was walking in and out annoyingly, about the room. Was the furniture normally like this? ("Look down, please," said the makeup woman.) Annie mesmerized me, her movements, which she noticed. "You're so attentive," she said mildly, bent down, squinting into her camera. I'm trying, I said, to understand why an Annie Leibovitz photo is different. She asked, "How many photographers have shot you?" I laughed. Only you, I said. Oh, and a few paparazzi. She made a vague noise of assent, focusing. Something was bothering her. And I was uncomfortable and nervous, and so to hide it I said in my strong voice, I'm sorry, but how long will this take because I *really* need to cut back my vibernum.

She lifted her head. "You garden?" she said.

It was a lovely shot, I am on my knees in the dirt. We'd stripped off the ridiculous gown, the pearls, most of the makeup, I had put on my usual things and gotten an enormous amount of work done, entirely finished the vibernum and almost completely pruned and repaired the spaliéd bouganvillea by the time she announced she had it. She said I was "a natural." I replied I was surely the most unnatural in the world: I had had to drown myself in something that made me utterly forget the camera, clicking away. She said being able to forget it was what made me a natural.

My favorite photo, however, turned out to be the one with Sam. You barely see him, in the living room, slightly out of focus and from the side and back, heading toward the kitchen door. The Volvo's keys dangle like dull platinum from his index finger. Yet somehow she had managed to make him the focal point of the portrait. Everything comes through, the teenage slouch, the sneakers. Howard, his arm around my shoulders about to be photographed, twists backward on the sofa to shoot Sam an order over his shoulder, and you can tell Sam is laughing as he talks back. A flash of white teeth. She had caught Howard in the act of preparing a pose but disrupted by the act of fathering. I am sitting, gazing at the camera's lens but clearly not concentrating on it, since it was the instant before my eyebrows went up and I said, Oh, Howard, he's been driving for six months, leave him alone!

It's quite brilliant, actually. I love this family portrait.

Poor Justin. He didn't put the phone down for four days.

The Browning anecdote David distilled nicely, following it with one dark anonymous quote ("Her political views are seductive; I think she's actually a crypto reactionary") and then Jeffrey Katzenberg: "Anne's politics are kind of a cipher," he said ("with a grin").

It was a revelation to me. I was a bitch (anonymous), I was one of Hitchcock's icy, thin, elegant, perfect blondes. (This from a pathologically insecure talent manager, who I had to admit did give a good physical description.) They were in awe of me, they loved me, they were frightened of me. I was a snob. No, I was sweet and caring "to those who really know her." (This from someone who didn't.) I found myself stunned by it, and fascinated. Howard has been written about hundreds of times, though never in anything close to this depth, and I startled him when he put his arm around me gently and asked, somewhat warily, was I OK? Reading what people said? People said anything, Anne, people were jealous and small.

I wiped at my eyes, and he moved to hold me, but I said, No, no, and he moved back just a bit and was surprised to see that I was wearing an elated expression as I struggled to express what I felt. I was trying to figure out what this was exactly. I said it was such a strange pleasure.

"How is this a pleasure?"

We'd read, "The thing you've got to know about Anne is she's married to Howard Rosenbaum, and Rosenbaum's an exec with fearsome connections. His New York bookworld contacts make him a real exotic, yet no one plays the home game better. Without him, she's nothing." And someone else, who said, "I wouldn't say she's an opportunist, necessarily." I was brilliant, and I was cold. Something (undefined) had made me frightened of intimacy, I kept people at a distance, everyone except Howard, whom I needed like air. I believed passionately in things, I was constantly thinking about "esoteric subjects"—they cited public school education policy. (I said to Howard, The education crisis is "esoteric"?)—you can't spend a minute with Anne without sensing the wheels turning. And the books! She's so goddamn well-read it's like, you know, she's lived a hundred lives in other places, and so sometimes you kind of think she's not really in this one. And she can say things in ways that people read as unfeeling or cold. Though that (many of the anonymous quoters were identified as intimates of mine; I didn't know I had so many intimates), that was just my surface, you know, and if you really *knew* me like they did, you understood that I *wasn't* cold or unfeeling. In fact, they explained, it made me very unhappy to be perceived that way. But I didn't know how to be otherwise. (This was in fact true.)

How is that a pleasure? I said to Howard that it was a pleasure because here, laid before me, was what others truly thought of me. Not every one of them. There were enough silken compliments and self-promotion using my name, enough self-interested protection of me and thus, carefully, of their connections to me, that, as Machiavelli would have pointed out, their respect was crystal clear. They wanted in, and I found myself in *Vanity Fair* terribly powerful. Yet I was guarded against flattery by their anonymously speaking the truth they could not tell me to my face. What a luxury, Howard, what a pure, unhoped for, rare luxury: To know what others truly think of you. It was, I said to him, a pleasure at the very least to know, if others are wrong about you, how they are wrong. And it is a pleasure to find out that some people, people I liked but had never tried to become close to, that some of these people had in fact come to know me very well. And they honestly liked what they'd found.

This was the way I appeared to the world, so much that was true, so much false, so different to each observer. It made me both sad and happy to see it, there in the magazine.

IT WAS IN FEBRUARY, AFTER David's interview but before the *Vanity Fair* piece came out, that we discovered the emails. It happened because the proceedings of the last two book clubs—the talent managers, then the advertising executives—showed up, more or less verbatim, in a message to several hundred people at the studios, the independents, all the major talent agencies (nine recipients each at William Morris and United Talent Agency), and production companies (eight people at Imagine alone), assorted scout outposts, a selection of literary agencies in London and New York (ICM, for example), and the admin offices in Orlando. These were apparently the seventh and eighth book clubs thus résuméd, and this had been quietly going on for two months. Justin placed a copy of the email on my desk and stepped back to await my reaction.

The operation was completely anonymous; the From address was bc ("S'gotta be 'book club,'" said Justin) @annerosenbaum.com, and annerosenbaum, it turned out, was merely a shell on a server registered to a nameless entity, "No Information Available." Not even the recipients knew the sender's identity; Justin had systematically tried to trace its origins. The unifying factor, Justin explained, appeared to be youth: Everyone on the e-list was under thirty. "And heat."

Heat? "Yeah," he said. The rising stars in the industry, the ones at the strongest outfits, with the big mentors. Pretty awesome. I should, said Justin, be flattered.

I was still reading. He waited, silently.

I said, They've misspelt a number of things.

He had other emails, anonymous quotes from people in my book clubs about what other people in my book clubs had said about *Babbitt* (some idiocies, and one brilliant, sardonic observation I actually remembered Robert Sillerman making about Sinclair Lewis and Democratic fund-raising in Hollywood), gossip about who I had invited (I never invited Tori Spelling) and who I hadn't, gossip on what people wore, lists of titles I'd assigned.

Find out, I said to Justin, who this is.

He looked uncomfortable. "I've tried," he said.

Keep trying.

Then after a moment, *Damnit*, I exclaimed, upset, there are detailed comments Ken Ziffren made in my garden. Who is talking?

"*Everyone's* talking. Why else go to a book club?"

To talk to each other, I replied, *in private*, about what they thought of the book, not to talk to the *Hollywood Reporter* about how so-and-so from Paramount had an opinion on—I glanced at the email—Steinbeck's view of violence that explained why the studio was putting Allan Loeb's latest project in turnaround.

Judging from his face, I was missing something.

Look at this, I said. There's even one that forecast the books I'm going to select next. I put my reading glasses on. "So you can get a jump on *The Charterhouse of Parma*," it read. ("Probability of her choosing it: 92%.") I took the glasses off.

"If they can't get into the room," he said. The sentence, to his mind, didn't even bear finishing.

Yes?

So he explained it to me patiently, as to a child. "People always want in, even the ones phoning in the lunch orders. Why should you shut out the worker bees?"

Well, I said. I hadn't thought of it that way. I drummed my fingers on the desktop. *The Charterhouse of Parma*, I said.

Justin found me working on the hyacinth. He was pleased with himself. It radiated; he was leading with his hips.

He laid it on the garden table, stepped back to brief me. Apparently the list was being run by an assistant producer at Miramax, a young woman named Carrie Fein. She was aggressive, talented; he listed the producers who had mentored her, the films she'd worked on.

Do you have a phone number?

He put down another sheet of paper: phone, address, email.

Brilliant. Well done, Justin.

"Hello, this is Carrie," she said when she picked up.

Right, this is Anne Rosenbaum.

It took several minutes for her voice to come down to its natural register. I said I was impressed by her work. I said this call was not retributive. I was perhaps a bit put out about the comments being broadcast, but I was not interested in the names of those who had passed on information, although I would be fascinated to know how she had gone about it in a general way. So why didn't she come to dinner. How about tonight. Howard would be home around seven. Was she free at eight?

"Oh!" she said. "Sure, I'm free." I heard her mentally rushing to cancel appointments. "I'll call Michael and Sarah, too," she said.

Who are Michael and Sarah?

She began backpedaling.

I assume, I said, that they run this little operation with you.

She was relieved to have them in play. Michael Schnayer at Sony. Sarah Adler at CAA. Please invite them, I said. Do you have a pen? Here's the address.

"Oh," she said, "I know where you live," and then instantly: Oh,

God, oh no, it made her sound like a stalker, like the *Scream* franchise or something, honestly—

I'll see you at eight, I said, smiling as I hung up. I turned around and called, Justin? Can you stay for dinner?

They had prepared a pitch. It came not quite at the end of the salad. I found the timing slightly aggressive; they could have waited till the main course. I had mentioned Paul McMahon (they were attentive; you could see them trying to calculate my interest in him) when some invisible clock ticked over in all three of them and the plan went into action as previously agreed. Fein led, strongly, with Adler on tactical support in facts and figures and Schnayer batting cleanup (which turned out to consist of charming Howard, to Howard's amusement, and stroking Justin, which Justin took as his due). They were well dressed and very, very smooth. Slightly mannered. They behaved, I remarked to Howard afterward, like they were in some conference room at a studio. "They were," said Howard. They acted chummy with Sam, who guardedly gulped it down (twenty-four-year-olds who took notice of him, astonishing) and overly solicitous of Denise, who ignored them completely.

How about if they expanded the club to a new medium? said Carrie. They wanted to put Anne Rosenbaum's book club on the Internet. "Officially," Justin added pointedly, and she acceded to this. But: They'd have an observer at each meeting, to be approved by me, of course, to do notes and reporting. All to be approved by me.

Both my eyebrows were up. Howard's look from the other end of the table made me snap them down again.

Howard asked mildly, "Anne, will you have time for this?"

I thought it over. Oh, by the way, I said, I had to congratulate them on the forecasting of my book choices, which was quite astute. The subject matter was perhaps overly narrow, but there was a decent literary range, and it had given me a number of ideas.

"That's my work," said Adler.

Fein shot her a very dark look. I saw Justin file this for future use.

Fein said that the report would be distributed to their list and only to their list, and posted to the new website, "which we can build in a week."

What would be the name.

They looked patient: www.annerosenbaum.com.

Sam rolled his eyes. "What did you think it was going to be, Mom?"

Obviously they had already taken the liberty of registering my domain name. Members would have password access and would post literary criticism, comments, thoughts. I would suggest the critical sources, they could do the research and were thinking of approaching the English departments at Harvard and Stanford and Brown (their alma maters) and (nod to Howard) UCLA of course to supplement, or guest star, as it were, tailored editorials from Stanley Fish and Harold Bloom and James Shapiro and so on. (The obvious choices.) And of course there'd be a forum for participant commentary, said Adler.

Commentary, I said.

"I got some terrific stuff from Lauren Shuler Donner on Merwin," said Schnayer.

Sam said something.

"What, Sam?" said Howard.

"Geoff Helprin's older brother's at Vertigo," said Sam. "He's on the list, and Geoff brought to class what James L. Brooks told you he hates about late Wordsworth. My English teacher had us write an essay on whether we agree with Brooks."

I was staring, truly openmouthed now, at Sam, who looked back as if all this were the most natural thing in the world. The unstated question—how the *hell* did Jim's comments in *my book club* get on the list—hung there. Fein took a breath. "I was in a meeting? With Jim? And he went into it in detail. You'd just done Wordsworth." She paused. She was anguished. "I know it seems like spying—"

It is spying.

"Mrs. Rosenbaum." Adler, strongly, on my flank. "You gotta understand, Jim didn't have any problem with—"

How would you know.

"He emailed us a post on your comment about Wordsworthian symbolism."

Ah, I said after a long moment. Then I said to Sam, Why didn't you tell me you were doing this in school?

He sort of shrugged. "Sorry." Then brightened. "It makes you look really good, Mom. Brooks thinks you're a genius."

"Plus," said Adler, "when two studios start racing to put a work into production, it gets really exciting."

Howard looked at me. I didn't know this?

Know what? I was now seriously cross.

"You said you like Bellow's characters. Paramount and Columbia are competing to rush *The Adventures of Augie March* into development."

No, I said, I didn't know, but I would never have picked that one. I would have chosen *Humboldt's Gift*.

"Really?" said Fein, Adler, Schnayer, Justin, and Howard simultaneously.

IT IS EARLY MARCH. HOWARD takes Sam to LAX, arriving just after 9:00 P.M. He has proposed taking him to dinner, but Sam has said no, Dad, thanks, and so Howard drops him curbside at Departures. Before Sam hoists his backpack, Howard, with an eye on the traffic cop, jumps out, runs around the Mercedes, gives him a quick but very strong hug and says, "I'm so proud of you." Howard is surprised (he will comment to me on this the next morning) at how emotional Sam's leaving for Israel is for him.

Sam pats his pocket to make sure the ticket and passport are there. He looks at his father. He says, "Why are you *proud* of me?" Howard—if he is conscious of the slightly peculiar tone in Sam's voice, he does not show it—explains that mothers feel love for their sons, but fathers feel pride.

A PRODUCER NAMED MARK SIEGAL takes me to lunch. He asks have I ever thought about producing. "I mean," he says, "your literary judgment, combined with our expertise: an incredible combination."

I put down my fork. Mark. I was under the strict impression we were to talk about Joyce.

He nods. "Exactly. Let's talk about Joyce."

Not about turning him into a movie, I say.

"Why not?"

Oh! He's so . . . What can one say? Not filmic. I start to give examples, bits and pieces of Joyce from here and there, which is how Joyce sticks to your mind, and he says, "There! You just made your first producing decision. No Joyce."

I attend to my tomatoes.

"Look, all's I'm saying," he says, "is concept this as a natural extension of your talents. This is what you do."

This is not what I do.

"But it *should* be what you do." He talks about his new production company, West 85th Street Films. What they had in development.

And then he mentions a figure. It is quite a figure. One has to wonder: How did he arrive at it? How many people had worked to come up with all these zeroes? He talks about books and stories. He talks about my name on the screen. Anne Rosenbaum. Except that it is Howard's name, I say. (For some reason, the idea of seeing it as a credit makes me voice this. It seems important, suddenly.) My name, I say, is Hammersmith.

"Oh," says Mark. "But your name *now*."

Well, I say. My name—now—is Rosenbaum.

"Well then," he says, and smiles.

It is just before I turn to walk to my car that I mention the screenplay. I've only skimmed it, once, I say, but it seemed very interesting.

Mark says, I'll send a messenger, and then, How do you spell this guy's last name?

Capital M, c, capital M a h o n. First name Paul.

IN MY OFFICE AT HOME, I put down Paul's screenplay and take off my reading glasses. I think it is very good, but I haven't read a screenplay in years, so I go to Howard's office and select a few from his shelves. I read them over. Yes, Paul's is at least this good. I make a copy of the script and put it in an envelope and tell Justin that Mark Siegal of West 85th Street Films is sending a messenger.

"Got it," he says.

One moment, I say, I'm going to write a note to go with it. I'm recommending this quite strongly. (I bend over my pen, avoid Justin's intensely interested look.)

That evening in the shower I find myself involuntarily thinking about Paul's script again.

Waking up I have what Howard would call a strong visual for the last scene. I give him the gist. I put a copy in your office, I say. Have you looked at it yet?

"Not yet."

Howard, I think it's actually quite good.

"Listen," he begins gently, "it's not really something I'd take on."

I know, I say, cutting him off, I just want your opinion. I tell him briefly about sending it to Siegal, about West 85th Street Films, their interest in my (I have to make myself say it) producing for them. It's just talk, I say.

"Huh," says Howard after a moment. His tone seems vague and ambivalent, but perhaps I'm imagining this?

I just—well, I suppose I just want you to tell me I'm not crazy. For liking it.

And (I add) *if* you were to like it, well, you might do *something* with it, right? You might *talk* to the writer . . .

He has put his hand on mine. I'm receiving his "you are utterly transparent" smile. "OK." He squeezes my hand, sits up in bed, and says "Bleh" very cheerfully to the beautiful morning.

SAM HAS BEEN GONE TWO weeks, and at Arrivals, the flight from Tel Aviv having touched down almost half an hour early, Howard hugged and kissed his son. "Christ, I still can't believe you're as tall as I am." Deposited the dusty backpack in the trunk and himself in the driver's seat, glanced at Sam, who had already buckled his seat belt. "What's wrong?"

"Nothing."

"What's the matter?"

"Nothing, Dad!"

So Howard held on to the steering wheel for a moment. "Seriously," said Howard gently. "Sam-o?"

Seriously, he was fine, he said to the ozone.

"Meet any girls?"

No. And then the boy asked: Was Howard hungry? He, Sam, was totally starving, they never fed you enough, it was lunchtime, right? Could they eat?

"Sure we can eat," said Howard carefully.

Two days later, Sam and I were driving to the studio for a screening he wanted to attend. Holding the wheel with both hands, Sam said to me, "Before you got married, did you ever talk to Dad about the Law of Return?"

I'd been reading. I stopped. I looked up at the traffic on Ventura. Cursorily, I said.

His eyes are fixed on the blue truck before him. He says nothing more.

The pieces of the story arrive from various sources. I collect them, fit each in its place.

He gets off the plane in Tel Aviv and heads immediately for Eilat, where he meets two American friends from L.A., Josh Weinberg and Ben Talat, at Josh's parents' vacation home. After three days of sun, he surprises everyone by announcing that he is leaving to wander the country. On the bus up to Jerusalem he happens to sit next to a girl with very curly black hair from La Jolla. The girl invites him to visit her moshav family on Moshav Amqa, up in Galilee, so he goes with her. It's a conservative moshav, completely kosher, not like the kibbutzes Howard and I knew. He stays three nights, picking avocados, then thanks the family, clips the blue-and-white *kippa* they've given him in his hair, and leaves.

Why the *kippa*? Well, it makes him feel different. He is now Sam Rosenbaum with a *kippa* on his head. He is tentatively trying out an identity. Israelis treat him, subtly, differently. Larry Talat got this intelligence from Ben, who'd got it post facto from Sam. His trajectory at this point seems random. He is in Haifa for a day, then moves down to Tel Aviv, then a lateral shift over to Jerusalem, where he checks into a cheap pension and disappears into the Jewish quarter. Gone to ground. He is off the radar.

He resurfaces one evening before the Western Wall, which is filled with people and their tortured trembling. Two things happen there. The first is an altercation. Two Norwegian couples, like four gentle blond giraffes, arrive like any other tourists. Their presence at the Wall provokes a religious Jew, not a black-hat but a black velvet *kippa*, and he begins screaming at them hysterically: "*Ani kadosh! Ani kadosh!*" This is translated in real time for Sam by an older English-

man he happens to be standing next to; the Englishman—he is perhaps some sort of Oxbridge scholar—with distaste at the intolerant
outburst, says to his wife, "It means, 'I am holy, I am holy.'" Before
several thousand people, the religious Jew mimes ostentatiously to
the Norwegian Gentiles that their presence dirties the purity of this
place. He motions to them with disgust, Go! Go! They lope away
disconcertedly, murmuring in Norwegian.

The second thing is that around ten minutes later he is approached
by a young, shortish man of indeterminate age. Wispy beard, a little
overweight, white-and-blue knit *kippa*. The young man asks him: Are
you Jewish?

Now, Samuel Rosenbaum is seventeen years old. And he says,
"Yes, I'm Jewish."

And the man, in a thick Israeli accent, recites (it is a set text that he
repeats hundreds of times a day, and he delivers it perfunctorily but
with force), "In that case, would you like to learn about your heritage
and your past? Would you like to understand who you really are?"

And Samuel Rosenbaum says sure, he would like to understand
who he really is. It is a crystalline evening under a blue sky, and they
are before the Western Wall.

The next morning he climbs, in the predawn dark and shivering,
into a white van and sees five other young men sitting there, looking at him. One from Sweden, one from Spain, one Italian, and one
Portuguese. The fifth is from San Diego. Each had been at the Wall
the previous evening, alone, and to the same two questions each had
answered "Yes."

They are driven very, very fast, the way the religious drive, through
Jerusalem and find themselves at a yeshiva. It is, behind its non-
descript wall, large and white and clean and self-contained. Judith
Weinberg puts together what she can extract from Josh and gives
me her guess as to which yeshiva it is, along with a sympathetic look;
"They're pretty hard-core," she says. They are taught some elemen-

tary prayers (Sam squints at the English translations of the Hebrew) and at 6:30 A.M. are given a kosher breakfast—it is explained that the breakfast is kosher, exactly how it is kosher, and why they as Jews should keep kosher. He is sent to classes. He tries. He is game. He feels, for example, a moment of true excitement when an intense, intellectual young man from South Africa with a knit *kippa* recounts to them his personal journey to observance. He tells them that his engineering training was remarkably easy to use in Israel when he made aliyah (it means "to go up" in Hebrew and denotes becoming an Israeli citizen; he makes sure they know this). There are jobs and a place for everyone.

At noon they send him to lunch, where he is fed kosher sandwiches—they explain what makes them kosher and why it is important for Jews to keep kosher. He sits next to the boy from San Diego. They talk about California, what're the best sandals, hybrids versus hydrogen, the pluses and minuses of the Arclight cinema. The boy mentions that he's Russian Jewish. Sam says that Oh, yeah, he's Russian Jewish, too, on his father's side. And English and Scottish on his mother's. The boy says, Yeah? Wow, because there aren't that many Scottish Jews, and Sam explains that they're not Jews, they're Scottish. Anglican. It is a moment before he notices that the boy's face has shut down. In fact it is drained of color. The boy gets up, leaves. Sam, chewing his kosher sandwich, looks around the lunchroom and wonders if the kid is OK.

That is when two large Israeli men appear on either side of him. They motion, no words. Leave the sandwich. He puts it down. Follow them. Sam obeys. They enter the office of the yeshiva's head rabbi, a somewhat portly, thirtysomething Australian Jew with a dark blond beard. The two large men take up positions on either side of the door. Sit. So, the rabbi asks Sam, where has he traveled? He's a long-term backpacker? No, Sam says cautiously, this is just, you know, two weeks. Spring break. He glances behind him at the men.

The next detail is given to me by Jennifer. She looks down at my driveway as she repeats what Sam told her. He had shown up unexpectedly the previous day just before her lunch break—she'd been delighted to see him—they had hung out on the studio lot in the shade of some trees. She starts by saying that he hadn't formally sworn her to secrecy.

I nod, acknowledging what this means. It's OK, I tell her.

Well, says the rabbi, looks at his watch for the fourth time, you really should get this book—he names it—fantastic, tells you where to find kosher food from the Ivory Coast to Thailand.

Why? asks Sam, looking back from the men to the rabbi. Why get the book? (The menace in the room is both frightening him and making him combative.)

The rabbi leans forward. So you can eat.

Sam had said to Jennifer that, weirdly enough, *that* had been the biggest shock of all to that point. What had been? she asked Sam, confused. It controls everything, said Sam. Like, if you don't have this book you can't *eat*. Presumably you—what?—starve? With food all around? Food perfectly good for everyone else, says Sam.

Jennifer mentions to me that she has already recounted this story to Howard. It seemed to her that Howard buckled slightly, but he'd had no reaction. And anyway they had a 2:00 P.M. in a few minutes. A potential new Pixar project.

The rabbi looks at his watch for the fifth time, and as he glances up again, Sam can see that his demeanor has transformed. You deceived us, he says to Sam, you told us you were Jewish, and you are not. You have caused us to sin: The Talmud prohibits teaching Torah to non-Jews. You are a traitor and a thief, and you pollute our yeshiva. He goes on for a while. It is unclear if the two big men understand any of this. (Somewhere in the middle of this icy tirade, Sam recalls hearing that if your mother is not racially Jewish, you're not racially Jewish. He remembers, as if for the first time, which is bizarre, the comments his grandmother made. He considers, as if for the first time, his mother's unexplained disappearance from seders and his father's determinedly cheerful silence and the fizzing, irritating interpersonal static like on a TV screen. Even as his mind is overloading, it's assembling data, putting the pieces together backward.) You are *trefe*, says the rabbi. You are unclean. You are impure. You are *not* a Jew. (He seeks to be clear on this point.) Understand that you are not a Jew. (Sam looks at him.) Your father has been part of the destruction of the Jewish people. Get out of this yeshiva, get out of Jerusalem, get out of Israel, and never come back.

Sam, moving now because he is propelled by the two large Israelis on either side of him toward the exit, turns for some reason to ask—again—about his father. Oh, says the rabbi, his Australian accent chipper now and seemingly unfazed by the shift in his position, your father should definitely make aliyah because there will always be another anti-Jewish genocide. He should be with his own people.

The two men march him out of the office. Sam sees now that the lunchroom has just emptied. It is the only passage to the street, so the business with the watch was timing, to avoid anyone's coming in contact with him. (And he then realizes that the boy from La Jolla turned him in to the authorities. He marvels for a second at the swiftness of the boy's instinctive reaction: Discover the impurity; eliminate the impurity.) They open the door and wait, wordless, for him to exit blinking into an empty inferno of sunlight. He takes a step into the street. Then the other foot. He hears the door slam behind him. He's alone before a tall white wall. He's squinting into this blinding vacuum, and he can't see anything at all.

At this point it becomes fuzzy. For an undetermined period he seems to lose a sense of where he is. The people have vanished from the city, and yet he hears voices. The street is packed dust, completely empty, although cars drive past. He must have picked a direction, walked, because after a while he is able to see figures moving about again. He is in a market somewhere. He spends an hour with two teenage girls he meets somehow. They are shopping for scarves, a

sweet girl from New Zealand and a snarky one from New York.
"Well," snaps the New Yorker, manhandling the scarves, "we've got
to *choose*, we can't be total *Japs* about this." Sam thinks this is sort of
funny.

He goes back to the pension, checks his El Al ticket. His flight
leaves the next morning. It is late afternoon. He falls into a very deep
sleep.

AS I FILL HOWARD IN, he stares at nothing. We're sitting in
the garden. Sam is out somewhere. I think in passing that Howard
looks older. It must be the light.

I hesitate. Are you OK?

He looks at his shoes, a strange look, as if mice were swarming
around his feet.

Howard, did you and I ever discuss Israel's Law of Return?

He says in a hard tone, "Why the fuck is Judy Weinberg gossiping
about our son."

I'm rather astounded. I peer at him. Howard, she's not "gossiping" about Sam. She's letting me know what—

"Never mind," he says. This time, by contrast, his tone is defeated,
wan.

I wait for clarification. Howard has indicated to me, without giving details yet, that he's already received some information from his
own sources. Since Sam isn't talking yet, I don't have the whole story.
If, I begin, we—

"What the *fuck* did he think he was doing," Howard asks my garden. It sounds like a plea. For an instant, I'm confused; I assume
Howard means Sam. Then it occurs to me that he is being more
precise: Howard means Sam's answering, "Yes, I am Jewish."

Not that I care about Sam's being Jewish or not. Or what it might
mean to whomever. I care about Sam, but I can attend to him later;
in the immediate it is Howard's tone of voice that concerns me, and

whatever is behind it, and I start by putting my hand gently on his shoulder and saying, "Howard," but he moves away from my hand, gets up suddenly and, very fast, walks away from me toward the house.

When I come in—I have spent a few moments in vague nothing—I see Howard on the phone. He is talking to his brother. I can tell this instantly by his tone and his expression. He stops talking when he sees me, and we look at each other. Then he says, "Stu wants to say hi."

He holds out the phone.

Hello, Stuart.

"Anne." Stuart talks a bit.

You sound distracted, I say.

"Nah," says Stuart. "Nah."

So when are you coming out to see us?

Afterward I ask Howard what he and Stuart had been talking about.

"Just stuff," says Howard, frowning at his hand.

SAM EXPLAINED HIS CONCLUSION TO me (apropos of absolutely nothing; it's nothing, nothing, nothing from them, Signal Unavailable, and then all of a sudden one evening they're standing in the kitchen as you're chopping ingredients for the salad, vehemently expressing their thoughts as you try to hide your surprise). The thing was, he said, if you really, you know, want to *maintain* this crap (he meant "if you want to perpetuate a tribe of people separate and distinct from all other people"), then you have to *do this* to other human beings. You, like, have to! (His voice was straining upward.) To look at all the people who aren't in your *club* this way and stuff. This totally extreme in-group, out-group social organization, all the fucking ethnocentric differentiation and the primitive identity cueing, and the—the *theological-slash-morality* that, you know (he gesticulates, searching among things he has heard in classrooms for a verb), *undergirds* it all philosophically. And you shore it up with this insane crap about what dishes you have to eat off or whatever and pretend that the Thing that created the universe seriously *cares about your dishes*. But it's all just about keeping your guys separate from everyone else's guys, because your guys are more—he gestured vaguely at the window—*valuable to God* or whatever.

He was very agitated, but the words came out in the end quite logically; he'd clearly been walking himself through it. He scoffed at the idea that a God would care if you were circumcised, which he called "disfigurement as tribal ID," a phrase that sounded like something he'd learned recently from a book. I washed lettuce and listened.

All the theological acrobatics, all the crap you've got to generate because all the rules you've laid down back you into it. And the thing is, said Sam, the rules were supposed to mean you were more moral. But actually, said Sam, they meant exactly the opposite: Doing this to other human beings was the most *immoral* thing you could do. Seriously, Mom!

It's like, he said, they used to pull this shit at some fucking racist country clubs in Alabama. His hand was resting on the counter over the dishwasher. But this is *religion*. This is *worse*. This is, like, "We're the only people with platinum-mileage status with *God*." So what is everyone else worth, then. Nothing!

From the living room, we heard Howard get up from where he had been sitting and walk back to his home office and shut the door.

Sam was silent. He looked toward the office.

I GOT AN EMAIL. WILLIAM Morris literary agency in New York. The agent represented the authors of two novels coming out soon, and she wondered if I might be interested in getting an early look at the manuscripts. Oh, and maybe I could give her my comments, she'd be very interested to hear. I was intrigued. I told Justin to say I would.

The next day, just after FedEx had arrived with the two titles, Justin found me on the stairs, still filled with the thrill one has at the beginning of a novel. This is quite promising, I said to him. "Good," he replied, "because they invited you to lunch." There were several authors of theirs who, they'd suggested, I really should meet. A salad at the Beverly Hills Hotel, next Wednesday. Someone from New York was flying in, and some of their L.A. office would meet us. I told Justin it sounded interesting. It is, he said, already turning back to the office, and he'd already accepted. He had also specified to them the two writers they were to place on either side of me.

The day after the William Morris lunch, ICM called. Their New York office had just signed a new fiction writer, a real whiz kid, he was right up my literary alley, they said to Justin. "Well," Justin replied smoothly, "I guess that will be Anne's call, won't it." I found this harsh. He put a finger on the mute button, mouthed, "Let me manage it." The finger turned the mute off. "So you're looking for a blurb from Anne," he began. It was the start of a negotiation. I have no idea what he thought he could extract from them. I left him to it.

When Howard got home and I started telling him about this, he was the slightest bit—I was surprised when I realized it—envious.

(The following day an editor called Justin to ask if I might slip a brand-new literary acquisition into Howard's hands. I had Justin call Howard and repeat what she'd said. I took the phone. You see? I said to Howard. They're using me to get to you.

Howard felt better but pretended he didn't.)

I realized Justin was now regularly signing for five or so overnight deliveries each day. The stout dirty-blond DHL woman had a terrible crush on him. He moved around my house with his lists and papers, his mod glasses and moussed hair and his Princeton tones (I heard him casually mentioning his undergraduate institution to someone at Universal on the phone) never above a certain decibel, with a masculine friendliness that told people he kept the gate. He was a perfect animal for the telephone in Los Angeles. He treated Sam like a younger brother; in that role as well he had eerily perfect pitch.

I WAS NOT OVERTLY CONSCIOUS of why I chose the Trollope and *Anna Karenina* for my directors of photography. One of them actually elucidated my own choice to me afterward.

The phone rings at 3:00 A.M. It is two years ago, I explain to them, and it is Sam, age fifteen. Howard is instantly awake on adrenaline, sitting up, grunting his terror at whatever lies on the other end of the line. But Sam is fine. It is the other boy, the driver, who has been arrested on Santa Monica for an expired registration. The boy was not drunk, not high, not irresponsible. He'd just had the bad luck to meet this particular, overeager member of the LAPD.

There are two young women involved. And then it turns out the policeman was, perhaps, not so overeager. One of the girls had drugs, or she didn't have drugs because she'd just swallowed them, wrapped in a plastic bag. We never get the full story. Sam was isolated in a separate room at the police station when they strip-searched her.

"This is his date!" Howard whispered to me, hand over the receiver.

No, mumbles Sam—too scared to be sullen at this particular instant; right now he needs us—she's the other boy's date. So the putative nondruggy is his then? Our first knowledge that Sam is dating, and we're hearing it, in effect, from the LAPD. It struck me as hilarious. Honestly: *This* is how I learn about my son's maturing social life?

Which drugs? I ask.

A pause. "GHB," says Sam's voice.

I give Howard a look: Do *you* know what that is? He has no idea.

"Is Mom crying?" asks Sam's voice, stricken.

"Yes," Howard barks. "You get home right now."

Actually I am trying not to laugh. Howard, on the other hand, is cross. He will wait up till the police car arrives in the driveway and march out to meet it.

Howard has been this way from the start, since the moment we brought Sam home. He understood innately Bacon's warning, "He that hath wife and children hath given hostages to fortune."

How do you protect them?

Howard bought him a Volvo.

Howard lies now in the dark, eyes on the ceiling. I sleepily stroke his ears. "Stop smiling," he says to the air above, "Jesus."

Nonsense, he's perfectly fine!

"He's not gonna be fine when he gets home," he says.

Bosh, I say to dismiss this, and I curl myself around Howard and fall semi-asleep as he auditions tones of voice in which to administer effective but not overly severe punishments. I feel like a casting director. Oh yes, *that* one, I mumble authoritatively as he rehearses. It just irritates him.

Howard obviously wanted Sam to have sex education, but in his view that came down in its entirety to this (Howard quoted it to the boy):

There was a young lady named Wylde
Who kept herself quite undefiled
By thinking of Jesus
And social diseases
And having an unwanted child

Howard, I said, this is ridiculous.

"Have *you* ever talked to him about birth control?" asked Howard.

Oh, of course I have, every boy is dying to have his mother explain how to put on a condom.

Howard gave me a Precisely! look. "So I have to do it."

He's fifteen, I said. Don't you think it's a bit early?

"All I know," said Howard, "is what they tell me on television."

Howard put the condoms in Sam's hand, stating our strong preference that they not become necessary any time too damn soon, OK? No, *really*: Got it? Sam mumbled a response. "Well," he sighed afterward, "you can't make them climb into the lifeboat."

And now our semisullen teenager was dating a girl who was snorting the alphabet.

Did he actually say he was dating her? I ask.

"Of course he's dating her! He doesn't have to tell his dad he's dating her! The dad knows!"

Do we all look back at our own matings and find them inevitable, or perhaps simply uneventful, which is indistinguishable, retrospectively, from inevitable? I worried deeply about how Sam would go about it. Some club on Sunset frequented by bleach-blond girls with silicone implants. So many ways to go wrong. "The kid," Howard says (it's a warning to me), "will figure it out."

I'm not so sure, I reply, Sam seems astonishingly dim sometimes. We'd noticed his dull, almost total reticence on this particular topic.

"What do you want to do, Anne?" Howard sighs. "He'll meet a girl, that'll be that."

One thing that helps me, I say to my directors of photography, opening up a book now, is remembering that none of this—our worries about our children, their sexual risks, their potential mates—is new. It helps, remembering that, I say. Tolstoy's world, for example, was absolutely ours.

Literature continually startles you with the fact that each book contains a time horizon beyond which absolutely nothing was known. The people reading these books and the characters inhabiting them crossed into the unknown future of 1741, of 1835, of

2048, and survived, and therefore so, perhaps, shall we. Take Tolstoy on marriage, I say.

"The old Princess's own marriage had been arranged by an aunt. The young man, about whom everything was known beforehand, had come, looked at the girl, and was looked at by the family; the aunt passed on the impression on each side; on an appointed day the expected proposal was made to the parents and accepted. Everything had taken place easily and simply.

"But with her own daughters, she felt it was not at all simple. How many arguments with her husband there had been over the marrying off of the two older ones, Dolly and Natalie. The old Prince, like all fathers, was irrationally jealous of them, especially of the youngest, Kitty, his favorite, who had just come out into society, and at every step he made his wife a scene.

"The Princess felt that in Kitty's case, the Prince's punctiliousness had greater justification. Social customs had been changing a great deal lately. She saw that girls Kitty's age went off to lecture courses, saw men freely, drove about the streets alone. A great many of them never curtsied and were completely convinced that choosing a husband was their business and not their parents'. 'Nowadays girls are not given away in marriage as they used to be,' all these young girls said, and so did even all the older people. But how marriages were then to be managed nowadays the Princess could not find out from anyone. The French custom—parents deciding their children's fate—was condemned. The English custom—complete liberty for girls—was impossible in Russian society. The Russian custom of matchmaking was considered monstrous somehow and was laughed at by everyone. But the Princess knew her daughter might fall in love with someone she was seeing a lot of, and it might be someone who didn't want to marry, or who would make an unsuitable husband. And no matter how often it was suggested to the Princess 'it's the young people who marry, and they must be left to make their own arrangements as best they can,' she could not believe it, any more than she would have been able to believe that the best toys for five-year-old children could ever be loaded pistols."

We want our children to have what we had, I say to my book club. At least we want them to have the best of what we had. And when marriage is good, nothing is better. The question is figuring out what a good marriage should be.

"You can't really do a damn thing to get them a good marriage," Stephen Schiff says to me, "other than, you know, raising them right."

True, I reply. But you can provide them a target. Although, I added, Anthony Trollope disagrees with me. (We all put down Tolstoy, pick up Trollope.) From a position as a postal worker—Trollope invented the mailbox—he rose to become one of the best-selling authors of his era. For one of his novels he received the immense sum of £3,525. And if not a writer of the first rank, I defy anyone to point out a writer who achieved a greater connection to the parts of our lives that we don't put in the movies. Compare Trollope's view in *Can You Forgive Her?* to Tolstoy's. Please read from the top of the page.

People often say that marriage is an important thing, and should be much thought of in advance, and marrying people are cautioned that there are many who marry in haste and repent at leisure. I am not sure, however, that marriage may not be pondered over too much. Nor do I feel certain that the leisurely repentance does not as often follow the leisurely marriages as it does the rapid ones. That some repent no one can doubt; but I am inclined to believe that most men and women take their lots as they find them, marrying as the birds do by force of nature, and going on with their mates with a general, though not perhaps an undisturbed satisfaction, feeling inwardly assured that Providence, if it has not done the very best for them, has done for them as well as they could do for themselves with all the thought in the world. I do not know that a woman can assure to herself, by her own prudence and taste, a good husband any more than she can add two cubits to her stature; but husbands have been made to be decently good—and wives too, for the most part, in our country—so that the thing does not require quite so much thinking as some people say.

I clear my throat. I tell them, a bit hesitantly, that in its little confidences of an age gone by, its lovely sweet optimism, it gives me hope for my son and the woman he will eventually find. It makes me hope for the woman's beauty and for her goodness, and for how he will love her, and she, him. Trollope is the poetry of things that just happen to us.

My eyes have become a bit wet, and I have to take a swipe at them with my hand. I hurriedly put the books away and clap my hands. Go on then, I say to them, off with you, no sitting around grinning like idiots.

As Howard said, "Sam will meet a girl, and that will be that."

Afterward, one of them stays for a moment. She assays me with a smile and says, very gently, "It really won't be so bad when he goes. I promise."

Yes, I say, he's prepared for the world, I think.

"I don't mean for Sam," she says, "I mean for you," and gives me a kiss. "You'll be fine."

But I realize that actually I'd been thinking of Howard.

IT WAS THE TENTH DAY after Sam returned from Israel. Howard had already started to change. The thing had happened, and now it started gaining force behind us, advancing to engulf us, and we were just beginning to turn and look back at it, trying to make

out its initial form as it gained ground. We had, at this point, no idea
what it would become.

At five thirty in the morning, I am awake, and I leave him sleeping
in the bed and make my way through the living room to his office,
watching myself move through the large, elegant, clean, cool hallways, knowing something will be there.

It is a booklet, a single sheet of paper, hand folded, in small print.
It looks vaguely strange, as if it had been printed on an antiquated
press. At first I think it is a poem. I pick it up.

. . .

If you are a Jew, we have a message for you, it says.

CONSIDER that the Jew, the symbol of Eternity,
who neither the fire nor the sword could destroy, is
today succumbing to spiritual annihilation.

CONSIDER that the Jewish people, who have
illuminated the world with the Divine Light, have
raised a generation in darkness.

CONSIDER that we are the people of the Book, the
nation that has given the Torah to the world, and yet
today, its wisdom eludes our grasp.

CONSIDER that the Jew possesses expertise in
every field, and yet his own heritage eludes him.

You are a Jew.

You have been given the unique mission of
proclaiming the one-ness of G-d.

You have traveled the corners of the earth.

You have known oppression, all forms of
persecution. Your memory fails. You have forgotten
your past.

But nevertheless, a still, small voice calls out to you, to discover your inner self, to bend your will to your Maker's, even if your intellect rebels, even if you do not understand why you should do this.

A still, small voice that gives you no peace, for within you courses the blood of prophets, martyrs, sages, and kings of Israel.

Who are your ancestors?

Where do you come from?

Why did G-d create you?

Your roots are sunk in eternity.

You are heir to a legacy over 4,000 years old.

Come home.

. . .

The paper is lying open and carefully smoothed out on the desk as if he has pressed it flat with an open hand to reread it many times.

Someone—I can't remember who—said that the only true paradises are those we have lost.

"READY?"

Wait. I'm sorry. These shoes are new.

He waits, hand on the car door, as I adjust them.

"Ready?" he asks.

Ready.

He nods, they open the door, and we step out onto the red carpet. The weird awed gasp of the crowd and the eerie bombardment of camera flashes, like a slaughter of soldiers in some strange war, explodes around us. We wear halogen halos.

"Anne! How are you!" "Anne, *finally*." "Anne. You look terrific," and then, as if hearing thunder lagging behind a lightning flash, "Hey, Howie."

"Hi," says Howard.

At the first opportunity, I catch his eye. He grins a self-mocking grin, which I have seen before, but then it slips, which I have never seen. I am still looking toward him, wondering if I should go to him as they take my arm, "Oh, Anne, come over here and meet the producer!" There are unfamiliar hands on the small of my back, guiding me. Not Howard's hand. "He's attached to the project," they murmur to me, "great guy!" and add as if it's the most hilarious, unbelievable thing, "He doesn't even know you and I are friends."

Howard seems to be paying less attention to me than usual. Or else he is busier than usual. He remains far away, and I, lonely among the hopeful who press, sequentially, to talk to the stars and the director, and now strangely enough to me, watch him in the swirl like a desirable, distant cloud, and wonder about this.

The young man jibes far away, then tacks toward me across the floor through the crowd. I've tracked his approach, and still he seems to materialize out of the air. "It's Anne, isn't it?"

I sip my tonic water. Isn't what?

Not a scratch. "You're here by yourself," he says. Nonchalance. Are you sure?

"Well," he says easily, "your husband isn't here." He looks around, the jaw cutting a perfect arc in the air, and then the eyes sweep down and land in mine. "I mean, not right here." The eyes are cobalt and magnesium.

If, I say, you know who my husband is, then you know who I am and that my name is Anne. What do you want?

"Help with Ezra Pound." He smiles; it takes my breath away. It would take anyone's breath away.

I say, Pound, 1885 to, I believe, 1972. Not very fashionable—the difficulty of the poetry, the textual complexity, plus of course the Fascist politics.

He clasps his fingers behind his head. The muscles in his shoulders pull back the fabric of the expensive blazer. He holds this position, grinning.

> *I have tried to write Paradise,* he says to me
> *Do not move*
> *Let the wind speak that is paradise.*
> *Let those I love try to forgive what I have made.*

(I don't know this. I turn over the last line in my mind.) You're well versed, I say to him. Why do you need me?

He laughs, a lovely, athletic laugh. "You know everyone," he says. "All these people." He indicates them with the chin, turns back again to face me, closer now. "I thought we might strike a deal." His voice is very gentle. He is looking at me, his head slightly cocked to one side. He is the other half of the deal.

Imagine all the unimaginable things. I say to him, You have the thickest, darkest sheet of hair and the most perfect teeth. They're rather astounding, actually, your teeth. Even your breath is wonderful. You're a beautiful man. It's also entirely possible that you are an actor of some talent, although as hokey as it sounds, they actually never really know till the screen test. Good-bye.

I set down the tonic water. I turn and walk out of the room, returning the waves of three people. At the corner, someone mouths "Call me" and I nod, descend the stairs carefully, my hand brushing the rail as a light control. I allow myself to swallow. I ask the boy at the valet stand for the keys. On second thought no, I'll get it myself, where is it? There? The left side? Thank you.

I find Howard's Mercedes, unlock it, get in, shut the door, put my purse in the passenger seat, and lock the doors. I will wait here for Howard. I sit still, eyes closed, and grip the wheel. The cobalt and magnesium eyes are still in my head.

THE NEXT EVENING. HOWARD COMES home late. I look up from a book.

Oh, I'm so glad you're here, I say, stretching luxuriously, I'd just started dying for bed.

He says nothing. I see his face, and I stop smiling. I watch him for a moment. What time is it by the way? I ask.

"Eleven twenty."

I look involuntarily toward the clock. So where were you?

He jingles the keys. He says something.

Howard, I can't hear you.

"I went to a temple," he says. He throws the keys on the table, then peers down. "Is this all the mail?"

Yes, I say. I actually think I've misheard. You went to a temple?

He is sifting through envelopes. He picks out two, but looks dissatisfied with both. He walks toward the bedroom, eyes on the mail. "Talked about the problem with Sam," he says, disappearing down the hallway.

I ORGANIZE A DINNER FOR Howard's colleagues. It's our turn, essentially.

We all sit in the night breeze on the restaurant's stone terrace, the fountain's water flows, and every so often the breeze picks up this water and washes us with fine, cold spray. Nothing connects tonight. I can see Sam, frozen in place, talking to no one, and he looks like he is waiting, but I don't know what for. He is opaque. I feel that every voice is coming from far away.

Howard pushes his chair back to talk to someone.

And then I understand that in that moment I am seeing Howard again as he was before. Smiling, happy. Talking with everyone. Fielding comments and making them. He fills the place with his joy. But I notice he never once looks at me, and he never once looks at Sam. And that is what Sam is waiting for.

But Sam is just beginning to figure it out. Howard has not spoken to him once about the yeshiva's view of what he is, his classification, but Sam is figuring it out. You can see it progressing across his face like a shadow.

We fly to New York, a short trip of forty-eight hours, planned months ago, Howard "just checking in on a few projects." He reads during the entire flight.

That evening we have scheduled drinks with Alex Ross. The lights of Times Square are holograms on the wall of glass enclosing this slick new bar on 46th and Broadway. Howard's choice. Too young for us, in my view, and too crowded.

"So," says Alex, "what are you drinking?"

They talk business, of course. What is Alex writing these days? He's writing on Strauss, he tells us. "Was Strauss anti-Semitic?" Alex's article will ask.

Howard does not look up, but the movement of his body suddenly stills over his tumbler. He is listening alertly.

"It's complex," Alex says. (Alex does not notice Howard's reaction. He doesn't notice my glance, the straightness of my spine. Alex is just describing the question.) Strauss, who when Hitler came to power accepted the presidency of the Reich Music Chamber because it was his chance to implement some long-cherished ideas he had about musical reform, particularly legislation to benefit "serious" composers, legislation he thought necessary in an increasingly commercialized culture. (Hitler, a lifelong fan, agreed.) Strauss, who was only interested in the music. Strauss, who refused to sign documents firing Jewish musicians. Strauss, who continued to work with his Jewish librettist, Stefan Zweig. Strauss, who wrote to Zweig with an audible sneer, "Do you think that I am ever, in any of my actions, guided by the thought that I am 'German'?" The letters were intercepted by the Gestapo. Strauss, who was asked to resign.

"This," Alex asked us, "was an anti-Semite?"

"Strauss's son," says Alex, "became a dedicated and ardent Nazi. But, to muddy the waters a little, his father fought him on it, and, to muddy the waters a whole lot more, the dedicated Nazi married Alice von Grab, a Jewess. They had two children, and Strauss adored his grandsons. Both boys were Jews according to Hitler's Nuremberg Laws that defined who, under Nazi Germany, was or wasn't a Jew. They are also Jews according to Israel's Law of Return, which defines who, under the Jewish state, is and is not a Jew."

Alex went to the town of Garmisch and met one of these grandsons of Richard Strauss. A tall, gaunt man, Alex reports to us. Not much came of the meeting, actually. He got, he tells us, only a single terse paragraph out of it. (He laughs, shrugs.) This Strauss is a Jew. His grandmother died in Theresienstadt. His given name is Christian.

"These are hardly simple matters," says Alex.

I hesitate. I think they are, actually, I say. (Alex looks very slightly startled.) I think, I say, putting the words together, that dying in Theresienstadt because of what you are born is a simple matter. I add, I think a law—anyone's law—that defines you because of what you are born is also a simple matter.

It is at this point that Howard looks down. He watches the way the oily liquid rolls in his glass as he swirls it counterclockwise. Alex is not sure exactly how to respond. He has connected my statement to Howard, and he now connects Howard's reaction back to me. He is uncertain of motive and causation.

I say that it seems to me rather clear that Strauss's sin was being loved by a maniac.

Alex considers this. Alex is not sure. Conscious now that there is between Howard and myself a backstory whose terrain he does not know, Alex carefully reserves judgment. And Howard doesn't say anything at all.

They return to Alex's work. In this same obsessive vein, Howard and Alex discuss Wagner's astounding genius, "which was fueled by his anti-Semitic hatred," says Alex. "This is the theory. The scholar Anthony Julius located T. S. Eliot's creative muse in anti-Semitism, too. 'A gruesome guide to poetic truths,'" Alex quotes Julius.

"It makes sense," says Howard grimly.

Alex sips, looks around the bar. People move around us inside this glass cage, talking loudly.

I observe, my eyes narrowed, that it is also of course the Jewish muse. Anti-Semitism.

Alex blinks.

Anti-Semitism, I explain, is the muse of Jewish religious truth and Jewish survival because it is the gruesome muse of Separatism. It drives the central Jewish genius, separation, the unique genius that has through millennia kept the Jews alive as a distinct tribe. A genius much greater than Wagner's, in a Darwinian sense.

Alex's eyes don't meet mine and, carefully, don't meet Howard's.

Well, why, I ask Alex, why endlessly discuss anti-Semitism's *possible* usefulness to T. S. Eliot and Wagner and other anti-Semites but not its *clear* usefulness to Jews? Why?

Alex glances at Howard. But Howard seems to be musing on something that makes him absolutely furious.

We walk back to the hotel and ride the vast escalators and the elevators that raise us into the curving colored glass tower over Eighth Avenue. In the room, we undress. How can I say it, I ask myself over and over, but no answer comes to me. He undresses faster than I, gets in bed. I'm sure Howard has understood what I was saying. Then I'm sure he has not. (I step out of my skirt, lay it on a chair. I take off my shirt.) I am, perhaps, still too shocked by what he said in our living room, or too uncertain, to state any more plainly what seems obvious to me. That there is no fucking problem with Sam. There is nothing wrong with Sam at all. Sam is perfectly fine as he is.

Howard snaps the covers up to his collarbone and shuts off the lights. I can hear him breathing in the dark. I stand, in the dark hotel room, in my slip and bra with my shirt in my hand, staring toward his still, shadowed outline. I am sure he can hear my breathing as well. Neither of us moves a muscle.

And the next day we go along, go to his appointments, and on the surface everything is normal.

On the flight home to L.A. we are strapped into our first-class seats, bumping gently toward the concrete lip of the JFK runway that will funnel us up into that evening's horizon. We are breathing the cool metallic gas. He has his half glasses on, a memo on a meeting before him. The engines are building. He stops reading the memo. As the plane lifts into the air, he takes my hand and holds it so tightly I am afraid he will break the bones, but I don't dare remove my hand; he does all of this without looking at me.

IN HOWARD'S STUDY AT HOME he has a framed photograph of himself with Judy Kaufthal and David Harris at a Salute to Israel benefit they coproduced. It is five years old. Howard had written a substantial check "to start things rolling." Judy and he have their arms around each other and are grinning. I enter the office. He is staring at the photo. When he hears me, he's startled. "Whadda you got," he says brusquely, reactively, as if I've caught him and he's going to bluff his way out of it.

I hesitate. Nothing, I say, surprised.

"What's the matter?" Terse.

Nothing's the matter, Howard.

He sniffs, vaguely now, wipes a finger briskly under his nose twice. Turns back to his desk. There are some papers at his elbow, a report from the National Population Jewish Survey on Jewish-Gentile intermarriage. Robert Abramson and the United Synagogue of Conservative Judaism.

The words *ba'al teshuva* are in bold. I notice that. I don't know what it means.

I move to the shelf over his desk that holds the regiment of screenplays and start to reach up toward the Paul McMahon script. I muster a light, dry tone: You haven't forgotten young Paul? My genius driver who finds us gardeners?

He claps both hands to his forehead—yes, he'd forgotten—and his tone is completely different. "I'm sorry, Anne."

I start to say that it's OK, I just really need him to—and he says, "I'm so sorry," and, seated, embraces me tightly around the waist. I freeze, my arm outstretched, hand on Paul's screenplay.

"I'm going to," says Howard from below. He's talking about the script. "I mean to," he says.

I go back to the kitchen. I remember an interesting point Nancy Franklin once made to me (she was working on a theater review) about fictional characters and the ways we view ourselves. Nancy had seen Barry Edelstein's production of Arthur Miller's 1947 play, *All My Sons*, at the Roundabout, and there was something she had found strange.

About the play? I asked.

No, she said, about the characters. "Any of us could make the mistakes of the businessman Joe Keller in *All My Sons*," she said. "But the tired, desperate Willy Loman?" This salesman, this Jewish failure. She tapped a fingernail against her coffee cup and smiled, thinking about it. "Innumerable people have said that they know someone like Willy Loman. But it's a good bet that no one—not even a traveling salesman—has ever recognized himself in the character."

Consider the nature of this problem, which is suddenly bothering me. Seeing oneself. As Nancy has so precisely outlined it. I do not know if Howard is able to see himself at the moment, and I have no ability to judge because at this moment I do not know what I myself am seeing when I see him. I'm recognizing less and less.

I think, Oh damn Nancy Franklin and her observations.

One can arrive at a certain point, and turn around and look back, and see differently, and with a strange, discomforting clarity, all the things that have come before. Things clicking into place. Clarity, it seems to me, is supposed not to be discomforting. But.

Year after year, we exited Ben Gurion International into warm and ancient evenings under Israel's skies of blue silicate, the wind in the growing dark an aluminum scalpel slicing the tissue of heat away from the land. All those flights Howard and I used to take to Tel Aviv. (Our last trip several years ago now.) Howard "wanted to help." He felt an obligation. All the evenings I remember of endless conversations, lawn chairs and fluttering flames of candles and the last bits of *pashteda* and *salat peirot* and *marak pitriot* littering the table, and they gave their opinions and picked at the food and argued and argued. I listened to them from the side. It was always the same: What of Israel? What of Israel? Besieged.

Surrounded by a violent enemy sea of fanatics who strap bombs to children, Israel's leaders necessarily fight back. They order assassinations in neighboring capitals—shootings, poisonings in Amman—as if ordering furniture. The country's founding history is a bomb's shudder, its borders are bullet paths. Its unending series of bloodlettings paint the biblical cities in corpuscles, catheterized with detonators: Galilee in coats of O-positive; Bethlehem, A-negative; and as for Jerusalem, any type you wish.

And they would sit, Howard's friends and acquaintances, the intellectuals and publishers and writers and three or four rich concerned Americans, at, for example, a long, outdoor dinner table in Jerusalem hosted by Ari Shavit, the liberal thinker of the left-leaning *Ha'aretz*, and moan and bewail the present, past, and future, like the bitterest of fortune tellers. View it this way, they would say. View it that way. They eat, they drink, and they talk and they argue. The hours tick by as always. I do not look at my watch. I try to find constellations in the sky. They do not talk to me. David Makovsky, whose *Ha'aretz* beat is diplomacy, sits next to Howard, who is listening to *Ma'ariv's* Shalom Rosenfeld, who interrupts himself, looks around.

"More wine, Anne?"

No, thank you.

He returns to the fray.

The tablecloth is stained with coagulated burgundy spots. I sit in the evening dark and wait, or go inside to read. Every so often someone enters to search for another volume of the *Encyclopedia Hebraica* or some other reference book and stumbles on me. "Oh! . . ." They need to verify some disputed, vituperative, ancient, anachronistic pseudo-datum. I remember once hearing, vaguely, David Bar-Illan roaring about Netanyahu, "One thing is to have an affair with a shiksa—but a married woman! With a shiksa, even the rebbes do it. But a married Jewish woman!" At this I close my book—I am suddenly unable to focus on the print—and wander outside again into the night and away from them, out of earshot. Howard is engaged in the conversation.

The Israeli press is pro-Labor, the immigrants are pro-Likud, the Ashkenazi are beset, the settlers have God and their Uzis on their side, and they and the Hasidim are as nutty, as someone describes it, as Snickers bars. I feel the hatred; it is palpable. I might look over at Amy Wilentz, whose loathing for the fanatics and the settlers seeps like acrid smoke from her *New Yorker* pieces. Someone would be loudly quoting Charles Krauthammer and saying in English, "At least *someone* understands!" I recall a comment that Abe Rosenthal writes "like a man shouting from a fire escape," but everyone talks that way here. It is exhausting.

When we were home, in Los Angeles, Howard and I never discussed it. It was important to him. I accepted that. I always went along: a few days' visit, perhaps a week here or there.

Once, sitting with Howard in David Remnick's office, I ask David: How was his trip. David has just returned from reporting a profile of Bibi Netanyahu. He looks haggard. David says, "Jerusalem is the City of Opinion. It rains opinions." He laughs bleakly. "The desert blooms on the moisture of harangue. The rarest phrase in the fifty-year-long history of Israel is 'No comment.'"

He looks as if he has imbibed all of these opinions and wants to vomit them back up.

Howard asks about the piece. You can't understand the son, says David darkly, without understanding the father. "What Bibi has inherited from his father is a keen notion of Us versus Them." And They will always, according to the father, act toward Us as They acted during the Inquisition in fourteenth-century Spain, when they devised a racial theory of the Jews as inherently different, inferior. (This particular racialist theory is, to David, self-evidently horrific.)

After David goes back to work, Howard and I will walk leisurely north hand in hand on Sixth Avenue. I will tilt my head at the images in a Neil Folberg exhibit in the International Center of Photography.

Howard reads David's articles and looks agonized. Howard says to David: Israel is a spectacular disaster. They mourn this together. We have met, Howard and I, a few of the founders who arrived to build a country of fraternity. We watch them survey the devastation of their dreams, poisoned by religion, riven by divisions among its people. And its failure is so pedestrian. Israel is now what it was never meant to be, a country like all the others, but it is worse because it is crippled by the weight of its failure, which hangs over it, invisible but deadly, something nations not crafted from dreams will never know.

That is what Howard thinks.

I think something very different. Even if I do not say it because, before, it never needed to be said.

What I think, what I have always thought, is this: The dream itself is poison. The country has a poisoned soul, an ideology of xenophobia that has traveled forward five thousand years like an unkillable ancient virus. A group of Middle Eastern nomadic tribesmen created a self-made pass through the terror and uncertainty of life by thinking up a god of segregation. Self and Non-Self. A cultural immunological system of breathtaking strength. A higher moral standard that axiomatically means for everyone outside the tribe a moral standard that is lower.

That is what I think.

The Ashkenazic elites abhor the Orthodox, loathe the Extreme Right, wince at the pervasiveness and politics of the military, denigrate the Sephardim, belittle the immigrants, and see themselves as a tiny bastion of civilization pressed on all sides by the fetid breath of medieval, irrational, superstitious hordes who reek of body odor, who know nothing of the Enlightened mind, who are clannish and inbred and practice a nepotistic theocratic totalitarianism. I agree. But. Howard once overheard Shimon Peres, the Ashkenaz, the educated, the secular, bitterly complaining that the Orthodox hate the Arabs, who surround them. And they hate *that* the Arabs surround them. But by God, said Peres, at least *they*—he meant the Orthodox—were surrounded by people exactly like themselves.

What, said Peres, what about us?

I remember Howard sympathizing with Peres. What about us, he and his friends lamented to each other, the nonfanatic Jews?

But I had been watching them for years, these friends of Howard's, and I had noticed that, like characters that Nancy Franklin observed in an Arthur Miller play, they had no ability to see themselves. It hardly took much effort, my noticing it. For example, it would go, year after year, basically like this.

It was afternoon. We had dovetailed with David, there reporting, and together were walking along a path at Hebrew University. David and Howard were hunched over, listening intently to Danny Rubenstein, the liberal, the intellectual, the writer on Arab-Israeli affairs. Danny inhabits the ever-thinning strip of coastal Israel that is the secular state, giving way gradually to the Middle Eastern, Oriental state, the theocracy. He shook his head. "For people like me and my friends, it's almost the end of the world. This new wave of immigrants— people holding values utterly not our own. We were brought up to work, and the new people, especially the ultra-Orthodox, don't give a shit about work. They're like the goddamn Moral Majority."

He was fiercely angry. He was already mourning the future. Next to him, Avishai Margalit, who taught philosophy, murmured, "It turns out that we, the secular community, are the dinosaurs: It's the end of a species."

Danny insisted to Howard, "The ultra-Orthodox don't respect us. They don't serve in the army, they don't care that we die." He choked on the insult. "They treat us with such contempt, like—" He was looking for a sufficiently disturbing image. It was getting late. The sun was a burning sheet dying in the sky. Some students walked past. Danny, the secular, the enlightened, found his sufficiently disturbing image. "They treat us as if we were *goyim*," he said. He was staring darkly at an invisible point in the distance, pondering this horror.

The students clanged a door behind us. Involuntarily I glanced right for an instant. David, apparently, had noticed nothing at all. I thought: OK, now I just have to move my eyes slightly left toward Howard. He will indicate to me that he has caught this, that he hears what it means. I moved my eyes. Howard was staring into the hot, dry air, contemplating the fact that Jews could treat other Jews as if they were *goyim*. (The word, spoken with the usual disgust.) After a moment I moved my eyes back to nothing.

Avishai had understood. But what could he do?

DRESSED FOR WORK, HOWARD WALKS down the hall. He passes Sam's door without stopping. He makes no sound, no whistling today. I hear the kitchen door open and his car keys fading outside.

Evening, he is still gone. He doesn't call. He arrives home at 11:28 P.M. and drops the keys quietly on the table in the hallway where he also leaves books and files for the office.

In the morning, when he has left and the keys are gone again, there is a flier that wasn't there the previous evening. He hasn't hidden it. He hasn't not hidden it. The address is a temple in Los Angeles. I see "Ba'al Teshuva" and after that the translation, "Returned to Faithfulness." Next to the flier there is an envelope with an Israeli stamp addressed to Howard. The letter that was inside it is laid neatly open and squared with the papers. I don't know the handwriting.

I pick it up. It is a letter from Avital Sharansky. "Dear Howard," she writes, and then there is a sentence or two about his health, and her health, and how was his son, Sam? And a reference to David and the movie project. And then, "I hope that you—and all the American Jews—will save yourselves and come to Israel. There is no life there. This is just who I am, but I just feel that way, in the sense of all the assimilation. You are not living fully. I have had the experience of not being in Israel, Howard, and I know that by your not being here you lose something of yourself. It's not real life, it's just spending time. It might be luxurious, it might even be interesting, but you must understand that real life is when you have your own place and you are with your own people and you have your own way of life and are not worried that your children will become something else."

Then a final paragraph that reads, in entirety: "Please, Howard, I don't want to offend you. It's just one Israeli housewife's opinion."

Howard, of course, is worried about exactly this. About the son who has already become something else. Who, without Howard's having perhaps given it quite the thought he should have two decades ago (although they warned him), was born something else. He hadn't listened to them then. He is listening now.

THIS I HEAR ABOUT AFTER the fact.

They are in one of the studio's marketing offices. The immensely proud DP is unveiling the movie's poster; with a small handheld camera he'd surprised the star in her underwear between takes, and the studio has, contrary to expectations, built the entire marketing campaign on that shot.

"Ta da!" says the associate producer.

"Whoa," says a development executive as someone whistles. "What's your MPA?"

"NC–17," says the marketer loudly.

The associate producer doesn't appreciate the joke. "It's an *R* movie," she assures the exec. "We got an *R*."

Howard mutters something.

"What, Howie?" asks the exec, turning.

"Kids see this thing," says Howard of the poster. "Children and women. *Respectable women* see this thing," he says.

Everyone waits for the punch line. They lean forward infinitesimally.

"How about some fucking modesty," Howard says, glaring at the photo. "She's completely uncovered." He averts his eyes.

The development exec is still waiting for the punch line. The DP and the associate producer glance at each other.

I WALK INTO THE KITCHEN and retrieve an orange for breakfast. Saturday morning. I am going to play tennis with a friend. I am holding yet another phone message from Mark Siegal. Justin has written a single word: "When?!" When indeed. I still don't feel comfortable jumping into this until I get Howard's take on the screenplay. I am wondering for the nth time if this is just silly when, from my position in the kitchen, I see Denise and José standing outside. They are having some sort of hushed discussion. When they spot me, they instantly suspend it. José squints at the garden as if surveying something. Denise folds her arms and scowls distractedly. It's then that I hear Consuelo crying in the driveway.

I call to cancel the tennis and change my clothes.

In the car, I get the full story. José and Sam sit in back. We take the Hollywood Freeway to the Santa Ana Freeway, going to Pico Rivera. Consuelo is sitting next to me, directing and explaining. José interrupts her every so often to clarify or stress a point she might be softening. Her younger sister came up from Guadalajara five months ago (this I knew) with her five children (this I didn't). She came with a man who is not her husband but who lives with her and who may or may not have fathered the fifth child. They found a bungalow in Pico Rivera, which is near Downey, which is where Consuelo lives. The man found work and was paying the bills. But Consuelo rarely saw Susannah in Pico. Susannah always came to her house (there was a relatively convenient bus). Everything was fine.

Consuelo got the address from a friend, secretly—it was to be a surprise—and bought a present for Pepina, since it was her eighth birthday. She discovered a house that was filthy, the children were filthy, they were unfed, and all of this because her sister was sick. The man, it turned out, was disappearing for weeks at a time—no, he had not found work, no, he was paying no bills, there was back rent since May. Since *April*, said José from the backseat. Consuelo corrected herself.

She is scanning the row of sagging houses, trying to locate Susannah's. She says apologetically, "I've never come from this direction."

The man wasn't violent, exactly. (Consuelo and José debate something, but I am missing the vocabulary or else it is slang. Consuelo puts her face in her hands.) "There was," says José directly to me, "a question of sexual behavior with the children."

I see.

Consuelo's voice is ragged from crying. Direct me, I say gently. She points, wordless. We pull up outside a dilapidated, old Los Angeles wood bungalow.

Inside it is dark and it stinks. The children, from five to thirteen, stare at us. Consuelo's sister lies on the ratty sofa. I ask if the electricity and water work. They do. Right. Here we go.

The car keys and three hundred dollars to Sam for cleaning products, trash bags, lightbulbs, toilet paper, rags from the *tienda*. José will go with him. Sam, keep the doors locked, park in front, you stay in the car and wait. The two littlest girls' dresses are not only grimy, they look bloodstained. I take each child into a bedroom, which is horrendous, and with Consuelo's help get their clothes off and examine their skin and genitals carefully. One has scabies; two others, crabs.

I wash my hands (I finally find soap), then get my phone out of my purse and call Dr. Zimmer. "Doctor's office." It's Anne Rosenbaum, I need to speak to David immediately, please. (David, who is almost seventy, was Sam's pediatrician.) While I'm holding, I start telling José and Sam what we need to get rid of: the sofa (lice infested), the giant, filthy unidentifiable wooden thing sitting in the main room, three of the four chairs (the fourth will do), and—David comes on sharply: "Anne, where are you?" I explain what I need. I can hear him uncapping a pen. "It's irregular."

I say nothing. Which he expects.

"Where do you want me to call in the prescription?"

I ask Susannah for the nearest drugstore. She remains silent. Consuelo blows up at her, most of which I again miss. We fix on a drugstore, and I give the address to David. Sam is watching me very closely. I catch his eye. He's wearing an expression I've never seen. I describe Susannah's symptoms on the phone. David stops me, asks about her diet. I ask Susannah. When she prevaricates, I have Consuelo leave the room and then question her rather sharply, translating her responses into the phone. "Oh hell," he sighs, "it's probably 90 percent malnutrition." He adds a dietary supplement for Susannah and we hang up. Consuelo leaves with Sam. Sam, you have your credit card?

"Yeah," he says. "*Tienes la lista?*" he asks Consuelo. She nods, gripping it. "*Vamanos,*" he says.

By the time they come back, José, with the children's help, has moved the sofa and chairs out and is dismembering the wooden thing with a crowbar. Consuelo and Sam have stopped at Kentucky Fried Chicken. The children fall upon the food like rats. We stand there, watching. This is the most disturbing sight so far. My lips are pursed. I tap my manicured fingernails on the tabletop.

I think about the next gubernatorial race. I mentally run through some things to talk to Howard about.

When they are sated—Susannah has been made to eat something and is feeling better—I put on latex gloves, hand pairs to Consuelo, José, and Sam, and we strip the children, the sheets, the bedding, and the towels. We put what is in decent shape in plastic bags and the rest in the trash. We put all the kids into the shower at once. The oldest, a boy, will not cooperate. Sam gets down on one knee, talks to him face-to-face. I hear a man's quiet tone of voice. Eventually the boy obeys. While I use the Kwell on them—the gloves catch their skin, but they are brave about it, and I tell them so—José drives the bedding to a laundromat. Very hot water, lots of detergent, and a strong shot of bleach. When I go into the living room, Susannah is up and has started scrubbing the floors. There is soap everywhere. She looks visibly better. The house smells of lemon and Clorox. Consuelo opens plastic packages of new sheets, towels, underwear, T-shirts and cotton shorts and plastic flip-flops. Later she will take them to Payless for shoes. José is sweeping. I start ripping down the dark, dingy curtains. Home Depot has cheap, white paper shades that will look nice.

At four o'clock I check my watch. I write a check for the back rent and the coming month and hand it to Susannah. (*Usted tiene un conto banquario?* I ask, and she nods.) I give Consuelo some more money and leave her there with instructions that she spend tomorrow here. She will look into the school situation. José is staying the night as well. Next Saturday he will bring the boy to our house, where Sam has told him there is a basketball net over the driveway. As we drive off, the children wave, including the boy. Sam waves back.

My son drives, putting us on the 10. I feel almost narcotized by the effects of the day. Sam is staring a bit glassily. Stunned.

Sam, I say. Listen: Italian words that do not exist in English: *scaramanzia, allappare (la bocca), freddoloso.* (I just love that one.) He thinks about them. I can see him focus. Almost imperceptibly, Sam smiles.

I am furious with Consuelo. I never tell her, of course; it is simply part of catharsis: why she didn't tell me till now, why she felt she had to keep it secret, the overall tragic state of the human condition, et cetera. When she arrives on Tuesday morning, she comes and finds me in the bedroom and we sit on the bed and cry together.

Howard appears at my elbow. I startle, then scrunch over a bit on the lounge. I put my lemonade down in the pebbles beside the tall grass, and after an instant of some sort of thought, he sits down next to me. "He was very impressed," he says. I find his tone ambiguous.

Did you talk to him?

He doesn't say anything for a moment. "I overheard him," he says. "On the phone."

Oh.

"He said you were, and I quote, 'totally defiant.'"

Strange word.

It is warm in the afternoon sun.

He gives a brief laugh. "This was authentic teenage 'Whoa, didn't know she had it in her.'"

Then he didn't know me, I say.

"He does now," says Howard. He thinks of something. "When her kid comes over to play basketball with Sam, Justin and I could go two-on-two."

Better not overwhelm him the first time, I say.

Howard hadn't thought about that.

He stands up to go. I say to him, You should have seen the way Sam dealt with things. He was wonderfully mature. Really fatherlike to those kids. You know, I didn't know him, either.

I say, maybe a bit too eagerly, Howard, why don't you talk about it with him?

For the past four weeks, Howard has been remarkably distant.

I've spoken loudly, so he can hear. He's walking toward the house. "Sure," he says, vaguely, back over his shoulder.

Howard is gone that night. I don't know where. When he comes back the clock reads 11:27 P.M.

I GET UP JUST BEFORE seven, brush my teeth and shower, then go to my office and sit down at the computer.

Justin has taught me how to sign in to annerosenbaum.com and how to navigate. (Never, I had said to him, our chairs scrunched together before the screen while he walked me through it as one would a child, Never in a million years. "Your password goes here," he'd continued patiently.)

I had created a Thomas Hardy thread, and Albert Brooks has become quite competitive over—"*So* predictable," Howard said to Jake Bloom—*Jude the Obscure*. Albert is adamant that Hardy is saying religion just comes from interpreting misfortune as divine intervention, but Grant Heslov is insisting that anyone with a brain could see the novel is *primarily* condemning social determinism and class structure.

I read over Albert's post. There are already eight replies on the

Hardy thread. Some nice work. I post some replies of my own. As I'm working on it, I forget the other things going on. I love this.

"ANNE FOUND A TERRIFIC SCREENPLAY," Howard announces to Stacey Sher and Joe Roth, "and I think she should produce it." It is Tuesday evening.

"Hey!" says Stacey. Joe looks his congratulations at me. We're all sitting together in a row at the back of the studio screening room.

I stare at Mr. Out-of-the-Blue. You finally read it, I say to him.

Owlishly: "I *did*," he says. "Whoever the hell this guy is."

I ran into a screenwriter, I explain to Stacey and Joe, who was running over my gardener.

"I mentioned it to Rob Greenberg," says Howard.

Howard, I'm supposed to call Mark Siegal before you do anything!

"You want *Mom* to produce it?" says Sam, slightly incredulous. He is sitting in the row just below us, his legs sprawled over the red velvet seats before him.

Oh, thanks, I say to Sam.

"Put your feet *down*, Samuel," says Howard. Then to me, "Seriously. Think about it." The screening room is filling up now, so Howard lowers his voice. "The guy's good."

"Do I know him?" asks Stacey. The writer. "Anything produced?"

No, I say, nothing.

Is he married to anyone in the industry? she asks. Maybe she knows his wife.

I say, He's gay, actually.

Sam looks up at me instantly. Howard's eyes, by contrast, seem suddenly locked on the screen.

His name is Paul McMahon. I think the boyfriend is an elementary school teacher.

"Oh, a teacher, good for him," Stacey says, "thank Christ some people are still going into teaching. How long have they been together?"

Howard says, "A teacher. To children."

His tone has changed. Joe looks over. Stacey is a bit surprised. Howard's eyes are still fixed on the screen. I'm a bit surprised myself. Down in front, the studio exec in charge of the movie is preparing to introduce the screening. Howard says to the screen, "Why do gay couples never last. It's a joke."

Stacey and Joe glance at each other.

I say, Howard. I wonder what he is processing here.

"Because," Howard says, "*il y a toujours un qui fait le con et l'autre qui s'emmerde.*"

I say: Howard . . .

Howard doesn't look at me. He repeats to them the explanation we heard from the boorish France Telecom consultant on a flight from Paris. The joke involves duplicate meanings of two different French words, both of them slang, the result a single sentence with two readings. One being "Because one of the guys is always a jerk and the other gets bored," the second, "Because one of the faggots always plays the cunt while the other gets shit all over himself."

Joe blinks. Stacey diplomatically pretends she's looking for a friend. They have heard about the incident with the DP's marketing photo. They add that to this.

I'm looking at Howard, who is still staring at the screen. Who is this man, what drives him to say such a thing? (This transformation, which I still don't understand, that seems simply to gather speed.) We hear the studio exec say, "Good evening!" He smiles a big smile at us. He's young, and this is his first major project. As everyone finds a place, Samuel, who is angry—almost as angry, we see to our surprise, as Howard—jumps up and walks four rows forward, slams himself down again, and puts his feet over an empty red velvet seat.

THEY CALL ME WITH THE proposal. Three of them, two on speakerphone at Spyglass Entertainment, Wendy Finerman conferenced in from her office. Quite enthusiastic. A private talk, they propose. It will be lovely, catered of course, perhaps six in the evening? at a beautiful home in Bel Air. (I've heard the man's name, an industrialist and his wife. They tell me he is funding a new shop headed by two former Castle Rock people.) So what did I think? they ask. They'd invite a nice, small selection of people, says Wendy—they mention a few names, some production companies, some titles.

And how about this for a topic, Anne. They'd love for me to speak about Why People Fear Art. Meaning literature, they clarify. Why do people fear books? (They are industry people, and they consider the question and its answer to cut uniquely in their favor. They assume they know what my answer will be.)

I honestly think it was the sheer solidity of the thing that made me agree and write down the date in my book. It sat there in neat black letters and looked like an anchor, something to steady me. On this date, at least I know I will be *here*.

Well, I say to them after I jot it down. I'm looking forward to it.

I felt I needed some anchors.

SAM IS SILENT THROUGH THE entire drive to the Farmer's Market. He feels vaguely angry, but I keep thinking I'm misinterpreting this. It is early on a beautiful Los Angeles Sunday spring morning, heading for 81 degrees announces 89.3 FM. For a week, since the trip to Consuelo's, he has been remarkably quiet. Howard and I have both noticed it. Howard pulls into the lot off Fairfax Avenue and asks him what he wants for breakfast, and Sam says, "Huh?" and looks around: Oh. We're here.

Howard wants apples.

They're an autumn fruit, I say, it's April.

"No, everything's everything now."

Strawberries then, I propose, a bit randomly.

Howard rolls his eyes. He decides we will start with beignets. "They're frying them over there," he says, pointing. "They smell terrific."

Yes, I say. They've added something to the oil.

"They flavor the oil?" He says to the cook, "My wife says you guys flavor the oil." The man sticks out his lower lip and shrugs.

"Do you ever wonder about me?" says Sam to us.

"You got cash, Anne?" Howard asks, digging in his pockets. "What are you talking about?" he says to Sam.

"I've never had a girlfriend," says Sam directly to his father. He looks him in the eye. The look—yes, I was right—is angry. "Like, never, OK?"

As if it will be a way into this, I say, *Please* don't say "like," Sam, it drives me to distraction.

The beignet man sugars three beignets generously, passing each in order to Howard. "Anne," says Howard, shuffling the first one, very hot, over to me.

Thank you. You've had a girlfriend.

"No, Mom," says Sam, "you read that onto some girl I was hanging out with." He's cool and remote. Sam says calmly and with almost no inflection, "That was good, at Susannah's."

Well, I say. (I wonder what, exactly, my defiance has awakened in him.)

Howard says a bit aggressively to Sam, "What are you *talking* about?"

"I'm gay," he says, to Howard, not to me, and adds, in a tone that combines nonchalance with steel, "but, you know, you probably knew that." He is looking directly at Howard, and it occurs to me that he is taking careful aim. I wonder if he overheard Howard referring to "the problem with Sam" and in the next instant realize that, well before that, much more than that, Sam actually intuited Howard's anger. The moment they closed the yeshiva's door behind him, Sam knew it would never be next year in Jerusalem. And Howard's reaction—this pulling away, this perceiving the problem to lie with Sam rather than with those who expelled him, Howard's leaving Sam before Sam can leave him, "What the fuck did he think he was doing?"—all of this has made him furious.

I think, So this is Sam saying to Howard, This is what the fuck I'm doing.

What Sam is saying does not, I realize, matter so much to him. He is, simply and directly, warning his father.

We move out of the way of the next people in line. Sam has chosen this public place to avoid a scene. Strategic. It seems so casual, but clearly it's not.

Howard, silent, is still holding Sam's beignet. Sam takes it from his father. "Thanks," he says.

I look around the market. It's as if they were filming this on a soundstage. The sunlight suddenly feels like it's being pumped onto us by a gaffer.

We walk, possibly toward the strawberries. Howard is walking ahead holding his beignet. He stops, turns. He and I regard our son. It occurs to me that Sam looks the opposite of how he looked when he walked into the house after the El Al flight—hollowed out, shell-shocked. Now Sam is defining Sam himself.

He looks remarkably calm.

IT IS MONDAY. I GET out of the car and put money in the meter. I begin to walk. I look down at my purse, to make sure I have it. I do. The afternoon sun is making me squint. At a certain point I realize I have been standing on the street corner. I look up at the blue metal rectangles: Melrose and Robertson. Now, why am I here? Certainly there is something nearby I need. I look about me with an expectant air. I have my purse. I am wearing black pumps. I have some cash and a few credit cards and a perfume and a lipstick.

No one comes. I peer at each store in turn. I do not need Thai noodles or sunglasses or CDs or coffee. For an instant I am angry. I don't need gasoline or air-conditioning. I turn around and go back to my car.

I pull up to my house. I sit in the drive for a moment, then go inside and find Denise. She watches as I down a whiskey. Then she takes the bottle from me and walks away. My face feels hot and uncomfortable. Twenty-five minutes later, she is driving me down Lankershim, and the windows are open, and I lean out and let the wind burn a bit of the alcohol out of me.

We go through the gates, showing the pass to the guards, and I get out in front of the Dwarf Building. She heads off wordlessly in my Saab to Pavilion for groceries. Jennifer is surprised when I walk in, immediately fearing she has overlooked an appointment. I smile quickly. He's not expecting me, I reassure her. Just let him know I'm here. Jennifer types a message in to him. I sit down and pick up *Variety*. A procession of deals and numbers and dollars and the names of our friends and acquaintances. My eyes move over them as over glass. He sticks his head out. We consider each other for a long moment. He says, "Twenty minutes?" OK. He watches me for a few more moments in the tasteful, taupe-colored, light-filled office, and his head disappears back inside.

Jennifer fields calls, walks back and forth to files, goes in and out. She indicates the phone next to me. I pick up.

"Anne, it's Ron Meyer."

Hello, Ron.

So! he says. How am I doing? I listen while he talks. Howard sticks his head out to make sure I am talking to Ron, whom (I instantly see now) he has just called and told to call me here. Howard disappears again. I'm fine, I reassure Ron. Ron doesn't mention Sam.

Howard drives us home. His Mercedes moves up and then

down the 101 as if on rails. We open the windows. He doesn't speak although—once—he looks over at me.

As the engine dies I open the car door, step out onto the driveway, and put my purse down on the paving stones, heated by a now-disappearing sun. I don't close the door. The safety light on the door's inside edge remains on, the handiwork of thoughtful German engineers who want you visible to cars coming from behind. Howard, standing by the car with his arms full of stuff, looks at me. He lays his briefcase on the stones, then piles on top of that his stack of folders, three scripts, a dozen faxes (in the car I saw fax numbers from Rome and Shanghai), and his pass for the lot. It all sits piled there, looking like a bonfire waiting to be lit. I want to show you something, I say. We leave the potential bonfire, the car doors open, the dashboard lit up; we want the car alert and expectant.

Maneuvering his strong fingers, I rub his fingertips over the lavender's delicate tips, swimming with bees, just inches from our faces, then hold the fingers up to his nose, and he inhales, holds the odor in his lungs. I take the fingers of his other hand and caress a pink rose with them, and we both smell his scented fingers. I crush one petal of a white rose between my thumb and index. He grips my wrist to hold the tips of my fingers a millimeter from his nostrils.

We lie on our backs on the grass.

I take his hand, which feels smooth and textured and warm like a very large pebble. After a moment he removes the hand and wipes the dirt from his fingers on the thick green grass under us. Consuelo and Denise peer out at us through the window. We lift up slightly, wave to them. They wave back to us. We return to our backs. They retreat to discuss the situation, their supine employers.

You're going to get grass stains, I observe.

"This is so peaceful," Howard says to the blue oxygen shell above us. But he sounds doubtful. After a moment he heaves himself to his feet. He clears his throat. He collects his things, tucks them under his arm, and walks inside.

He does not look at me. I sit on the grass, now by myself. It is not peaceful.

DENISE SAYS, "HE YOUR BOY?"

Yes, I say.

"He my boy, too." Her spine is stiff. She levels a gaze at me. She cannot predict my reaction, but that doesn't concern her. "Seven. Teen," she points out, punching each syllable. This includes every day of his life on earth. Seventeen years. She has been here in this kitchen every day he came home from school. I place my hand on the back of a chair. She waits. Consuelo watches us, arms folded.

"He kill someone?" No, I say. "He *gone* kill someone?" I assume not. "He using?" No. It was she who found him with a joint at age fifteen, and he mouthed off, and she smacked him in the face and gave him such a talking to that he cringed. Howard said she should have hit him harder for the mouth. Who knows what we owe her for that. "He a decent person?" Yes, I think he is.

Long pause. Tired irritation: "What you *whinin* about."

I sigh, sort of laugh. OK, I say vaguely, and Denise's face hardens. She knows it's not OK.

Consuelo does not look convinced on the merits, she juggles her personal permutation of Catholicism and its moral teaching, social norms and expectations, the problematic translation of Denise's reasoning into Spanish, and the equally problematic translation of the values of this culture she happens to live in. She watches TV like the rest of us, but she doesn't buy it all. No. Even though it's Sam. Denise is aware of this. She shoots Consuelo a warning look. They have been going back and forth. Denise thinks: *Two* damn fools.

OK, I say, and if it were Kelvin.

I've flung it at her, my voice bitter. She won't disarm it with a flip retort, though part of her would like to do that. She takes it seriously: goes through the scenario, calls up various images of

Kelvin (Consuelo and I wait), Roy's reaction, her friends' reactions, Kelvin bringing a man home, perhaps holding this man's hand in front of them, and methodically measures her responses. When she is done, she addresses me. I want, she prefaces, to stipulate that I in no way say this lightly. (She waits for me to acknowledge this.) She says in effect: Were this all I had to face, I would consider myself extremely lucky.

OK, I say and let out a breath. Consuelo glares at the cabinets. Her back is to us now as she washes dishes that are only going to go in the dishwasher. In her view, it is not natural. There's what her priest has told her, and there's what her husband says. Denise glares at Consuelo, drying a bowl that is dry, her gesture saying, The hell with the Church, and your priest, and your ignorant husband. She may break the bowl. I, for my part, am looking for nothing at all in some drawer. We are silently being together in the kitchen, pretending we're doing things.

I CALL HARVARD-WESTLAKE. THE SCHOOL always talks with a completely straight face about its "commitment to holistic counseling," which is why Howard refers to it as "the sanitarium." I've always found it a bit rich myself, but apparently they assign Sam a dean to counsel him in both academic and social matters, and when I ask, I am put right through to an affable man. This is, I suppose, a social matter, I begin, and explain. Ah, yes, says the dean, he and Sam discussed this briefly a few months ago. Sam mentioned it to his friends last year apparently. The dean's casual tone communicates everything: the boy is fine, nice weather we're having.

And, I say dryly, we're the last to know.

I can feel the dean smile. "Don't feel bad," his voice says. "This is pretty standard coming-out procedure for most of the kids. Honest."

I suppose I find this reassuring. Sam has been nicely protected by the sanitarium. I will have to mention to Howard this vindication of their astounding tuition.

At the group on Thursday I am quiet. No one mentions it, everyone has heard, and no one ascribes the least importance to it.

Jim Berkus hangs around afterward, and the rest obediently vanish. He says, "Listen, if you want me to talk to him—OK?"

And I start to say no, no, but then realize something, and it startles me. Jim means talk to Howard. I add two and two, and I realize that they think, mistakenly, that the change they've recently noticed in Howard has to do with Sam's coming-out. It doesn't, but I now see that the juxtaposition of the two is confusing. Both to them and, I'm starting to realize, to Howard.

For a moment I think about explaining the real cause of the problem to Jim. Sam's being expelled from the yeshiva. Howard's guilt. His mother having recently died, the seders I no longer attend. This question of Sam's impurity. The problem with Sam. It is when I reach the impurity issue that I think: No. Better not.

OK, I say to Jim. Thank you.

"He'll figure it out," Jim says comfortingly. I nod. It is very sweet. Even if his aim is wrong, it is very sweet. He says, "Well!" The car keys in his hand jingle.

When he's gone I wonder briefly about the implications of their having noticed the change but misunderstood its source. At the time, it doesn't seem particularly important.

HOWARD FLINGS THE HOMOSEXUAL PORNOGRAPHY on the table in front of me. It spills open. It is well read; you have to assume someone had it before Sam. Men with penises in each other's mouths, ropes of sperm.

"Under his mattress," says Howard.

Well, I say, he's not very original.

Howard points at it, once, a finger stab. "Look at it, Anne."

He turns, leaving. Wait, I say, and he stops. I am searching for what I want to say to him. From the back, his arms bulge slightly from his sides with anger, but this is merely puffery, a mask of the pain he feels. So, I think dryly, Howard is a man after all. Yes, love made him strong, but fear, it turns out, makes him weak. A man.

I know he hates speaking to me this way, he hates the anger in his voice, and he hates the panic he feels at finding it all out of his control. And I appreciate that, but I hate this, too.

He waits, caught in between for a moment, but then he disappears.

I think: Right, so that's your tactic; then you and I shall discuss this another way.

I put the pornography in the trash. I check my watch and see that I have more than enough time to find a particular Wharton passage I have in mind.

When everyone is seated, I say to them, Before we get to tonight's reading, I have something new. Edith Wharton. She wrote this in 1922. An example of heterosexual sexuality, I say. A father performs cunnilingus on his virgin daughter.

She hardly heard him, for the old swooning sweetness was creeping over her. As his hand stole higher she felt the secret bud of her body swelling, yearning, quivering hotly to burst into bloom. Ah, here was his subtle fore-finger pressing it, forcing its tight petals softly apart, and laying on their sensitive edges a circular touch so soft and yet so fiery that already lightnings of heat shot from that palpitating centre all over her surrendered body, to the tips of her fingers, and the ends of her loosened hair.

The sensation was so exquisite that she could have asked to have it indefinitely prolonged; but suddenly his head bent lower, and with a deeper thrill she felt his lips pressed upon that quivering invisible bud, and then the delicate firm thrust of his tongue, so full and yet so infinitely subtle, pressing apart the closed petals, and forcing itself in deeper and deeper through the passage that glowed and seemed to become illuminated at its approach . . .

"My little girl," he breathed . . .

I lower the page. It's heterosexual pornography, I say, to make sure they understand. Incest porn.

They add up the elements with lightning speed. By the next morning Howard, via Jennifer, has received the exact details—the Wharton text, what I said, my tone of voice, and their interpretation of what I was saying to Howard. Honestly, Howie, they said, straight, gay, what the hell's the difference. (This is what they think I'm saying.) They tell him, with complete confidence, Look, Anne's *totally* right on this one, c'mon!

They think Howard is upset about Sam's homosexuality. I myself have reluctantly concluded that it is a sincere result of his new religious beliefs.

And I am more apprehensive than I would like to admit about a question that has recently occurred to me. What will they do when they discover what this is really about? Whose side will they take? Because I have now invested my heart in them, and they are thus a second point at which I stand the chance of having it broken.

I receive no response from Howard. My little victory is hollow.

WE GO TO A PARTY at the Bel-Air Hotel.

A group of seven of us are in a corner of one of the large rooms. I know all of them except the man who puts his drink on a coaster on the piano and sits at the keyboard, preparing to play. Which sends a *frisson* through the air.

You're a top,

he sings jauntily,

You're a Roswell probing
You're a top, you're a disco strobing

Then I realize and say to Howard, It's that Broadway composer.
I've seen him on an awards show.

Howard, who is usually in the thick of these things, says nothing.
Doesn't even glance over.

You're a Chippendale, an XL male, a stud
You're a ten-inch wonder, a genetic blunder, a can of Bud

Alan Menken and his wife are grinning ear to ear, looking over
at the piano. How many times have we, all of us, heard these songs
at parties, the music. Two gay men are doing a doo-wop backup, in
tune, precise.

You're as big as the big bonanza
You're as gay as a Garland stanza
I'm a passive Greek, someone to shout, "Don't stop!"
But if, baby, I'm a bottom, you're a top!

A woman leans an arm on Howard's shoulders for support as she
laughs. Howard does not laugh. He is rooted to the spot. Someone
next to me asks, Did Marc write this for Bette?

You're a horse, you're my gonads tappin'

No, says his neighbor, a benefit review they're developing.

You're divorce just about to happen
You're the box that gives Fire Island Pines a rush
When you wear your Raymond Dragon undies you make Jeff Stryker blush

At this line, the backup singers (I think: They don't look like Sam, not in the least, they are effeminate and wriggly) almost collapse onto each other. Only they understand it. No, wait, the Luffmans have gotten the references, and they laugh, making their comprehension clear. For this, they are envied. They have the keys to this tribe. One more tribe for us to be in or out of. I see David and Ellie Trachtenberg on the other side of the room, and they are looking directly at Howard.

> *You're a top, you are Geffen's money*
> *You're a top, you are clover honey*
> *I'm a tricked and treated overheated slop*
> *Oh, but, babe, if I'm a bottom, you're a top!*

Why doesn't Howard move away from this. Why don't we just go. Should I push him? Should I lead him?

> *You're a jones, you're a magic johnson*

Someone yells something in response to this line. Laughter.

> *You're the vaulter's pole that shoots above the bar*
> *You are adipose, you're Streisand's nose, Speed Racer's car*

David leans over, says something in Ellie's ear.

> *You are whipped like an ice cream dinner*
> *You're equipped like the derby winner*
> *(spoken: "And I don't mean the jockey!")*
> *When your trou are down I've got no glottal stop*

Howard turns and walks away, including away from me. He doesn't glance in my direction. People are arriving, attracted like moths, and he pushes past them. David and Ellie fall back from the crowd to pursue him.

You are hung, you're endowed like Harvard
You're as long as from port to starboard.

I watch them as if they were other people. Three figures, all in motion, three trajectories.

I think, Move, Anne! But I'm afraid to move.

I turn and push gently past a couple. Excuse me.

I'll cry "deeper, deeper!" till you go and pop!

I find them in the bar. Howard is taking a scotch from the bartender. He has apparently just said something to David because David replies, "So now you know him." David glances at me.

I think: More mistaken aim.

We move, the four of us, in an odd group movement away from the bar. Howard's face doesn't change. He holds his glass. He doesn't drink it. As if to the far wall, he says softly: "Easy for you."

"I'm only saying," says David, "that you need to consider your position."

"So self-righteous," says Howard vaguely.

"Don't be a prick," says David.

Ellie is aghast. "What are you doing?" she hisses.

"It's *his* kid," David says to her, leaving it, turning away.

She replies, "David, it's his *kid*." A rewrite of the line. A strong rewrite—with merely a change of stress she has retained the original dialogue yet fundamentally redirected its meaning and, neatly, the entire thrust. Ellie makes a lot of money doing this.

Howard is a totemic presence. A waiter with a silver tray approaches, picks up the signals, instantly tacks toward a group pretending not to be listening to us. They lift things off the tray. Ellie glares at them.

Howard is breathing audibly through his nose.

David takes a deep breath and speaks earnestly and low. "Don't *fuck* this up with Sam, Howie. Or I'm telling you, buddy, you will regret it the rest of your miserable life."

Ellie says, "Anne." She is pleading with Howard via me. Like a minor saint improvidently called upon to route a matter to the very top, I weigh my powers of intercession here. But I don't know this stone god before me. Not his face, not his voice, not his language. And it occurs to me that I have not known Howard for some time now. Since, say, around 11:00 A.M. almost six weeks ago when Howard left the house for LAX to meet Sam's flight from Israel.

It is Sam who returned, from Howard's perspective, different. But to me it is Howard who is different now. You, Howard, but not you. Without moving a finger, I feel him arc away from me at speed, like some furious charred angel abandoning a burning earth. He is leaving me behind, and I am paralyzed and terrified and helpless to stop his going.

Ellie realizes I have not said a single word during this entire exchange. She tries to interpret me and fails. We watch Howard turn abruptly on his polished heel beneath an impeccable navy blue suit, a ship cutting the tide.

One can measure his force by the number in the room, disturbed by his wake, who turn toward him, then plot his trajectory back to the wake's point of origin. Their lookouts spot the three of us, stranded there. Gleefully, these tiny boats bob in the ripples, beginning their analyses. Information is radioed out. I calculate dissemination and retrieval times. I try to estimate where Sam is. I look at my watch, a motion these eyes note. It is almost my first physical movement other than blinking.

David and Ellie need absolution and then explanation. I am not sure I will give them these. I am not sure exactly what I will do the next moment. Do I have the keys or does he? Where did we leave the car? What does one do?

"Did he leave?" asks David. I see Bob Broder making for us fast, rescue in his eyes, but on seeing David's lips move Bob cuts his engines and floats at a distance, uncertain.

I have no idea, I say. He's never done this before.

Ellie gets an inquisitive look. "Really," she says.

Really, I say, returning the word with a bit too much force.

She follows me into the hallway, catches my shoulder, says, Howard *must* understand, he must this, he must that.

I say to Ellie: This is not what it appears. And she stops and looks at me very closely, waiting. But I falter. They are religious, she and David. Kosher, observant. They go to temple, and if she knew what Howard was becoming, I wonder whether Ellie Trachtenberg would be saying that Howard must understand, must this, must that. She might in fact be saying something very different.

He finds me standing in the northern corner of the Bel-Air's parking lot. He approaches, crosses his arms on the car's roof, and buries his face in the arms. I can't see his face, hidden against the metal sheet, though of course I can feel the agony that radiates from him. The back of his neck is slightly hairy, he needs to go to the barber. I reach out and stroke his neck.

He turns instantly and enfolds me in his arms and I feel his beard scratching my cheek and catching strands of my hair. I still can't see his face. Held in this position, I look up at the clouds lit just so by the moon. I hold on to him as tightly as I possibly can. It is my desperate hope to make him stop changing. (I call him softly, Proteus, Proteus. The name of the god. This god in the midst of his transformations, trying to escape. I was promised that, if I can keep tight hold of him, these transformations will stop. He will resume his proper form.)

The car's metal skin is cool, Howard's skin is warm in the chill.

"I need time," he says.

They had asked me a question in my garden one evening. Did I feel at home here, having left Britain? I've thought about it constantly over the years in the way all of us immigrants do. But it had never occurred to me to ask myself whether Howard felt at home. With me, I mean. Not to be defensive, but Howard never gave me reason before to think the answer might be anything but yes.

Now I see it differently. Unlike myself, Howard never changed passports. On the other hand, he had married me. I'm the one who saw home Auden's way, the place we have chosen, wherever we might be somewhere else, yet trust that we have chosen right.

But Howard always said he saw it Frost's way. Home as the place where when you go there, they have to take you in. First of all, that's slightly different.

The flower girl sloughs off her native dialect and acquires a new tongue and leaves her old world, and she may well have done it scientifically, she may indeed have believed entirely in that process, it may be thoroughly real. But what if her previous world, vengeful, comes back to reclaim her? What if one ducked briefly into the old territory for a visit, as one had for years, without thinking about it, but on the way out was stopped unexpectedly at customs, the guards with lowered guns. What if one is surprised by an inability to leave? Like Auden, who left Britain for a chaotic New York, shedding his old identity, Howard had chosen to leave Brooklyn and instead join Auden's tribe, the determinedly origin free. Marrying me had made Howard nameless. I made him nameless.

But his son had crossed a checkpoint, and they'd seen that his papers were wrong, and they were coming after the father, laying claim to him. They had his previous name on file.

And I suddenly think to myself that it is strange I've never thought of it before. Howard had changed passports after all.

THE NEXT DAY, HE LEAVES at dawn.

That evening, he sits in a lawn chair, watching the sun sinking over Catalina. I come up behind him. I say, "'I cannot heave my heart into my mouth.'" It is Cordelia's response to Lear's demand for a protestation of love. (Tell me you love me, Lear commands his daughter. Why, she replies, is this a test?)

He will know the line. He teaches it. He doesn't turn around, doesn't move. I can hear a distant helicopter. He shifts his buttocks slightly on the teak chair. "You're saying that or I am?"

For an instant I have to think about it. I assumed you were, I eventually say to the back of his head. To Sam.

He says nothing. I'm surprised at having to spell it out for him. I mean it sympathetically, Howard. (Perhaps he has misunderstood me.)

"So blond," he murmurs, "and so untender." At least he can joke. (Shakespeare's line is, "So young and so untender.") Lear with a whiskey on ice.

I reply, So blond, my lord, and true.

Suddenly his shoulders stiffen under my hands. "You think" (he pulls away from my hands, rises, turning toward me, holding the drink, and I see with a chill that his face is flushed with fury), "you think I would stop loving him." He is ashen, staring at me, a poisonous suspicion passing behind.

He raises the tumbler and slurps the liquor from it. He specifies the line he's thinking about. "'*Here I disclaim all my paternal care*,'" he says, Lear heartlessly banishing Cordelia, "'*propinquity and property of blood, and as a stranger to my heart and me hold thee from this for ever, thou my* sometime *daughter*.'"

I had somehow forgotten that these are the king's subsequent words. *Stupid*, Anne. No wonder Howard has arrived at this reading of the text. The oversight makes me extremely irritated with myself. That's not what I meant, I say.

Howard blinks. "I'm not Lear," he says. "Jesus, Anne."

I think, but do not say, that to my mind at this particular moment Sam is, on the other hand, Cordelia. Cordelia, who refuses to feign love. Who is honest about who she is and pays a price. I say nothing.

We listen to the ambient noise. The helicopter is gone. Then a soft pinging in the garage. José? Then no sounds.

I wait for a moment. I lift my chin, glance around clear-eyed. I have a block on "propinquity," I say. He walks over and with the hand that is not grasping the tumbler grasps my upper arm. At his touch, I feel the breath go out of him and out of me. He is staring down at Los Angeles, covered in the red.

"'Nearness of relationship or kinship,'" says Howard without any air. He does not come nearer, but he grips my arm tightly.

Ah, I say.

DURING OUR EARLY YEARS HERE, when he was just establishing his foothold. Howard used to call and say, "We're invited to dinner, is that OK?"

OK, I'd say. I knew he needed me there. That was part of his job. My dislike of these rituals I set aside. That was my job. I would ask: What time? And: Shall I meet you there?

I had been prepared for dining in Los Angeles by Tolstoy. When I was seventeen, I first read the dining scene near the beginning of *Anna Karenina*. It takes place in 1870s Saint Petersburg, Oblonsky and Levin on their way to the Hotel Angleterre in a sleigh. "As they entered the restaurant, Oblonsky took off his overcoat, giving orders to the Tatars in swallowtails, who clustered around him." We would wait for the two or three from the studio, or for the director, or for the producer arriving with the star. We walked among the diners toward our table, and as we passed I felt people's upward glances, like butterflies flying across your back. "Oblonsky bowed right and left to acquaintances, who as usual were delighted to see him. 'This way, please, Your excellency, this way!' said an old, specially eager white-headed Tatar, with broad hips and coattails separating over them." (I loved that.)

All those evenings in the golden food boxes on Sunset and Melrose. One of the men from the studio would have reserved the table. It was his table. I never understood what made it different from most of the other tables, but to these people it was very different.

I found it hard to get the hang of it at first. It was much more than eating. It took me time to understand this. Salad, I would say. "*Just* salad? Listen," he would explain, "it's my treat!" Yes, I would say, not showing that I was taken aback, I know. Thank you. "So, Howard. I wanna say two words to you: Negative Pickup. If the studios can do it, why not the independents?"

"I agree," Howard would say, "but what do you do about the writer?"

They would discuss the writer. "He can be fired," the woman from United Artists would say. And when they had discussed the writer, and how to fire him, we would order, and then we would discuss the director's back end.

I would sit with them as they talked. "Oblonsky said to the Tatar, 'Well then, my good fellow, let us have two—no, that's too little—three dozen oysters.'"

We in the industry feast under our palm trees on reindeer, ostrich, assorted snake and reptilia, molluscae and delicate sub-species of avians. We have regressed: The menus of tonight's Los Angeles read like nineteenth-century naturalist tracts, the seasonings like the treasures of plundered exotic cultures, powdered pearl, moondust. We are culinary Magellans. In our opium-free opium dens along Beverly and Robertson, our porcelain plates are test tubes into which they pour the reagents, sauces and spices hauled by elephant down from Thai mountains, rare plants cut by Peruvian Indians (and given a 400 percent markup by this evening's chef). We systematically sample every phylum, every genus, like evolutionary biologists, yet there are only so many species to eat. I quietly ask Howard, as that evening's waiter hands us yet another list, printed in nonpolluting soy-base inks on chlorine-free paper, when will we get to rat?

"What makes you think we haven't?" he mutters, staring at the menu.

"The Tatar darted off, his coattails flying; five minutes later he flew back with a dish of opened oysters in their pearly shells and a bottle between his fingers." Tolstoy gives you nothing of the interim, notice; the important thing is the ebbing and flowing of the Tatar.

Howard and I sit facing an immense metal tray of ice they have just placed on our table. The cool marine smell washes over me. Marvelous. The oysters are being paid for by an Englishman with a large amount of money meant to acquire "literary properties." Oh, I say lightly, scripts. The Englishman doesn't reply to me. He squeezes lemon over the bed of gleaming, silver-gray, gelatinous cells. He addresses himself to Howard: "*Right* then."

I would excuse myself sometimes and walk out into the blue evenings and sit slightly to the side and watch the movies walk in and out, the well-known faces from the screens, their expensive Italian sportscars being parked by the young valets who moved like short, athletic members of a Hispanic corps de ballet. Then I would go back in, careful to approach them from the direction of the ladies' room, and sit, and Howard would take me by the hand and draw me into the conversation. They would compliment me, "That accent, that's terrific," as if it were a great tan. But they were energetic, and over time I started to revive and blossom, and I grew used to nights and nights of these lacquered restaurants, became casual about them, came to know them, slipping into their sateen seats with familiarity, until things shifted in our favor, and my presence became my own decision.

Back then, I would think of this scene from Tolstoy not for the food or the opulence but for the connection. Things would be fine, and then abruptly the deal would hit a snag and the conversation would founder, their slick L.A. talk would fail, and you would feel the strange, sudden loss of bearings as they attempted to navigate the sea of laundered white cotton between them. Tolstoy foresaw it. "Levin sighed and was silent. And suddenly," Tolstoy writes, "Levin and Oblonsky both felt that even though they were friends, even though they had been dining together and drinking wine, which should have brought them still closer together, each of them was thinking only of himself, and neither had anything to do with the other. Oblonsky had already had this experience more than once, of the extreme estrangement instead of intimacy that takes place after a dinner, and he knew what had to be done."

"'The bill!' Oblonsky shouted, and went out into the neighboring room where he immediately met an aide-de-camp he knew and started up a conversation about some actress and the man who was keeping her. And in the conversation with the aide-de-camp, Oblonsky instantly felt relief and relaxation."

As the electronic banking network in back sucks on the credit card, the players prepare to part, the deal undone, the studio and the producer unreconciled, the director still frustrated, the star (as stars always are) unfulfilled. Despite all the food, which is already forgotten anyway. It takes an eternity for the valet to bring the Porsche back from wherever they park them, huge hidden warehouses maybe behind Fairfax Avenue packed with ludicrously expensive steel and leather. No one ever knows. No one asks.

I have known scorched partings, stumblings. Coldnesses that swam on and on with iced gills while you stood there. The sudden estrangement from them instead of intimacy, even though having dined together, even though (sometimes, sort of) friends. Neither having anything to do with the other.

I never once imagined that those estranged people would ever be Howard and me.

ON THURSDAY, HOWARD GOES TO New York. Saturday around noon he arrives back in L.A. Just after sundown the phone rings. I pick it up in my office. "Hello, is Howard Rosenbaum there?" asks a strong, pleasant male voice. I think, It must be an actor. I have just begun to say, Yes, he is, when somewhere else in the house Howard picks up fast and says, "Yeah," a bit awkwardly, as if he were winded.

The man is slightly confused. "Uh, Howard?"

"I got it," says Howard's voice. The man starts to say something peremptorily, but I hang up. Somewhere in the house, Howard very quietly but firmly closes a door.

IT WAS A SPECIAL CAREER project the school set up for the seniors. Private audiences with mothers and fathers in their suites and bungalows and clinics. Sam had chosen a law firm on Beverly Drive, a midmorning meeting. The partner (they stared at his plush office) was representing a client, an old man, a Hungarian Jew, who had been through the Holocaust, recovering his money in Switzerland. The client was, it turned out, a thoroughly nasty, petty, cruel human being, "but," said the lawyer from his large leather chair, "we can't judge him because we've never lived through having everyone we know die."

Sam sat up and said, "Some gay men—"

Four teenagers stared at him, but the lawyer was furious. "That's different," he exploded, "they brought that on themselves."

"That's what they said about the Jews," replied Sam.

It is 5:15 P.M. and already the story has been carefully repeated in precise detail by someone to Howard. Sam's little performance has had its intended pyrotechnic effect. Howard stands before me, inflamed. "To a *disease*, God help me! . . ."

I think: Well, Sam does know how to get to him.

I stand up from the kitchen table and start to leave, but he leaps, spiderlike, and is in front of me before I can blink. Grasps my wrist. Don't, I say. His face is inches from mine, and I add, Touch me. I pull away, just like in the movies. Yank the wrist sharply down and away with a snap. Lower the shoulder for extra force. His eyes are filthy green cataracts.

He strides past me, his shoulder brushing mine, and disappears down the hall. Though he has not raised his hand an inch, I feel that he just missed putting a fist through the light fixture, or the wall had he aimed at my face.

English words that do not exist in French:

Bracing (as in a sharp slap).
Don't (the imperative form).

Three hours later, and Howard stands outside in the dark, dangling his car keys. He has arrived from somewhere. Perhaps he has just been driving around. I stand opposite him in the dark driveway. We can barely see each other.

"You used to be on my side," he says to me.

I take a breath. I've never had to fight for you. So I could afford to be uniquely on your side.

He says nothing. I wait.

You used to have great confidence in expressiveness, Howard. Now you seem to have renounced it.

"Well!" he says, ignoring what I've just said, responding to the other comment, "This is a big change."

I don't think so, I say.

"Oh," he says in a voice I don't recognize, "I do. I think you're a very different person from the woman I married."

In a few minutes I watch the taillights of his car disappearing back down our drive.

I tracked down the person who had repeated the lawyer's office conversation to Howard. It wasn't difficult. A Wilshire Boulevard colleague of the lawyer's who, for reasons I could guess at, was trading in destruction. We'd met once. I called him.

"Why shouldn't Howard know what his son says," he replied blithely. "He's the boy's father."

What the hell are you trying to do, I said, my voice iced.

He hesitated. His job depended on industry contacts. Then he didn't hesitate. "Anne," he said, unimpressed. "You're losing your touch."

"I'm afraid for him," Howard yells. "What do you want for him? Aren't you afraid?" He mutters why am I so goddamned obtuse, can I not see the dangers?

And why my obsession with *talking about it*?

And then he hangs up the phone.

It isn't *Sam* who is in danger, Howard. It is you and I. This danger you perceive is not your son with a man. It is you with me. That is what you fear, and you don't realize it. (But the phone line is dead.)

Because Howard will not allow me to speak to him, I give him my answer via the directors, and then I ask him a question.

Now, we'll start this evening with Edward Lear, the nonsense poet. The first photocopied pages? On top? Yes, the screenwriters read him a few months ago. Anthony Lane described it this way, I say to them. (I find my place in Anthony's article.) "Lear was odd, eccentric. A man who seemed to love no one. His verse impenetrable as Yorkshire taffy, and why?" (I am conscious of speaking a bit fast.) "Because he felt, one of his female biographers has politely suggested, a sexual longing for a man named Franklin Lushington, with whom he toured Greece in 1849." (The directors' eyes move quickly to me, then back down to the page.)

"Lear and Lushington decorated their hats, coats, and horses with spring flowers as they went. But longing never bloomed; in Lear's mind, and in his awkward body, desires were something to be buried deep, stuffed down until they became a tangle of roots."

> *Down the slippery slopes of Myrtle,*
> *Where the early pumpkins blow,*
> *To the calm and silent sea*
> *Fled the Yonghy-Bonghy-Bò*

Would you (I asked them) wish for one you loved that he flee, like the Jumblies, to a silent, lonely sea in a sieve? (But I was not referring to Sam.)

I told them how, the previous evening, I had called Anthony in London. He had sighed. How much they have always been hated, Anne, he said, these odd people. Edward Lear, inadvertently perhaps, opens up little wormholes to that hatred: into the macabre laughter, the violence pokes its gray claws.

> *There was an Old Man of Whitehaven,*
> *Who danced a quadrille with a Raven;*
> *But they said—"It's absurd, to encourage this bird!"*
> *So they smashed that Old Man from Whitehaven.*

(Brad Silberling is rereading this carefully. It of course speaks to him.)

Look at Auden. (Next photocopy.) Auden was relentlessly self-critical, partly, no doubt, as a result of the guilt programmed into homosexuals by British society. He felt, he said, embarrassed in the presence of anyone who was not in some respect his superior. "'It may be a large cock,' he explained. 'It may be sanctity.'" Isn't this *really* why Auden was so hated by the English? (I look toward Nick

Hytner; he of all of them should know.) Among the English, the given justification, the one you could speak in public, was that he had abandoned England in her time of great need. It was in 1939 that he and Christopher Isherwood left for New York.

In my head I hear the pain in Howard's voice. I see them sitting all around the garden, on chairs and the low stone walls with their texts, completely still.

For a moment, I'm not sure what to say next. I clear my throat. I ask them: Would anyone like more lemonade?

After a moment, someone says, "I think we're fine, Anne."

A. E. Houseman, I say. From *The Invention of Love*, you all have the text, so, right, Bryan, could you read for us, please? Bryan Singer lifts the photocopy I've made. "'Your life is a terrible thing,'" he reads. "'A chronological error. The choice for people like you was not always between renunciation and folly. You should have lived in Megara when Theognis was writing and made his lover a song sung unto all posterity . . . and not *now!*—when disavowal and endurance are in honour, and a nameless luckless love has made notoriety your monument.'"

Thank you, I say when Bryan finishes.

Houseman's sister Kate Symons observed after his death, "He very much lived in water-tight compartments that were not to communicate with each other."

Listen, I say to them. E. M. Forster's only homosexual novel, *Maurice*, was not published till long after his death, his shame for the brilliant child of his hidden self ensuring that he would never see it born. Virginia Woolf's lesbianism was passionate and isolated and carefully unspoken of for years and years. Henry James wrote tortured love letters of increasing desperation and pain to Morton Fullerton, the dashing Paris correspondent for the London *Times*. "You do with me what you will," James wrote in September of 1900. "You are dazzling, my dear Fullerton; you are beautiful . . . you are tenderly magnetically *tactile*." In December 1905, chokingly: "I can't keep my hands off you." For decades James biographers took pains to explain that he was speaking metaphorically.

When we had finished, when they had gone, Howard alone would know what I was saying. I was saying that there are, in fact, all sorts of forbidden relationships.

Do you yourself want to set off, Howard, like the Jumblies, to a silent sea? Would you truly turn from love, Howard? When did disavowal become an honor to you, when did our love, yours and mine, Howard, become a notoriety? Why, Howard, do they forbid you from loving me because of who I am?

The given justification, the one you can speak in public, is abandoning the tribe in its time of great need. That's not good enough, Howard. Do you not see the guilt programmed into Jews, the poison by those hermetically self-sealed off? Do you not see all this buried deep inside you, stuffed down until it has become a tangle of roots? Do you not see this?

Later I will hear that someone debriefed Howard in his office. In detail, including what I had looked like, the quotes, how I'd spoken.

THE MOONLIGHT IS LIKE MILK when he wakes me. He says nothing (he never does), his hands moving strongly, automated with the urgency of sleep and his erection. My reaction is instant, this spike in me, though it comes from somewhere utterly different this time, I know that, but I turn toward him, naked already, I've put the jelly in myself, and he mounts me. He fills me and puts his whole weight on me, which is what I love, and we rock back and forth, the sheets slipping back and the milk from the moon spilling over us. He slips out, or pulls out, and then he comes in a bit lower, by accident, or by intention, and raising my hips with his large hands he enters me further down, and a huge sound escapes from him, very low, as he takes from me what he has never before taken. And we move.

We lie in silence. I look out the window. The moon is directly south, heading toward the Pacific, large and alien white. That's what they do, I say. And you loved it.

I don't tell him it hurt. It was worth it for Sam.

I can feel his body instantly grow cold against mine. But I don't care.

THEY ARE ARGUING OVER THE next book selection when Denise leans down. A phone message, but I don't understand. I'm distracted. Denise says more loudly, "Rabbi Stern."

Rabbi Stern? I say, and several heads turn in my direction. Just then Consuelo comes and whispers in Denise's ear. Denise grunts, irritated, marches back to the kitchen.

Consuelo is embarrassed. "The message is for *Mister* Rosenbaum," she clarifies. "Before I no unerstan."

Ah, I say. I see.

Howard calls. "I'm not going to be home this evening." He attempts to mitigate it. "Sam's never home Friday evenings anyway."

But I am home Friday evenings, I say.

"I'll be back late," he says and hangs up.

Consuelo is gone, and the house is quiet. I ask Denise, Aren't you going home? She taps a foot on the floor. She has work, she says after a moment.

Go home, I say. You don't have any work.

"Nobody there. They gone to see," and she names some team.

I look at my garden, but it says nothing to me. What if I waited till he came home, she proposes.

No, I say to the garden, very softly. Go.

I hear nothing for a moment. "Got some of that good soup in the freezer, lobster meat and all." She disappears, comes back. She has her car keys and purse. Do you know where he is?

No.

I think we both suspect this is a lie, that we do know where he is.

I take out the lobster soup and look at it. It is a chunk of congealed salmon-colored ice in a zippered freezer bag. I open the bag, dump the heavy chunk of ice into a pan, set it on a very low fire, cover.

One thinks one wants an evening alone, no husband, no son, no maids, no gardener. And then one is lost in large, airy rooms on a long, curving street, up a trembling driveway, a magic, expensive treehouse that has lost its pirates and fairies. The flowers call plaintively from their prisons in the soil. Poor, pathetic things.

Some couples have scales on which they live their lives. The scales rise and fall in increments of emotion and sensation, and the couples live in seeking balance and equilibrium, adding or subtracting bits and pieces: one kiss, two airplane tickets (surprise), three children. Howard and I are not this. It is not a scale, though it encompasses balance. It does not rise and fall, though motion is involved. When I open my eyes, under a sky that the last stars have not quite yet relinquished, those stars lacing the pale ghostly early clouds, he is next to me, and I am, at that moment, very happy. Then he opens his eyes. We examine each other, and I realize that I am alone for the first time in however many years with this man. He touches my cheek. I hold my breath. His eyes flicker. But there are the invisible radio signals that only he can hear, and he focuses his antennae on them now, I vanish before him, and he withdraws his hand. As it recedes, I feel my heart spinning. Vertigo.

I sink into softness because the soft points of light in the twilight still above call softly and pull me under. I wait far below the surface until the stars, modest to a fault, flee higher into the azure and onyx oxygen veil and disappear. When I again emerge from sleep, slit the membrane of early white-yellow light, the stars are gone, and so is he.

IT COMES, WHEN IT COMES, from an unlikely source. A director. I don't remember him, though he insists we've met. We stand in the sunny parking lot where he has approached me. He wasn't "insinuating" anything, he said (I think he meant to use another word), but he had happened to notice Howard there, sort of hanging by himself, because, well, it was Howard! Also because Howard was acting *so intense* during the service.

(I ask not a single question. People give you this sort of information in the hope of receiving information from you. They tell you a long, involved question, essentially.)

And he was simply awed. The fervent devotion. The way Howard had bowed his head over the books. The way he'd stumbled over the Hebrew, using his finger like a little kid, trying to keep up.

Ah, I say, only because he has paused to hear what I will say.

The way Howard looked around at the candles and blinked. (It is simplistic, somewhat juvenile imagery, but he is infamous for being a manic storyboarder.) Envied the guy! Seriously. Searching. Frowning at the stuff he didn't know, visibly self-conscious about it, he was bar mitzvahed, yeah?

Yes.

He chuckles. And now he didn't know a *Baruch-hu* from an amidah. Amazing, huh. Here's this guy on a Friday evening, pretty far from his house, the Beit Yisroel synagogue over in Santa Monica, they do a lot of outreach to *ba'al teshuvas* like Howard—Jews going back to observance, it's a real movement these days!—and we lived up by Mulholland, right? The one with all the French doors and the big garden, right?

Yes.

So anyway when the service is over Howard makes a beeline for the rabbi, young guy, young-*ish* for a rabbi, great speaking voice, sounds like an actor, which is very important, you know, he throws Howard this huge grin, Well done! see how easy that was, that kind of thing. Howard grabs at him like he's drowning, and Rabbi Stern pulls him up, hauls him around, they confer a bit privately, he pats his back, then sets Howard safely in a corner and starts greeting people. Except of course everyone is noticing, Hey, wait a minute, isn't that Howard Rosenbaum? Has he been here before? Someone asked, Where's Anne?

(I don't rise to it. I'm wearing my sunglasses, which gives me a tactical advantage.)

So there was that pushy woman from HBO and of course that jerk at Millennium Films and some big shot from DreamWorks, they all go over and start talking to him, welcome blah blah even though it was *clear* he wanted to be alone and just sort of take it all in. Which is why he himself hadn't gone over, although Howard was unfailingly gracious and even seemed to be a little glad for the human contact, so then he was sort of kicking himself for not going over. But whatever.

(I wait. He is talking and watching me in equal parts.)

And then Rabbi Stern says *Shabat Shalom!* to everyone and puts his arm across Howard's shoulder really warmly and they duck back to the rabbi's office and close the door. And that was that. It was a pretty beautiful thing, seeing a guy getting back to his faith, like that, you know, the— He searches for it. That return story? It's the, you know, *essence* of the thing, after the years of being lost, you can't—

He's reaching for words.

"*For this, my son, was dead,*" I say, "*and is alive again; he was lost, and now is found.*"

He looks at me, startled. *Exactly*, he says, really, really pleased.

An ancient story, I say.

And a powerful one, you gotta admit, that's really—wow, your

Talmud is *good*, you (he laughs) you've always got those references, Anne. You always know exactly—

It's New Testament, I say crisply, the parable of the prodigal son. Spoken by Jesus.

His body moves not a millimeter, and yet he recedes from me at the speed of light.

AT 9:40 A.M., THE PHONE rings. When I answer, Jennifer is very concerned. He has missed his 9:00 and his 9:30. No, I say, I don't know where he is. The 101 is more or less clear, she says, Lankershim as well, and he has not called. His mobile is off. She hesitates. "Has something happened?" She knows the answer, at this point. She is asking for more.

Well, yes, I say. Actually, something has happened. And now, apparently, something else is happening. Call me in an hour, I say and hang up. I pick the receiver up again and call Howard's brother in New York. "Oh, hi, Anne," says Stuart's secretary. He's just left for lunch. She apologizes. No, he didn't take his cell phone, but she'll have him call me.

Jennifer calls an hour later. Still nothing.

Stuart calls back. I give him an update. He seems concerned but just asks me to keep him up to date.

At 12:30, Jennifer calls again. "He's here."

Where was he?

There's a beat. "He said he was driving on the PCH, up to Malibu."

Jennifer, I say, none of this is your fault. You're not responsible for him. What he's doing is thinking.

"All right," she says, grateful and extremely uncertain.

May I speak with him?

He comes on. "I'm in the middle of something."

Clearly, I say.

Silence.

I'm joking, I say very softly.

"I'll talk to you when I get home," he says.

Sam arrives home at 5:30 P.M., walks into the kitchen, car keys jingling. He looks guarded. "Jennifer said Dad wasn't in the office this morning."

No, I say, he wasn't.

He stands there. He sets down his pack. "Are you upset with me?"

I think about upset. No, I say, the right words escape me.

He grunts, exactly like Howard grunts. He says, to the wall, "First time you ever said *that*." (Just like his father.)

Neither of us knows what to do right now.

He picks up his books and slings them over a shoulder and walks out of the kitchen.

"Sam," I say, but there is no answer from the long, clean, cool California hallway.

I open my eyes and look at the clock. It is 4:18 A.M.

I was thinking, I say to the figure moving about in the darkness of the bedroom, how prominent a role time plays in family crises.

He considers this, lying facedown in his clothes on the bed onto which he has just climbed, his shoes on the sheets spilling sand, smelling of sweat and car exhaust and Malibu sea air. "Counting minutes," he says into the bottom sheet.

Not exactly. Noticing specific times. 1:50 A.M., 2:47 A.M., 3:22 A.M. And now (I glance) 4:19 A.M. I roll onto my side toward him. Where did you go?

"Back to Malibu, the beach."

You're becoming a regular park ranger.

He mumbles something about park rangers.

How did you work the meetings out?

"Jonah'll come back," he says. "They're such assholes at Gersch, this goddamn chip on their shoulders." Something distracts him, he flickers over several distant mental islands, returns to dispose of the subject at hand. "Jennifer can extract me with delicacy from anything." He pauses to cough, continues, "She just told them I was having a mental breakdown."

Is that true? I ask. I sit up in bed. The window is wide open, and the moon vine is bright on our windowsill.

He gets up and starts shedding pieces of clothing. "What do you think?" he asks. Shoes, trousers, shirt, one sock.

So I clear my throat and say, Who has the life he wants? Wystan Auden did, you could argue.

Howard cuts in savagely, "We're not fucking talking about Auden, Anne."

I am, I say with a calm I do not at all feel, talking about Auden.

After a moment, I realize Howard is crying, his shoulders shaking beneath his stained, unbuttoned dress shirt, his chin down almost to his hairy chest, bobbing up and down with every sob, his fists clenched. I am so stunned I cannot move for a moment, but then I jump out of bed, I take him in my arms, and I am pushed back and forth.

I know, of course, what the crying is: I am now, for him, a different kind of person, and so he has lost me, and he is mourning my death. He is in shock, his system is in overdrive, trying to accept this, and the pain is acute. Howard has realized that Sam, too, is a different kind. It was inadvertent—Sam never intended (Sam who is asleep down the hall) to lead Howard to the conclusions that have brought him to standing here in the dark, covered in cold sand and half-naked and sobbing—but inadvertent hardly matters now.

I have watched Howard suffering, and here in the dark I finally, truly, see it. Somewhere inside him, this ideology rooted itself at the earliest age. Howard, despite everything he has said to me, despite all his professed universalist beliefs (despite, for example, his marrying me), has carried this infection from the start, it has slept, latent, in him, and Sam has woken it from its slumber. It is in his bloodstream now, and he is reacting. Self versus nonself. Sam has begun to understand. But unlike myself, Sam feels no sympathy, only anger. The product Howard produces—I don't mean to assign too much importance to the movies, but they have taught Sam to assume that everything he wants or is or does is his natural right, that plot works out, that characters reconcile, that he is entitled to being right *and* to a happy ending. These things are, in his naiveté, identical to him. Sam is seventeen years old, and he has not yet experienced the destruction of his beliefs. He gives no thought to the radioactive poison that ancient, dying moral systems leave behind after they and their cherished certainties are exploded over pale emotional deserts, no thought to large men, naked except for a single sock, sobbing at obscure hours before dawn. But I am older, and I have this large, crying man on my hands, and I'm glad that my son is happy and certain, but there are other dimensions to this. There is Howard. And there is me.

Howard, I say. Howard.

He takes a swipe at his nose with a forearm. He turns away from me. Somewhere inside me the first tiny flecks of true panic spark to hot red life.

Oh, Howard, I say. I'm so confused. You've left me at sea.

"It's bad," he finally says, his back mostly to me.

I retreat the tiniest bit. What do you mean, bad?

"No," he says, "I mean it's really bad."

I am holding him. He won't let me see his face. After a few minutes his back straightens. He takes in, then quickly releases, a huge breath. He turns toward me. I see that it is some other man, a man I don't know, and I pull my arms away from this man's waist.

"I've thought a lot about it," says the man. He fills his lungs, and his eyebrows descend pensively over his eyes and he turns away again and looks out over L.A. "I don't know," he says. "I really don't know." He pauses, frowns. "I can't help feeling like I did something wrong."

You mean we, I say.

He doesn't say anything for a moment, and then he says, "No, actually I mean I."

Too small for a commercial flight, the taillights of a tiny plane draw a dashed straight line across the sky.

I hear the "I." I feel something very cold start to climb. The man in front of me says, "There was something wrong before, and I see it now." He raises a hand like Caesar and says in a very loud voice, "Don't argue with me, Anne." And then we both fall still, listening to hear if we have woken the baby, the tiny baby whose room is no longer the nursery next to our bedroom, the baby who is now seventeen years old, who is snoring with his mouth open, whose armpits are hairy now and smell when he doesn't shower and who has an erection in the morning and who has probably thrown his dirty shirt and underwear on the floor.

The baby who is a half-Jew. And I the wrong half.

Howard has understood this now. He has decided that he made an error. And having made his decision, he wrestles the old suitcase, the big one we never use anymore, down from the high shelf inside the walk-in closet and, agonizedly, opens it.

Slowly, each movement the force of pure will, he opens the drawer of his dresser. Socks. Underwear. T-shirts. He scoops them out. I watch his deliberate movements. Can you at least tell me why you're doing this?

"There's something missing, Anne." (He's speaking so softly his voice is like falling ash.)

There was never anything missing before.

"There is now." (From the closet, five button-downs. He quickly puts on clean clothes.)

I think about this. From the person who was quite happy before.

(Heavily.) "Yes." (He fights back a shudder of a sob.) "Listen," he manages to say.

I'm listening.

I'm still listening, Howard.

The navy suit. The gray suit. Three ties. His face is kept together through determined concentration.

Articulate it, I whisper to him, tell me what you're thinking.

Oh, Howard! I implore, I can't bear these silent bits!

"It's not necessarily rational," he says in a very low voice. The words are halting, but pushed out with a huge force. "And to you that means it's suspect, Anne. I used to feel that way. Now I don't."

He begins to speak about having left an island long ago and wandering in the wilderness but the little island never forgot him, about longing without realizing he was longing—and my saying, How can you long without realizing it? and his digging in his heels, putting his head down like a bull, his voice rising by several decibels as if sheer willpower could win the argument.

But, Howard. Where does that leave me?

He seems not to have considered this. The response is, somehow, at once automatic and confused. "You're my wife," he says. "I'm your husband."

And I say: No.

I explain: If you are now a Jew and I am now a Gentile, you have now placed me in a fundamentally different category of human being from yours. We are divided.

And his not answering this.

He has finished packing the suitcase that lies on the foot of our bed. Wrapped some black shoes in felt. Next to it is a suit bag, and he's put the suits in it.

Who will you be staying with? I ask.

"I'll be in touch," he says.

He hefts the suit bag. Glances at the dresser to check if he's forgotten something. He prepares to walk out of our house.

Who will you be staying with? I ask.

I WAKE UP EARLY AND lie alone in wait for an idea. It has been floating in my mind, but now I snatch it out of the air and slip it on.

He answers quickly, a bit wary given the hour. "Paul McMahon?"

I say merely, Paul, but he instantly recognizes the voice. "Oh!" he says. "Hi!"

Please come over, I say. I'm sorry to tell you that no, it isn't about your screenplay. Which, I hurriedly add, is excellent, by the way. We'll talk about that. But it isn't about that. His disappointment is alloyed with a wary, intense interest. He seems instantly a bit intoxicated, which reminds me what this looks like from his perspective, a summons from the queen. It is always odd when we are made to see ourselves. A cardboard queen. Paul is talking breathlessly, young and optimistic. On second thought, I say, I'll come to your house.

"Oh, well," he says, panicking.

Don't worry. It won't be worse than my son's room.

"Right," he says unevenly, thrown by the mention of Sam. He has obviously heard either about Sam's announcement or Howard's putative reaction to it. Justin had mentioned it was a topic on Internet gossip sites.

He's the reason I want to see you, I say.

By now Paul is so at sea that he simply assents. He gives me directions. I thank him and hang up.

I go to wake Sam to tell him about his father and stop dead on seeing him in the hall, barefoot and slightly dazed with sleep, waiting for me. I realize, first, that I haven't a clue as to what to say to him and, second, Sam knows.

You felt it?

He nods briefly, uninterested in the phenomenon, as if this were entirely normal. (Well, I think, that's astonishing. But I suppose one can feel an absence.)

Sam's gaze is fixed on me. He is easy to read. I go to him, and he crosses to me and puts his arms around me, and I say in response, I'm OK, I really am. I can feel him nod against my shoulder. You?

"What time'd he leave?" he responds, ignoring my question, as I assumed he would.

This morning, around five thirty. He has his cell, of course. I hesitate, which destroys it completely but I can't stop myself from saying it. He'll call you soon, I'm sure.

Sam's face instantly goes dark. "Asshole," he says. I brush some lint off his shoulder. Look, I say to him, Samuel. He needs time. I want you to remember, I say, that you did nothing at all wrong.

He gives me a bitterly sardonic look that says he knows exactly what's going on, it's the yeshiva incident, he's perfectly aware what's in Howard's head, I should not treat him like a child. He gently pushes away my little gesture with the lint, as Howard would. I realize that he has gotten my coloring, my looks, my hair, and Howard in everything else. Don't go anywhere, I say to him as he heads back to his room, I'm bringing someone by.

Sam becomes instantly wary.

I get in the car and start the engine and think, but only for an instant, Anne, what are you doing?

At 1403 North Laurel Avenue I park under a hyperthyroidal palm. I walk up the steps, 1960s slabs of cement that someone has optimistically painted coral pink and set on metal rails, and refer to the small white paper in my hand, then to the numbers. I turn left. No, the numbers are going down. I walk the other way and hear a voice from somewhere saying, "Anne?"

Yes, I say, and then, Speak, Lord, for thy servant heareth. I laugh, leaning against the stucco wall. When I turn the corner I see him, watching me, in his socks, halfway out his open door, alarmed. I understand the alarm. Hullo! I say in my best chipper British. I am giddy. I feel dangerous.

"Come in," he says.

I consider the amount of money represented in this living room and the sum sitting in ours.

"It's a mess."

It's very nice.

A dog barks in the bedroom, once. "Oscar!" he says to the dog. Then, "You want some coffee? I just made it."

Thank you. No milk, just sugar.

He busies himself with it.

Where is your partner? I ask. Does one call him a partner?

Despite himself he is amused. "You make him sound like a cowboy."

I think about what I should say. I suppose I meant to make him sound like a husband.

"Then that's the word."

I suppress my irritation. Fair enough, I say. Paul points, and I see a photo of the two of them. In fact, I say to him, looking at the photo, I suppose this is why I'm here.

He's waiting. I'm not sure how to proceed. I clear my throat. My son, as I imagine you're aware, is just seventeen, he's in high school, and he— Again, this problem of words. He recently told my husband and me.

He absorbs this for a moment—the connection between it and my presence here—and then breaks out into such a huge grin I want to step back, as if from the sun. "You're so great!" he says. "Wow!" He says, "I don't believe it!" He nods his head. "So you want me to help you out."

I'm sorry?

"Show you the ropes."

Well, no, I say. No, no. I laugh. I want— (What do I want?) Not me. I want you to help Sam. Sam.

He looks at me. "Why?" he asks. "You don't think you need help?"

I was not expecting this. I'm fine, I say.

He considers that. Then switches to another tack. "Why me?" He's not at all thrown. He's actually amused. And interested in my response. He crosses his arms and cocks his head, waiting.

I know you, I say. I add, truthfully, You seem like a good and decent and open person.

He will counter this, calmly. "You don't know me," he observes. "We spent three hours together under really weird circumstances."

Best way to know a person.

"OK. But, like—my credentials as a homosexual." His logical suspiciousness is making me crazy. "You know Scott Rudin, Rob Marshall, people like that." He adds, "Bruce Cohen."

These are not people I would go to in this case.

"Why?"

(Why must he perseverate?) Don't you know what their lives are like? (No. He doesn't. Never mind.) In any event, they're acquaintances of my husband's.

"Your husband, Howard."

Yes. My husband, Howard. (What does *that* mean? Oh!) Oh, I'm terribly sorry he hasn't contacted you about the script, Paul, I say. He thinks it's quite good. But it—

"I'm thirty-six," he says. Which means: Let's move on. He moves on. "What does Howard think of this?" My being here.

This is my decision, I say.

"I'm not old enough to be the kid's father," says Paul.

The kid, I say, already has a father.

"And where is he, this father? Howard Rosenbaum, movie executive."

He's at the office. Where he works.

He waits a moment, to let me know he knows perfectly well he's put his finger on it. I let out an impatient breath, which has always made people tremble, but this young man is of a sudden quite calm and not afraid of me at all. He reaches out a hand—I watch it approach, frowning at it—and takes mine. "Anne," he says. "I'm sorry." I have an instant of absolute fury and panic at having my life exposed to the world in this way, and then I am simply overcome with sadness. I am alone.

I turn my head far to the side. I am squeezing my eyes shut. I try to say, I'm very sorry, too, but only half of it comes out before I have to cut it off. Paul smiles. I wipe the tears away with my hand. Afterward, we sit awkwardly at the not overly sturdy dining table. I watch my coffee. After a moment I say, So. Sam.

"So, Sam," he says.

He smiles. I take a very deep breath and feel a weight lifted. We watch the morning sunshine falling like snow on the asphalt.

Paul changes clothes twice before settling on T-shirt and jeans while I wait. "What the hell do they wear? Those stupid baggy jeans." What they wear is irrelevant, the question is what are you going to wear. "I don't want him to think I'm some geek." Well, you're not going naked.

It's a beautiful Saturday morning. As we drive up Laurel Canyon, I think about Howard, his performance at the screening and Sam's reaction. I ask Paul if he knows any gay jokes. Paul thinks about it. "What's the difference between a vagina and a bowling ball?" What? "If you absolutely have to, it is theoretically possible to eat a bowling ball."

That's good, I say.

In my living room Paul stands awkwardly. Stop it, I say.

"What?"

Just relax.

"Every time I'm with you," he observes, "I'm living some kind of crisis."

Sam enters the room as if hauled in by invisible ropes, glaring at both of us. He shakes hands with Paul, his eyes slits. Paul affects nonchalance and goes into the handshake a bit too hard, which makes Sam roll his eyes, and Paul grins at this totemic display of teenage *Weltanschauung*. He relaxes.

Sam turns to me and says in Italian, "This guy is supposed to be my fucking babysitter?"

Sam and I measure each other for a moment. My son is now four inches taller than I am and perhaps twenty pounds heavier. Without moving my eyes from Sam's I say in English, He wants to know if you're supposed to be his fucking babysitter.

Paul appraises Sam coolly. "Tell him," says Paul, in English, "that his mother did me a big favor, and now I want to do one for her."

I translate this into Italian.

"Tell him," says Paul, in English, "that he is an ungrateful little prick."

Sam flushes. I translate this, a sentence actually easier to say in Italian than it is in English.

"Tell him," says Paul, "that his mother is trying like hell, in her own way, to deal with the bomb he's exploded, but he's so self-centered and immature he's not giving any thought to its effect on her." Paul's eyes are on Sam. "He only thought about getting himself to where he wanted to be, and getting back at his father, but now she's dodging fallout, shoring herself up, dealing with a husband who's freaking out, and yet *still* she has a plan, because this is a woman who always, always has a plan, and at the moment I'm the goddamn plan. She's decided that if her son's a homosexual then by God he's going to be a squared-away homosexual. Not standing around some dark bar with a shaved head and tattoos and an ear stud, a cynical smile leaching the freshness out of his face. She's decided he's going to get to know some decent people and be at least slightly protected as he enters these strange waters, in particular now that the father has pulled out, so he doesn't drown his sorry ass leaving the dock."

Paul sighs and stretches his right arm by pulling it with his left, which makes him look quite athletic. His elbow seems to hurt. "I played tennis," he says, "too hard."

Sam is looking at Paul.

"You guys are coming out," Paul says, sincerely resentful, "and you're still babies."

Sam grins sideways. I am dumbfounded. How did Paul do this? "I'm late," mumbles Sam, "compared to some. There's this kid in, um, ninth grade."

"Shit," says Paul briskly. For a moment he views some interior film of his own life, and Sam and I imagine the years gone by and the regrets, and we wait for him. Of course, I think apprehensively. Sam, free and young and handsome, is for Paul a symbol of complex and powerful things. I suddenly wonder if I have chosen wisely.

"How old are you?" Sam asks Paul.

Paul gives Sam the summary of how he met Steve at Pink's liquor store on Sunset late at night after a disastrous date, a handsome guy who had left him on the sidewalk. He was crying in his rum and Coke, Steve sat down on the concrete, dumped the drink down the storm sewer—Paul had alcohol poisoning by this time—took him home, and put him to bed. Steve teaches seventh grade, public school, in Jefferson Park, all sorts of kids, Cambodians and Guatemalans and an Asiatic hill tribe, who the hell knew what. Little kids with straight black hair. Good kids. Paul takes out a photo and shows it to us. Sam examines the photo with interest. Steve looks surprisingly army sergeant–like for a teacher, handsomer and smaller than Paul. Dark, some Indian blood. A few gray chest hairs.

So what did Paul do?

Screenwriter. (Sam darkens.) Unproduced. (Sam brightens.)

Paul checks his watch, puts a fist on Sam's collar and starts dragging him out of the house backward like a potato sack. "We're late, we gotta pick up Steve." In my general direction he says, "We're tak-ing him to the mountains today. He'll be back by midnight. You have my cell number."

I nod, but Paul is not facing me. Sam is, and I watch his face as he recedes. They go out, and the door closes. I stand alone in the living room, looking at the front door.

The door opens again, and Sam rushes in and attacks me. Actu-ally he brusquely puts his arms around me and buries his face in my shoulder. He has to lean down. Then he bolts out the door.

FOUR DAYS LATER ON A Wednesday, the book club starts at 6:30 P.M. There's a small change, I say. Given things, they are not at all surprised.

I have supplemented their reading. I hand out a series of pages, which they accept and look at intensely as if I'd put details of How-ard's leaving in it. I have something to say, and I am not exactly sure what it will be. But when I start to speak, it comes out fluidly.

William Golding, *The Lord of the Flies*, I say to them. I want to add something.

When my father went into the army, it was, I think, a severe shock. We recall World War II as "the good war," but this is stu-pid hindsight. If you are expecting the upstanding adventures of *Chatterbox*, modern warfare disappoints. People argue that the Great War destroyed the upper classes, but for my father, Matthew Ham-mersmith, who joined up in 1939 at age twenty-five—and for Brit-ain, I personally believe—it was the Second that truly did it, because it underlined the whole goddamn, bitter thing. It killed (finally) the concept of the gentleman, it finished off the fields of Eton, which had only just begun bleeding to death in 1914, the brave school lads marooned on islands, and so on. It was the death of a moral belief, and the death of a moral belief, by gun or science or literature, is the cruelest death of all. From time immemorial people have had detailed belief systems, carefully organized in their heads, and they have all died, and it has, always, been agony. It made Kipling cry out, "What comes of all our 'ologies.'"

I do not refer to Howard.

Instead I say to them: Golding makes it clear that it is more painful for our beliefs to die than it is to die ourselves, because (I will lay this on the air, which will carry it to them, and they will carry it to Howard's ear) our lives are simply our lives, but when we retreat to a set of beliefs, no matter how stupid or crazy they may be, we turn these beliefs into the very purpose of those lives. And that is a perversion.

You could think of Auden, I said to them. I picked up the piece of paper on which I'd printed the poem from the Internet and read it out loud. From "September 1, 1939." The title itself—the date Germany invaded Poland and began the war—was more than half the poem, but then context is arguably everything.

> . . . *Accurate scholarship can*
> *Unearth the whole offence*
> *From Luther until now*
> *That has driven a culture mad,*
> *Find what occurred at Linz,*
> *What huge imago made*
> *A psychopathic god*

We would all soon plunge again, of course, into the agonies of dying belief systems—Auden writing just before this plunge, Golding just after—of certainties drowning, all under the glassy gaze of the psychopathic god, the French in the lead over that distant, tropical, suicidal Indochinese cliff, in 1954, when I was seven, and then the Americans after them, and so down into the darkness. But as

I have said the unimaginable sits, just beside us, at an infinite distance.

I put down the paper and stare at it. I take a deep breath.

MY CELL RINGS JUST AFTER eight on a Saturday morning. When I put the trowel down and answer, he says, "It's Mark Siegal, from West 85th Street Films," as if I'd never met him. Yes, Mark, of course, how are you. "Listen," he says, "Anne, the screenplay you sent me by this McMahon guy. I really *like this*."

Wonderful, I say.

"No," says Mark, "I *really* like this."

Yes, I say. I see.

West 85th wants to make this picture. (I imagine Paul's reaction, the cry of joy. I am already preparing to hold the receiver away from my ear.)

I do a rapid calculation—it's been weeks since I sent the script over (I think, You, Anne, who are supposed to be so hot)—and despite myself I start to make a slightly acid comment about this.

Smoothly, he cuts me off; he has anticipated me. Look, he's well aware that the standard practice is to call up and effuse immediately, but he'd wanted to lay the groundwork first. Ah, I say. With coolly calculated effect, he lists all the executives and producers and directors who have, during these weeks, read the script. I had no idea. None. (Casually, he communicates that this was part of his plan. He's a real impresario.) The list is impressive. I realize I have the cell pressed to my ear. Most of them, he tells me, are extremely enthusiastic about making this picture. Making it with me. We (emphatic) are going to make this picture. I will have to join the production company, he says, how's coproducer as a title (we can discuss that), pitch dates, we're thinking in two weeks, they're pitching it already to Sandy at Fortis, and to Nancy, perfect for Flower Films, and Bonnie Bruckheimer's gonna go crazy. He's sent it to a big director as well—he mentions the name casually—who is reading it, he says, "avidly." (This I take with a grain of salt.)

I shift the phone to the other hand and sink my trowel under a delphinium, squinting at the sun. I'm sorry, Mark, I missed that.

He repeats: "There is money, obviously." Oh yes. And there is art. There is *literature*, there is creativity.

I wipe my forehead with my trowel hand, sprinkling a bit of enriched dirt in my hair. The receiver asks, "Who is this guy, by the way?"

I explain Paul. "Hm," says the receiver, thinking. "Well, do you trust him?"

I smile. Yes, I say, I trust him.

"Well," says Mark, "get him onboard! There, that's your first assignment as coproducer. Terrific screenplay, going to be a terrific movie."

Oh, hey! (he has timed this idea that has just occurred to him), now here's a thought—perhaps I might want to host a book club or two at West 85th's bungalow on the Warner lot. I am about to respond when Mark says, very casually, that of course Howard will be involved.

I freeze. I register, in milliseconds, my fury, humiliation, and something I'd never thought I would feel: their particular terror; I want to make this movie, but apparently I have to deliver the one variable that is out of my reach. I now realize Howard was one of Mark's targets all along. I hear him say as blithely as can be, Hey! Come to think of it (you can almost hear his fingers snap), Howard might—well, why hadn't Mark thought of this earlier—*Howard* might want to join West 85th Street Films. Leave the studio. Mark Siegal and the husband and wife producing team of Anne and Howard Rosenbaum, after all a guy outgrows that fucking bungalow they've got Howard stuffed in, Jesus. The line statics, and I lose a bit of this. I move off my knees, put down the trowel, and sit down with my spine very straight. I think about my grandmother in her dining

room in Kensington, a tall white Edwardian ceiling, "sit up *straight*,
Anne"—so, let's see, Mark is saying, should he just *call* Howard to
propose this or maybe I wanted—

I'll do it, I say very quickly.

He seems startled to hear me speak. Oh. OK. And disappointed.
He had been angling to make that connection personally. The importance of this particular play is clear from the frustration in his voice.
I attempt to recalculate my true worth to him. He knows Howard
has left me. Perhaps he's betting it is temporary.

Mark, I say, I had better go.

"Call that screenwriter," he says, "we're on the pitch."

I call Paul. Steve answers. "Oh, hey, Anne," he says. I met him briefly
a few weeks ago. A very sweet compact drill sergeant. "You wanna
talk to Sam?" ("Sam!") he says. ("It's your mom.")

("Oh") says Sam, and there's some shuffling across a room. "Hi,
Mom." He's happy. "Cut it *out*," he says to someone. "We've gotta
go," he says to me breathlessly, "we're gonna be late. Cut it out!
Jesus." There's barking. He is talking to the dog. "Oscar!" says Sam,
and to me, "Oscar's a girl, by the way."

That's original, I say.

The phone is passed off, there is muffled loud talking.

Paul comes on. "We're going to some appalling-sounding movie
he really wants to see." He tells me its name. A movie of explosions.

"Howard could get him into a screening for free," I say. I add
hurriedly, "All of you."

Paul says, "We'll see it like normal people." He says it nicely.

Well, I owe you one, as they say, it's supposed to be horrendous.

"You do," he says. "*Sam*. Put Oscar in the bedroom."

"Well, have a good time," I say, involuntarily. I don't want to sully
Paul and his lovely dreams. But wouldn't he want to know? Is it support or cruelty to say this, given all the uncontrolled variables? I clear
my throat and add, "Incidentally, Steven Soderbergh is reading your

script." There is dead silence. I won't for the moment mention Siegal's current gambit. He should enjoy this, I think. I can hear Sam walking noisily out the front door, and I add hastily, "But you need to go, Paul, I shouldn't have brought it up now."

"Soderbergh?" says Paul.

Oh, bollocks, I say, smiling at the sound of his fresh excitement. My timing is usually impeccable.

"Ahhhhhh!" he shouts, and I laugh willingly.

"So what next?"

We wait.

"That I can do," he affirms energetically. "I'm the Olympic champ."

Yes, I say, this is Los Angeles. The best in the world at waiting wait here.

THE PHONE RINGS, AND I look at the number. It is either Ellie or David. At the last moment I flip it open. "Anne," she says. We exchange a pleasantry. Her tone is gentle but opaque. "Can you come over?"

I blink. I look down at my watch. I suppose so, I say. Yes.

As I leave the house I run the traffic in my head. I take Mulholland, then south on the 405, which oddly enough is flowing beautifully, the Sunset exit, left to San Vicente, right toward the beach. David's car is gone. I park in their drive.

Ellie and I sit in the living room, the doors thrown open to the deck and the sea breeze. They own an enviable house on Ocean Way with a view of the Pacific. Rachel is out. "Practice," Ellie explains, not specifying the sport. She has brought me a glass of water, and because she is a practical woman—which is one reason I've always liked her—she sits down directly opposite me and asks, "Do you know what a *shidduch* is?"

No.

Her finger taps her water glass. "It's a setup. An introduction of a man and a woman with an eye toward marriage. I think technically it's something done by a rabbi."

It takes me a moment. Once I've understood, I have nothing to say.

"Being married is a religious obligation," she says. "A mitzvah." At the word, she looks at me questioningly.

That one I know, I say, Howard's parents used it. I add after a second, They said Sam was a mitzvah when he was born.

She gets the point. She stands up, walks behind my chair toward another room. From somewhere behind I hear her saying, "A *ba'al teshuva*, a Jew recently returned to observance after years outside, would have many mitzvot to make up." She's looking for something. "He would be obligated to get married as soon as possible. It's supposed to cement the thing in place." I hear her pick up a piece of paper. She comes back into the room. "And have children with her. Jewish children are another mitzvah." She is administering this inoculation under the theory that the more complete and rapid it is, the less painful it will be. She and I both know it's just a theory, but it's as good as any other, and I respect that. She's going to push me through this fast, applying velocity as an anesthetic.

She hands me the paper.

Beit Yisroel Chabad on 21st Street in Santa Monica. An Orthodox synagogue, it says. Howard is to fill out the form. They've typed his name on the top at the left. I read "Shidduch Profile." A list of items followed by blank spaces. Name. Hebrew Name. Date of Birth (Month/Day/Year). Telephone: Home, Work. Height, Weight. Gender (circle one): Male Female.

Part 2. Education and Occupation. Please circle your level of secular education.

Marital Information. 5a) If divorced, please give the name and phone number of the Rabbi who facilitated the Get.

Do you have children (circle one)? Yes No.

Are you (circle one) Ashkenazi, Sephardi, Other.

Are you (circle one) Observant from Birth, Ba'al Teshuva (returned to faithfulness), Convert.

If you're a Ba'al Teshuva, how long have you been completely observant (Shabbos, Kashrus, etc.)? How long has it been since you began your Ba'al Teshuva process? (please supply details)

Do you: Go to Movies? Yes Never Sometimes

Do you participate in mixed swimming? Yes No Sometimes

Do you participate in mixed dancing? Yes No Sometimes

Do you: Eat in non-kosher restaurants? Yes Never Sometimes

Women Only: Do you wear pants? Yes Never Sometimes

Women Only: When you are married, will you cover your hair?

Men Only: Would you be comfortable with your wife wearing pants? Yes Never Sometimes

Men Only: When you are married, what are your plans for learning Torah?

Current Synagogue Affiliation. Name and Telephone Number of Rabbi.

Do you smoke? Yes No

Are you willing to date a smoker? Yes No

Men Only: Are you willing to date a woman taller than you?

Would you like the person we introduce you to be (circle all that apply): Observant from Birth, Ba'al Teshuva, Convert

Photo. (Please include a recent photo of yourself.)

References.

Someone will contact you within two weeks after receipt of this application to arrange an interview. Please return to: Young Israel of Los Angeles–Shidduch Committee.

Knesset.

I look up at the wall. Ellie hesitates. She considers coming over to me, then decides to stick to the original plan. Fast and clean. "This is

a copy for you," she says. "We have it because Howard asked David
for a reference. David, not me, since David is a man." She says this
a bit tightly. She adds, "Normally Howard would start divorce proceedings with you before getting too deeply into this. But as far as I
can tell he's not thinking with great clarity right now."

My voice is hollow. I thought, I say, at first that I was imagining it.

"Well," she says flatly. Her tone means that this doesn't surprise
her. "It's the walking time bombs that make the screenplays work,"
she says. A professional archetype.

I smile briefly. I'm imagining Ellie pitching Howard in an office
on Lankershim.

She tucks a foot precisely underneath her. "After he left home,"
she tells me, "Howard stayed with us for a few days." I look up at her
sharply. She holds my gaze, perfectly even. We are poised there. The
question is whether I will consider this a betrayal. After a moment I
nod. So that's done. She is not too proud to give me a glimpse of it:
She's relieved.

She says, "I may not have been quick on the trigger here, but he
finally opened his big mouth and told us."

About Sam and the yeshiva.

"Except that's not the way Howard tells it. He talks about a religious reawakening."

Of course.

She has to add, for the record, "It was David who was sure the
problem was Sam's being gay."

I nod. That's the way Howard has presented it, I say. Although I
don't think it was conscious on his part. I think it was more just the
timing. For a little while it gave him something to channel it through,
but that's finished.

"I felt like an idiot, of course," says Ellie. "When you'd said,
'This is not what it appears,' I thought you were—" She hunts for a
description.

Speaking metaphorically.

"Something like that." She comes to it. "Why didn't you tell me, Anne?"

I think about my answer. I say to her, You keep kosher.

It's what she suspected. "Well." And then she says, "Things change." Her eyes are hazel in the late afternoon light. She begins to tell me about conversations she and David tentatively started having a few years ago. A discussion that seemed to present itself to both of them. Rachel was dating a Mexican American boy. She and David adored him. Ellie explains their decision to no longer keep kosher. "The rabbi was very unhappy," she says, adds, with emphasis, "We also stopped going to temple."

Ellie speaks, firmly and quietly, about their increasing conscious- ness of the meticulous separation of human beings into two classes. "And then," she observes with irony, "we pretend to be surprised when they dislike us." I realize as she talks that there are relatively few people to whom she can express what she has come, over time and at a cost, to understand. She has experienced isolation, even if self-imposed, perhaps for the first time. She and David have been understandably circumspect, among their friends and inside the industry. But, Oh!, there'd been this one truly great moment. She'd been in a script meeting with Nina Jacobson and had tenta- tively, and a bit indirectly, brought it up, her evolving thoughts on the problematics of eternally dividing people. The instant Nina had gotten it, she'd simply waved a hand, cutting it off to dispose of it. "So, what?" Nina had demanded. "They're wrong and we're right?" She'd scoffed, her distaste brief and dry and definitive, and they'd returned to the script. Ellie laughs as she tells the story. She loves Nina for this.

She stretches and looks out over the ocean.

Where is he? I ask Ellie.

"I don't know who he's staying with now," she says. "He's not really speaking to us anymore." She has an afterthought. "That's why Howard left, by the way. The rabbi told him our house was unclean." She smiles to herself.

What strikes me is that as Ellie talks, I cannot tell if this change she and David have experienced, which came from a shift in their views and their perceptions, originated from her or him or both of them equally. I think that my not being able to tell this is a mark of a good marriage. They have come to this new place together. For a moment I can taste my envy.

Ellie turns her gaze from the ocean. "When I wondered, later, why you hadn't told me at the party, why you hadn't simply picked up the phone, I explained to myself that you couldn't have known how I would react. We haven't really talked in a long while." She laughs at the classic Los Angeles excuse. No time, traffic's terrible, we never see each other. It is a substitute for her real accusation, which is that I had not trusted her.

I haven't trusted anyone, I say.

We both sit back and let the golden light take over. I get up and walk through the doors to stand on the deck, and the breeze goes through my hair. She comes to stand next to me and takes my hand and squeezes. Then she moves to the edge of the deck to glare down at the neighbor's trash cans. "Son of a bitch," says Ellie.

The ocean is so pretty, I say.

She shrugs. "At least there's that."

He has come back to the house for a moment to get some clothing. He is going through some papers at his desk. It's dark.

Do you wish you'd married a Jewish woman?

He twists away from the question, like an animal looking for an exit from a trap. He has no desire to hurt me. When he replies, his voice is strangled. "Yes," he says. But he sounds unconvinced.

I lay the photocopy of the Shidduch Profile on the desk and step back. He stops moving. We stand there, next to each other, his back to me, both his hands resting on the desk, his head down. I watch his back rise and fall. "Anne," he says, and I can barely hear his voice. "I'm so sorry."

When he has gone, I look again at the Profile. At the bottom of the page is a quotation, Lamentations 5:21: "Turn us to You, O God, and we shall return; Renew our days of old."

I think of Denise's wall behind her battered screen door in Compton. The little frame holding Romans 9:25. "I will call them my people which were not my people." And then I remember the second part. "And her beloved, which was not beloved."

THE CURRENTS PICK UP EVERYTHING. The words Howard speaks, the expression he wears, are borne to my ear on the tides, reliable as clockwork, and what I say these tides bear swiftly back out to sea to other ears on other shores.

So I say to him what I would have said were we face-to-face. What would we, all of us, be to a god? I asked them that evening at my book club as we sat, gathered in my garden. How would a god see us?

(They were a little startled at my opening approach to the text—I have given them James Joyce—but game enough.)

None was more acquainted than Joyce with the Troubles. In *Ulysses*, Leopold Bloom, a Hungarian Irish Jew, sits in a Dublin pub. The talk takes a political turn. Bloom complains that the history of the world is full of persecution, which perpetuates "hatred among nations." Someone asks him, "But do you know what a nation means?" Bloom answers: "A nation is the same people living in the same place." And then adds, "Or living in different places."

OK, their faces said, waiting. The paperbacks sat, poised, on their knees.

Bloom, I said, escaped "nations" because he understood a better way of grouping ourselves.

An absolute adherence to culture, I said, is as stupid as an absolute adherence to nation. Cultures are merely what we decide they are, and thus they change constantly. As we mature, we leave things behind all the time.

In my garden, they lean forward with the copies of *Ulysses* on their knees. What are you saying? they ask me.

I am saying, I say, that the problem with a nation is that it demands that identity be taken seriously.

I am saying that a god—I use the term figuratively, I specify to them (Howard, when the tide carries this back to him, will understand me)—of goodness would never buy a Nazi ideology of racial purity and superiority of one group of people over all others. People would, yes, because these ideologies of us and of them are adaptive human nature. But human nature can be overcome, to a degree.

I am saying that as far as a god would be concerned, all of us are human. I am saying what James Joyce said: A nation is the same people living in the same place. Or else living in different places. And if we choose to be—*if we choose*—we are the same people.

They sat back. They said this was just beautiful. They nodded to each other, and they nodded to me. They did not understand, of course they never prescribe to themselves what they prescribe to everyone else. But they loved what they thought I was saying.

ONE OF THEM HAD UNDERSTOOD me. It was, perhaps not surprisingly, someone who has over the years been a guest in our home, someone in whom we took real pleasure. The man (it doesn't matter who) saw me in the lobby of a building. Immaculate suit and tie. He approached, and we exchanged a greeting.

"It's how he feels, Anne," he explained to me. "You can't condemn someone for how they feel."

Actually, I said, you can't really condemn anyone for anything else.

He assessed me. He said, in essence, This is ultimately very dangerous, what you are doing, and I would counsel you against it. Why don't you just let him go.

I registered the strength of his reaction. I replied, I cannot.

"If you continue, you will lose me as a friend." (It was putting me on notice.)

And I swallowed, although I tried not to show it, and steeled myself and replied, You are not my friend.

He was trying to work me out. He said carefully, "Anne, you and Howard and I have been friends for fourteen years."

And I said: Let me restate. You like me, and I've always liked you, very much. You and I are quite happy to see each other once every four months at a party. But you confuse friendliness with friendship. And if you would advise me to live apart from him, you don't know me at all.

I look at the fine cloth of his suit, the shoulders precisely squared.

I say, This is why your threat is empty. I could be wrong, but it seems to me that none of you can hurt me.

He considers this. "And Howard?" he asks.

He has taken me by surprise. I say, Yes?

"Losing him would hurt you."

The words escape before my mouth can close over them. More than anything, I say.

"Ah," he says, nastily, and with satisfaction.

Perversely I find that the farther I go, the more of the armor I shed. As I open myself bit by bit I feel more and more protected. How is it that as I am increasingly visible, a target making itself ever clearer, I am safer than I've ever been before. I never, ever would have imagined this.

I overhear someone saying that "shiksa" derives from the Yiddish word for blemish. I'm not certain whether they know I am within earshot.

JUSTIN IS HOLDING THE COPY of *Variety*. He hands it over warily. "Literary guru of Hollywood," they have written, "wife of Howard Rosenbaum," "exclusive book salon," "has parlayed renown into a coproducing deal with West 85th Films." "Rosenbaum brings a project to the table," "scribe Paul McMahon." All the ridiculous, campy language they use. Mark has not (as Justin knows from Jennifer) spoken with Howard, nor did he get my OK to release this.

As if he has some sort of sensor, Mark's call comes during the only hour that I am not at home. Justin takes it: Listen, says Mark, someone leaked the deal, didn't know who but whatever, forget it, done now—and it had sparked considerable interest. Ride it, just ride it.

It has its predicted effect, like heroin in the bloodstream. Todd Black calls to say that he is devastated, he'd been prepping a proposal, could we meet immediately? And Jon Liebman and Gary Levinsohn both send notes, Dan Aloni and Bob Bookman leave messages to say that, look, now I really *did* need representation. And someone from the *Hollywood Reporter*, and someone else from *Variety*.

And Paul McMahon (now known as "my" screenwriter), breathlessly saying that he's been "personally called" by Elaine Goldsmith-Thomas and, twenty minutes later, by Arnold Rifkin, and they've both sent messengers, he's just sent them treatments, OK? not scripts! not scripts, Anne! for other ideas, which are being read even as he speaks. Paul assumes (hopes?) this was OK with Mark, and where the hell am I, he's been trying to reach me all day.

JENNIFER DOESN'T CALL. SHE JUST arrives.

Sam sees her car from his window and runs out to meet her. They hug in the drive with an easy American intimacy that I will always find remarkable. She took him to Venice Beach, thus eternally establishing her cool quotient, and on the new Universal ride when he was thirteen and she twenty-two. Standing beside her car, they confer intently. I can see that she is holding a manila folder. Sam gets very heated and angry. She puts a hand on his shoulder, and he calms down. She glances at her watch, then up at the house.

"Hi, Anne." She hugs me, and we look at each other as if to check for damage.

So. Howard has made a request. Would I bring him something. A letter mailed by accident to our house.

Neither of us knows what to make of his inventing a reason to see me.

Jennifer thinks I should go, in part because she believes I need to, in part because Howard needs to see me. She takes care of him. Sam doesn't want me to see the son of a bitch, and Jennifer and I both know that he does. I already know that I'm going.

I leave them and, in Howard's office, quickly find the ostensible reason. I carry the thin white envelope back to the kitchen, where we ignore it.

Jennifer proposes the following day, 2:30 P.M. She has his agenda in her head. He suggested Canter's Deli, she says. Fairfax between Rosewood and Beverly.

Rosewood and Oakwood, I say.

As she leaves, Jennifer passes her manila folder to me. She makes no comment at all on the contents. This is fine. She is guiding me, telling me things I need to know.

There is a recent photograph from a newspaper—not the *L.A. Times*, I assume it's a local paper—of Howard sitting across from Michael Steinhardt and next to Charles Bronfman, "of the Seagram's fortune," it specifies. "A main sponsor of the $210 million 'Birthright Israel' project," reads the caption, "which attempts to deepen the commitment of American Jews." The article starts by quoting a demographer: There has been "a vigorous effort by organized Jewry to reverse recent demographic changes . . . to get large numbers of Jews to change their family-related decisions—that is, to marry young, marry each other, stay married, and have many children." Then it quotes Bronfman: "You can," he says, "live a perfectly decent life not being Jewish, but I think you're losing a lot—losing the kind of feeling you have when you know [that] throughout the world there are people who somehow or other have the same kind of DNA that you have."

I read through it. There is a statement by Mandell I. Ganchrow, president of the Orthodox Union, saying that intermarriage is sweeping young Jews "out to sea." It goes on to describe the differences in approach: The ("rather successful") Orthodox policy is segregation of Orthodox children from American society in day schools. "Play is discouraged," writes the reporter. The Conservative movement, by contrast, uses suasion; their website, says the article, promotes an anti-intermarriage book called *It All Begins with a Date*. Various websites that will send your Daily Torah Portion by email (*Parshas Metzora, Parshas Tazria, Parshas Shemini, Parshas Tzav*), an exhortation to save your family from assimilation.

I look at the photograph again. Howard's face is turned toward Bronfman as he speaks. Abe Foxman and Mortimer Zuckerman sit on the other side of the platform. There are two or three other studio people I recognize under the banner.

The following day I turn left off Crescent Heights onto Rose-wood. Residential streets. I can't remember whether Canter's has parking. Ah. It does.

We sit at the back. Although if he's trying to hide our meeting, which his rabbi would of course disapprove, I can't figure out why he would suggest this place. He has ordered a tea. And I'm very sorry if his hands begin trembling at the sight of me, and I'm sorry that he is in so much pain, but when he extends a hand across the table, I can't take it. He has needed to see me. OK. I need to say something to him.

I say to him: Take Jennifer. Your protégée. It would never occur to her that she is a different category of person. It never occurs to her, when the Jewish executive asks her out, takes her to the little restaurant he knows by the beach, gets her into bed, that he might see her as ineligible. No, that would be racist, and she's a good, liberal person. So it doesn't occur to her until she learns late some evening in her driveway, where they are fighting and she is trying with great frustration to *get* his reticence, this sudden out-of-nowhere desire of his to "cool things down." She's trying to understand through his stumbling words why he's thinking it doesn't work after all. And only when she really, really pushes him and he says that well, if she were Jewish . . . "What?" she says to him in the dark driveway. And that is how she learns about this. (She is indeed a bit naive.)

She is shocked. She is stunned, and yet still (because she considers herself "open-minded," because she recycles her glass and plastic and tries to conserve gas) she thinks, OK, wait, it's his religion, right? It's his culture, right?

(So why does it feel like bigotry?)

But no, no, she must be wrong about that.

In her bed, alone, sleepless, she thinks: Then no more Jewish men. But that makes *her* the bigot. Right? But—wait. He's not a bigot when he does it, but I am when I do?

She is sweet, but she is not quite intelligent enough and not quite brave enough to add the parts together and reach the logical conclusion. She rationalizes it until she falls asleep, tearful and newly single, near dawn.

Howard says nothing.

Say there is a woman, Howard. Say she's black. She has a degree from some ivy-covered East Coast college. She works in a steel-and-glass tower, manages twenty-three people, plays office politics (which she hates) with some dexterity, and earns a salary her parents still can't believe. She would (if forced) call herself a centrist Democrat, though on taxes she's more with the Republicans (the problem is that she worries about the environment and is adamant about choice and so she just "votes the person"). She gives to Emily's List, she bicycles on the weekends, she tries to attend gallery openings. These she goes to alone, mostly. She wonders if she'll ever meet the right man. She watches the various single men looking at the paintings and glancing at her. And from this aforementioned list of facts about her, any—any—of these choices she makes, any of the values she holds, any of the things she does, could in her opinion legitimately disqualify her in the eyes of these men.

Except one. The one she has no control over. Her having or not having the same kind of DNA that they have. If they disqualify her for that? She knows what kind of people they are.

Howard, I say, is it true you're keeping kosher now?

"Stop," he says.

He picks up his cup, noisily swallows some tea, puts the cup down a little too hard. He puts his hands in his lap in a ball.

I think about our lovely kitchen in which he no longer stands, the stove, the glassware, the sink. The counters where Denise and I have made us years of meals. All of it, to you, polluted now. Our sink is polluted. Our kitchen is unclean, and you can no longer eat there.

"Stop," he says through his teeth. Howard's need was to see me, said Jennifer. I am making sure he sees me.

If they don't accept my son, I say to him with freezing rage, they can all go to the goddamn ovens. If that means mass cultural suicide through the intermarriage that they, the racists, hate so much, then mass suicide it will be.

As I watch his competing needs violently drowning each other in the storm in his head, I feel satisfaction that comes from my own anger and an utter, complete, black emptiness. I suppose I should not feel surprise when he closes his eyes and whispers, "*Shut your hole.*" He leans forward. "*Shut your fucking hole.*"

I tell myself, This is expected. I walk toward the front door of Canter's blinded, seeing nothing, the light refracting my vision.

I SEND OUT AN EMAIL assigning my screenwriters' group a novel called *A Soldier of the Great War* by Mark Helprin because, I tell them, it contains the best description of religion I've read.

When they arrive, I see that they are looking at me differently now. There is a wariness. I grip the book and begin.

I tell them that years ago I took this passage and said to my young son: It is what all literature does, Sam, literature describes what we experience. Nothing more. You know, the first time I read it I felt delightfully light-headed, like the way you feel when you really, truly understand something Dad tells you about a poem, or when you sink the perfect shot. That's the way we feel when literature makes us gasp and say, Yes. And look here. It involves a boy, like you.

"The protesters filled the rain-slicked streets as if they were the cobblestones. Apart from what they were saying, the chanting itself brought Alessandro to a high peak of excitement, and he wanted to join them.

"'Go ahead,' his father said, not looking up from the desk. 'It can't hurt. It might even help. Let me caution you, however. You imagine that you will make a speech.'

"'No I don't.'

"'Yes you do. I can see it in you. At the Campidoglio you'll step forward and, suddenly, Cicero. But Alessandro, they won't let you, and even if they did, you would be speaking to a thousand different conceptions. Everyone has a self-made pass for travel through the terror and sadness of the world, and because, in the end, nothing is sufficient, everyone wants to share his own method, hoping for strength in numbers.'"

He read it himself (he was nine, he could do it). "They take the self-made passes," I explained to Sam, "and build their numbers, and they call them religions, Sam."

He nodded.

"They're just people clinging to each other for comfort and defense. In the end, this pass you've made disappears, and it's just you alone. You with all the rest of us."

My writers look back at me. They know I'm speaking to Howard. They are starting to figure out what I'm saying.

STUART AND I ARE SITTING at the kitchen table. His bag is on the floor, the LAX tag still on it. I haven't even shown him to his room yet. "Nah," he says politely, "no tea, nothin." It's so good to see him it hurts. I am dying to put my arms around him and hold him tightly, but I don't.

Howard's little brother. I've promised myself that I won't ask him where Howard is staying. He's going to see Howard tonight. For dinner?

"Yeah," says Stuart. He names a restaurant.

I don't know it, I say.

"Yeah," he says, "I think it's nondairy."

He is facing me as he says it, but I can't really read him.

Ah, I say.

His eyes move away. We wait. "I understand it," says Stuart quietly in response to the question I have not asked. "Even if I don't *get* it. You see what I'm saying?"

He understands it. How nice for him that he understands it. No, I do not see, not at all. Stuart's calm density has, in a single instant, enraged me. I reel from the emotion, which feels like the first hit of morphine that merely makes you nauseous without removing the pain.

I clench my jaw. Stuart, I have to know, I say to him. Are you for me or against me?

Stuart moves his head sideways the way Howard does. "I'm for Howard," he begins. He's speaking carefully. "I'm always gonna be for Howard."

But I don't let him finish. I start to cover, the way the English reflexively do with brisk movements of the hands and face meant to convey cool indifference, always pathetically transparent. And then, as if the bottom has fallen out, all the brisk movements fail me, and I jerk upward and stumble out of the kitchen through the hall, knocking over a framed photograph that cartwheels glassily and smashes in slivers on the narrow hall table, and Stuart, whom I love and who has betrayed me so that now I am truly, truly alone, has leaped up and is pursuing me, a hunter and a deer. As I flee, I am making some sound I don't recognize, of panic perhaps. The pursuit traverses the living room, I knock over a lamp and the cord rips from the wall, I turn into the hallways beyond, where Stuart finally grabs me and holds my arms against my body in a steely embrace as I kick and scream, sobbing, my arms striking him wherever and as hard as I can.

"Anne," says Stuart. "Jesus Christ, Anne," Stuart says, pressed against me, and I realize that he is laughing. He's rocking with laughter. "A fuckin' *nondairy kosher restaurant*," says Stuart. "Are you *kiddin'* me?" He's roaring with laughter. "That fuckin' nutcase!" His shoulders mound in waves with the absurdity. He staggers against the wall with hilarity, me in his arms.

I start to laugh and choke. I hold him as tightly as I can. Stuart's a bit smaller than Howard, but it's a very similar feeling.

I feel him sigh as his arms surround me, and I cling to him.

Oh my God, I say. Oh my God, Stuart, oh my God oh my God.

We sit on the sofa. Both of us in bare feet. Mine are tucked under me, Stuart's on the floor, and he looks with interest at his toes. "I've never been married," he remarks calmly. "Never get to climb into the bed with some woman I love. Every night I pull down the covers. I get into the bed. I pull the covers back up over me. I go to sleep. I wake up, and I lie there, and I think, 'OK.' I look at the walls, and I think, 'So. Here we are again.'" He shrugs. "Howard sees that," says Stuart. "He knows what love is, what he's got. But he isn't able to feel it right now. Not since he wigged out over Sam being the wrong half."

He knew it perfectly well, I say. Before Sam was conceived he knew it.

"Yeah, he knew," says Stuart patiently, "but he didn't *know* know. That asshole rabbi in Jerusalem, he kicked Howard in the fuckin' teeth. By kicking out his kid. *His kid*, 'k? Which is, they're kickin' out his love, his wife, everything Howard's got, they're throwin' it in the toilet. And these are the people our parents taught him were" (he audibly stresses the distinction) "*his*. You kidding me?" He makes a face. "And he never saw it comin'! A lifetime of conditioning hits you. You feel like you've betrayed your mother, who just died, your father—" Stuart gets a wry look. "He was due for a midlife crisis," he says with a grin. "But *this*! Wow, *How*ie."

I try to say something to him. Your mother, I begin. But I'm not sure how to finish. I see by his face I don't need to. Yeah, yeah, he knows. His mother, his mother. He sticks out a lower lip, says, "Eh." But, I burst out, but—then why don't *you* believe all this, Stuart!

Stuart's face doesn't darken. He thinks about all the things he could say and then says simply, "She's dead." He shrugs. "And even if she wasn't. She's just not that, for me. She's just not the fucking Body Israel or whatever these crazies believe. She had these absurd ideas. '*God hates bacon*.'" He puts it in audible quotation marks. "Oh, fuck, please." Dismisses it. Back to Howard. "Look. She was from that culture, they were completely programmed, she passed it on to him, and it stuck in places he didn't know about, and a couple decades later there were four good triggers, and it blew up."

Hamotzei, I say tentatively, the blessing for bread. (It's the only one I remember.)

Utterly uninterested, Stuart waves it away with a bored hand. "For our parents, that was the way of ordering the world. Now Howie says that he thinks it's that for him, too. And maybe it is, I dunno. Whatever. For me?" Stuart grins pointedly. "There's another way of ordering the world. It's simple. Listen." He's mimicking me; he's seen me murmuring my words to Sam's ears. "Assorted vocabulary." He mimes opening a book. He skims his finger down the invisible columns, stops at a word. "There it is." he says. "See under: love."

JUSTIN IS TALKING ON THE phone in my office. His back is to me as I enter. It is raining, a gray day.

Well, he asks the gatekeeper on the other end, can I meet him on Thursday? (He listens.) His flight gets in at three? (He listens.) How about Friday? (She is questioning him closely now, but he keeps his cool. I hear the tension in his voice, but she probably can't.) Yeah, he says, Anne spoke to him about me.

I am not supposed to be here. I am supposed to be out till evening. Justin has laid open my personal address book on the desk.

I move forward. He jumps, and his face drains. I glance down at the name in the book. I am impressed with his audacity. He has gone directly to the top. I hold out my hand, and he passes me the headset, which I put on. Christy, this is Anne, is Ron free Monday morning?

Christy comes alive now, I hear pages turn. Tell him, I add, that I meant to speak to him about this.

She sets up a meeting for Justin with Ron Meyer on Monday morning.

I hang up, write the number on a piece of paper, snap shut my address book, hand Justin the paper, his jacket (which is on a chair), and his cell phone (which is sitting on my desk).

Now get out, I say.

I assume Justin calculated that his window of opportunity was closing. His instincts are probably correct, as usual. That is why it unnerves me so deeply. After I hear the front door click shut, I sit down in my chair at my desk and watch the rain.

WE ARE ON AN EMPTY cement sidewalk at a bus stop on Normandie Avenue. Apparently he is living in one of the houses near here.

"'And when she had weaned him,'" Howard recites, his voice like smoke, "'she took him, with three bullocks and one ephah of flour and a bottle of wine, up to the temple in Shiloh. And she gave the child to Eli, the priest, to be raised in the temple. "As long as he liveth he shall be lent to the Lord."'"

I say nothing.

"Why were you always reading him that story from the Book of Samuel?" he asks me. It is a grim plea. He needs an explanation. He holds our divorce papers in his hand, which he has signed. He has asked me to come here because I am supposed to sign them. I have not touched them yet.

I think: I could never have imagined this, not in my wildest dreams.

Hannah was barren, Howard. And I had all those terrible fertility problems, and they had given me those horrendous drugs. And we wished so desperately for a child. That was all it meant to me.

He is sitting on the bus stop bench. I am standing. I say to him, If that insane woman wanted to surrender her child to a religious cult, that was her business. People do all sorts of things. I would never— never, Howard, never—*never*—wish for my son to find favor with anyone's fucking *god*.

I clench, unclench my jaw. I am nauseous with disgust.

"But when you were infertile," yells Howard, jumping up, coming at me, "why did we pray for him?"

I never prayed for him, I say.

Howard turns his back. "I did," he says after a moment.

I don't believe you, I reply, after I've thought about it.

His back is to me, his face buried in his hands. "Don't hold on to me, Anne," he says into his hands, his voice suffocated. "Let me change. Let me go."

I gasp. I am not sobbing, but it feels like it. "I am stronger than the monster beneath your bed," I say with all my might, "I'm smarter than this trick they are playing on your heart."

AT THE STUDIO BUNGALOW, HOWARD is walking down the hall past the door to the conference room where they are prepping a meeting. (Jennifer will mentally record all the details.) It must be his peripheral vision that spots Barry. He stops, turns into the room. Barry looks up from the page he's annotating. "Hey, Howie," he says. Jennifer is standing to Barry's left, bending over the page. She is tracking the lines of dialogue the studio wants cut, and she straightens and gives Howard a smile.

Howard looks down at Barry.

Barry, uncertain, is trying to gauge this. "What's up?" he says.

Howard's jaw is clamped shut. He looks out the window, he looks back at Barry. He walks abruptly to the broad, polished cherry table, takes a sheet of paper and writes something down, folds the paper once, twice, three times, and throws it in Barry's face. He leans in after the paper, right up close, says, "Here's her fucking number. Give her a call."

Barry edges backward into his chair. Howard is much larger than he is. Jennifer stares at Howard. Because she is very attractive, and given Barry's reaction, she intuits the backstory, the character relationships, and the plot, but not the theological subtext, not the motivation. Two associate producers arriving for the meeting are frozen in the doorway.

Howard says, "You *prick*." Barry eyes the words. Howard's shoulders sag and his eyes unfocus. "You goddamn fool," he adds to empty space.

He turns and the producers at the door press against each side of the doorway as Howard walks out between them, down the hallway, out the door, and gets into his car. They hear the engine roar and the sound vanishing.

The producers look at Barry, sitting there.

"What was *that*?" says Barry.

No one believes him.

When Jennifer will recount this to me later, both of us standing on an asphalt parking lot far enough from the studio that no one will see us (our two cars parked at odd angles, like FBI agents meeting covertly on this empty expanse), she will say, "I think I know why Howard called him that."

A fool? I will ask.

She nods.

I will say very briskly, It's that Howard sees the risk of a man like him falling in love with a woman like you. Which is to say of making the same error Howard made.

She smiles simply because she is learning this. "And," she will reply evenly, "the equal risk to the woman of falling in love back."

For some reason I think of Ellie peering down at the trash cans. "Well," I say, "at least there's that." A non sequitur feels appropriate.

"He misses you," she says. "I feel like he's suffocating from it." We hear the cars driving past on Lankershim. "He's so torn up," she says.

I steady myself on the parking lot's cement wall. How do you know he misses me? I ask her. How do you know?

She loves him, too, actually, and I suddenly see the sadness this is causing in her. "It's in every gesture he makes." She will frown. "He's had two"—(she's trying to remember the word *shidduch*, which I supply)—"two of them." A pause. "You know that the rabbi has forbidden Howard to have any more contact with you."

I assumed so.

"He took both women to the same kosher restaurant in Beverly Hills. He found the food mediocre and the conversations brutally uninteresting." (I can hear Howard saying these words.)

"He looked at the women," Jennifer says, "at their long skirts, at the wigs they wore, nodded while they talked, and thought about you."

We will each be getting back into our cars when through my windshield I will see her say, "Oh!" and she will run back to me across the parking lot. I roll down the window. "Anne, what are you reading?"

I will think: Yes, I suppose he would want to know that. I will say to her, Tell him that I've stopped reading.

THE PHONE RINGS, AND WHEN I pick it up, there's nothing but a man, breathing.

Howard, I say. I love you.

I listen to his breath, and he listens to mine. We are not allowed to talk, but we can listen, and so that is what we do. Outside the stars turn overhead.

When he puts the receiver down, it is very gentle. Like a kiss goodnight.

I BEGIN MY LONG-SCHEDULED TALK on Why Do People Fear Art (meaning literature) this way: When it happened, I say to the audience, we were on a small cruise ship in the Mediterranean, an archaeological tour run by an Israeli outfit. The incident was reported later by AP.

(I am standing in an exquisite outdoor space. The evening is a yel-

low and red liquid over the ocean, an opalescent blue inland. There
are no stars yet. A private talk to a select group at a large private
home in Bel Air. A wooden Japanese templelike structure is above
us. A small cascade of water plunges into a black swimming pool.
There is no podium. I stand before them in a simple charcoal dress. I
am relaxed. There will be an elegant reception afterward. The caterers are setting up, the wine has been plunged in ice. It is just after
6:30 in the evening, and it is a Tuesday night.)

Our ship had left Tel Aviv on the tour, sailed to Luxor, I believe it
was, and we were heading to the Sinai for two days. Then Turkey for
three. The ancient world. We were sitting in the lower dining room
on the tacky gold-colored chairs, listening to a lecture about Knos-
sos. The visitors walked in as if they were bored houseboys. They
put a shot in the ceiling. A single bullet hole. We peered up at it with
confusion. One of the Americans, Zimmerman, a Miami carpeting
mogul, demanded What did they want? and couldn't keep his voice
from shaking. The leader—he was clearly the leader—did not bother
to respond. They escorted us all to our compartments to get our
passports. Once we had them in hand, without consulting them, they
began dividing us up in a first pass.

They put the five Brits and the two Swedes and the Norwegian
family with small children in the breakfast room above. The lower
lecture room they filled with the Italian scholar and her husband, the
sole Turk, the only other family onboard—Mexican—and a hon-
eymooning Argentine-Peruvian couple. An eclectic bunch, but we
were all in it for the archaeology and were thus self-selectedly rather
serious minded. The two Germans were in the tiny disco with the
five Japanese, the Spanish couple—he a violinist, she an alto—and
the Canadian graduate students.

Americans were, at twelve, the largest single group. We sat in the
game room and did not speak.

Then they did a second pass. This time they checked the passports.

They came and took out Zimmerman and his wife, both somewhat portly and fussily dressed. From the deck breakfast room they extracted Dr. and Dr. Wolfson (from Bath, England), with whom we had discussed Greek mythology the night before. From the lower dining room they took Sr. and Sra. Carlos Steinberg, the musicians. The Japanese remained untouched and utterly mystified. They alone, one of the Canadians told me after, while conscious that there was a system of assortment, could not divine it.

They came to the Levys from Miami. "Ah," said Mr. Levy, enunciating each word since we had no idea how good their English was (they had barely spoken), and pulled on his damp collar, "you see, my wife is not . . ." The young man with the machine gun pointing at us watched him with detached, clinical interest; perhaps in Egypt or Saudi Arabia he did entomology when he wasn't doing this. "My name is Levy. But my wife's maiden name is Hanson." He attempted to point at the U.S. passport held above him, the blue cover and stamp with the State Department eagle. "Under 'maiden name,'" he explained helpfully. And when the young man with the gun remained opaque, he added, "She's from Wisconsin." I was furious. I said to him, They even have them in Wisconsin. He vaguely turned to me and looked nauseous. His wife was trembling. They sent both the Levys outside.

They took Howard's passport and my passport. Howard looked at me. I would never, not for an instant, have allowed him to separate me from him due to my last name, and after a brief moment, he nodded at me, and we turned to face them together. A tall one with a thick beard fingered through our passports, bending the pages into blue, ink-covered arcs, and then, with a little moue of the lips, motioned after the Levys. We stood. We walked out. We, all of us who had been sorted according to the system, American and Spanish and English and one Canadian (Margulies, a postdoctoral in Upper Paleolithic art), we all sat on the top deck, as instructed, in deck chairs in the sun. We watched a small plane fly up close, circle the boat once languidly, go away again. We held light-green cotton deck towels over our heads to try to block the sun. After about two hours, we began to think the visitors had gone. We didn't move. We heard nothing. Then the crew came up from below, blinking at the light, and restarted the diesel motors. I don't even know how AP got the story.

I always marveled that Levy would not enunciate that word *Jew*. I assume it was because other people could hear him. Death was staring him in the face. But he was a highly socialized creature.

We never found out what they were. I suggested IRA. Everyone looked at me blankly. Black Irish, I added. One of the Dr. Wolfsons coughed. If that's your idea of a joke . . .

Of course it was my idea of a joke.

We continued to Sinai, then Turkey. We flew home. No one noticed. Not even CNN. I saw one report, in Turkey, which said (I asked someone to translate) that the guns were fake. But there was the single bullet hole in the ceiling. Maybe it was fake.

Here, I said to them in Bel Air, is the one and only exchange my husband and I had about the event.

My husband: The fucking Arabs divided the Jews from all the other groups, from everyone else.

Yes. Precisely.

My husband: A very long pause—What does that mean?

It means precisely.

Howard: Anne—

That is precisely, exactly the division that Judaism makes.

How could you say that, he said.

Howard, I replied. Don't be ridiculous. You're an adult.

I paused at that point in my lecture. I stared up at the Japanese trellis overhead because I was formulating words, and it was tricky.

We may, I said, standing no more than a single centimeter from another person, glimpse vast sights they do not see, whole worlds hidden to them a mere movement away. What you do, I see. I see many of you spend your entire lives avidly, constantly making exactly this division, imbuing it with the deepest meaning, positing it your central tenet of what you call worship. And then I see you shocked when people you've divided from yourselves notice. Shocked when other people draw this same line. Yet you are adults.

I don't even mean, I add, the more obvious aspects of Jew-ish theology, the dietary laws and so on. The practice of the rites ostensibly for the benefit of some deity but actually meant simply to perpetuate an ancient idea of an us. And, just as importantly, a them. What is called "Judaism," both the religion and the culture, consist in their practice of this division of all human beings into these two groups. The disgust for *trefe* being of course not a disgust for shrimp but a disgust for non-Jews. What compounds this is the ludicrous idea that this division must always and only work in one direction. How convenient and good racialism is when you're doing it, when it's you keeping you a separate, integral, coherent group. How inconvenient and terrible it is when others are doing it to you. This is the live by the sword, die by the sword problem. Hypocrisy and so forth. This is what I want to discuss. This is the reason people hate literature.

The evening is now twilight, the horizon over the expanse of ocean a nuclear rim above dark water. It faces an approaching sheet of violet. Now there are a few stars. One glows through the wooden lattice above us, laced with shadowed wisteria.

I was asked, I say to them, to talk about why some people hate literature. Why some groups, regimes, systems, religions fear it.

(I pause to drink from the water glass at hand.)

The reason is obvious, of course. Literature shows us who and what we really are, whether we like it or not. This isn't an original observation. But there it is. I think the most important thing to note this evening will be something Auden wrote from New York to his father in England. Auden was conscious of his position, and he began by saying that (I've taken out my three-by-five cards, neatly arranged, and I read) "if he wants to be the mouthpiece of his age, as every writer does, it must be the last thing he thinks about. Tennyson for example *was* the Victorian mouthpiece in 'In Memoriam' when he was thinking about Hallam and his grief. When he decided to be the Victorian Bard and wrote 'Idylls of the King,' he ceased to be a poet. What an age is like," (I look up at them) Auden added pointedly, "is never what it thinks it is, which is why the best art of any period, the art which the future realizes to be the product of its time, is usually rather disliked when it appears."

Auden's identity is Namelessness. (I stress the word.) And it was hated, and it *is* hated and feared still. (I pause.) For instance, you hate it, I say to them. (A few eyes either widen or narrow, and someone shifts in a seat.) Auden rejected the traditional classifications of country, race, religion, and so on. I had always known I instinctively embraced this. Until something happened to me recently, I say to them, taking a breath, I never quite realized how deeply I am nameless, too.

Now, art—let's use a specific example. You hear or read or see something, some piece of art, and you think, "Ah, this means that." Look again, and you frequently realize it means something completely different. This may well be the artist's intention. For example:

All good people agree,
And all good people say,
That all nice people, like Us, are We
And everyone else is They:
But if you cross over the sea,
Instead of just over the way,
You may end by (think of it!) looking on We
As only a sort of They!

In my own book club it did not occur to many otherwise good, decent, educated people that this is literature adamantly opposing the idea that we should order our lives by (I glance down at a three-by-five card) "the feeling that throughout the world there are people who somehow or other have the same kind of DNA that you have."

In my opinion, I add, neither cultural pride nor theological kinship offers guidance that is morally satisfactory. And yes, I fully realize that secular spirituality's dark and dubious places are more numerous and obscure than those of religious spirituality. But I expect us to be big boys and girls and to get to work and deal with them. Not to retreat, pathetically and incoherently, like frightened children to religion's atavistic fairy tales.

When, I say, I realized to my utter astonishment that this question of who is and who is not a Jew was actually going to play a role of importance in my life, I did what I've usually done, which is lug books from the library—in this case the Los Angeles Public Library—to my garden. I wanted first to look up Hitler's Nuremberg Laws, which in Nazi Germany answered this exact question of who is a Jew. Now, who, I asked them, wrote in 1933 in Berlin, Germany (another three-by-five): "We want assimilation to be replaced by a new law: *the declaration of belonging to the German nation and the German race.*" (Italics in the original, I said.) "A State built upon the principle of the purity of nation and race can only be honoured and respected by a German who declares his belonging to his own kind. . . ."

Obviously, I said, the National Socialist era produced a volume of such quotes, from Hitler to Goebbles to Goering and so on. But this was said by Rabbi Joachim Prinz, a famous Berlin rabbi. And the actual quote was this: "We want assimilation to be replaced by a new law: *the declaration of belonging to the Jewish nation and the Jewish race.*" (Italics in the original, I said.) "A State built upon the principle of the purity of nation and race can only be honoured and respected by a Jew who declares his belonging to his own kind. . . ."

Israel, I said, is a racial security state with a hybrid democratic-theocratic government, overtly racialist citizenship laws, a particularist, exclusivist legal system of apartheid that distinguishes Jews from non-Jews in everything from immigration to public services, and a national philosophy of ethnicism. The United States is a universalist, inclusivist, constitutionally secular, antiracialist and antitheocratic multiethnic democracy, one that outlaws racialist citizenship and immigration policies, and has the most racially diverse population on earth. And the problem is that to Jews in the United States, the definition of Jewishness is the same as its definition in Israel, which is to say racial, which is to say that it is morally identical to the Nuremberg Laws of Hitler's Third Reich. The disconnect is intellectually worsened by the fact that Jewish American liberal thought (which largely defines American liberal thought, "liberal," "progressive," and "educated" being euphemisms for Jewish influence) has since 1945 been the denunciation of anything even remotely associated with Hitler and Nazi-like thinking. This ranges from the antiracist principles of the black civil-rights movement to antisexist feminism and throughout Jewish organizations like the ACLU. The irony is that there is one and only one exception to the antiracism of American Judaism: Judaism. Specifically the Jewish definition of Jewishness. Which is not only identical to the Nazi definition; much more importantly it agrees with the Nazis' basic philosophical premise that such a definition should—indeed must—exist.

(I finish that thought and clear my throat. There is nothing before me but a vast inchoate darkness. I know it is simply the brain racing to process thoughts, but it is a bit disconcerting.)

Exactly how the racialism of historically authentic Jewish thought can be logically reconciled with the antiracialism of liberal Jewish thought remains a topic little explored, but since it is relevant to me personally, as I imagine you are all quite aware, and given the literary topic tonight, I wanted to simply point something out. The Nazis believed in the moral superiority of their group, and in their racial purity. If the Nazis were wrong about the Jews, then the Jews are wrong about the rest of us.

This goes equally, I say, for other versions of the Nazi idea. Such as the Jews are not superior, God simply holds the rest of us to a lower moral standard. My husband, Howard Rosenbaum, will get that reference when he hears it, I tell them. When, I say, Christian parents oppose their child's intermarriage to a Jew, they are bigots. When Jewish parents oppose their child's intermarriage to a Christian, they are something else. (My face is flushed. I am not so relaxed now. I do a quick mental inventory of my talk. Next is Mann, yes? Yes.)

Thomas Mann, I say, had an answer to why people hate and fear art. (Three-by-five. Keep the hands still, Anne.) "Art," he said, "has a basically undependable, treacherous tendency; its joy in scandalous unreason, its tendency to beauty-creating 'barbarism,' cannot be rooted out." Actually my own answer would be just slightly different from Mann's. Art, as something that is only interesting to the degree to which it shows human beings not as we would have them be but as they are, leads us to throw over the control structures others build for their benefit. Literature shocks not because what it shows about us is inherently surprising. It does the exact opposite. It is shocking because it breaks down what we would be and shows us what we know we are. Dividers of each other into races and groups. Ethnicists. People who hate others via these concepts. And then why this is problematic. Because (this is the way I would rephrase Mann) art's treacherous tendency is to show that we all bleed, and in the long run you will not withstand art's construction of life, which is Shakespeare's construction of life, a construction that ultimately finds all human persons fundamentally human, regardless of religion or biology.

(Quick breath in and out. I register for some reason a caterer, a boy in black tie carrying a neat tray of clean wineglasses.) Obviously this is not the point this evening's organizers were counting on. Well—I should be more precise: This is exactly the point they were counting on, but they were not counting on its being applied to *them* and the immoral ways in which they organize themselves. But then that too nicely supports this evening's point.

Harold Bloom says that he would locate the key to Shakespeare's centrality in the canon in one very specific aspect of one single character, Falstaff. "It is," says Bloom, "Falstaff's capacity to overhear himself. And, thereby, the man's capacity to change. It is the most remarkable of all literary innovations."

I agree. The capacity to change is, indeed, one of the most remarkable aspects of literature, and one of the most remarkable, perennial capacities of human beings.

And, I add, if a person can change, he can also change back.

I am standing in an exquisite outdoor space. It is night. The ocean and the sky are now the same darkness. Stars above the wisteria. The little cascade of water into the black pool.

I unfold the photocopied page I made of the script I got from Howard's shelf. I clear my throat and read.

GOETH in his Nazi uniform. His eyes track
HELEN HIRSCH. She's cornered. She glances
right, left. He murmurs:

> AMON GOETH

I would like so much to reach out and
touch you in your loneliness. What would
that be like. I wonder. I mean—what
would be wrong with that?

> *(a beat)*

I realize you're not a person in the
strictest sense of the word.

> *(she doesn't respond)*

But, well . . . Maybe you're right about
that too. What's wrong isn't us. It's
this. I mean when they compare you to
vermin, rodents, lice . . .

      (she doesn't respond)

I . . . no, no, you make a good point. A
very good point.

      (he caresses her)

Is this the face of a rat? Are these the
eyes of a rat? Hath not a Jew eyes?

     (his hand moves to her breast)

I *feel* . . . for you, Helen.

He leans in to kiss her. She is frozen
with terror. And revulsion. And he sees
it. Stops.

       AMON GOETH (CON'T)
No, I don't think so. You're a Jewish
bitch. You almost talked me into it.

There are people who tell you that you are a kind of person, I say. Not a person. A kind of person. And that all other people are another kind. Who take your desire for good and your talents and your spirit and twist and twist till you instinctively say, "He is one of mine. He is not. She is one of mine. She is not." And then convince you that there is a god sick enough to want this. Or, if you've no use for the god, that there is reason to perpetuate this culture. That evil is good. That lies are truth. That a heart should close.

I stop. My vision has faded to black now. But in my sharp imagination, I'm in a large, dark vastness before a towering wall of dirty white. He sits on the other side of this tall, ice-colored wall between us where they've put him. I see the ugly thing crouched on its haunches above his head, hanging to the top of the chair, whispering into his ear. It is the only thing he can hear.

I can see him. He leans toward me, and I love him so much, I love him so infinitely much, and I struggle in desperation to move myself to him, to touch him.

But then he leans back. No. He doesn't think so. I almost talked him into it.

I realize, I say to them, that in my beloved husband's new view of things I'm no longer a person in the strictest sense of the word.

And then I begin to sob.

No one moves as I turn and run. My heels sound rapidly on the beautiful slate stones. I run as fast as my sobbing will permit, but I am shuddering and sick with it. This is the path to the drive. I will somehow find the valet, he will give me the car keys.

NO ONE calls throughout the evening.

The next morning, I explain briefly to Sam. He nods, asks a few questions. "OK," he says.

Later that afternoon when he gets home he looks shaken, rather badly. But he also looks resolute. We talk for a bit, mostly me confirming or correcting what he's heard from people or gotten via text. I find I have to explain nothing, merely fill in details and counter misinformation. I talk about Howard.

There's a silent moment as Sam considers his father. Sam has something to say about this. He says: "'Here—we—are,' said Rabbit very carefully, 'all—of—us, and then we wake up and find a Strange Animal among us.'"

I laugh. Yes, I say, indeed. I feel a thousand things lifting from me, spinning away. Such strange feelings we both have for Howard, Sam and I. An animal, I say, of whom we had never heard before.

(Sam had forgotten this. He agrees it fits.)

I say, I'm not letting go of him, Sam.

He nods. He thinks this is good. Who knows what will happen. Sam, too, is a fan of perspective. He returns to last night. "Why didn't you warn me?" He doesn't look so shaken anymore.

What makes you think I knew beforehand, I say. He knows I don't mean it on the more literal levels, but I mean it in some real way, and he accepts this as I've not experienced him before. He is more present to me and at once more distant than ever. Wonderful and sad.

So. He sits back. "Anyway, you went out with a hell of a bang."

I smile. All ruined, I sigh. Oh, dear.

"Maybe. Maybe not."

I'm sorry, Sammy. I really am sorry.

"S'all right," says Sam, and smiles. "Don't worry, Mom. Seriously."

I call Ellie. "*Christ!*" she says. And then: "Has he called?"

No.

I hear her inhale. She lets it out. Do I want to come over? David is making dinner. I say maybe tomorrow. She mentions, wryly, that their guestroom has availability. Yes, I say, I'd heard that.

I call Stuart. He has heard via two colleagues. Accurate accounts, it turns out.

He says, gently, "I haven't spoken with him."

I nod. OK.

"You couldn't've just called the guy?" and immediately, "Annie, I'm *joking.*"

Yes, well. (I smile, briefly.) There's silence on the phone for a moment. You know that he doesn't take my calls anymore, Stuart.

I can hear a horn from the street in Queens. "Listen," he says.

"Anne. You need to believe me when I tell you this. He heard you. Every word."

But you haven't spoken with him. How do you know?

"Every word," says Stuart. "Trust me."

I'M RETURNING TO MY UPSTAIRS table where I am eating by myself. An agent just leaving comes too close; a greeting is unavoidable. And then she must turn to the woman she's lunched with, must introduce me. Anne Rosenbaum. The woman's smile hardens, white paper burning in seconds to dark ash. Ah, yes, says the woman. The very diplomatic Anne Rosenbaum.

Well, I say. I think about this matter of diplomacy. I suppose, I offer forthrightly, I'm not exactly Talleyrand. (Napoleon's deft foreign minister.)

No, she says immediately, maybe Ribbentrop, though.

The faint clink of dishes. It takes me an instant to process it; Ribbentrop, yes, Hitler's chief diplomat. Two busboys scurry around us. I smile. Nice, I reply, intellectual, even slightly arcane and yet extremely vicious at the same time. Though *subtly* so. Very nice. Two points.

I DON'T CHECK EMAIL. THE faxes I glance at and throw away.

Then I decide to check email. There are a few cancellations from assistants for the book club tomorrow night. Some bitter tirades and several freezing-cold single lines. When I reach an email that consists of one word—"Nazi"—I delete the rest without looking at them and shut down the computer.

For my last book club, only two come. Both are Jewish, as it happens. One of them married an Italian Catholic and loves her deeply. The other was Orthodox and is now, as he puts it, "just a person."

The weather is overcast. We don't read. It would be a farce. We drink lemonade and talk about how to transplant flowers. The key is water, I say.

The one with the Italian wife tells us how to make plants thrive indoors.

It bothers me that the clubs would end so abruptly. It bothers me because we had several good books coming up. Well—that is, of course, an absurd lie. What bothers me is how much I will miss them. I will miss the people, their words, the warmth of their presence, the way they crowded me. The arguments and the interaction. I can't think about it, but then I know I must think about it, their going away, leaving me behind.

I tell these two that I will miss them all terribly, and that I need them. I didn't need you before, I say sternly, and we laugh. Now I do. It's a bloody awful thing, I say, I had always managed to avoid it, my entire life, I'd always very carefully managed not to need people, but there you are.

They smile. We sit together and just talk, about everything.

I OPEN THE DOOR, AND it is Justin.

"I came to pick up my things," he says. He is steeling his voice. It's a brave little effect.

I smile. I say, Come in, and I walk with him to the office. He is a young man with the Hollywood disease, but it is explained by his youth and counterbalanced maybe (maybe) by his character. When he realizes what I'm offering, he is astonished, not by the content of the offer—we both know it is not a plum position anymore—but because he never expected it. He has braced himself for an impact and is spinning from the lack of one. He convulses once, the way boys sob, his face in the tight contortion of crying, then releases it in a gasp of air. "I'm sorry," he whispers. Before he can go on, I say, It's OK. Just please don't do that again. (It has become obvious to me where it was not obvious before that some things are so ephemeral.)

We let this sink in for a moment. He looks exhausted now, but calm. He takes a deep breath. He can't possibly tell me he wants to be in my corner while I need him, so he clears his throat and just says, "Four more weeks?"

Certainly. That should be just right. I deleted a lot of emails. I perhaps shouldn't have.

He nods, he'll look at it. "Hey, Sam."

Sam is frozen midstep. "Hey!" says Sam, pleased, then, suspiciously, "You, uh—?"

"Shut up," says Justin, laughing, and wipes a wrist rapidly across an eye.

Justin has a lot of work to do. I want things closed down correctly. Michael Schnayer and Carrie Fein, my young Internet entrepreneurs, have both moved to Warners, and my website has disappeared. Justin calls Michael about it, Michael doesn't return the calls, and then he does and says that, well, you know.

"Yeah," says Justin.

When Justin recapitulates this, he tells me, "You never owned the URL, Anne." Then he explains what that means. I just nod.

I compose an email. I can't decide between "canceled" or "finished." I choose "canceled," then change it to "ended." Justin sends it to everyone.

He gives me my call list, and I make the few calls, but everyone happens to be out. This makes us both smile.

AT CLOSE TO 2:00 A.M. on West 72nd and Amsterdam, Howard sits in the booth of a Greek diner. Alex sits opposite him. The large Formica-covered interior is empty except for the cook and a waitress. The buildings around them are filled with cleaning staff and sleeping people.

Stuart sits next to Howard. "Comin' on business," Howard had announced to him the previous evening on the phone.

"So, Howie," Stuart says, "there's something Alex thought you'd find interesting."

Howard has not asked why nor how his brother would have been talking to Alex Ross, nor what they discussed. He's asked nothing at all.

Alex glances over at Stuart. Almost imperceptibly, reassuringly, Stuart nods.

"Howard, I was thinking," Alex begins. "This odd thing. Did you know that Wagner isn't played in Israel?"

Howard lifts his coffee cup. He seems to be focusing on the coffee.

"The music is considered tainted. You can't put your finger on the taint, but it's in there, in the notes, infesting the chords."

Howard is motionless. Relaxed as a cat, Stuart's head is slightly tilted, he focuses on Alex.

"And Wagner was an anti-Semite," says Alex, "no question. In 1850 he wrote of Jews: 'a swarming colony of worms in the dead body of art.' The man is clear." He adds, "But there is, of course, an irony."

Howard is listening. Not looking, but listening.

"The irony," says Alex softly, "is that the Israeli ban seems to follow the same logic as Wagner's own edicts on Jewish music." He quotes a musical scholar: "'If we dismiss Wagner's diagnosis of "Jewishness" in music as the bigoted drivel it seems to be, how do we go about ascertaining "anti-Semitism" in music?'"

Howard picks at something on his sleeve. Far away in Los Angeles, I have no idea this conversation is going on. Stuart has always been extremely discreet. With a translucent clarity Howard has, inexorably, come to a stop before the only possible conclusion: Perhaps you don't get to do both.

In the white fluorescent light, Alex seems to be contemplating something, searching for a small bit far away. Stuart wears the trace of a smile. The meaty palms of Howard's hands are pressed to his temples, his elbows on the Formica.

Alex returns, offers the small point. "When Pfitzner, the raving anti-Semitic German composer, tried to persuade Mahler the Jew that the most essential feature of Wagner's music was its 'German-ness,' Mahler responded that the greatest artists leave nationality behind," says Alex. "This, the secret of artists dropping outmoded identities, was elucidated by a Jew." After a brief moment Alex adds, rather boldly, considering the context, "A nonobservant one."

Howard takes a deep breath in. He grunts a laugh. Exhales. He gets Alex's point.

They wait for Howard's response. Two taxis flow past outside. Howard says to the black diner window, "I miss the earth so much. I miss my wife." He sits in the booth, the song's lyrics a murmur. "It's lonely out in space."

Alex puts a finger on a spoon. Turns it slightly, examining the angle. He hums the next few notes of the melody.

Stuart says nothing. He is sitting next to his brother. It is after 2:00 A.M. and Howard's eyes are bloodshot watching the taxis, flashes of yellow in the dark over the pavement.

THERE'S A MESSAGE FROM WEST 85th Street Films. Mark's first call in a week.

There are some problems with the screenplay, says the answering machine. He lists them, cursorily.

I replay the message, twice, just to experience my own uncontrolled descent. I close my eyes and listen to the violent rush of the wind against my wings of feathers and wax.

I dial Paul's number. Paul, it's Anne.

"You heard from West 85th," he says.

I'm so sorry.

He laughs, briefly. Sighs.

I say, It's not dead yet, you know.

"*Anne*," he says flatly.

I'm *so* sorry. . . .

(He's smiling, I can tell.)

But you were collateral damage, I say.

"Yeah," he says. It's a shrug.

I think about what I want to say to him. I want to take him in my arms. Or I want him to take me in his. I say: I don't deserve you, Paul.

"Yes," he says firmly, "you do."

I FIND A LETTER IN the mailbox. A single sheet of paper is inside. Written out by hand is a careful description of a man slowly drowning. It is (I look it up) from Byron's "Don Juan, Canto the Second."

> *And first one universal shriek*
> *Louder than the loud Ocean, like a crash*
> *Of echoing thunder; and then all was hushed,*
> *Save the wild wind and the remorseless dash*
> *Of waves; but at intervals there gushed,*
> *Accompanied by a convulsive splash,*
> *A solitary shriek, the bubbling cry*
> *Of some strong swimmer in his agony.*

It is Howard's handwriting.

"ANNE," HE SAYS QUICKLY, "IT'S Paul."

I think: Is this panic in his voice or laughter?

"Listen," he says. "Howard just came by." He pauses as if out of breath.

I wait for more. I realize he's waiting for me to respond. I manage, Ah.

"He sat at the breakfast counter. Chatted a little with Steve."

Yes?

"He just left." He pauses.

Sam wasn't there?

"No. I think Howard thought he was, but when I told him he wasn't, he hung around anyway. He had three cups of coffee." Paul hesitates. "I don't think he's OK."

I think he knows that, I say.

THE PHONE RINGS. SAM ANSWERS. He listens for a moment, then hangs up. He goes to the door. "Dad wants to talk to me," he says. "He's in his car down the driveway."

OK, I say. I nod.

Sam is gone a long time. I go to the window once and crane my neck, trying to see the car, but I can't.

When Sam comes back, he is different. The word that comes to mind is *soft*.

Howard sits before me. The car keys are in his hand. His mouth is closed and I can hear the breath moving in and out and in his nostrils, making a very, very tiny whistling noise. Do you remember "When You Are Old" by Yeats, I ask him. He says, "No." The breath goes in and out and in.

> *And bending down beside the glowing coals*
> *I murmur, a little sadly, how Love fled*

And paced upon the mountains overhead
And hid his face amid a crowd of stars

I've done nothing but wait, I say.

He nods briskly. "Well," he says. And then he starts to cry.

I wake up. It is night and the living room is dark. We are squeezed onto the sofa, fully clothed. Howard has both his shoes on, one of mine has fallen off. He is snoring into my left shoulder. My arm is asleep. I shift it and almost fall off the sofa. He startles awake. He stares blankly, panicked, and when his brain realizes it's me he clamps me in his arms.

HOWARD IS GOING TO REPLACE the basketball hoop next weekend, although Denise can't see the point, and I agree with her.

He has gotten phone calls. Some people are vehement, a few plead. They call from the temple, mostly, but they call from elsewhere as well. Howard puts the receiver down slowly, a calm, distant look in his eye, and the voices, still insisting electronically as they pour like birds through the wire, are cut off, leaving us in peace. Against the voices he seems armored. He seems in fact oddly burnished by the friction. He glows. But he doesn't smile. He hasn't recently. I asked why not. He thought about it and said maybe people don't smile after suffering a great fright.

Once, as he lowered the receiver, the only word I heard was " . . . *fuck*?" Here, I said, taking his hand, leading him out the French doors to the garden, look at the moon vine. The stars are out, and it's just the right time for the blossoms to open.

Sam had a few volcanic blowups with Howard. The normal detritus, I said. It will pass. Howard merely nodded; he absorbed the blows.

I told Stuart that Howard and I had escaped from nations. Our own tiny new virtual country is located in a house on a hilltop up a curving drive, the hilltop populated by some lovely palm trees and a well-tended garden, overlooking a large desert valley, high above the 101.

West 85th stopped using my name. Justin called from his new job at Endeavor to let me know. A number of them have not called or spoken to me, but it's only been a few weeks. It concerns me. "Don't worry about it," Ellie says very firmly.

I'm not.

"I know you're not," she says. "But don't anyway. It'll work out."

I don't know, I say, and we leave it there.

Ellie says I am a clairvoyant who can see the past.

Howard marvels at first how easily the system moves on, but then he just shrugs. There is a new star on the cover of *Vanity Fair* in an ivory sheath, UTA got a director an astronomical deal at TriStar, and Stacey was reported to have a falling-out with Mark Gordon over a property represented by Bruce Vinokour, and the town took sides until the three of them lunched together at a new place in Century City to quell it.

Jennifer has Howard on a 7:20 A.M. to New York next Thursday. A meeting with David on *The Afterlife* movie. Natan is trying to rearrange his schedule and may be there.

Howard told Paul that his old screenplay was "DOA for obvious reasons, but," he said, "what else you got?" Paul took a breath and made a pitch and has written sixty-seven pages, mostly in Howard's office, though a few times Howard and I have gone to Paul's house, and Steve and I made dinner while the two of them worked. They sit and argue about characterization, but on the plot they are in complete agreement, and that, says Howard, is what will count for the sale. I comment that plot is the least important part.

"Thank you for sharing," says Howard and exchanges a look with Paul.

"So, Howard," continues Paul from the sofa as if I haven't said anything, "this goddamn problem on page thirty-six."

Sam has gone. He packed and he flew away, as they do. He's cautiously excited about his roommate. He embraced us both at LAX as they called final boarding, Howard a moment longer than me. Howard's shoulders didn't heave until we were just outside the terminal, and I put a hand on the small of his back, gently but firmly, and my hand rode his shoulders as they rose and fell. Sam, who these days has to lean down a bit toward Howard when he hugs him, had whispered "I love you" into his father's neck.

Howard, I say. Listen:

English words that do not exist in French: Infatuation. Mind. Picture.

Assorted vocabulary: tabescent, coruscating, propinquity ("nearness of relationship or kinship").

A line from a Walter de la Mare poem: "Our dreams are tales told in dim Eden by Eve's nightingales, silence and sleep like fields of amaranth."

Acknowledgments

Much of this novel was written at the New York Public Library's Mid-Manhattan branch on Fifth and 40th. Thank you, and thank God for the NYPL.

Debbie and Jim Fallows, Scott Baldauf, Aileen Cheatham, Devon Burr, Stephanie Newsom, Richard Pillard, Anne Lester, Norman Carlin, Alexia Brue, Lars Yockel, Jay Marcus, Brett Thorn, and Chetan Raina read various drafts and provided crucial comments.

Jennifer Lyne and Adam Watstein gave crucial moral support. Robert Attanasio and Lee Stein were the warmest of hosts. Yorick Petri was and is a wonderful friend. Joe Tomkiewicz held the lifeline.

Two people took extraordinary roles. Michael Strong both quite literally saved my life and dedicated himself to guiding the text in the right direction. And I had the rare fortune of a thing I'd never actually conceived of, an editor who takes hands-on charge of the development of an evolving novel. It is difficult to know which is greater, the dedication that Lacy Crawford of narrativemagazine.com gave me or the perceptiveness and precision that she applied.

Eric Simonoff, super agent, superduperagent, transparent enigma, beacon of hope, voice of sanity.

Eadie Klemm, superstructure.

Shannon Ceci, production editor, who made it go.

Laurie McGee, copy editor, who sifted it all.

Beth Silfin, Ecco's dedicated, pointillist, thoroughly professional legal eye.

Allison Saltzman, genius designer.

Greg Mortimer, visionary, architect, and Matt Canale, construction manager.

Dan Halpern, publisher and lover of dark scents.

Abigail Holstein, always there, tireless, without whom? Forget it.

Most important of all, Lee Boudreaux, my editor. The velvet fist in the iron glove. Refiner's fire. True believer.

Source Notes

The anecdote concerning Samuel Goldwyn and Maurice Maeterlinck is adapted from A. Scott Berg, *Goldwyn* (New York: Knopf, 1989), p. 96.

Anne's comments on James Boswell are informed by Adam Gopnick's "Johnson's Boswell" (*The New Yorker*, November 27, 2000).

Aspects of Anne's Mamet book club and her statements on elitism are paraphrased and quoted from John Lahr's "Fortress Mamet" (*The New Yorker*, November 17, 1997) and Calvin Tomkins, "The Importance of Being Elitist" (*The New Yorker*, November 24, 1997).

Anne's visit to the Juilliard class and, later, her comments on punctuation to her book club at Orso both use ideas and quotes from John Lahr, "Speaking Across the Divide" (*The New Yorker*, January 27, 1997).

Anne's conversation with Howard about her taking U.S. citizenship and her lecture on "Why People Fear Art" adapt ideas and quote from Nicholas Jenkins, "Goodbye, 1939" (*The New Yorker*, April 1, 1996).

Anne's book club discussion of homosexual writers adapts sections and quotes from Nicholas Jenkins, "Goodbye, 1939" (*The New Yorker*, April 1, 1996) and two pieces by Anthony Lane, "Rhyme and Unreason" (*The New Yorker*, May 29, 1995) and "Lost Horizon" (*The New Yorker*, February 19 and 26, 2001).

Alex Ross's comment to Anne regarding the Salzburg Festival is a quote from Ross's "Portfolio" (*The New Yorker*, May 25, 1998).

Howard and David Remnick's discussion of Natan Sharansky is adapted and quotes from David Remnick, "The Afterlife" (*The New Yorker*, August 11, 1997). **The letter from Avital Sharansky to Howard** is, with the exception of Howard's name, a direct quote from this Remnick piece.

Howard guarding the entrance to Hollywood as described by Mark Singer quotes from Mark Singer, "Sal Stabile, for Real" (*The New Yorker*, August 11, 1997).

Both of Anne's book clubs on Edward Lear are adapted and use quotes from Anthony Lane's "Rhyme and Unreason" (*The New Yorker*, May 29, 1995).

Donald Kuspit's quotation at the Jewish Museum is from Simon Schama, "Gut Feeling" (*The New Yorker*, May 25, 1998).

The quotation about Jews being held to a higher moral standard is from Lawrence Weschler, "Mayhem and Monotheism" (*The New Yorker*, November 24, 1997).

The Ba'al Teshuva text is from: https://www.hineni.org/inspirations_view.asp?id=17&category=15&CatName=Jewish%20Issues.

Alex Ross's discussion of anti-Semitic classical composers is adapted and quotes from three pieces by Ross: "The Devil's Disciple" (*The New Yorker*, July 21, 1997); "The Unforgiven" (*The New Yorker*, August 10, 1998); and "The Last Emperor" (*The New Yorker*, December 20, 1999).

Nancy Franklin's comments about Arthur Miller's *Death of a Salesman* are adapted from Nancy Franklin, "The Cost of Success" (*The New Yorker*, June 2, 1997).

Discussion of Bibi Netanyahu and Israel is adapted and quotes from David Remnick, "The Outsider" (*The New Yorker*, May 25, 1998).

The Shidduch profile is from http://www.yibrookline.org/shidduch_profile.html.

About the Author

About the Book

Insights,
Interviews
& More...

Read On

Meet Chandler Burr

© MICHAEL STRONG

CHANDLER BURR is the *New York Times* scent critic and author of *The Perfect Scent, The Emperor of Scent,* and *A Separate Creation.* He has written for the *Atlantic* and the *New Yorker.* He lives in New York City. ❧

Q and A with the Author

This Q&A was adapted from interviews with the author by Clara Castelar (bibliolust.wordpress.com) and Marie Cloutier (bostonbibliophile.com).

You or Someone Like You *has been described as "the controversial novel of 2009." Is this what you meant it to be?*

I know some writers design novels to be controversial. What happens to Anne Rosenbaum—her husband's leaving her to become religiously Jewish—leads inexorably to the conclusion that being observant (Jewish or, I should emphasize, being any other organized religion) is morally unacceptable. That's automatically controversial. Anne believes that no perceptive reader of literature can come to any conclusion other than that all human beings are equal in the eyes of a deity, if there is one—personally, I don't believe there is—and that literature correctly read shows that calling yourself a Jew, Muslim, Christian, or Hindu is irreconcilable with being good and moral. Say that to almost anyone, and you'll generate controversy.

What inspired you to pen a novel on the topic of religion, instead of, say, an essay or a nonfiction journalism piece? Was there something you thought you could say better through fictional characters, truths you felt could better be expressed through fiction? ▶

Q and A with the Author *(continued)*

It's interesting. I've been asked this numerous times, and it seems quite clear to me by now that when people ask this particular question, they're interested in the intellectual problems the novel raises. The people who don't ask this question talk to me exclusively about the characters, their feelings about them, the shadings of emotion and meaning of the experiences the characters live—the ideas are merely a component inside the greater fictional work. I just got an email from a woman— Jewish—who wrote, "I love Anne! I KNOW her! It amazed me how well I know her." She mentioned, sort of in passing, that she agreed with me that one cannot simultaneously claim to believe in Judaism and claim to oppose racialism, tribalism, and separatism (she added, "And I consider myself extremely Jewish!"). But fundamentally she talked about the characters. She's an example of a reader who responded to the story. And that's my answer: to me there was never a question but that I'd write this as fiction. You can write nonfiction, and it's fine for laying out your truths in one way. But fiction communicates those truths in an utterly different way. Infinitely more complexity, subtlety. It always felt, and feels, so obvious to me that these particular truths can be much better expressed through fiction for a simple reason: they are so deeply, irrationally, viscerally, utterly human.

You must be aware of how sensitive the topic is that you've chosen. What made you decide to go at it as aggressively as you have?

Incoherence and hypocrisy and superficial thinking and the corruption they create are exceedingly dangerous. And if we are not rigorous in our thinking—we who believe that the value of a human being has nothing to do with what god they do or don't worship or what they are or aren't born—if we are not rigorous, then corruption starts spreading like gangrene. Argue something incoherent on one point, and ultimately you can become thoroughly corrupt. Look at the grotesquely insane politics of the extreme right and left both.

Archaic religious identity threatens the existence of the world, as Bill Maher noted in *Religulous*. If we do have a nuclear war, it will most probably be started by religious people.

4

***What challenges did you face as you wrote the book, either
internally or externally?***

Um . . . none externally, I guess. Well, I was worried about my
agent's reaction. I dedicated the novel to him. He's been my rock
for two decades. I'm deeply indebted to him. He's Jewish and
married to a gentile woman, and his kids are the wrong half like
me, and when I sent him the first draft it turned out he agreed
with every word of my novel. I'd been concerned about that for
nothing. Even my Jewish family has basically dealt with it. At least
so far. Internally: I think just the usual novelist's struggles.

Is* You or Someone Like You *a novel about rejection?

Yes, it is very much about Judaism's fierce rejection of non-Jews,
which is exactly what the ancient men who concocted the religion
designed it to do: Judaism is a social immune system solidly
engineered to reject anyone "non-self," a mechanism crucial, in the
extremely harsh, dangerous, resource-poor ancient Eastern
Mediterranean, to the survival of this wandering Semitic tribe. It
was necessarily and brutally efficient in an ancient, brutal world.

The problem is that this theological immune system is still
functioning in the twenty-first century, where it is now
disastrously maladapted to a much, much smaller, resource-richer
world and to the liberal, open-society, anti–organized religion,
antiracialist democratic humanism that is a vastly more advanced
way of organizing and valuing human beings than Judaism. But
this prehistoric machine, blindly moving forward on its automatic
pilot, is still detecting, isolating, and rejecting. It carried out its
programmed, unthinking function with my fictional seventeen-
year-old Sam Rosenbaum because he was non-self, both
theologically and racially. This is Judaism. And according to what
you, I, and everyone we know believes today, this is grotesquely
immoral. So Judaism's core religious belief is immoral.

And so is Christianity's core belief (the ridiculous idea of a
petulant, capricious, vindictive god, damning those who don't
recognize him to hell), Hinduism's (the hideous belief that there are
human beings so theologically polluted they are untouchable), ▶

and Islam's (all human beings not in *Dar-al-Islam*, the House of Peace, are in *Dar-al-Harb*, the House of War, and must be either conquered or slaughtered). None of them works.

But the novel is also about another kind of rejection, this time a wonderful one. W. H. Auden rejected exactly these anachronistic, tribalist, racialist, separatist ways of identifying ourselves. The best way to say it is this, from pages 87 through 89 of the novel:

At some benefit dinner in New York—at the NYPL on Fifth, I believe—[Stanford literature professor] Nicholas Jenkins once said to me it seemed likely to him that Auden would turn out to be the only poet of world stature born in England in the last hundred years. I said to Nick that this struck me as harsh (for England), but the "born in" was certainly crucial in his case. The soles of Auden's feet took him from England . . . to New York City, where he started the process of getting an American passport. . . . Auden had a concept of home, and it wasn't a particular place. He had transcended physical location. He had made a choice. . . . Howard and I talked about it, of course. Perhaps because Howard never changed passports, or because he encountered the Robert Frost lines first, in high school, Howard sees it Frost's way:

> *Home is the place where*
> *When you have to go there*
> *They have to take you in.*

But Auden's view, I said to them, is a bit different from Frost's. And I myself hear Auden's voice more clearly because it involves choice . . . Auden, Nick observed, had gone from one mental place to another and discovered in going there that he had arrived nowhere in particular. That he had shed everything and constructed something nameless.

Auden meant [that] you shed the old names and assume[d] new ones, and the new names mean what you want them to. In 1942, just three years after he arrived in his new home, Auden wrote that home is—the meter alone makes me weep—

> A sort of honour, not a building site,
> Wherever we are, when, if we chose,
>   we might
> Be somewhere else, yet trust that we
>   have chosen right.

Auden remarked to Benjamin Britten that New York was one "grand hotel in a world so destabilized that everyone had become a traveler." I am a traveler, and that my son does not share my accent bothers me in the end not at all. I was and am that thing Auden described, feared, and in the end loved more than anything. I was—I am—nameless.

I am not a Jew, a Christian, a Hindu, or a Muslim. I reject those. I am nameless. So are all people, everywhere in the world, who have transcended the old, now anachronistic, destructive identities, these giant international theological conglomerates manufacturing their poisonous products, these mindlessly rapacious dinosaurs. We have to be better than that.

The experiences of the gentile in the Jewish world is not a topic that one finds often in literature. What made you decide to write from Anne's point of view instead of Howard's?

For precisely that reason: The experience of a gentile in a Jewish world is indeed not a theme you read often, if ever, I would say, in literature—it's virtually always the reverse, and if you're going to write this story, it seems to me evident that you write it from Anne's point of view, not Howard's. Jewish culture is astonishing in producing, in numbers hugely disproportionate to its size, people who become great writers and novelists and scientists and philosophers and academics and politicians and businesspeople and every other occupation that requires brilliance and guts. And Jewish culture is explicitly designed to ferociously inculcate in Jews an obsession with "what is Jewishness." Thus there is a huge ▶

amount of literature by Jews, and it is hugely about Jews from the points of view of Jews.

Obviously this is true of the literature of most cultures—Junot Díaz writes books about Dominicans in the U.S., Jhumpa Lahiri writes about Bengali Americans and so on—but pile Mailer on Roth on Bellow on Doctorow on Myla Goldberg and on and on, and there's an insanely large amount of Jewish point of view about both the gentile and Jewish worlds. Which, again, is why it would be sort of stupid for me not to write on Judaism and the Jewish world from, for once, a gentile's point of view.

Flaubert once said, "Madame Bovary, c'est moi." Who is Anne Rosenbaum?

Obviously to a degree Anne is me ("is I," technically, but I disagree with Anne about the predicate nominative). But Anne is also, very much, in her movements and responses and reactions and perceptions and mental processes, several women I've known. My very English grandmother Marjorie Stewart. My friends Aileen Cheatham and Anne Lester and Anne Sikora.

What is a writer's main responsibility?

Now, that's a question. To tell a great story. To change one's perception of things. To surprise. . . Tikkun olam, to repair the world. To be a better mirror. Whichever of those a reader wants. Or maybe it's whichever the writer wants.

Anne Rosenbaum seems to be someone to whom things happen rather than someone who makes things happen. Why?

I never thought about her that way, but I can see why you would if you're thinking about the fact that she doesn't really give a damn about any of it—all the glitz, the movie stars, the expensive houses, the exclusive parties. And there really are a few people like that. I've known some of them. But Anne is deeply if subtly active throughout the novel—so I have to pretty completely disagree with you on this one; she's someone who makes things happen

constantly—and after the novel takes its 90 degree turn, she's
ferociously, overtly active. Maybe you'd agree that the things she
cares about are the things she makes happen.

*You have a character in your novel, a rabbi, who says that the
teaching of Judaism is forbidden to gentiles. In real life this is
inaccurate. Is verisimilitude important in fiction?*

With all due respect, this is one of the four things the Orthodox
rabbi at the Jerusalem yeshiva said to me when he expelled me.
"You caused us to sin by teaching Torah to a non-Jew." Is
he "wrong"? I couldn't possibly care less. Post-temple Diaspora
Judaism is designed to make everything debating material,
and I'm not interested. In this particular work of fiction,
this is an example not just of verisimilitude but of direct
reporting.

How much, if any, of You or Someone Like You *is
autobiographical?*

That I can answer very specifically: the scene where Sam goes
to Israel, goes to the moshav, then to Jerusalem, is invited to
the yeshiva by a guy doing kiruv (outreach to nonobservant
Jews), the details of how he's expelled, all of this is completely
autobiographical. Down to every detail. (I was twenty-three, not
seventeen, and I didn't start at a friend's Eilat apartment; I
backpacked in, then got on a bus, but it was on that bus that I met
the girl from La Jolla, and the direct autobiography starts there.)
Everything else, everything that happens in New York and Los
Angeles, is fiction. Obviously the Hollywood parts are informed
by my experience "taking meetings" on screenplays and television
series and so on. But it's fiction.

The yeshiva experience must have been terrible.

People say this to me, and if they're Jewish they frequently say it
apologetically, and I really do appreciate that, but it was just
something that happened. It was unnerving at the time. It freaked ▶

me out for a few days. But terrible? No. It forced me to think about things.

Is universalism the answer to global problems?

If you call it Audenism, then hell yes.

If Judeo-Christian ethics are outdated, should they be abolished?

Yes. I could also write a hundred thousand words to answer this, but here let's include Islam and Hinduism and just go with "yes." Well—"abolished." I'd say "transcended," which is a fancy way of saying we have a better way of thinking about ourselves now.

Is assimilation a cultural imperative for Anne?

This is something very important. Anne is not a cultural assimilationist. Cultures are profoundly different, and they create profoundly different outcomes, some cultures leading to wealth and knowledge, others to chaos and poverty. Jared Diamond demonstrated that in *Guns, Germs, and Steel.* Anne isn't opposed, at all, to Jewish culture. Not at all. She's opposed to any theology that holds that "God divides people into two." Which is every theology.

On the other hand, if you want to call educated, freethinking universalist humanism (or however you want to name it) a culture, then yes, she'd like to see the fundamentalist Christians, Jews, Muslims, and Hindus assimilate into it.

Anne implies that anti-Semitism is clearly useful to Jews. How useful to Jews was the Holocaust?

Immeasurably, in terms of the effectiveness the Holocaust has had in keeping Jews together as a people. John Podhoretz once said to me, "A little anti-Semitism is good for the Jews." This is not at all paradoxical, nor is it unusual. British violence against Indians and white Americans' violence against black Americans just after that were crucial to those rights movements.

The AIDS epidemic has been hugely good for homosexuals in terms of the force it has generated for gay rights. AIDS, the Holocaust, and Separate but Equal are and were horrific, terrible phenomena in terms of their brutality, violence, and loss of human life. But if your goal is to ensure that ethnic Jews identify as Jews, which John's goal is (and which mine is explicitly not), then John is obviously right that anti-Semitism is good for the Jews.

Is Anne a genius or a fool?

I don't think you have to be a genius to see the obvious. You simply have to be able to think and see clearly and (and this is the hard part) say what you see.

What is a good reader?

Ask Harold Bloom. Understanding literary references is an example of part of Bloom's answer, and I guess mine, but I actually do have Anne give another part of the definition. She's speaking to her book club: "Half of any book, I say, is just a mirror in which you do or do not see yourself. . . . The best readers try to fit themselves into the writer's mind rather than the reverse. Take a step toward your authors, and they will repay you twofold."

"There is truth. And we must find it. We must take what we see and we must judge to find the truth." How would you like your novel to be judged?

As a literary work, I suppose. For the characters? For the word choice and the writing? Hell, that's up to every reader's taste. Nothing more. For its ideas? I hope the ideas will be understood and debated coherently. And that it's judged in this way to have been helpful to all of us. ∽

A Reading Group Guide for *You or Someone Like You*

1. Why did the author choose *You or Someone Like You* for the title?

2. In his author's note, Chandler Burr writes about the power of observation: "What is our capacity to step back and see ourselves as we actually are?" How is this question made manifest in the story? How do each of the Rosenbaums—Anne, Howard, and Sam—see themselves? How do their perceptions of themselves and each other affect their relationships with one another and with the outside world?

3. What is the significance of literature— books—in Anne's life? What role do they play in Howard's? How does this couple define themselves through words? Do books ever fail them? What does literature mean to you?

4. Why do you think the author set the book in Hollywood? How might it have been different if he had set it in New York?

5. What does Hollywood mean to Anne? To Howard? What does having a reading salon in the power- and celluloid-obsessed culture of Hollywood do for Anne? What does it do to her? How does it affect her marriage?

6. How did Anne's book club become the height of fashion in a town where "nobody reads"? What are your impressions of Hollywood from

reading the novel? Does Chandler Burr like Hollywood? Why or why not?

7. Anne calls W. H. Auden, "the adamant universalist who saw all people as the same kind. He called the human species 'New Yorkers,' and to him they were otherwise nameless." What does this mean? Why does Anne find comfort in Auden and in being "nameless"?

8. The daughter of an American woman and a British diplomat, Anne has always been an outsider, a person without a homeland, so to speak, yet a woman at home within herself. How does her background and experiences shape her attitudes? Going back to an earlier question, does it help her see herself—and others—more clearly?

9. For Anne, Howard is her "one strong, anchored island" on which she stayed "safe and contented." Does her reliance on her husband make her marriage stronger? What does it mean for one individual to anchor her- or himself to another? What are the benefits—and the drawbacks—of doing so? What were each for Anne?

10. Does Anne care about what people think, especially about her? What is your opinion of Anne? Think about her relationship with her in-laws. Was it good that she stopped going to Brooklyn to celebrate the holidays with her husband and son? Is she ultimately a good role model for Sam?

11. Anne put her faith in Auden's idea of home as the place we have chosen. "But Howard always said he saw it Frost's way. Home as the place where when you go, they have to take you ▸

in." Compare these two views and their influence on the events in the book in relation to each—and both—characters.

12. Talk about Howard. What do you think of his character? How did Howard's background shape his attitudes? How does he change—and change again?

13. Pondering her husband's bond with their son, Sam, Anne says, "I'm fully aware that Howard thinks of Sam very much in terms of his own flesh, because in everything Sam is and everything Sam does, Howard sees himself." What effect does this have on Howard after his son's experience in Israel? And when Sam tells his parents that he is gay?

14. Anne tells her readers that *Pygmalion* is the single most important work of literature of the twentieth century. Why? How would you compare the central premise of this novel and that of *Pygmalion*?

15. Anne advises her readers, "A book is like a person, and one's reaction to a person invariably has more to do with one's own personality and life experience than with the actual person herself." Do you agree with this? Do people forget that when they are scrolling through Internet sites perusing starred recommendations? Talk about this in reference to your own experiences as a member of a book club.

16. Analyzing Robert Browning, Anne tells a group, "There is truth. And we

must find it. We must take what we see and we must judge it to find the truth," to which they respond, "everyone has a point of view, and all points of view are equal." Comment on both statements. Can we judge without being "judgmental"? Are all points of view truly equal?

17. Anne argues that anti-Semitism is the muse of Jewish religious truth and Jewish survival. What is she trying to convey with this statement? How might this extend to racism? Sexism? Homophobia? Can it be applied to these other forms of oppression? What might Anne say?

18. Anne splits her diverse following into groups on different days: "producers with producers, studio people with studio people. It made them at once more competitive, which was to say sharper, which I enjoyed, and more relaxed, since among their own. They mix very poorly, these people." By doing this, isn't Anne refuting the very ideals she believes in?

19. Why do you think going back to observance—for Jews and members of other faiths—has become so popular in recent years? What does this offer people? How can it be detrimental? Can rationality and faith coincide? What circumstances might make this so?

20. Art, culture, family, marriage, love, religion, identity, and moral belief are interwoven into the narrative. Choose one and explain its relevance in the story. Use examples from the novel. ▶

21. At the beginning of *You or Someone Like You*, when Anne and Howard first meet, they discuss writing. Howard tells her, "Turgenev stayed the hell out of his stories, and that was the way to write literature. Present the characters as the world sees them and get out of the way." How might it be limiting to write fiction in this way? Is this the style Burr adopts in *You or Someone Like You*?

22. According to Anne, "the capacity to change is, indeed, one of the most remarkable aspects of literature, and one of the most remarkable, perennial capacities of human beings." What was the most important thing you discovered from Anne and her creator, Chandler Burr?

23. Literature is Anne's passion. To her, it is a 360 degree mirror that offers a complete reflection of who we are: "Good literature is strong opinion, intelligently expressed. . . . It has long been observed that literature, if it is not ruthless, is nothing. . . . Literature, well done, illustrates the reality of human nature. . . . Literature describes what we experience, nothing more. . . . Literature shows us who and what we really are, whether we like it or not. . . . Art is shocking because it breaks down what we would be and shows us what we know we are." Has Chandler Burr succeeded in upholding Anne's viewpoint? Has reading *You or Some Like You* altered your perceptions of yourself, of books, of the world? ∼

Don't miss the next book by your favorite author. Sign up now for AuthorTracker by visiting www.AuthorTracker.com.